NINTH CYCLE
ANTARCTICA
JC RYAN

BOOKS

By JC Ryan

Rossler Foundation Mysteries

The Tenth Cycle

Ninth Cycle Antarctica

Genetic Bullets

The Sword of Cyrus

The Skywalkers

The Phoenix Agenda

The Rowen

Termination

Vinci Books

vinci-books.com

Published by Vinci Books Ltd in 2025

1

Copyright © JC Ryan 2014

The author has asserted their moral right to be identified as the author of this work in accordance with the Copyright, Designs and Patents Act 1988. This work is a work of fiction. Names, characters, places and incidents are the product of the author's imagination or are used fictitiously. Any resemblance to actual persons, living or dead, places and incidents is entirely coincidental.

All rights reserved. No part of this publication may be copied, reproduced, distributed, stored in any retrieval system, or transmitted in any form or by any means, including photocopying, recording, or other electronic or mechanical methods, nor used as a source for any form of machine learning including AI datasets, without the prior written permission of the publisher.

The publisher and the author have made every effort to obtain permissions for any third party material used in this book and to comply with copyright law. Any queries in this respect should be brought to the attention of the publisher and any omissions will be corrected in future editions.

A CIP catalogue record for this book is available from the British Library.

Paperback ISBN: 9781036700393

The EU GPSR authorised representative is Logos Europe, 9 rue Nicolas Poussion, 17000 La Rochelle, France
contact@logoseurope.eu

Chapter One

FORGET YOU EVER SAW IT

Lieut. Cmdr. Jack Neville sat back, stunned, after watching the video he and the rest of the rescuers had found among the scattered gear of the TV crew that had disappeared in Antarctica a week before. The transition from rescuer to detainee had been so abrupt that he could hardly believe the events of the past twelve hours. He fully expected to be released once the video had been aired for the four men in the room, but why he and his men had been detained in the first place was a mystery to him.

His companion, a junior officer, was also silent after watching the video. Although it was unedited and occasionally dizzying to watch, the missing TV crew obviously had found something unexpected in the Transantarctic Mountains. Neville found it almost impossible to believe what his eyes were registering.

What appeared to be a city, though the architecture was strange, was clearly shown in many frames. Closer examination revealed no people other than the TV crew themselves, posed here and there for proportional reference. The city, if that's what it was, seemed to have been constructed for occupants of a similar size to modern men. And yet, no one had inhabited Antarctica when it was discovered in 1820. Only in 1895 had anyone set foot on the continent, and even now, the year-round population was scattered among several countries' research stations and not considered permanent. Most left during the winter months.

Cmdr. Neville and his crew had been dispatched from McMurdo Station on the failed rescue mission three days before. When the TV crew failed to report in, their home office contacted their embassy in Washington, D.C. The request took a full twenty-four hours to navigate the red tape and make it to McMurdo, and then Neville's team had to attempt to locate the missing crew in a vast wilderness that quickly covered tracks if they weren't constantly groomed. The only trace of the missing TV crew had been some expeditionary equipment, discarded polar gear, and the professional-quality camera in which the video had been found, a few hundred feet from the compressed-snow road they called the McMurdo-Amundsen highway.

There were no large predators in Antarctica, if you didn't count the few thousand human beings scattered across the continent in various research stations. Only the weather might account for the disappearance of five people with no trace, but the weather had been calm for weeks, November being mid-summer at this latitude. What had happened to them would remain a mystery.

Upon radioing their discovery back to McMurdo, the rescue team was shocked to be told to stay put for extraction by chopper rather than continuing the search. Within a few hours, the sight of six fully equipped Navy SEALs running toward them left them wondering even more just what they had gotten themselves into. Now, only Neville and his second-in-command were allowed to view the video, along with a captain that he didn't know and a civilian from McMurdo. The civilian was the first to break the silence.

"You realize we can't allow this to be reported by the media," he said to the unknown captain. Ignoring both Neville and his second, the captain responded.

"I'm taking this video into custody and recommending it be classified at the highest level. No one in this room," he said, glaring at the other three, "may speak of it again. The best thing you can do is forget you ever saw it."

It was the last time that Neville ever saw any of his team. Within hours, he was transferred to the North Atlantic without explanation. Nor did he ever hear from any of the others. But, he never forgot the sight of the strange architecture he remembered from the video. A naval officer who wants to advance his career doesn't ask questions when the questions are obviously unwelcome. Neville put the incident out of his mind and didn't think of it again for many years.

Chapter Two

ADMIRAL PIRI REIS

Dr. Charles Summers walked along the hallway toward his office in the history building on the University of Boulder Colorado campus, speaking with his research assistant.

"I'll need you to review any material you can find on the Piri Reis map from 1513 and several others," he said. "I'll give you a list of the others in a day or two."

"Just what is it that you're looking for?" his assistant asked.

"I came across a lot of anomalies when I was working on my thesis," Dr. Summers explained. "There are a number of them that are quite impossible, and yet they exist."

"How so?" Dr. Summers recognized that his research assistant was skeptical. And who wouldn't be? Maps that were more accurate than modern maps, even though the tools for cartography had not been invented for centuries at the time they were drawn. Quite impossible. The paper he was preparing for the prestigious Rossler Foundation Journal for Modern Archaeology would require careful research into the purported dates of the maps he wanted investigated, alongside the known history of cartography and of modern human understanding of the geography of their world. To his research assistant he only said what was absolutely required, since his theory was as yet unformed.

"There seems to be some difficulty regarding the dates of these old maps vis-a-vis what was known of world geography at the times they were purportedly drawn. I want you to verify the authenticity of the dates. Once we have a list of those for which the dates can be verified, I'll compare it to the history of world exploration to try to explain the anomalies."

"But what anomalies?" The research assistant insisted.

Irritated, Dr. Summers said, "For one thing, how were they able to draw accurate maps when they knew nothing of longitude and latitude?"

Recognizing from his tone that Dr. Summers was done with his questions, the research assistant nodded and said, "I'll come by after my 3 o'clock class for the list, if that's okay."

"That will be fine."

In fact, Dr. Summers had more questions some of which were not very sophisticated. For example, how was it that mere mortals were confident enough to sail into a vast, uncharted ocean with no maps? And, since they had no maps, how did they ever find their way to and through new worlds, and then home? Cartography wasn't Dr. Summers main area of expertise, but the sight of a map dated 1513 that showed the continent of Antarctica, when there were no previous records of a confirmed sighting before 1819, had puzzled him for years.

With the astounding discovery of a code left by a previous civilization in the Great Pyramid at Giza, came the possibility of an explanation. Dr. Summers' intention was to debunk the dates of those maps that had perhaps been forged, and search the Library of the 10th Cycle for an explanation for those that could be validated. Later that afternoon, Dr. Summers placed a call to Daniel Rossler, who had become a good friend since locating his foundation in the Boulder area.

Rossler and his wife Sarah were responsible for the work that broke the code placed by an earlier advanced civilization within the Giza pyramid to convey their knowledge when their civilization fell. Rather than amassing untold wealth from their discoveries, the pair had created a non-profit organization to translate the entire contents and give helpful technologies to the world. At the same time, the Rosslers were working with the US government and some allied governments to suppress technologies that could do more harm than good, especially in the hands of terrorist or criminal organizations.

"Daniel, it's Charles," he said, forgetting as always that Daniel would have seen from caller ID who it was.

"Hey Charles, to what do I owe the pleasure?" Daniel asked.

"I was hoping you could let me dig around in the library," Charles said. "I'm finally ready to write that paper we discussed, and as soon as my research assistant has validated the dates of the maps in question, I'd like to compare them to what was known of the globe in the 10th Cycle."

"You know the library is always open to you, Charles." Daniel said. "It's been a pleasure to work with you, as we've told you frequently. You were one of the first scholars to embrace the notion that we had turned history on its head. Why else would we have made you a Fellow of the foundation?"

"Man, I was never so happy as when all those pompous evolutionists had to eat their words."

"Would you be interested in having some help? I could ask Sinclair and Raj to give you a hand, and if you'd like a gopher, I've just hired my little brother and he could use an assignment." Daniel had never gotten over the habit of calling JR his little brother, even when the 'little' no longer fit after JR grew to his remarkable six-foot-ten height.

"Yes, that would be very welcome."

"When can we expect you?" Daniel asked.

"I'm thinking I'll have enough to start with by the end of the week."

"Very good. Sarah and I will be glad to see you, as always."

Summers' immediate acceptance of the information held within the coded 10th Cycle library, despite skepticism from many of his colleagues who studied ancient history, had earned him the enduring friendship of the Rosslers, not to mention the coveted Fellowship and unlimited access to the Library. That the latter was expanding every day as translation continued, was an even bigger bonus.

His call completed, Summers quickly typed out the names and purported dates of the maps in which he was interested. The most intriguing, however, was the 1513 map clearly showing Antarctica. Quite impossible. What a disappointment it would be, if the map he had spent years thinking about turned out to be a fraud.

Shortly after three, the assistant returned to find the list on his desk. Among the references was the Zeno map, drawn in 1380, showing the exact latitude and longitude of a number of islands, despite the fact that the instrument required to determine longitude had not been invented until 1765. A Chinese map on stone from 1137, formed on a spherical grid, as was the Camerio map of 1502, despite the fact that it was accepted in the Middle Ages and into the Renaissance that the earth was flat. The Orontius Fineus map, drawn in 1531 and The Zauche map of 1737, showing Antarctica, the existence of which was not verified until 1819, but free of the overlying ice sheet. The graduate student's head was spinning. There were more, but for some reason, Dr. Summers had circled one, the Piri Reis chart of 1513. It seemed to be the main object of study. How were these maps possible?

By Thursday, Summers had confirmation that the Piri Reis map was genuine. Even if all the others turned out to be misstated or actually fraudulent, this one piece of evidence would give him plenty of material for a paper for the Journal. Summers chuckled to himself. If he had been doing this research he would have carefully eliminated the less interesting subjects before researching the most interesting. A difference in methodology, to be sure, but a major one. He would have to have a talk with his research assistant about making assumptions. But, this time it had panned out.

Summers placed another call to Daniel, verifying that he would be available at ten the next morning when Summers intended to present himself at the headquarters of the foundation to begin his research.

"Well, I had planned to take Sarah to Paris tomorrow morning," Daniel joked. "But I guess we can postpone that." Summers laughed.

"Have you still not taken her on that honeymoon you promised?" he asked. After breaking the news that they had cracked the Pyramid Code, Daniel and Sarah had barely found time to get married, and he'd had to give her a rain check for the fabulous honeymoon. He was lucky Sarah was a good sport, Summers thought. Any other woman would have gone straight from the altar to divorce court.

"I still haven't," Daniel said. "But we've been to more exotic locales than you can shake a stick at. I ought to have declared one of those trips our honeymoon."

"You'd better treat her right, or one of these days I'm going to beat your time with her." Daniel knew it was an idle threat. Summers knew as well as he did that Sarah was a one-man woman. And Daniel was that lucky man. The next day, at the foundation headquarters, Daniel stood to welcome Charles in his office. Daniel had invited his top researcher, the world-famous linguist who'd been the one to finally read the code, Sinclair O'Reilly, to join them, along with his IT director, Rajan Sankaran, aka Raj. Summers had met the two men before, and greeted them now with pleasure.

"Daniel tells me you're quite excited about a 16th century map," Sinclair said. "What do you expect to find here in the library that can throw light on such a modern document?" Summers reflected for a moment on the gestalt change over the last several years that could now refer to a moment nearly five centuries in the past as 'modern'.

"I'd like to keep this confidential until my paper is out," he said. Seeing the others nod, he went on. "Unless I'm mistaken, this map depicts the new world as accurately as any modern map, and yet, Columbus had only discovered the New World a couple of decades before. Furthermore, it appears to show the continent of Antarctica." Summers assumed that the others already knew the history of Antarctica, but was glad to explain, when Raj asked the significance of that.

"It was nearly two centuries after that map was drawn, when the first mention of land to the south of Tierra del

Fuego is mentioned in the historical record. It seems that Capt. James Cook crossed the Antarctic Circle in 1783 and caught sight of land masses that were previously undiscovered, but from the descriptions, he apparently only saw outlying islands in the Antarctica Peninsula, rather than the continent itself."

"So, let me get this straight. When was Antarctica first discovered according to the historical record you mentioned?" Raj asked.

"As far as we know in the history of this cycle, the first human being to set foot on Antarctica was an American sealer named Capt. John Davis, in 1821."

"Is it possible," asked Sinclair, "that parts of the historical record are missing?"

"Anything's possible, but when scholars came across this map in Turkey in 1929, they speculated that it had been drawn from even earlier documents that are now unknown. My thought is that perhaps those earlier documents dated from the 10th Cycle somehow. What I'd like to find in the library is confirmation that the 10th Cyclers knew of Antarctica, and perhaps that they left representations of the geography of the globe that were known earlier in our own cycle."

"Well if anyone can help you find evidence of that, these two guys are your best bet. Sinclair, do you and Raj have time to assist Charles?"

"Absolutely. We are always happy to assist one of our most loyal supporters," said Sinclair.

"Charles, here is an ID pass that will get you in the front door twenty-four/seven and a key to a guest office. Make yourself at home, and let me know if there's anything else you need."

"You mentioned giving your younger brother an assignment to assist me," Summers said. "Is that offer still open?"

"Stick around for a minute, and let's discuss it."

Just as he had avoided giving his research assistant the whole story, Summers had deliberately left out the information that most intrigued him about the Piri Reis map. Not only did a good part of it look very much like the coast of Queen Maud land, which was a section of Antarctica, but when compared with the most recent maps of the same region, it matched nearly exactly the shape that had been discerned only through the use of modern seismic equipment and satellite imagery. In fact, it depicted only the land mass of Queen Maud land, which had been covered with a thick sheet of ice extending out into the ocean for what scientists insisted was tens of thousands of years. The shape lacked the overlying ice.

The question was not, as he had described it to the others, how the mapmaker had known of the continent at all. The question was how did he know of the shape of the land mass when it hadn't been seen within our current cycle, and perhaps since before even the height of the 10th Cycle, perhaps 35,000 or more years ago? Was it possible that the admiral had discovered or been in possession of maps predating the 10th Cycle calamity? What he hoped to find in the records of the library were clues if not answers to these questions.

Summers debated revealing the rest of it to Daniel, and decided that there was no need. When he had found what he was looking for, there would be plenty of time to discuss his next project. That is, *if* he found what he was looking for.

Taking his leave of Daniel, Summers located his guest office, and noted with approval that it was equipped with a state-of-the-art workstation from which he would be able to retrieve any translated records by keyword.

Raj, with whom he was the less familiar of the two men he'd be working with, must be a real genius with the organization of data. After only a few minutes' perusal of the introductory files, he was ready to begin his search. Sinclair's help would come in if he found records mentioned in the index that had not yet been translated.

Summers was not yet sure what use he would be able to make of Joshua Rossler, known as JR according to his brother Daniel. Apparently, the young man had an undergraduate degree in archaeology, but could be erratic. That was what Daniel had asked him to take into consideration after Sinclair and Raj had left them earlier. He would meet JR on Monday. Between now and then, he would try to think of something useful that the boy could do for him. It was the least he could do to thank Daniel for the courtesy the Foundation was extending to him.

Summers was eager to get to work, but before he had even had a chance to take a look at the index, Sarah Rossler knocked at his door.

"Charles, I just wanted to say how happy we are to have you here again," she said. "And to invite you to join us for lunch."

Even though Charles wanted nothing more than to begin his search, it would have been ungracious to refuse Sarah's invitation. Charles shut down his workstation and stood, saying, "Lunch sounds great." He stepped to the doorway and kissed Sarah on the cheek, stepping back just in time to hear Daniel's objection.

"What's this? Are you making a pass at my girl?" Sarah laughed, as Charles winked.

"I told you you'd better treat her right or I'd move in," he retorted.

After lunch, Summers returned to his guest office and was at last able to take a look at the index. He wasn't certain where to look, whether in the sections marked geography, history or archaeology. Rather than disturb Sinclair or Raj for such a basic question, he started at the top of the geography index and read through it. As always, it took a while before he got over the disorientation occasioned by the 10th Cyclers' use of different names for the landmasses in their world, not to mention that different areas of the globe had been home to populations in a different distribution than that of the 11th cycle, our own.

Even now, after several years of advances made possible by the 10th Cycle material, it was hard for some people to believe that before our history began, a more advanced civilization than ours had begun, flourished and died in a cataclysm that geologists and others still hadn't identified. Or that before that, nine others had done the same thing, if the 10th Cycle record was to be believed. The same people, or their children, who'd once insisted that the manned landing on the moon was a hoax, now believed that the Pyramid code and everything learned from it was an elaborate hoax, perpetrated by unknown villains on an unwary populace.

That the cataclysms that ended each cycle had rearranged the land masses of the earth was mind-boggling. Perhaps less so was that the 10th Cyclers would have had their own names for them, rather than calling them what we, the presumed 11th Cycle now named them. Of course the different shapes of the land masses meant different weather patterns, and a different path of development and migration for the earliest humans to emerge from the catastrophe to repopulate the earth after being literally thrown back into a Stone Age existence.

Sinclair's translation team had done a great job of providing the current name for anywhere that was recognizable with respect to an 11th Cycle perspective, but Summers realized immediately that he would need a Mercator-type projection map of the 10th Cycle globe to refer to as he researched. He made a note of the request so that on Monday he could ask JR to acquire one, assuming such a thing existed.

Stymied for the moment by his inability to visualize the world of the 10th Cycle as it existed physically, Summers turned to the history section. Once again, the fuzzy nature of his search left him unable to formulate a sensible query of the index. He could do nothing but examine it line by line for a clue. Several hours passed before he realized that the hum of activity that had accompanied his studies was no longer loud enough to hear. He glanced at his watch, to see that he had worked long past his usual dinnertime, and that it was now nearly eight p.m. It was time to go home and try to forget his work over the weekend, a constant battle against overwork that he fought valiantly. In fact, one of the reasons he'd been so drawn to the Rosslers was their mutual enjoyment of the nearby mountain recreational options.

Summers briefly considered calling Daniel to see if they would like a hike the next day, but thought better of it when he realized the trails would be quite muddy, and vulnerable to erosion until the early spring thaw had finished and the brilliant sun and dry air had dried them. Too late for skiing, too early for hiking, he would have to find something else to keep his mind off his research.

Chapter Three

THE ORION SOCIETY

In an ancient ruined castle in the even more ancient city of Würzburg Germany, four masked and robed figures sat around an ancient table as their predecessors had done for centuries. Each of them went by a codename that represented the quarter of the earth over which their families claimed dominion. At the head of the table, Septentrio, representing the North and the acknowledged leader, and then clockwise with Oriens to his left, Auster opposite, and Occidens to his right. This was the quarterly meeting of the Orion Society.

The powerful and secretive society dated from before the birth of Christ, and, despite the fact that relatively few had heard of it and lived, they controlled much of the wealth and resources of the earth. Their unsuccessful attempts to kidnap Daniel and Sarah Rossler before the Pyramid Code was translated and disseminated had come near to exposing them, necessitating the honorable retirement of Septentrio's father, which he accomplished by throwing himself from a turret of this very ruin.

Now, the current Septentrio presided over the quarterly meeting to hear reports of ongoing projects, and to report concerning his own project.

"As you are aware, my father failed in his mission to secure the contents of the Pyramid Code for our use only," he said. "I am happy to report that we have been able to plant operatives within the staff of the Rossler Foundation. Their brief is to report back to me any discoveries of note, particularly any hint of a formula for ultra-longevity, as we have been searching for that since the beginning of time."

"And what have they reported so far," Auster sneered. Her personal mission was to discredit and depose the leading family, Septentrio's, and take the lead herself. She never failed to look for an opportunity to point out any of Septentrio's shortcomings. Unfortunately, he was performing quite well in his capacity as a Society leader. It was in his personal life that he fell short of their collective standards.

Auster's spies had reported that Septentrio's private entertainment included several male prostitutes at a time, several times a week. His ruthlessness in questioning traitors in their own organization and informants from rival organizations was without question. Septentrio the elder, himself a ruthless despot, had laid out the approved method for questioning with prejudice, even with extreme prejudice. However, the son had been twisted by years of physical and mental abuse at the hands of his father because of his sexual orientation. Once he attained the power that his deceased father had wielded, he spared no compunction in avenging himself on the enemies of the society. Auster anticipated a time when Septentrio would go too far and leave himself vulnerable to her coup.

"What is the status of our assets in America?" she asked.

"We continue to maintain watchers who are aware of our interests, but not of our identity, within all major institutions of higher learning, major governmental and unofficial intelligence gathering organizations, as well as within research laboratories and large corporations throughout the country. I've just told you of those we have finally been able to plant in the Rossler Foundation itself."

"And how are you processing the information stream from all these assets?" Auster pressed.

"Information from the first line assets is funneled to several regional coordinators, who all report to our CIA operative, Latet. Only he knows how to reach me directly, and he analyzes and verifies all information before passing it to me."

Auster had to hand it to Septentrio, who she still thought of as a boy in spite of the fact that he was beginning his sixth decade. If nothing else, he was efficient. No wonder he had time for his disgusting recreational activities. She made a note to forward her spies' reports to her counterparts from the East and the West. They were even older and more conservative than she; when the time came, she would be able to count on them for support, and of course Latet would keep her apprised of important developments even before reporting to Septentrio. The latter's organization, in fact, played into her hands perfectly.

When the meeting had ended, each of the members of the Orion society returned to their homelands, except for Septentrio, who lived in Würzburg as his family had for over 2000 years.

Septentrio divested himself of the heavy robe and stifling mask that were the trappings of his office. His pale, pudgy body sank into the steaming waters of the spa he had

had installed in his quarters, and he rang for his manservant.

"Send me some playmates," he demanded.

"Yes sir. Right away," his manservant agreed. As he dialed the number of the brothel where Septentrio's favorites were employed, he also coded a note for delivery to Auster, as she had required of him. He wondered what would happen if Septentrio ever discovered his perfidy, and dismissed it as too trifling to worry about. His master was a weakling, not to be feared. Had the manservant known of the fate of his own predecessor, he might have had a better idea of how to protect himself.

Chapter Four

JR IS A PROBLEM

On Monday morning, Charles found the Rossler Foundation humming with activity again. Before going to his office, he knocked on Daniel's door, and stepped in at Daniel's invitation.

"How was your weekend?" he asked.

"We worked," Daniel said. "It's becoming a bad habit."

"I thought about inviting you guys out for a hike, but then I realized the trails would be too muddy."

"You're right, but that would've been fun. However, we had a ton of applications to process."

"How's it all going?" Summers inquired. "I should have asked last week. I was so intent on my own research that I didn't think to check up on how it's going overall."

"It's going. Sinclair has a full complement of translators working two shifts, and the more we find, the more there is to find. I still can't get over how cleverly these 10th Cyclers were able to arrange the blocks so that hundreds of thousands of facts were nested in such a small number of symbols."

"I've never quite understood how that worked," said Charles. "Can you run it by me again, slowly?" He grinned. "Pretend I'm an idiot. I know that won't be a huge stretch."

"Don't sell yourself short buddy, if I can understand it anyone can understand it. But, we don't really get too specific about it. If we did, anyone could do it, and then the idea that we can keep harmful information out of the hands of criminals and terrorists would go by the wayside. But, in general, it involves a technique I read about in a book that made me think about taking every few symbols and making words that way."

"How'd you ever come up with that?"

"It was almost an accident," Daniel said. "It's hard to remember now why I was doing it, but about the time we hit on the idea of the individual stones representing symbols, I learned about a school of thought that used this method on the Torah to reveal prophecies. When we applied it to the pyramid, though, what we discovered was the greeting and the index. Then we knew that there had to be an entire encyclopedia, if you will, hidden in the stones."

"That story never fails to boggle my mind," said Charles. "And then to think that you outwitted international criminal organizations to save it for the world."

"Well, that was the Mossad that did the outwitting. We were lucky to have their help."

"Luck. Yeah, right. I'm a big believer in making your own luck, and I'll bet that's what you guys did. Well, I'd better get to work. Thanks for the rundown."

Charles had heard the story before, but never from the horse's mouth. Somehow Daniel's understatement of both the effort it required to figure out how to break the code and of the danger he, Sarah and the other researchers had faced made it all the more dramatic.

Dr. Summers' day was barely begun when Joshua Rossler, the younger of Daniel's two brothers, known to most as JR and sometimes to his family as Josh, presented himself for Charles's assignments. The latter was startled when the young man loomed in his doorway, freakishly tall and built like an athlete. Charles didn't think Daniel was anywhere near this tall, but that was a curiosity that could wait for exploration.

"Come in, JR. It's nice to meet you. I'm Charles Summers, but please call me Charles."

JR sauntered into the room and dropped his lanky, athletic frame into a chair situated at the front of Charles's desk. Summers noted the resemblance to Daniel, but in the super-sized version. The kid had to have been nearly seven feet tall, with the same unruly brown hair as Daniel's and the same blue eyes. But there the resemblance ended. Something was bothering him, and it showed in his alternately sullen and cocky expressions. Summers shook off his natural tendency to be intimidated by much taller men and wondered why it seemed JR wasn't comfortable either. With that physique, he could have dominated anyone, but instead, his shoulders were hunched, he didn't offer to shake hands and his eyes were downcast.

"Daniel says I have to help you with whatever you need," said JR. Charles thought it was an inelegant way of putting things, but accurate nonetheless.

"I understand you have a degree in archaeology," he said.

"Yeah." This conversation was going nowhere fast. Charles tried once more to get a responsive answer.

"Do you know anything about cartography?" He asked.

"Mapmaking? A little, I guess. I learned to map archaeological sites in school." Encouraged, Charles smiled.

"Do you happen to know if anyone has made a map of the 10th Cycle world with something like a Mercator projection?" JR's blank expression dashed Charles hopes again. Then he asked a question.

"Is that, like, where they make a round thing, I mean, the globe, look flat?" It was perhaps not a scholarly explanation, but it would do.

"Yes, exactly. To understand what I'm reading in the pyramid record, I need to have a picture to look at that's accurate for the 10th Cycle, but a familiar concept to my 11th Cycle mind," he smiled.

To Charles's surprise, given the young man's almost sullen demeanor, JR smiled in return.

"Okay, I get that. I don't know if anyone's done that, but I can ask around. Anything else?"

"Not at the moment. It would be brilliant if you could find one, but is there any chance of getting one made if no one's done it yet?"

"Let me see if I can find one, and if not I'll talk to Daniel."

"Great!" Charles said, turning to his computer without dismissing JR. JR stood for a moment watching Charles as he worked the keyboard, and then left the room.

JR took a detour before continuing on his errand for Dr. Summers. Despite the chilly March wind, he stood on the outdoor patio smoking his second cigarette since arriving an hour before. JR knew that Daniel was aware he smoked out here, and Daniel hadn't said anything about it, so JR figured it was okay. His ten-minute break stretched to fifteen and then twenty before he went back inside.

"Hey, Sinclair!" JR shouted as he entered the translation department bullpen. Twenty translators raised their heads to see who was creating the disturbance. Seeing JR, most went back to work, though a couple of the girls grinned at him. He waved at them, and grinning in return, wandered down the aisles toward Sinclair's office.

"Is he in?" he asked the person nearest him on the last row of cubicles.

"I think so. Just knock," came the answer.

JR opened the door without knocking and said again, "Hey, Sinclair."

The older man jumped a little, not having heard the door open. "Oh, hey, JR. What can I do for you?"

"Do you know if anyone has drawn a mercury projection of the 10th Cycle geography?"

"Do you mean a Mercator projection? I'm not sure, why?"

"Summers wants one. I'm supposed to either find one that's already been done or get Daniel to have one done."

"Sounds like something that might be useful. Give me an hour and I'll see what I can find out."

His errand successfully passed on to Sinclair, JR made his way back through the cubicle farm, detouring to pull the hair of a redheaded girl, one of those who'd smiled at him when he came in.

"Want to get a drink?" he asked.

"My break's not for another hour," she replied.

"It's okay, you're with me. I'm family," he boasted.

"Well, if you're sure."

Sinclair watched the exchange through the blinds of his glass-walled office. That boy was interfering with his department. He'd have to speak to Daniel again.

When Sinclair had joined the research effort, no one knew what a big deal the Pyramid Code would be. He was the first translator to make a breakthrough, but the sheer volume of the data had required a veritable army of assistants, and even with two shifts of twenty working on it, they'd barely scratched the surface. Sinclair sighed and made a few calls to the research department, looking for anyone who could tell him whether a map such as Charles Summers was requesting had been made. When he couldn't find one, he made a call to Daniel, unconsciously doing the other part of JR's errand for him.

"Daniel, can I order a Mercator projection map of the 10th Cycle geography as we understand it? Summers needs it."

"Sure, sounds useful."

Sinclair called the research department back, this time asking to talk to Nicholas Rossler. The old man, Daniel's grandfather and a noted archaeologist in his own right, had come out of retirement in his eighties to work with the Pyramid Code revelations, and was in charge of the research department. He often told his wife that he hadn't had so much fun since he was in his early seventies and had to quit going on digs because of the University's darned liability policy. Bess was happy that he was happy, but just as glad that he was no longer climbing in and out of kivas on potentially rotten Anasazi ladders.

Naturally, much of the research was being carried out by people like Charles Summers, but a cadre of graduate students under Nicholas's direction was working on extracting core information about exactly what the Library contained, as fast as it could be translated.

"Nick, could you assign someone to work up a map of the 10th Cycle world, ASAP? An outside researcher has requested it, and Daniel just okayed it.

"No problem, but I don't have a cartographer on staff. I'll have to send out an RFP and hire one."

"Jeez, can't we just do it the old-fashioned way?"

"Sorry, buddy. With all the government funding that comes our way comes red tape, too. A request for proposal is the way to get it done."

Sinclair muttered under his breath.

"What was that?" Nicholas asked. "I didn't quite hear you."

"Never mind," said Sinclair. "Bess would have to wash your ears out with soap if I repeated it out loud."

After ordering the map Summers needed, Sinclair left his office for a face-to-face consultation with Daniel. He liked JR, they all did. But the kid was often out of control, and just as often lazy. Sinclair's translator still hadn't come back from her unauthorized break, but Sinclair laid that at JR's feet.

"Knock, knock," Sinclair said, opening Daniel's door. Daniel was on the phone but waved Sinclair inside and ended his call as soon as he could.

"Hi! You'd think we'd see more of each other, working in the same building, but I seem to be on the phone 26 hours a day." Sinclair's ascetic face took on a look of commiseration.

"Not what you anticipated when you were talking about escaping international spies and cracking ancient codes, was it?" Sinclair asked.

"Not at all," Daniel said, "but I've got to admit that I'd do it again. The good we've done in four short years far outweighs any personal inconvenience. Sarah and I agree on that."

Sinclair raised his eyebrows. "Are you implying that there are areas on which you don't agree?"

Daniel shrugged. "What marriage has no points of disagreement? Don't worry, we're solid. Most of its pretty minor, and we have always been in agreement on the really big stuff like setting up the foundation here in Boulder near family."

Sinclair sensed that he would get no more, nor did he really wish to hear of even the slightest trouble in paradise. Especially since he was here to raise a bone of contention with Daniel, himself. As he gathered his thoughts to determine how to approach it, Daniel sidetracked him for a minute. "What about you? I thought you'd have persuaded Martha to move out here by now. Aren't you tired of flying to Providence every couple of weeks?"

"You let me worry about that, boyo. Sure and I love the woman, but it's hard for her to leave the house she's lived in for thirty years and more for the likes of me." Sinclair had the habit of dropping into a fake Irish brogue at random times in honor of his forebears, which often made his hearers guffaw at the mixture of brogue and the tangy vowels of a New York accent.

Daniel understood it to mean mind his own business this time. He dropped it in favor of the reason Sinclair had come in the first place.

"What can I do for you?" Daniel asked.

"Well to be brutally honest, I'm here about JR." Sinclair said. Daniel hunched his shoulders ever so slightly and a frown began to knit his eyebrows.

"What's he done now?"

"Daniel, you know that I've been behind you all the way when you asked us all to give JR a break. It's great that you can give your brother a safe place as he recuperates from that god-awful sandpit." Sinclair began to digress a bit, unconsciously, as he went on. "Why our government in all its wisdom sends these boys back there fighting a pointless, endless holding action against terrorists on their own ground over and over again until their minds are ruined I will never understand."

Daniel's eyes darted around the room seeking an escape from the hard realities of JR's Marine Corps experience. The sunny, bright young man who'd had a potential future in the NBA and a more than passing interest in archaeology had quit school in the last semester of his senior year and impulsively joined the Marines when his girlfriend broke up with him right after Valentine's Day.

Even that wouldn't have been so bad, as the young recruit had acquitted himself well on his first two deployments, rising to the highest noncom rank available in a little less than three years. It was the final deployment that had broken him.

JR still refused to talk about what had happened, but Daniel could read between the lines. He had been in Afghanistan himself, embedded with a Marine Corps battalion as a young journalist. No matter how carefully intelligence was gathered, there was always the potential for a terrible mistake that cost the lives of innocent civilians. Daniel suspected that JR held himself responsible for such a mistake, though he had no evidence.

Even if there wasn't just one thing, long deployments in a war zone tended to eat at a man, especially if, like Daniel, JR had seen buddies horribly wounded or killed. JR wasn't alone in carrying mental scars; it seemed that this condition was more the norm than not among this generation of soldiers. Probably had been in previous wars, too, if the truth were known. Only this time, it was being acknowledged. Bringing himself back to the present, he urged Sinclair to finish his thought.

"The thing is, the boy's devilishly handsome," Sinclair observed. "Even a crusty old mick like me can see that the girls fall over him. My problem is that they're doing it on company time. This is the fifth or sixth time that JR has come into my department, teased one of the translators until she's agreed to join him for coffee and then disappeared with her for the rest of the day. It needs to stop."

Daniel sighed heavily. "I know, I can't tell you how many times I've called him on the carpet in this very room and told him he had to quit messing around with the other employees. In the first place, it's a liability, since he's family. No telling when one of these girls is going to slap him with a harassment suit or worse, a paternity suit. I'll talk to him again. Sorry, man. I just hope he straightens up soon. I can't fire him, you know, that would be like throwing him to the wolves."

As Sinclair left the office, he reflected that Daniels troublesome younger brother might be one of those areas where he and Sarah couldn't come to an agreement. Sinclair had seen Sarah press her lips together firmly to keep from saying something during meetings when JR's erratic behavior was discussed. Daniel had a blind spot when it came to that boy, Sinclair thought. He just hoped that the kid didn't bring the roof down around their ears.

Once Sinclair had left, Daniel decided to visit Charles in his guest office and see if there was anything he needed other than the map he'd requested. While he was there, he planned to ask Charles if he felt comfortable taking on a sort of mentor role to JR, since he was benefiting from JR's assistance. He found Charles staring intently at the monitor on his workstation, his lips moving as if he were reading to himself.

"Yo, Charles. How's it going?"

Charles looked up, startled. He smiled when he saw Daniel in the doorway.

"It's going well, thank you. I've reached a stumbling block in my examination of the maps so I've been going through the history section looking for anything about exploration or mapmaking that I could find."

"So I heard," Daniel said "I'll look at getting that map made for you as soon as possible but I'm afraid there's a little red tape involved. So have you had any luck in the histories?"

"There's so much here," Charles answered, "I haven't even finished reading through the index for the category. I may have to press your younger brother into service and have him look at certain sections for keywords I'm targeting. By the way, I haven't seen him since I asked him to find that map for me. Does he have specific work hours, or do I need to jot down anything I'd like him to do for whenever he turns up?"

"That's what I actually came to talk to you about," said Daniel. "I wasn't exactly forthcoming with you when I saddled you with him as your assistant. I apologize." Daniel missed Charles's look of surprise, because he could not meet the other man's eyes. He rushed on, hoping he hadn't damaged their friendship by offering what seemed to be a favor but was instead a babysitting job.

"I should have told you that JR is suffering from PTSD. He's erratic, sometimes angry and often irresponsible. He did set in motion your request for the map you need. But he did it in a way that shuffled off responsibility to someone else. I've come to set the record straight, apologize and ask if I can enlist you in our campaign to rehabilitate him."

Charles didn't know quite what to make of the request. He was a guest researcher, nothing more, and certainly not qualified as a counselor to a young man suffering from a mental illness. He opened his mouth to object, then realized that it would be unkind if there were any way he could help.

"How do you see me helping?" he said instead.

"Just keep him busy, call him on his bullshit when he needs it. If he gets out of line in a way you can't handle, don't hesitate to call me and I'll deal with it."

Charles thought he could manage that, since it was more or less the way he would deal with any research assistant. "He doesn't get violent when he gets angry, does he?"

"He used to, and we do try to keep him from drinking too much, because that does tend to bring out his anger issues," Daniel replied, "but, he hasn't lashed out in that way while at work. He's getting better almost every day, so if he hasn't done it yet I doubt if he'll do it in the future."

It wasn't a ringing endorsement for the young man's good behavior, but Charles was inclined to grant his host's request.

"I don't see a problem then," he said. Charles began making a mental list of the errands he'd give to JR; nothing that would jeopardize the research if it didn't get done, but hopefully interesting enough to keep the young man engaged. *Pity about his condition*, Charles thought.

No sooner had Daniel returned to his office, than his private, direct-line phone rang. Only his family had this number, and it was understood that he was not to be disturbed with personal business during work hours unless it was vitally important. Therefore, it was with some trepidation that he answered.

"Daniel. It's your dime."

"Hey Daniel, Luke. I've got some news regarding your old friends," he said. The way he emphasized 'friends' told Daniel that Luke was talking about, not friends at all, but the group that had plagued him and Sarah and almost cost them their lives as they labored to crack the Pyramid Code. The damn Orion Society.

"I thought we had crippled them when we captured their mole," said Daniel.

"Oh, you know, counterespionage is like housework. It's never done. So, we're seeing some activity that has their fingerprints all over it," he said.

"What kind of fingerprints?"

"The usual. Corpses with their heads and hands missing, disinformation showing up in unexpected quarters after we plant it, missing agents." Daniel's sensibilities weren't all that delicate, but he couldn't help shudder when Luke described the mutilated corpses. The CIA agent who, as far as they knew, was helping them during the height of the code research, turned out to be a ruthless killer who had used similar methods of disguising his victims' identities. Daniel and Sarah counted themselves lucky to have come through that phase with their heads on their necks and all fingers intact.

"So what are they up to now?" he said, weariness overtaking him at the thought that they may yet again have to take evasive action.

"We know that a new mole took over David's role as soon as we picked him up," Luke reminded Daniel. "We've been trying to ferret him out with a disinformation campaign. With no luck so far, I'm afraid. But, we did pick up a fragment of conversation that leads us to believe you may have at least one mole in your organization."

"We aren't researching anything that we don't intend to disseminate freely as soon as we have results," Daniel protested. "Why would they need a mole in the Rossler Foundation?"

"It's more likely to be someone in your translation department," Luke said. "The idea would be that as soon as anything you might be required to suppress turns up, the mole would steal it and convey it to the Orion Society before anyone knew it was missing. And of course you realize that they're after the method you're using to extract the information to be translated, as well."

"Causing us to be in violation of our contracts with all of the governments who signed the 11th Cycle Treaty," finished Daniel. It was a possibility that had been discussed when the treaty was being drawn up. What if information in the Pyramid Code would be a danger in the hands of terrorists or criminals?

The countries who had signed the treaty, virtually all major world powers and the majority of the rest, agreed to fund the Foundation and its translation efforts each according to their ability, with the condition that a committee consisting of representatives from each would have oversight as the translation progressed. This committee would have sole discretion when it came to suppressing dangerous information.

Neither Daniel nor Sarah had particularly liked the condition, but it was something they had discussed prior to breaking the code. They and their advisers, which included both of their families, Sinclair, Martha Simms and Raj, agreed that some sort of control had to be exercised. The rules governing the committee's decrees were complex and intended to keep only such knowledge as weapons of mass destruction, chemical warfare and biological warfare under wraps. Everything else, even if it could possibly be used for a nefarious purpose, was to be made available to anyone who asked. Of course, they had reserved the knowledge of the extraction method for the coded information to those who already knew.

"So, what do you suggest we do about it?" he asked Luke now.

"Nothing at the moment. We'll be inserting counterintelligence agents into your translation department to try to catch out any mole that the Orion society has managed to plant, I just wanted to let you know about it."

"Will I know who your agents are?" Daniel asked.

"If you can give me a compelling reason why you should, otherwise no. They'll be more effective if no one there knows or suspects their role. Think about it. You would probably unconsciously treat them differently from the other employees, yes?"

"I suppose I would, yes." Daniel mused. "Say, Luke. Sinclair was here just this morning complaining that my brother was interfering with his team. You might want to warn anyone you embed there not to get caught up in his shenanigans. I'm trying to rein him in, but you know the issues."

"Don't say anything to him about our suspicions," Luke cautioned. "I wouldn't want him to get caught in the middle of a situation that he's unprepared to handle."

"I'll keep it confidential. But, if your operative has their eye on someone that JR seems to be getting too close to, especially a woman, can you give me a heads up? He's been through enough, I don't want him involved with an OS plant."

"Will do," said Luke.

"Anything else?" Daniel asked.

"No, that's about it," Luke said.

"Would you and Sally be free to join us for dinner along with Ryan and Emma on Sunday?" Daniel asked, speaking to Luke as Sarah's uncle now, rather than his head of security.

"I'll check with Sally, but I don't know why we wouldn't. Thanks. Unless you hear differently, I'll see you then." Daniel was always happy to see his in-laws, but the real reason for the dinner party was to mend fences with Sarah. Ever since he had hired JR, Sarah's silent disapproval had haunted their relationship.

He understood Sarah's misgivings, and today's events had borne them out. But, JR was his baby brother. He had been dealt a bad hand, and Daniel felt obligated to help him if he could. Sarah also understood Daniel's position, they had talked about it. She wasn't pressuring him to fire JR, but she couldn't help but worry that his acting out would reflect back on the Foundation.

She couldn't help but wish things were back the way they were before JR had joined the Marines. He had a bit of a brotherly crush on her, which caused him to forgive her for whipping him regularly at billiards. He'd been so sweet. She could hardly relate the sullen, angry and irresponsible man of today with the boy she'd first met.

It wasn't uncommon for Daniel to receive a phone call from a sympathetic police officer asking him to meet them somewhere and take JR home himself rather than booking him on a drunk and disorderly or disturbing the peace charge. Not for the first time, Daniel thanked his lucky stars that pleasing Sarah by locating their foundation in a relatively small town was working to JR's advantage. But, even

Daniel had to admit that JR could cause them real and serious problems.

At the end of that day, Daniel was very grateful when Sarah dropped by his office to tell him it was time to go home. She dropped a kiss on the top of his head, and gave him a flirtatious look. Even after four years of marriage, her smile never failed to set the butterflies in his stomach aflutter.

"Anyone around here want to go home with me and get jiggy?" She said.

"Jiggy?" Daniel repeated. "What does that even mean?" Sarah gave him a slow wink and pretended to pull her top down over her shoulder, which she rotated like a 1920s flapper. Daniel's eyes lit up.

"That's the best offer I've had all day," he said.

Sarah immediately gave him her most severe schoolmarm look. "And who else has been offering?" she asked, pretending anger.

"Oh, you know, the usual. Groupies, women who think I'm devastatingly good-looking, news anchors, random homeless people," he said with a smirk.

"Then I've got no competition," Sarah laughed.

"You knew that."

On the way home, Daniel related Luke's call, and then told Sarah that he had invited Luke and Sally to dinner on Sunday.

"I thought we'd have just your family, your mom and dad and Luke and Sally. Does that sound okay?"

Sarah leaned over to kiss his cheek. "Did I ever tell you I love you?"

"Hmmm, I don't remember," Daniel said, making a comical puzzled face.

Sarah smiled. "I guess I'll have to make it more memorable tonight," she said.

"Sounds good, babe," Daniel breathed. "But don't get me fantasizing while I'm driving. We'll have a wreck."

His mood brightened even more when he heard her giggle. It had been a typical Monday, but going home with his Sarah to spend a quiet evening together would put his world back on an even keel. He reached for her hand and squeezed.

Chapter Five

THE NINTH CYCLE

The next time JR presented himself in Charles's office, Charles was ready for him with a number of research requests. Until the new map was available, Charles had determined, with a little help from Sinclair, that he himself would continue to look through the history section, but he would give JR the responsibility for finding anything he could that mentioned geography. After Daniel's talk with him, Charles was unsure that JR would be able to do a thorough job, but Sinclair put his mind at ease.

"The boy's actually brilliant," Sinclair had said. "I'm friends with his grandpa, so I know how well he did in archaeology as an undergraduate. In fact, his marks were good enough to allow him to receive credit for the courses he was taking when he flew off the handle and joined the Marines. Don't take my word for it, talk to Nick himself. He's still hoping that JR will go back for his advanced degrees and make something of himself."

"That will actually be very helpful. I'm glad you told

me." Charles said. He did remember that Daniel had said JR had an archaeology background, but he didn't think the brilliance had been mentioned. Only JR's problems.

Charles made sure to describe his research requests to JR in a way that conveyed their importance to his project. He was gratified, therefore, when JR came back with several references at the end of the day.

"Excellent work, JR. Tomorrow, I'd like you to pull the narratives and read them. That will probably take you the rest of the week, but if you'll give me a synopsis of each reference at the end of each day, it will save me a tremendous amount of time. This way, I won't have to go through anything that doesn't actually forward my project."

"What exactly are you looking for?" JR said. Daniel had asked the same question, but by now Charles had solidified his original theory. If JR were to be a real help, he would need to know what Charles was thinking.

"While I was researching for my doctoral thesis, I came across the mention of a map drawn in 1513, called the Piri Reis map. Some researchers had discovered it in a Turkish archive in 1929. They were startled to see a representation of what appeared to be a continent at the South Pole. The kicker was, nobody saw that land until three centuries later, or if they did, they didn't leave historical record to say so. I've been thinking about that map for over a decade. The researchers who found it in 1929 speculated that it was drawn from even earlier sources. I'd like to find those sources, and I have a hunch that they might have survived from the 10th Cycle."

"How?" JR began. "Wouldn't anything that a map would be drawn on have been destroyed in the 10th Cycle calamity?"

"As an archaeology student, haven't you ever wondered

why all the pyramids that we know of are lined up along meridian lines? Haven't you ever wondered about Stonehenge? Everyone else in the world has. Who's to say that a map of the world from the 10th Cycle perspective didn't exist on stone or some more permanent material than our maps today? How would we know? The Sahara desert was once a lush valley. We still don't know everything that's under tons of sand. Besides, we know that some people must have survived each calamity, or the first one would have left the Earth as lacking in people as the moon. Why couldn't a map have been preserved and handed down at some point?"

JR was rapt as Charles spoke. It had been several years since the curiosity that had interested him in archaeology as a boy had made an appearance. For a moment, excitement made his blood dance, before he realized that he had blown his chance at an archaeology career when he joined the Marines. Still, this project sounded like it might be fun for a while.

"Okay, boss. I'll start on that tomorrow. So, what you want me looking for is any mention of a durable map or globe of the world?"

"Yes, that or anything that you see that strikes you as out of the ordinary. I'd rather see too much than too little."

With a mocking half salute, JR made his exit. Charles thought, the kid could actually be an asset. Maybe everyone was being a little too hard on him. He seemed fine, not at all like the brooding veterans Charles had seen on street corners, with signs pathetically and pitifully declaring, 'Homeless. Hungry. Veteran. Please help.'

By Friday, Charles had read three days' worth of JR's surprisingly well-written synopses of the sections of the records that he'd identified. It was only late in the afternoon when he discovered something that he would have thought JR would bring to his attention immediately.

It was an account of an expedition to map or survey all the landmasses in the world, about 1,000 years before the 10th Cycle calamity, as nearly as Charles could identify the time line. Maybe 10,000 years ago, or a little less? Several teams of cartographers and archaeologists had been dispatched to the four corners of the earth. One of the reports electrified Charles, and he knew that he could not wait throughout the weekend to see the original for himself.

Recognizing that he might already be too late to catch Sinclair in his office, Charles nevertheless jogged down the hall and into the translation department. There he found the second shift working, having startled all of them by bursting through the doors in his headlong race to catch Sinclair. Charles paused to catch his breath. He addressed the room in general, asking if Sinclair was still in.

"I'm sorry, sir," one of the young translators answered. "Sinclair has gone to Rhode Island for the weekend. Is there anything we can help you with?"

"I'm not sure. Do you have access to the translation database? I have a reference here, and I'd like to read the full text."

The translator who had offered her help nodded once, beckoning Charles to follow her. She let him into a server room that had several carrels with workstation monitors in each.

"If you have a pass that allows access, you can swipe it on the card reader here," she said, showing him the device on the back of the monitor. Charles picked up his ID on a lanyard around his neck and held it up with a questioning look.

"Yes, that's the one. If you have rights to access the data, it will be recorded in the security strip," she said.

Charles swiped his card, holding his breath. To his delight, the screen came to life with a search field highlighted, and the caption 'Index Reference' blinking under it. He quickly typed in the reference that JR had noted. The translator forgotten, Charles avidly read what was on the screen. It was even better than he had hoped. Noting a print icon, he clicked on it, only then remembering that he had company.

"Where do I pick up the hard copy?" He asked.

"I'll show you," she said.

Charles left with a couple hundred pages to read over the weekend. Unless he missed his guess, he had just found the key he had been hoping to find in the 10th Cycle Library.

On Monday, Charles arrived at the Rossler Foundation building at eight am... What he had read over the weekend was groundbreaking information. Not only would he have a scholarly article for the Foundation Journal; if he could get funding, he would instigate an archaeological expedition that would rock the academic community. He might even get a book deal out of it. First, he would set JR to following every strand of information from the reference in question, to try to narrow down where in Antarctica they should focus their search.

Charles was hard at work by 8:30, making notes on what he needed to do next, and waiting for JR, when Daniel stuck his head in the office.

"Just checking in with you," he said. "Is JR working out?"

"Great timing! I've got something here that looks significant, thanks to JR. I've not heard of anything similar in any of the translations I've read about."

"Is that so? What have you found?" Daniel asked, his heart speeding up as it had done many times before when his team was on the verge of a breakthrough.

"Unless I'm misinterpreting what I'm seeing here, it seems that the 10th Cyclers knew of some of the remnants of the 9th Cycle that either survived their calamity, or perhaps it was just their records that survived."

Every nerve in Daniel's body fired at once as a surge of adrenaline swept through him. "My God, that's the first I've heard mention that the 10th Cyclers knew any specifics about the previous cycles. Everything I've seen indicates that they were merely leaving a record of their own accomplishments in the library. Where exactly did you find this reference?"

Charles had not been thinking of it in that way, though now that Daniel voiced it, he could see why it would be so exciting. But, because he was focused on the history of the frozen southern continent, it was the mention of a ruin or abandoned city on Antarctica that had caught his interest. As far as anyone from the current cycle was aware, Antarctica had never been inhabited prior to the modern exploration bases being planted there.

"Daniel, what I'm thinking is that this is going to require an expedition. Is there any chance that the Foundation would consider funding it?"

"I'm sure we'd consider it. I can't make any promises on my own, but if you'll get a proposal together, I have no problem presenting it to the Board," said Daniel.

"We have no time to waste, you know," said Charles. "The optimum time for expeditions to Antarctica is between

October and February. Getting an expedition together this year is going to take some doing, since it's already March."

"Then let's get the proposal before the board by the end of next week," Daniel said. "I'll call a special meeting to consider it. Can you have a presentation ready by then?"

"I'll do my best."

Daniel left, only a few minutes before JR's arrival. JR looked as if he had had a late night. His eyes were bloodshot, and he had apparently forgotten to comb his hair. Charles ignored his appearance as he rose from his chair and rushed around the desk to embrace the other man. He stopped short of his goal when JR flinched.

"Oh, sorry. I guess you shouldn't rush at a combat veteran unexpectedly," Charles said.

JR gave him a hard look and, without a word, whirled and rushed out of the room. Charles mentally kicked himself. He had needed JR's assistance, and now it appeared he could forget about it, at least for today. Instead of dwelling on his blunder, Charles went back to his lists and notes.

He was relieved when JR came back after only a couple of hours, wearing a forbidding frown. Charles would have liked to apologize, but a look at JR's face persuaded him that now was not the time.

"Hi, JR. Ready for a new assignment?" He asked, pretending that the incident had never happened. JR's face smoothed and he nodded. Charles handed him the printout of the notes he'd made for the tasks he had laid out for JR. He didn't know whether JR had a good grasp of PowerPoint, so he had to ask.

"Yeah, I guess," JR responded, without much enthusiasm. Charles decided to take him into his confidence, reasoning that if they were to work together, he had to trust the young man.

"JR, I want you to know that it was your excellent work last week that has put this in motion. One of the references you found indicates that the 10th Cyclers had knowledge of a 9th Cycle civilization on Antarctica. Do you understand what that means?"

JR shrugged. "I thought Antarctica was uninhabited," he said with disinterest.

"Everyone did. What you found was a record of a civilization we've never suspected. I'm putting together a proposal for the Foundation to send us on an expedition to find the ruins."

"Us?" JR repeated.

"Well, me. Of course, I'll have to have a team, but I haven't worked out who all we might need. All that needs to be decided within the next few weeks. I'm going to need your help to organize it."

"Okay, boss. So, you want this PowerPoint to present to the Board, I guess?"

"Exactly. Can I count on you?"

"As long as I don't have to go to that deep-freeze with you," JR said.

"Oh, I doubt that we'd take you," Charles said, unaware that he had just uttered an insult to the sensitive man.

The rest of the week was hectic for both of them, as well as for Sinclair's and Nick's departments, both. Less urgent lines of inquiry were dropped, as everyone lent a hand to finding every last scrap of information that would be of use to the expedition. JR had more than a decent grasp of PowerPoint, it turned out. When he set his mind to it, JR could master virtually any software for which he understood the purpose. It was a knack that most of the generation growing up in the computer age shared.

Given an important role in the planning of the expedition, JR, to Sinclair's appreciation, stayed out of the translation department and out of the panties of the translators. He even refrained from drinking himself into a stupor during the week nights.

Too soon, the board meeting was upon them, and they had to convince themselves that the presentation was in order.

Chapter Six

LET'S GO AND FIND IT

Most of the board members, along with Nicolas Rossler, Sinclair O'Reilly and Raj Sankaran were on hand for the presentation. After virtually-free electrical power and the cure for most types of cancer, this was the most explosive discovery to come out of the pyramid material since its discovery. That an expedition would be approved was almost a foregone conclusion. Only the details and the funding remained to be sorted out. By unanimous vote, the Board approved the expedition, along with the request that the money be raised through subscription by the various countries that claimed any sort of interest in Antarctica.

There were a few dissenting discussions. The cost would be prohibitive, as all the exploration equipment would have to be acquired, adapted for the harsh conditions, and then transported. Furthermore, their time constraints would make each phase even more expensive due to the rush. There hadn't been time to establish the budget, so some members of the Board felt that they were signing a blank check.

Dr. Summers' conclusions regarding the origin of the information that informed the drawing of the Piri Reis map were questioned. Was it not possible that the earlier maps upon which it depended were in fact early 11th Cycle maps, not necessarily 10th Cycle? What confirmatory research had he done on the 10th Cycle exploratory expeditions? Did any of them mention a great southern continent? Other than the cities, how was it described? After all, it was known that the western part of Antarctica had broken away from Australia…had that happened already by the 10th Cycle, and if so, where was Australia on the 10th Cycle map?

Dr. Summers fielded all the questions he could, and allowed Nicholas or Sinclair to answer some that he couldn't. The fact was that no one was certain of the nature of the 10th Cycle calamity. That had of necessity been left out of the library, as it destroyed the civilization that built it. And no one knew for certain that the current cycle was the eleventh, though it was assumed so because of the resemblance of the languages and the assumption that there would have been more change if one or more cycles had intervened. Nevertheless, that was all speculation, until more study could establish the historic timeline within the geologic record.

His arguments in favor of the expedition were few and simple. The benefits that Dr. Summers presented were convincing; now that it was known that other civilizations had flourished and then died in world-shattering calamities, anything that could be gleaned from previous cycles might help the current civilization prevent its own calamity, widely thought to be frighteningly close to occurring.

Even if our own calamity was many centuries in the future, an understanding of human history and origins was always beneficial. And finally, if the 9th Cycle city known to the 10th Cyclers could be found, would it contain records just as important to us as those the 10th Cyclers left? It couldn't be known without the expedition.

In the end, the objections were overcome through Daniel's famous powers of persuasion, and even the question of whether the parties involved in the Antarctica Treaty would agree was put to rest. After all, the overlap between the countries signing that treaty and the one governing the use of the Pyramid Code was almost total. It only remained to complete the budget proposal, arrange funding, and of course put the plans in motion.

The U.S, Great Britain, Australia and, surprisingly, Chile, responded with generous funding offers and the expedition was set to go. Dr. Summers was elated, but he also knew that the approval was the easy part. Now would come extensive planning, recruiting and training, all to be accomplished before the short Antarctic summer began in October. It didn't escape his notice that it was already the end of March.

The first order of business was to develop a more detailed budget to replace the estimate he'd presented to the Board. While that was taking place, formal applications to use scientific facilities of the Antarctica Treaty countries were being filled out and sent for approval. JR was proving quite cooperative in the repetitive task of filling out the pesky applications. Meanwhile Charles Summers was up to his ears in specifications for ground transportation, polar gear, and calculations regarding how much food a team the size of theirs would need during the planned five-month expedition.

Included in the budget, was payroll for the team, transport to and from McMurdo Station in Antarctica, communications costs and all supplies. The final figure was staggering. Summers debated whether to forgo a salary, but in the end decided he deserved one, and wrote it in. He had applied for a sabbatical year to plan for and lead this expedition, which the school had granted readily, expecting the prestige of their faculty member to carry over to the University.

Summers estimated that he would have to provide transportation, food and sometimes overnight lodging in state-of-the art polar tents for his team of approximately fifteen people. Two Tucker Sno-Cats, each capable of carrying up to eight people, alone cost over a quarter million dollars, not to mention the cost of transporting them to Antarctica. In addition each would need to tow a sled capable of carrying at least twenty tons of equipment and food. The research required to determine all of the equipment needed, along with food that would be appropriate for the conditions, took more than a week. When at last the budget was done, Summers submitted it to Daniel, who submitted it to the countries that had subscribed to the funding for the expedition. A committee of representatives from each of those countries met to go over and approve the budget, after which Summers was given the go-ahead to carry out the rest of the planning.

A wrinkle had developed in his plans when representatives from each of the countries that were funding the expedition made a formal demand of Daniel that their own personnel be among the expedition members. Therefore, rather than simply recruiting the best that could be had of each specialty, careful selection had to be made among the available pool put forth by the countries involved. It was thanks to Daniel, whose legendary powers of persuasion served the Rossler Foundation well in cases like this, that Summers wasn't stuck with a hodgepodge of members that represented a strict division of personnel from each of the countries in question. How Daniel had managed to sort that out, Summers couldn't imagine. But the outcome was fortunate for the expedition. At least he now had a fighting chance to recruit competent team members.

Summers had a bit of natural bean-counter in him, so each day he went home with a sense of accomplishment as his planning moved forward. By mid-April, he had finished the preliminary planning and was ready to begin recruitment of those members of the expedition whose expertise would contribute toward the more detailed planning that would be required before he could begin ordering supplies.

Summers recalled that one of his original questions had been how early explorers, not only from the current cycle that was believed to be the 11th, but also from the 10th, managed to make their way to distant lands before maps had been drawn, and then home again. To his list of team specialties, he added 'cartographer'. Antarctica was mapped already, but nothing had ever indicated that a city or cities might be hidden under the ice. A cartographer was essential to map any ruins that they found.

His original research had been subsumed in the larger discovery that Antarctica had been populated. How was it possible, he thought, for such a forbidding climate to support a large city, or cities? Could it be that the climate had not always been so forbidding? What had changed to make it so? As an archaeologist, he was mainly interested in the ruins he hoped to find, and the civilization that had created them. But he was almost as curious about the geologic questions. Opening the appropriate window on his project management software, Summers again added a specialty, geologist, to his list.

By now, the new map that Summers had requested prior to his momentous discovery had been delivered. Surprisingly, what Summers thought of as the 'tail' of South America was missing from the map, as well as Australia and the Antarctic Peninsula. On the other hand, the African and South American continents as they were arranged during the 10th Cycle bore a strong resemblance to maps of Gondwanaland that Summers recalled. He couldn't remember exactly how long ago the supercontinents were said to have broken up, but he thought it was millions rather than thousands of years. Summers made a note to discuss it with the geologist he recruited, which would be one of the first team members he'd need. Maybe the answers to his questions would hold clues to the nature of the calamity that had destroyed the 10th Cycle.

Chapter Seven

THE RECRUITS

Summers had plenty of experience of his own in recruiting archaeological teams, but deemed it a privilege to work with Nicholas Rossler, who was legendary in the field. Nicholas turned his own work over to his assistant for the time he needed to be able to help Summers. Together they created a list of characteristics that each member of their expedition must possess to be eligible for selection.

First and foremost, the ability to work within a team. Both men had seen disastrous results from archaeological expeditions in which prima donnas were secretive about their finds, or argumentative with their fellow expedition members. Second, not only because it was good practice, but also because the harsh conditions required it, each member had to have a high level of intelligence and self-sufficiency. Even in summer, Antarctica could be fatal to someone who found himself alone on the ice without support. Summers was determined to bring home his expedition intact. A few would be required to have leadership skills, and Summers had his own ideas about which specialties should be represented by a natural leader.

A study of any failed exploratory project, in fact, any failed human endeavor, would likely identify too many leaders and not enough followers as the reason. The opposite problem, that of few leaders and all followers wasn't so likely to happen. Leaders almost always emerged in times of necessity, but the old phrase 'too many chiefs and not enough Indians' was descriptive of what happened when everyone was a born leader.

There was even a name for the syndrome, Apollo, based on the findings of Dr. Meredith Belbin. Dr. Belbin had been one of the original gurus of teambuilding. During his tests, he selected teams of highly analytical individuals and then tested them against teams that were selected in traditional ways. It was expected that the Apollo teams, as he called them, would perform at a higher level than the others. However, that was not always the case. In analyzing what had gone wrong, Belbin determined that those of his teams made up of highly dominant individuals were ineffective at the tasks because those individuals were less likely to yield to the suggestions of others. When his Apollo teams did do well, it was because those teams lacked dominant individuals or had only one or two. As interesting as that study had been, making a mistake of that nature could be fatal to some or all in the case of an Antarctic expedition.

In addition to those qualifications as well as expertise in the relevant specialty, Nicholas and Charles determined that each member of the team must speak fluent English, no matter what their native language was. Charles jokingly asked Nicholas if his scientists had not yet found records in the 10th Cycle library to make a Universal Translator such as the Star Trek crew had utilized.

"You'd be amazed at what the translators have found," Nicholas responded. "I wouldn't be surprised if they did find specifications for such a device before they finish translating everything. If they find the specs, my researchers should be able to develop it."

"Will either of us live to see the day when the entire library has been translated?" asked Charles.

"I've heard it said that some people believe the secret to lives as long as Methuselah's could be contained somewhere in the library. If that's the case, maybe you will live to see that day. I'm not sure I want to preserve this old body for that many years," he joked. "Now, if all this had come about when I was young and full of vinegar, it might be a different story."

Charles sensed that Nicholas had given this very idea some thought, however, he did not want to pry into the other man's personal philosophy.

That brought up another question, though.

"Shouldn't everyone be in peak physical condition?" asked Summers.

"Oh, I would think so," Nicholas responded. "You don't want people getting sick or otherwise dragging the team down. How's your own conditioning, Summers?"

"I'm sure I can hold my own, I hike, snowshoe and ski as often as I can."

"No wonder you and Daniel get along so well. I know he's in his element now that he's moved to Colorado. It sounds to me like you'll do fine."

"I suppose we should have some sort of physical and psychological testing, and it probably wouldn't be a bad idea for me to undergo it as well. Not that I would stay behind," he laughed.

Nicholas gave him a serious look. "All joking aside,

Antarctica can easily kill you. Be sure you really are in peak condition. You have several months to train for it; I'd recommend you start immediately."

"Not a bad idea," Summers agreed.

The last thing the two men specified was a background check. Nicholas was all too aware of international criminal organizations, that devil's spawn Orion Society among them, that would love to either steal the research or sabotage the expedition altogether. Summers agreed that anyone whose background included gaps or questionable associations should be eliminated immediately. In that way, they wouldn't waste time and money further testing them for inclusion. If they had consulted Luke, he would have warned them that background checks could be fooled. However, they naively assumed that all background checks are created equal and would always provide a reliable and flawless result.

As with the budget, Summers presented the final list of membership requirements to Daniel for approval. However, Daniel indicated that as long as Nicholas was satisfied, so was he. Summers insisted he read it over, anyway. Afterward, Daniel commented that it seemed to be very complete and was satisfactory to him.

Summers made arrangements to put out the call for applicants in the newsletter of the Rossler Foundation, as well as several other respected scientific communiqués and on the website of the Rossler Foundation. The application page had barely gone active when applications from all over the world began pouring in. Raj was enlisted to program a way to eliminate unsuitable applicants without human intervention. In short order, he had linked the application database to a query that automatically eliminated those who didn't speak English, could not present credentials in the specialty for which they were applying, or answered 'no' to certain of the physical condition or health questions. Of course, that would not eliminate the liars who thought they could game the system, but it did cut down the applicants by nearly half.

His task of sending out applications to the Antarctica Treaty nations for permission to use their bases had been completed for quite some time, so JR needed a new job. Summers gave him the job of responding to email after an auto responder had notified each applicant whether they were eligible for further consideration or not. Naturally, there were many who answered angrily when they received the email that they were not eligible. A second auto responder sent out a generic letter stating that one of the three considerations, language, credentials or physical inability, had been the reason for their elimination, a courtesy that was not appreciated by some. It was JR's job to personally answer those who persisted. The rest received emails directing them to various agencies within their respective countries where they would be fingerprinted, and told to wait for further communication.

The next step was the background check, which eliminated perhaps a quarter of the remaining applicants. At this point there were still several thousand applicants for the fifteen or so spots on the team. These applicants were directed to a secure website where they took the first batch of several psychological tests, including the latest version of the Minnesota Multiphasic Personality Inventory, and several others that could be administered without personal interviews. Once again the pool of applicants was reduced by at least a quarter, based on acceptable ranges that were determined by psychologists contracted for the purpose.

Those same psychologists would personally interview those applicants who passed the physical tests.

The task of helping Summers develop a battery of physical tasks fell to Daniel and Sarah's personal physician, who turned out to be a Renaissance person in an attractive female body, with degrees in general and sports medicine as well as a psychology concentration in her undergraduate background. It was Dr. Rebecca Mendenhall who assisted Summers in determining what psychology tests could be administered online, as well as the tests for physical conditioning.

Rebecca was the younger sister of Sarah's best friend Cindy, but had become a good friend in her own right when Daniel and Sarah moved to Boulder. In an ironic twist, Rebecca more strongly resembled the tall, brunette Sarah more than she did her own much shorter blonde sister. The three often joked that the stork had brought Rebecca to the wrong house. When they were kids, Rebecca was an annoying little tag-along, but now she formed the third leg of a solid triad who did what Daniel called 'girly' things together; shopping, for example. When Sarah tapped her for the expedition planning role, she was happy to help.

At this point, with still far too many applicants, it was decided that physical testing would begin in countries that had funded the expedition. Only if suitable applicants could not be found in these countries would teams be sent to physically test applicants elsewhere. This not only reduced the expense of testing everyone who had passed the initial psychological testing for their physical condition, but would satisfy the demands of those countries to have representatives on the expedition. Consequently, three teams of two personal trainers each would be sent to London, Melbourne and Santiago, to administer the physical conditioning test.

American applicants were required to travel to one of four regional testing facilities.

Surprisingly, another quarter of the remaining applicants were eliminated simply because they declined to make the trip for testing. Summers was philosophical about that, saying that anyone who wasn't willing to move heaven and earth to get to a testing center was likely not to be suited for the expedition anyway. When the physical testing was complete a manageable one-hundred and eighty-seven applicants remained, spread almost equally between the three largest countries, with about twenty living in Chile. These applicants were invited to travel to Boulder for a week of more in-depth psychological testing, with their expenses subsidized upon request.

Summers had been exhausted by the pace of the testing, being involved at every step in numerous decisions, some of which he had not anticipated. Fortunately, each time he had required a consultant to assist him in making those decisions, Daniel's network had supplied one that was eager to be a part of this endeavor.

As he watched the lithe young woman putting the testers through their paces and correctly performing the physical tests herself, Summers wondered if he could recruit her as the team doctor. As soon as she returned to his side, he asked her as if casually whether she spoke a second language. As a man, he couldn't help but admire her beauty and pleasing figuré, noting that she bore a strong resemblance to Sarah Rossler, though she denied being related.

Rebecca's warm brown eyes sparkled with health and enthusiasm for life, and Summers thought she would make a great addition to the team if she would go. Since they expected to have some expedition members whose first language was Spanish, it would be helpful if the expedition doctor spoke it, even though those members also spoke English. That way, any lack on either side could be filled in by either the patient or the doctor.

"Spanish," she answered. "You can't practice medicine in the Western US without having a passing knowledge of Spanish. I chose to learn it well, so that I could volunteer in free clinics in my spare time."

"That's very commendable, Dr. Mendenhall. Do you actually have any spare time?"

She laughed as she answered, "Not much."

"I had a crazy thought," Summers said, speaking slowly to feel his way toward the answer he wanted. "Would you consider, maybe, applying for the spot of team doctor?"

"I thought you'd never ask!" Rebecca cried, throwing her arms around the surprised Charles. "I just have to get one patient's approval."

"Oh? Who would that be?"

"I'm afraid that's confidential, Dr. Summers," she twinkled. "But, I'll ask her to tell you herself."

Mystified, Charles just smiled. "I hope you receive her approval, or if not, that she will allow me to persuade her. I think you would be a great asset to our team. Assuming you can pass the psychological tests," he grinned, winking.

Rebecca excused herself and left Dr. Summers watching the personal trainers perform the tests that they would administer the following week. Looking behind her, to see she was not followed, she found her way to Sarah Rossler's office.

"Knock, knock," she said.

"Becca! What a nice surprise," Sarah said, using the shortened form of her name that Rebecca preferred from her friends and family.

"I'm not so sure you'll think so when you've heard what I

have to say," Rebecca said, though her smile indicated it was good news.

"Oh, I'm not sure I like the sound of that."

"Sarah, I know we talked about me delivering your baby, but just hear me out." Sarah crossed her arms, but she thought she knew what was coming. Her eyes twinkled as she listened without responding.

"Okay, I'll just say it. Dr. Summers just asked me to join the expedition. I won't be back before your due date."

"You didn't tell him…"

"No, no. I told him I had to get one patient's approval. He asked me who, but I told him it was confidential. I did say I would ask her to tell him herself."

"Daniel and I agreed that we would wait until the beginning of my second trimester before we announced it to the staff," Sarah said. "But, I'll admit I'm having trouble keeping my mouth shut, and it's almost July. I'm so happy!"

Rebecca smiled fondly at her friend. "You deserve to be," she said. "How's Daniel at keeping secrets?"

"The man is a crypt, you wouldn't believe it. But, I could tell you stories! So, I guess you really want to go on this expedition?"

"I've never wanted anything more in my life," Rebecca said. "This will be the adventure of a lifetime."

"You be sure to come back from it, Becca. Even if I have to have someone else deliver my baby, you're still one of my best friends. I can't do without you."

"I intend to not only come back myself, but bring everybody else back with me," Rebecca laughed.

When all the planning was done that could be done without the required experts, Summers had a list that included an expedition coordinator, who would be responsible for all of the logistics for the expedition, since Summers himself would be busy with research projects. In addition a medical doctor was essential, and Rebecca Mendenhall had expressed her interest in that position, pending psychological testing. Summers had no doubt that Rebecca would pass that test with flying colors, as easily as she could pass the physical test.

For the research part of the expedition, Summers included a biologist, an anthropologist, a geologist and the cartographer he had added at the last minute. Two Rossler Foundation research assistants would continue their roles on the expedition. Support staff in the persons of an electronics engineer, a civil engineer, a couple of mining experts, an explosives technician, a communications and IT expert and a cook would be required.

Although Summers had researched the volume of food required for such a group throughout an arduous expedition, his coordinator and the cook would be tasked with determining exactly what supplies to bring, including the food. Their selection would need to be made almost immediately, so that they could get started on their preparations. Summers asked JR to read over the applications of the applicants who had passed the preliminary testing, to find someone whose CV matched the characteristics they'd identified as essential for the expedition coordinator. It would need to be someone who had a strong grasp of logistical considerations, a track record in teambuilding and leadership qualities.

As for the cook, the main characteristic would be experience in plying his or her craft in sometimes primitive and often trying circumstances. JR joked that his grandfather had often complained that all cooks were antisocial, and couldn't be trusted not to poison the expedition members, unless someone watched them closely. Summers hoped to find someone whose personality was not too unpleasant, simply for the sake of peace in camp. If he were also a decent cook, it would be a bonus. Summers had been thinking in terms of all expedition members being male until he invited Dr. Mendenhall. Now he wondered if there would be more female members when all was said and done. Without the slightest intention of being sexist, he felt some doubt about it. Dr. Mendenhall notwithstanding, the physical conditions might prevent most females from qualifying.

It turned out that among all the applicants, only three had the required experience for expedition coordinator. Those three were invited to Boulder to complete the remaining psychological interviews and physical tests beyond those they had already passed. Among them were wall climbing, bouldering, free solo-climbing and cross-country skiing evaluations. Summers anticipated that even non-researchers would be required to keep up in physically challenging conditions. The candidate who tested the strongest turned out to be a Frenchman, Paul LeClerc, who accepted the job offer with alacrity. Summers immediately gave him the task of selecting the cook. Who better than a Frenchman to select a skilled cook?

Next on the agenda was filling the researcher roles. Summers tasked JR with interviewing the Rossler Foundation research assistants to determine their interest in joining the expedition and to coordinate testing of any who expressed the desire to do so. Meanwhile, Summers himself combed through the CVs remaining to locate his research scientists. He found his biologist, Antonio Santiago, among the Chilean applicants, the anthropologist, Cecil Stone, in Great Britain and, to his delight, Robert Cartwright, the geologist, in Australia.

That had been a bonus, he thought. In addition to being from one of the funding countries, perhaps the man would be more familiar with geology in the southern hemisphere than a North American or European. For balance, he eliminated all cartographers except those hailing from the United States, at least for a preliminary pass. Once again, a round of testing as guests of the Rossler Foundation in Boulder ensued. Summers counted it auspicious that his first selections passed the testing with flying colors. His research team assembled, Summers set them to describing research objectives and listing supplies or equipment that those objectives would require. All were housed temporarily in a small apartment building that the Foundation had acquired for the purpose. All were also given guest offices in the Foundation headquarters building.

Now, all that remained was to recruit support staff, and it was imperative that this happen as quickly as practical. The six months between approval of the expedition and the planned departure date were now half gone, and there was still so much to do. Summers, Nicholas Rossler and the cartographer, Angela Brown, were spending hours poring over both ancient and recent maps of the southernmost continent, discussing routes and potential locations for a city to be hidden under the ice. While JR, assisted at times by Daniel, located suitable support specialists, Summers and his helpers labored to determine how the expedition would proceed. That would be important to know once the specialists were on board, so that they could requisition the supplies and equipment they would need.

Once all of the scientists and support staff had determined their needs, it still remained to acquire everything on the list. Summers often thought that the undertaking was as massive as if he had been leading an expedition to a hostile planet. In fact, though their destination was on old, familiar Earth, it was indeed a very hostile environment into which he would lead them. Temperatures would average about 36°F during the peak of their summer expedition, though extremes at night could drop to only 14°F or rise during the day to a balmy mid-50s. Wind, altitude and latitude as they explored would cause these temperatures to be highly variable. In addition to determining their supplies and equipment requirements, it would soon become necessary to begin training all of the expedition members in polar safety measures as well as how to handle strenuous activity under harsh conditions.

It was almost at the last possible moment that Summers realized he needed to transport his entire team to the Andes for the most strenuous training. In Colorado, it was summer and even the 14ers, that is, the peaks that topped 14,000 feet, had little snow or ice. And yet, traversing the Transantarctic Mountains would require the same skills as hiking or skiing 14ers. The logical answer was Chile or Argentina, whose ski season extended from mid-June to mid-October. A hasty consultation with Daniel and a few other advisers drawn from Foundation staff or the Board achieved consensus. Within a month, the expedition members would be dispatched to a ski resort in Chile to continue their training, while Foundation staff members took over the remaining tasks in outfitting the expedition.

One thing Summers had not anticipated, though, was the surprise that Daniel sprung on him when he let Summers know he expected JR to be included in the expedition. Summers arranged a meeting to discuss the possibility privately with Daniel as soon as he heard.

"You understand, Daniel that we have created a team specifically recruited for their psychological fitness within the team environment, as well as their expertise and physical fitness, yes? JR has not gone through any of that testing, and he's shown no interest in going."

"Yes, Charles. Of course I understand that. But you must understand my position. When you agreed to use JR as your assistant and then involved him in every aspect of the planning, I understood that to mean that he would be joining the expedition. He maintains his physical training, and in fact was already more fit than many of your team, due to his Marine training. I get that he is sometimes difficult, but again, because of his Marine training, he's not unsuited to a team environment. Not only do I think he will be an asset to your expedition, but I must insist that you take him. I'd hate for us to have a big difference of opinion on this."

"Does my funding depend on my cooperation?" Summers was maintaining a cool exterior, while starting a slow burn of indignation inside.

"I wouldn't want to put it that way, and I hope that our friendship would mean you wouldn't make me." Daniel said. "But, assuming we're now in agreement, I would ask you to keep it to yourself until I have a chance to put it to JR. We haven't discussed it yet.

It was plain to Summers that, though he wouldn't say so, Daniel was taking a stand from which he wouldn't lightly back down. It was rather surprising and puzzling. Rather than argue the point with Daniel, Summers tried an end run, appealing to Sarah to intervene. While she disapproved of including JR, which she only privately confessed to Summers, she declined to get involved in the controversy.

"Charles, you can't ask me to do that; I'm Daniel's wife. And he has a point. JR is lost, and he needs some guidance to find himself. Maybe he wouldn't pass your psychological tests right now, but if you'd known him before, you'd know that it would have been a slam-dunk for him then. He needs a chance to renew his self-esteem, get back to the JR he used to be. He has a strong sense of self-preservation. He won't slow you down, and if you'll just maintain authoritative control, he'll be fine. Besides, he's done good work in helping you get ready hasn't he? Being allowed to go would be a reward for him."

Summers had his doubts, but he had more important things on his mind, such as the health and safety of all seventeen of his team, including himself and JR. He could spend no more time worrying about it. In only two weeks, they'd be transferring to Chile, and he had to be ready.

In the time remaining before transferring the team to Chile, Summers insisted that they start doing things as a team. He wanted to observe their interaction and have Rebecca do the same. All in all, he was pleased with the results. With both his cartographer and the doctor being female, the other scientists were on their best behavior, while having females in both the electronics engineer and the communications/IT specialist roles had excited only a little sexist grumbling from the others before the team met each other. That both of the latter women were young and attractive quieted the grumbling once and for all then.

As they got to know each other, their quirks and habits,

likes and dislikes, set them apart as individuals. Santiago, the paleobiologist, loved to play poker, but was no good at it. He cheerfully lost to JR on a regular basis. JR, on the other hand, blithely unaware that he was slated to go with them, took part in the social activities because they were fun, and fun was his middle name.

JR constantly practiced his billiards game, as his sister-in-law famously slaughtered him every time they played. That Sarah also slaughtered Daniel and their brother Aaron mattered not at all. He was determined to gain the skill to beat her. The Brit anthropologist, Cecil Stone, read ancient Greek erotic poetry, translating aloud any time he could attract the undivided attention of anyone at all, especially one of the women. As far as Summers could tell, they would be a compatible and interesting group with which to spend five relatively isolated months.

One more female was included on the team, a research assistant that Charles was unsure of, though she seemed competent at her job and had passed the required tests. He didn't know why he had an aversion to the woman, unless it was her ridiculous name—Misty Rivers—or perhaps her unidentifiable accent or her slutty clothing and swaying hips. She just made him uneasy, never more so when he saw her leave the building arm in arm with JR half an hour before quitting time one afternoon. After that, he took a look at JR's notes to identify a replacement if necessary. However, other than the taking off without authorization, he couldn't fault her. She had even clocked out properly, so she couldn't be accused of time fraud.

The cook was among his favorites. LeClerc had found a brawny, hairy, foul-mouthed Cajun who could put a meal on the table that was fit for a king with nothing more than a few vegetables, some butter, flour and any kind of meat or seafood, including some disgusting little creatures that he called crawdads. They looked like large roaches, but tasted like lobster, and Charles had become reluctantly addicted to the little bastards. He hoped that Deveau, whose first name, Bartolome, was quickly shortened to a more appropriate and descriptive 'Bart', had laid in a supply of them to take to Antarctica with them. Somehow, he doubted if they were native to the region.

Aside from his inappropriate attention to the questionable Misty, JR was giving him no trouble so far, though he privately thought that would change if JR knew he would be going with them. Despite Sarah's belief that it would be a reward, there must be a reason Daniel was treating it as a delicate subject. JR did as he was asked, did a good job for the most part, and was pleasant to the other team members. Discreet inquiries by Dr. Mendenhall revealed that everyone liked him, even she did, although as a friend of the family she knew all too well how volatile he could be. Summers wondered belatedly if she was in on the secret, or if he'd just let the cat out of the bag with his questions.

Before they left for Chile, the team was trained in first aid and polar survival techniques, the use of their protective gear and rescue equipment, and some were cross-trained on essential but non-specialist skills in case the designated specialist was unable to perform his or her duties. Nothing was left to chance, no eventuality unexplored. Even stress-reduction techniques such as yoga and meditation were in the training regimen. JR avoided the stress-reduction courses, claiming that he didn't get stress, he caused it. He saw no reason to participate when he wouldn't be going on the expedition, and he didn't believe the techniques were effective anyway. They hadn't helped his PTSD at all.

Meanwhile, since the archaeologists and Angela Brown

had identified a few likely areas to explore, Summers called in the civil engineer, Dan Littleton, to get an idea of how they might expect the traverse of the icepack to go when there were no roads available. Robert Cartwright, the Aussie geologist, was the only one of the team ever to have set foot on Antarctica before, so he was included in the planning. He warned that the ice flowed in sometimes surprising ways, and that they would have to look out for crevasses as on any glacier.

Tunneling would be a risky proposition, and blasting would be even more so, though the expert they'd recruited had a reputation as the best at his specialty and had worked in a variety of conditions, including pipeline work in the Arctic, for ten years. Still, with the ice pack up to three miles thick, if they hoped to find a ruined city on bedrock, they'd probably have to dig somehow, just to get to it. Finding it in the first place was another story.

To aid in that task, the group did their best to compare the ancient maps, especially the Piri Reis map that had started Summers' fascination with the idea of a populated Antarctica, with modern satellite maps. The resemblance of the shoreline to today's shoreline, visible under the ice only through a technique that pulled information from satellite imagery, radio echoes to determine ice thickness, seismic techniques and cartographic data, was astounding. It could only have been drawn either during a time when the ice was not present, or by using similar techniques, which certainly weren't available during the time of the Piri Reis map.

Everyone on the team was acutely aware that, based on the map of the 10th Cycle world that Summers had commissioned, considerable tectonic shift had occurred, possibly in a catastrophic way at the end of the 10th Cycle. What that had done to the interior structure of Antarctica was up for debate, and much of it centered on the Transantarctic Mountains.

According to the 10th Cycle map, Australia either had not existed or had not been explored, though they all thought the latter was unlikely given the long history of the 10th Cycle. According to modern geographic theory, the western portion of Antarctica had broken away from Australia and moved toward the eastern portion of Antarctica via tectonic drift and seafloor spreading, until the two portions collided, pushing up the continent-dividing mountain range in the process. Summers, backed up by Cartwright, suspected that the most likely place to find a buried city was within the disturbed area, though it may mean that the ruins were shattered beyond recognition.

The next most likely scenario was that the ruins were instead under the Admiral Byrd glacier, the lowest point in Antarctica at 1.7 *miles* below sea level. This, however, presented the difficulty of ice so thick that discovery of any ruins was doubtful, and reaching them almost impossible if indeed they still existed.

No, with luck, they'd find what they were looking for within the mountain range, though doing so might prove difficult. In any case, locating and reaching the target sites would require bivouac on the ice at times, and would test the stamina and resolve of the team as much as any exploration had ever tested pioneering explorers in history.

The last piece of the puzzle involved permissions from the Antarctica Treaty nations for scientific exploration and support from the various permanent bases on the continent. Because the expedition intended to travel through sections claimed by several different countries, JR's first task had been to fill out the applications to do so. The Treaty governed behavior by the signing countries, everything from preserving the natural treasures to the polite fiction that the land mass belonged to no particular country. However, several countries laid unofficial claim to sections of the continent. Great Britain claimed a large slice that included the Antarctic Peninsula and subsumed the section claimed also by Argentina.

Continuing clockwise around the continent, Norway claimed about one-sixth of the continent, contiguous to Great Britain's claim on the east and abutting Australia's claim on the west. Australia claimed about one-third, but a narrow slice claimed by France intersected it. New Zealand claimed just under a sixth, which territory included the Ross Ice Shelf and McMurdo station. McMurdo station itself belonged to the United States though the US made no claim on territory. Just over one-sixth was unclaimed, leading around to the Chilean claim that took in half of Great Britain's supposed territory and a bit more.

In addition, thirty or so countries that were signatories to the Antarctica Treaty had planted permanent scientific research stations, mostly on the coastlines. It was a welter of confusing and conflicting political quicksand that had to be carefully negotiated if they wanted to cover the most likely spots for the ruins of a Ninth Cycle city to be found.

Finally, though Daniel had promised support from his permanent staff to finalize the logistics, delivery of the large equipment had to take place before leading edges of the Ross became unstable with warming temperatures. The plan was to have the two heavy Sno-Cats and their trailers unloaded at McMurdo and to drive them from there up the Transantarctic Highway. A couple of Australian volunteers known to Cartwright were standing by to meet the equipment before the expedition arrived and see it safely stowed on solid ground before the summer temperatures caused the ice shelf to retreat for the season.

Everything else was well in hand. Staging on a California wharf would begin early in September, and the container ship would steam down the west coast of the Americas toward McMurdo, stopping at various locations to take on the more perishable of the foodstuffs before meeting the group on October first. It seemed both no time at all and a very long time since Summers had made his discovery and proposed the expedition, but it was finally becoming real. The first stage would be a short six weeks of conditioning high in the Andes, followed by the dream of a lifetime: exploring a largely-unexplored continent for ruins that no one had previously suspected existed. For Summers, it was the culmination of a lifetime of reading adventure novels along with his scientific study and dreaming that he'd be the one to find something extraordinary. Better than Jules Verne, better than Clive Cussler; this one was all his.

Summers was getting anxious about keeping JR out of the loop regarding him joining the expedition. He went to ask Daniel when JR would be told just a few days before embarking for Chile, only to find that the brothers were out to lunch together.

Daniel had been trying to think of a way to tell JR without causing a blow-up. Sarah's insistence that it would be a reward seemed the best stance to take, though Daniel knew it was disingenuous of him. JR didn't like being told where he had to be or what he had to do, and despite this being an adventure that Daniel himself would have loved to join, he doubted that JR would feel the same.

For his part, JR had sensed that something was up for weeks. Summers was always starting to say something, and then backing off, claiming it was nothing. Daniel watched him as if he were an unexploded grenade, and Sarah kept giving him these looks of half-pride, half-pity that drove him crazy. After they gave their food orders, he waited tensely for Daniel to speak.

With the expedition leaving, was Daniel about to lay him off from working at the Foundation? Suggest he enroll in graduate school? What? The reality knocked him back a notch.

"You want me to go with them? Are you crazy?" JR could see no earthly reason why he should go, and he didn't particularly want to. It stunned him that Daniel was presenting it as an ultimatum. What had he done to deserve that?

Chapter Eight
THE CHOICE IS YOURS

JR's penchant for trouble caught up with him even before the team left for Chile. Daniel was summoned to the police station one night after midnight to deal with a drunk and disorderly charge, leaving a furious Sarah in bed. By now, she was nearly five months pregnant, and the couple had announced the happy news about the time she started showing. JR had been 'celebrating' every chance he got for the last six weeks, but this was more about digging his heels in and not going on the expedition as Daniel expected.

Daniel arrived at the jail to find the place in pandemonium. He could hear JR yelling and making a racket with something on the bars of his cell. Familiar faces swam by, officers who'd arrested JR time and time again and then released him into the custody of his famous brother. This time, they weren't looking very friendly. Daniel tried to ignore the commotion at the back of the building as he spoke to the desk sergeant.

"Sarge, what's going on?" he asked. "Do you want me

to take him home, or are you going to keep him here until he calms down?"

"Mr. Rossler, I'm afraid it's a little more serious this time. One of the patrol officers found him and a young lady in a state of indecent exposure on a park lawn, and attempted to arrest them. The young lady ran and escaped while your brother took a swing at my officer. Unfortunately, he connected. The officer is being treated at the emergency room for a broken nose. He looks like he was in hand-to-hand combat with a freight train. That brother of yours sure packs a punch, even when he's drunk."

"Oh, shit!" was Daniel's heartfelt response.

"Yes, sir. I'm afraid that's what's hit the fan," the sergeant said, not without sympathy or humor. "Our guy's going to be okay, but assaulting an officer is a serious charge. We called you as a courtesy, but your brother is going to have to stay until he's arraigned. Sorry."

"Don't be sorry, you guys are just doing your job. I'm sorry we can't seem to keep him under control."

"Have you considered getting him into a treatment program, Mr. Rossler?" the sergeant asked.

"Been there, done that. It doesn't stick, so I've had a better idea."

"Oh? What's that, sir?"

"I'm sending him to Antarctica."

"That ought to cool him off," the sergeant quipped.

It would have amused Daniel, too, if he hadn't been through this routine more than a dozen times since JR's discharge from the military. The diagnosis was PTSD, but Veteran's Affairs had been all but useless. Yes, they had treatment programs, but they weren't effective for everyone. And, unlike many, whose physical wounds were more visible and more treatable than JR's mental ones, he received less tolerance from almost everyone except his loyal family, precisely because his wounds *weren't* visible. Furthermore, his imposing physical presence, at 6'10" and hard-bodied due to his training, was frightening when he was inebriated and in a rage. In a word, he scared people.

Each time this happened, Daniel went through another mourning process for the happy-go-lucky baby brother who'd grown taller than himself by the age of fourteen, unfortunately having had just enough talent to aspire to but not be acceptable to the NBA. The disastrous love affair in his senior year of college had made him terribly cynical about women, all but Sarah, who he loved as a sister and was more than half in love with as an object of romantic worship. That she was also untouchable, as his brother's wife, merely added to his torment.

Daniel knew all of this, and couldn't find it in his heart to even be angry at JR, not any of the other times and not now. But he did despair about what he could do for him. The kid was adrift and getting further out to sea. Daniel felt he needed to get JR out of town for a while, and maybe this would be his opportunity to persuade JR that the expedition would be good for him.

The judge had seen more than enough of this sometimes violent young man, and was not inclined to forgive a charge of assault on a police officer. He remanded JR to the city lockup for ten days and set bail at a quarter of a million dollars pending trial. He would hear motions from the prosecutor and JR's lawyer regarding speedy trial when JR returned to enter a plea at the end of the ten days. Daniel was stunned. After JR was led away, he asked to see the judge in his chambers.

"Your Honor, I'm the brother of the young man you just sentenced."

"I know who you are. I hold you partially responsible for your brother's actions. I'm not unaware that the police have given him a pass on quite a bit of misbehavior due to your prominence. What have you done to put a stop to it? Apparently nothing," the judge said.

"Your Honor, that's not entirely true. We've sent him to treatment programs, we've had medications prescribed. He's suffering from PTSD because of one too many deployments to Afghanistan. But I'm not here to plead for leniency. I know he has a problem and that he needs to take accountability for it. What I'm here for is to ask you to allow me to do as I'd planned already, and send him to Antarctica as part of an archaeological expedition. He'll be out of Boulder and out of your hair. But I need him out of jail in a week."

Daniel stopped then, aware that less is more when negotiating with an angry judge. He was confident that the idea of getting his problem brother out of the judge's city would be appealing, but it would require the judge to find a way to save face before he'd let JR out early.

"Can you put up the bail until he's gone?" the judge asked suddenly. "If you'll get him out of Boulder and I can get a good report of his behavior on the expedition, I'll consider letting him out early. If he keeps his nose clean, and the officer agrees, I'll drop the charges when he gets back. We can consider it probation."

Daniel gulped. He could put up that kind of bail, but he wouldn't without consulting Sarah. That was too much money to gamble, and he wasn't entirely certain he could count on JR to cooperate. "I'll have to talk to my wife, sir. But, if I can, do we have a deal?"

"We have a deal if you can come up with the bail money. Otherwise, no."

"Yes, sir."

If only he could persuade Sarah, everything would be fine. However, Daniel knew quite well that Sarah was one of the few people who were immune to his powers of persuasion. It would have to make sense to her, and she already disapproved of JR's inclusion on the expedition team, even though she'd been loyal enough to turn down Summers' request for help in that regard. It was going to be an uphill battle, made even more dangerous by her fluctuating hormone levels. Daniel went home from court with less confidence than he'd had for years.

Sarah appeared to be torn. Yes, she thought it was a mistake to send JR on the expedition, simply because he was capable of so much destruction and self-destruction. On the other hand, her beloved husband was at his wits' end to find a way to get through to JR. Daniel, the beloved husband in question, took full advantage of his puppy-dog face to tell her of JR's sentence and the judge's offer of a bargain.

"A quarter million! Daniel, can you be certain JR won't skip bail? That's a lot of money."

"I know it, but we could get a bail bondsman to put it up; that would only cost ten percent for now. And it's only until he gets on the plane to Chile. As soon as I verify that, the judge will release the bail money. Sweetheart, if he misses that plane with the others, I'm not sure I dare send him alone. There are no direct flights; he could disappear in Dallas or Miami and who knows when or how we'd find him."

"You have a point. All right, honey, it's your choice; he's your brother and I understand your need to help him. I just hope he comes back more responsible. We'll have our own baby to worry about by then, and I don't know how tolerant I'll be if he's still a screw-up."

Daniel took Sarah into his arms to kiss her and thank her for understanding. "Have I told you that you've never been more beautiful, sweetheart?"

"Yes, but tell me again. I'm beginning to feel like a blimp."

"You've never been more beautiful. And if you feel like a blimp now, wait until you're nine months and counting the hours."

"Way to go, champ, you ruined it," she laughed, swatting at him to let her go. But the faint flush on her face told him he'd pleased her.

Daniel hedged his bets a little, waiting to arrange for bail until JR had settled down and had a chance to think about his position. After a few days, he visited for a heart-to-heart talk through the glass of the visiting room.

"Well, buddy, you stepped in it this time," he started. JR had the grace to look abashed, but he had nothing to say.

"Here's the deal, JR. I've talked to the judge. If the charges aren't dropped, you're looking at a Class 5 felony, minimum. That's if the officer agrees that it was a 'crime of passion', rather than intentional."

JR opened his mouth, but Daniel rode over whatever it was he had to say. "A Class 5 felony has penalties of up to $100,000 in fines, or one to three years' incarceration, and if he wants to, the judge can impose both. That's not jail, JR, that's prison." He waited for it to sink in. When JR's defiant body language slumped, he offered the alternative.

"The judge is willing to drop the charges, assuming the

officer you slugged agrees, but there's a condition. You go to Antarctica, and Summers gives the judge a good report of your behavior while there."

"So, you found a way to get rid of me after all," JR said. It broke Daniel's heart that the look in JR's eyes was of despair. But coddling him only made things worse. It was time for tough love.

"You brought it on yourself, bud, but it's your choice. I won't pay your fines for you, so if you think you can do the time and that it would be better than the expedition, it's your call."

"How do I know that the officer will be willing to drop the charges?"

"For some reason, the cops here have a soft spot for you, you asshole. He's willing to accept an apology, and will go along with the judge's decision when you get back. The plane leaves in two days, so I'd suggest you make your decision quickly. If it leaves without you, you'll go to trial, and with the officer's partner as a witness, you haven't got a prayer at a not guilty plea."

Daniel rose to go, but JR's knock on the glass stopped him. After apologizing to the deputy who monitored the visiting room for touching the glass, JR gave Daniel his decision.

"I'll take the deal. Shit, at least it won't be hotter than blue blazes and sandy."

"There is that," Daniel remarked. "I'll come and get you in a few days."

"A few days! Daniel, I've been here too long already. Why not today?"

"Because I'm risking the price of a house to get you out, JR. You're going straight from here to the plane. Take it or leave it."

"Daniel?"

"What?"

"I love you, bro."

Daniel examined his brother's face for sarcasm. Finding none, he replied, "I love you, too, JR. See you tomorrow."

The next hurdle turned out to be Summers. Daniel thought he'd put Charles's objection to rest, but it hadn't been possible to keep the arrest quiet, especially when it turned out that the young lady who'd escaped the night of the incident was none other than Misty Rivers, the research assistant.

JR's unfortunate last-minute incarceration couldn't have come at a worse time, when Summers, already overloaded with responsibility, had to sort out whether JR had received approvals or not. His search of the boy's desk turned up not only all the approvals, thank goodness, but also a number of highly unsuitable photos of Misty Rivers that would keep Charles from meeting her eyes for weeks. The girl was a menace, he thought.

Summers wanted her off the team, too, but unfortunately there was no one to take her place at this late date.

"Charles, be reasonable. We've discussed this, and I've already made arrangements with the judge. JR has to go, and that's all there is to it."

"I won't be responsible for him, Daniel. It's bad enough that his drinking is out of control. His involvement with this Rivers girl is too much. We're going to be in an ultra-dangerous environment. Any distraction could cost one of them their lives. At least get me someone to replace Rivers."

"I think you're exaggerating. In any case, we've already

settled it. JR goes, and that's final, and I don't know who we've got that we could send in Misty's place. Jeez, I snort every time I say that name. Sounds like a stripper."

"Looks like one, too. Should we get her sterilized before we go, or are you prepared to become an uncle?"

"Very funny. Look Charles, I've got no time for this. I say JR goes."

Charles slumped. He'd never known Daniel to be unreasonable before. It seemed that when it came to his family, though, he had blinders on. Charles's next move stretched their friendship almost to the breaking point.

"I say he doesn't, and that's *my* final word on it."

"Charles, I asked you not to make me do this. I'm sorry, but it's a condition of your funding."

"Do you care to put that to a vote of the Board?"

"There's no need. I have full authority to override the Board in certain matters. I can't *spend* money by overriding them, but I can and will *refuse* to spend it. Take it or leave it, Charles, but know that we've already spent millions. If you throw it away now, I can't speak for future funding for your projects."

Charles weighed the real risk against his friendship with Daniel and any future projects he'd want to run through the Foundation. Defeated, he acquiesced. "I can only hope that you won't live to regret this, Daniel. I have grave misgivings about JR's ability to fit in with the team, and if he can't, his life is at risk in Antarctica. Remember that."

A shiver of premonition took Daniel, but he shook it off. He had plenty of confidence in JR's ability to survive anything this world could throw at him. He'd done three deployments in a worse hell than Antarctica, by Daniel's estimation. Charles was wrong, and JR needed this opportunity. But, just in case, he'd have a talk with JR when he picked him up from jail.

Chapter Nine

BAD THINGS HAPPEN IN THREES

The last few days before departure for the training ground of Chile were more hectic than Summers could believe possible. First, their explosives expert was involved in a crash in his car, resulting in a broken leg. A scramble for a replacement took two days, but fortunately a Russian had the necessary qualifications and was willing to drop everything and join the group in Chile. Dr. Mendenhall would perform the psychological and physical tests there, and they could only hope he'd pass.

After that, the second of the research assistants came down with a mysterious virus. Charles was ashamed of himself, but he wished it had been the Rivers girl. They'd already determined that no other employees of the Rossler Foundation who were willing to go were suitable, so a hasty call for volunteers among the previously-screened applicants went out. They were lucky to find a Chilean microbiologist who, though overqualified for the research assistant post, was willing and able to go anyway. She would meet them at the airport when they arrived in Chile. The one bonus was that their other Chilean biologist specialized in paleobiology, so the breadth of knowledge between them was expanded with her addition.

Bad things happen in threes, Charles reflected, *so we should be good to go now.*

Charles knew intellectually of the Orion Society, a near-mythological criminal organization whose interference had almost sabotaged the decoding of the Pyramid Code, the basis for the 10th Cycle Library that was driving most scientific research nowadays. However, it didn't occur to him to think that they might be responsible for at least some of his bad luck. He and the team would be already in Chile before the police investigation of the explosive expert's car revealed that the brake line had been cut. Nor would Daniel consider it necessary to tell him of it. The expeditionary team was already on high alert for danger. There was no need to spook them when nothing could be proven.

In fact, the order to place their own explosives expert on the team had been Auster's idea. If it became necessary, the man would stage an accident that wiped out the expedition and left the OS as the only organization that knew any secret it uncovered. Septentrio, not to be outdone, arranged for the viral infection, not realizing that another of Auster's operatives had already been successfully placed on the team.

After centuries of success, the Orion Society was unraveling, though most of the four didn't realize it. Auster's overweening ambition combined with Septentrio's weaknesses had set up a dynamic that seemed destined to encourage a coup attempt. Auster's belief that a discovery by the Rossler Foundation expedition would give her the final, perfect opportunity to topple Septentrio's family from the leadership role in favor of herself was what led her to plan to sabotage it in secret. That fool Septentrio was too engrossed in his hedonistic lifestyle and boyish playmates to notice opportunity if it came and twisted his nose, she thought. If someone didn't do something, their cartel would collapse. She couldn't allow that to happen.

In a videoconference that Auster initiated without inviting Septentrio, she secured the passive agreement of Oriens and Occidens that if Septentrio's plans went awry as had his father's, they would support her bid for leadership of the group. Neither Oriens nor Occidens wished to go against the powerful family that had spawned Septentrio, but they would not oppose Auster.

Septentrio's father had been ruthless, competent and intelligent. Only a series of unfortunate circumstances, none of which were his doing, had forced his retirement when he lost control of some of his operatives, with disastrous results. That retirement had thrust his debauched and some would say mentally ill son into the position. Only someone who was mentally ill would have entertained some of the depraved pastimes in which Septentrio indulged. The three other members of the group suspected that they knew only the tip of the iceberg, but that was bad enough to make them not wish to know more.

The opposing forces within the powerful organization were set to cause its collapse, but they were still in a position to wreak havoc.

Chapter Ten

CHILE HERE WE COME

After all the other last-minute glitches, Summers didn't know why he was surprised that JR pulled one final and nearly unforgivable foul-up. On the morning they were to board a plane for the first leg of the trip to Chile, he was nowhere to be found, having been rescued from his jail cell the afternoon before. A frantic Daniel organized a search party that checked all his favorite haunts, including bars that were closed still so early in the morning. It was social media that saved the day.

The Rossler Foundation's Twitter account was pressed into service, asking if anyone had seen the prodigal JR in the past twenty-four hours. Following clues in the handful of answers, a surly JR was pulled from the bed of a University of Colorado coed, who was too wasted to notice. Daniel was furious.

"You little bastard," he said, failing to realize the insult to his own mother in his anger. "You knew I had posted bail. You knew the conditions. After all I've done for you, how could you pull this stunt? I've a good mind to take you back to jail."

"All you've done for me, huh? What you're doing for me now is forcing me to go to a godforsaken frozen wilderness. You just want to get rid of me." JR looked for all the world like a stubborn two-year-old, whose favorite word was no.

Daniel was at his wits end, and very near the end of his patience. He turned to his ashen-faced wife in a mute plea for her help.

"JR, honey, we don't want to get rid of you. We want you back. The JR we got back from the Marines isn't the real you. Please, please, don't make Daniel take you back to jail. We really feel that this will be good for you, or we wouldn't be sending you," Sarah pleaded.

JR had always had a soft spot for Sarah, since the first time his older brother had brought her, as his fiancée, to meet the family. At the time, he was an irrepressible undergraduate, star of his college basketball team, with NBA aspirations in spite of his knowledge that he was neither talented enough nor physically capable of a long NBA career. It was ironic that his hitch in the Marines had corrected the latter problem, but nothing would overcome the fact that there were only a few spots for rookies each year in the NBA and talent was all-important. Even now, though his PTSD had changed his personality for the worse, Sarah could usually get through to him.

JR was still angry, but Sarah's appeal silenced him. The whole group stood outside of the secure area, many wondering if they were going to make their flight as the first call for boarding came over the intercom. Summers went to speak to the airline representatives about delaying the flight, while the rest tried to sort out the issue. Surprisingly, it was Misty Rivers who tipped the balance. Daniel thought it was fortunate that she didn't know where JR had been found, or she might not have been so eager to step forward and persuade him to come along. When he took in her short skirt and low necked blouse, JR's eyes lit up and his sullenness disappeared. His charming smile spread across his face as he said, "Sure, baby."

Summers, who also had an opinion about her inappropriate attire, given that they were about to travel into a high Andes winter, was nevertheless grateful that it apparently enticed JR enough to end his objections.

"JR, I hope you have everything you need. If not, call us when you get to Chile, and we'll ship whatever is missing." Daniel said, hoping that his tone didn't set his brother off again. He didn't want to threaten JR to get him on the plane, but if that's what it took, he would. Not only because it was a condition of his release, but because Daniel genuinely believed that the experience would go a long way toward restoring JR's confidence. He knew that the cocky attitude and acting out was a front for a deeply shaken young man who had seen too much tragedy in Afghanistan.

Most of the team had gone on through the security checkpoint at Daniel's urging. Only Summers, Rivers and Dr. Mendenhall remained to help persuade JR to get on the plane. Now, barely scooting through the rally port in response to last call, the last four boarded. A slight scuffle ensued when Rivers realized that the seat assignments paired Mendenhall and JR. Mendenhall, having no wish to be seated next to JR for any length of time, even for the short flight to Dallas, thought to offer to trade seats. However, before she could do so, the flight attendants made the announcement that everyone should remain seated and fasten their seatbelts for takeoff.

From Dallas, the team would board a flight to Miami,

deplane again, and finally board the flight for the final leg from Miami to Santiago, a trip that totaled nineteen hours. From there, ground transportation would take them to the ski resort where they would spend four weeks acclimatizing to the cold weather conditions, as well as practicing their cross-country skiing skills and snowshoeing technique. In addition, they would attend a two-day avalanche rescues skills class, and spend their evenings watching video of polar conditions to give them all a healthy respect for the continent whose dangers they would face.

The trip was long enough to try anyone's patience, but many of the team spent the time discussing their thoughts on the adventure on which they were embarking, or in some cases getting to know each other through the usual small talk. JR and Rebecca spent much of the time in silence, either because JR was asleep, or because they simply had nothing to say to each other, though JR would have liked to flirt with her. He wasn't unaware that he was a screw-up. A beautiful and brilliant doctor was beyond his reach, almost certainly. It was ironic that her thoughts were on how good-looking he was, and what a shame that he couldn't seem to straighten out. Sarah had told her what a great guy the old JR was, the one who had gone to Afghanistan with such a promising career on hold. Rebecca would like to meet that JR.

Everyone on the team worked hard, even JR, once they got to Chile. Summers worried that the luxurious accommodations at the ski resort gave them little preparation for the much more primitive conditions that would prevail on the expedition. However, seeing his team begin to expertly navigate by snowshoe or by skis in the backcountry, he felt that their preparation was as good as it could be. After a communal dinner each night, and the obligatory videos, Summers regularly dismissed his team at about eight o'clock each evening. He spent most evenings conversing with LeClerc, who turned out to be a pleasant conversationalist and a worthy chess opponent.

The fact that neither of the leaders of the expedition spent much time chaperoning the younger members meant that the hours between eight p.m. and about midnight were left for adventures that would perhaps not have been approved had they known. Most of the expedition members made their way to clubs where they danced and some drank until awareness of an early wake-up call drove them to their rooms for a few hours' sleep.

JR and Misty had paired up again, despite someone spitefully telling her of JR's last minute fling. They were the two most guilty of alcohol abuse. JR frequently started his morning with a Bloody Mary to shake off the hangover from the night before. Only his superb conditioning and youth kept his excesses from the notice of Summers.

The other research assistant, Carmen, developed a crush on the handsome Aussie, Cartwright. However, he had his eye on the very attractive Dr. Mendenhall. As the weeks went by, little jealousies and even professional rivalries flourished without the notice of Summers or LeClerc. No one was willing to risk being removed from the expedition, so there was a conspiracy of silence that kept them unaware that the team was already in danger of not being as cohesive as it seemed.

Adding to the illusion, more often than not, they all managed to have a good time, even while experiencing rigorous training. Races on skis or snowshoes made the daily training treks more interesting. Even professional or romantic rivalries were set aside in the good-natured contests. Snowball fights, practical jokes and shopping kept the group relatively happy. One of the worries that LeClerc had expressed, that the women would develop cliques and possessiveness over the men they claimed as their own, didn't appear to Summers to have developed.

After some jockeying for position, Angela Brown, the cartographer and Cyndi Self, the electronics engineer decided to join forces and became fast friends, prompting the others to start calling the pair Cyngela. The male members of the group were disappointed because neither girl would hook up with any of them, preferring the company of handsome Chilean ski instructors, at least for now. The female members of the group, except for the jealousy Carmen had for Dr. Mendenhall, were relatively content to remain polite to each other, even if some relationships were cooler than others.

The time passed quickly, and at last the time had arrived for the expedition to start in good earnest. Summers and his team posed for pictures on the tarmac in front of their chartered plane, with news media from across the globe on hand for the momentous occasion. None of them gave a thought to a future in which those pictures would reappear with the headline: "*Expedition Members Missing and Feared Dead*" within a few short months.

Chapter Eleven

ANTARCTICA HERE WE COME

The twelve-hour flight from Santiago to Christchurch, New Zealand would be only the first leg of the journey, since McMurdo station was on the opposite side of Antarctica from the nearest point in Chile to the continent. To the North Americans, north and south became relative terms when discussing directions, as maps failed to give them a good visual idea of the relative positions of Australia and New Zealand to Antarctica. Being told that McMurdo was about 2,400 miles south of Christchurch, but 850 miles north of the South Pole created a mental block similar to trying to figure out a Moebius strip; it just didn't compute when viewed on a flat map of the Southern Hemisphere, which often showed all of Antarctica *north* of New Zealand and conversely, showed the South Pole north of McMurdo according to map-reading convention. Fortunately, the point would be of no consequence once they'd landed. *Everywhere* was north of the South Pole.

If they hadn't been training and studying for several months, most would have also been astounded at the size of

Antarctica. Though the width through the center of the continent was about the same as that of the US, the total area was nearly twice that of the fifty contiguous states. Antarctica was the coldest, windiest continent, and on average the highest. It was also the driest. The latter had been a surprise to some of the expedition members, who imagined it snowing constantly for six months of the year. In fact, much of the wind-driven snow featured in movies and videos of Antarctica was picked up from the ground and tossed in the strong winds, rather than falling from the sky. Another surprising fact was that it was the brightest continent, despite being in darkness for most of six months of the year. That was balanced by it being daylight for the other six months.

Each member of the expedition had high hopes for adventure, even JR if he'd only admitted it to himself, rather than resenting that it was forced on him. Most also relished the opportunity to take in Antarctica's pristine and wild beauty in person. Each also had a secret fear, carefully hidden during the psychological tests for the most part. Most of those had to do with unremitting cold or being lost and alone in a vast white wilderness. Most of them knew that the fears were irrational as long as they followed procedure. As such, it was a healthy fear, the kind that kept them mentally alert for real danger, but didn't cripple them.

The first leg of the flight was mostly over an endless stretch of impossibly blue ocean. Most of the group was happy that their few numbers in the large airliner afforded each of them a window seat, from which they spent many hours just staring at the expanse of water below them. JR was an exception. He'd had more than enough transoceanic flights between the US and Afghanistan. A superstitious horror of ditching far from land kept him in his seat and trying to both sleep and keep down the breakfast he'd foolishly eaten before flying. He knew better, but Misty's argument that there would be no in-flight meal convinced him he'd better eat despite his anxiety.

Four hours into the flight, as the others broke out snacks and veritable picnics of food they'd brought aboard with them, JR groaned and retreated to the tail section to get as far away from the smell of food as possible. What he needed was packed carefully in his luggage; two fifths of single-malt scotch that he'd managed to smuggle aboard, knowing that it wouldn't be nearly enough to last for five months.

Toward the front of the plane, a party atmosphere prevailed. All the months of training, the rigorous testing, and the work to prepare side experiments that they'd carry out as they explored for the ruins were over. In less than twenty-four hours they'd be at McMurdo, and shortly after that they'd be on their way to the adventure of a lifetime. Even the stoic and taciturn Russian explosives expert was infected with the hilarity.

Misty had become impatient with JR, who was a damper on her fun, and was flirting with the Englishman, Cecil Stone. JR observed from his position to the rear of the plane and resolved to punish her by withholding his attention, completely oblivious to the fact that it was lack of attention and fun that had caused her desertion in the first place. About halfway between JR and the party, Summers and LeClerc sat together going over everything once again.

Summers was happy that the team was getting some of their hijinks out of their systems before the serious business of the expedition began. He wouldn't deprive them of whatever fun they could have on the trek, as long as they remained safe, but he'd insist that they keep their minds alert to danger, as it would surround them at every moment.

Antarctica wasn't to be taken lightly, and he felt responsible for every member of the group, especially since the majority were several years younger than he. Watching them now, he had the crazy thought that he was leading a bunch of nursery school kids into grave danger.

Later in the flight, with everyone getting a bit cranky from being cooped up in the plane, the talk turned to what they'd do with their last night in civilization for a while. Robert Cartwright had spent a little time exploring New Zealand and was suggesting they take in some of the nature paths, especially since they wouldn't see anything naturally green again for five months. JR, however, had recovered at last from his indigestion and was advocating a bar trip, since they wouldn't have that chance again for five months, either. There was nothing to prevent the group from splitting up according to the members' preference, so in the end, some did one and some the other.

JR, Misty, Carmen, Antonio and the Russian, who'd been dubbed 'Roosky' because JR found his name difficult to pronounce, were bar-bound not long after the group had been transported to their hotel. Mikhail Stefanovich Maxhulin, aka Roosky, as the oldest and therefore presumably most responsible, was enjoined by Summers to make sure the group got back to the hotel by midnight, as they had an eight o'clock flight and a forty-five minute drive to the airport. Roosky wouldn't dare miss the flight, for reasons of his own, but he hoped to find a willing woman for the evening. Vodka wasn't all he'd be missing for five months, unless one of the young and lovely girls on the expedition would agree to warm his bed.

Misty persuaded JR not to overindulge for a change, reminding him what a terrible experience flying with a hangover was, so it was relatively easy for Roosky to shepherd them all back to the hotel with twenty minutes to spare. Misty's bed went unslept in, though, as she joined JR, abandoning the stuffy Englishman for the familiar JR. Her roommate, Carmen, noted her absence with disapproval, but said nothing.

The nature group all turned in early, themselves thinking of what they might be missing for the next five months—sleep in a warm, comfortable bed.

After that night and part of the next day in Christchurch to allow the team to stretch their legs, they again boarded their chartered aircraft for the final leg of the flight, to a landing strip near McMurdo called the Annual Sea Ice Runway, the only one of the three that operated at various times in the area that was open as early as October. It was serendipitously also the only one that would accommodate their chartered airliner.

By noon the following day, the Rossler Expedition for Discovery of Ninth Cycle Artifacts was approaching McMurdo station, with all souls crowding the windows of the plane as they approached the ice-clad shoreline. Even JR, cynical as he pretended to be, could not fail to be moved by the contrast of incredibly blue ocean to sparkling white shore. They were blessed with a sunny day and no wind to achieve that remarkable welcome to their home away from home. Transport to McMurdo was awaiting them at the landing strip, as promised. A short ride in several small Sno-Cats would deliver them to McMurdo just in time for lunch.

McMurdo Station had been originally constructed in the mid-1950s, but expansion and modernization had resulted in a surprisingly comfortable, though utilitarian, facility. The Rossler Expedition was among the first to arrive for the summer scientific research season, so there was plenty of room for them all, a condition that wouldn't last throughout the summer. Depending on whether they doubled back here for any reason, members of the expedition might find themselves paired with complete strangers as roommates, but for now, only those who wanted to stay in the same room had to. The rest had private rooms since they'd only be there a few days, but always subject to an unexpected roommate.

On the other hand, plentiful food was free for the taking, with the polite reminder that they should eat whatever they took. Internet access was also available. Most members of the expedition took the opportunity to email their loved ones at home with a greeting from the bottom of the world. JR declined, as he was still miffed at Daniel, along with the rest of the family for supporting Daniel's ultimatum.

Their sojourn at McMurdo was short. As soon as their supplies were delivered, everyone was pressed into service to unload small items, while heavy equipment took care of the larger items. Members of the station staff sometimes came out to lend a hand, glad to get even the low-angle sunlight after their long winter of near-total darkness. Several expressed doubt about the success of the expedition, which was like searching for a needle in a snow-covered haystack. Others actually scoffed and declared that they'd heard lost-city myths before, and they were always fairy tales.

They would remain at McMurdo for a few days, loading their supplies on the sleds in such a way as to leave accessible what they would need to reach first. LeClerc came into his own for this project; his expertise lying in how to outfit and run an expedition with as little physical effort as possible. This was necessary to conserve calories. Though the expedition members would travel in relative comfort in the cabs of the big Sno-Cats, strenuous work would be required sporadically, and the effort of maintaining reasonable weight in the extreme cold would also require that their physical effort be carefully conserved for the times of necessity. To the surprise of most of the group and the delight of the women, his last task before departure and every morning thereafter was to distribute large bars of chocolate to each member, admonishing them to consume at least half of it before they stopped for their next meal.

On the afternoon of the third day, they set out along the South Pole Traverse, bound for Amundsen-Scott station at the South Pole. Along the way, they'd use the sensitive equipment they'd brought to explore the ground on either side of the packed-snow track to a distance of one hundred feet once they reached solid ground. If a city were to be found along this road, it would be a bonus, but they didn't expect it. They were merely being efficient by exploring as they traveled, though the majority of the route was over the Ross Ice Shelf and therefore they would travel that section as quickly as possible. Heavier equipment took about forty days to reach the Pole from McMurdo, but the expedition, with lighter equipment that was the most advanced to be had, planned to make the first part in three weeks. Then they would break off to explore the mountains through which the Leverett Glacier was the pathway for the highway. It was here that Summers had the highest hopes for locating the 9th Cycle city referred to in the 10th Cycle Library.

First, though, they had an arduous trek across the Ross Ice Shelf, nearly 1,000 miles of ice with all the characteristics of a glacier, to cross. Crevasses, melt pools in later months, average temperatures well below freezing, combined with a constant headwind of five to eighteen miles per hour would combine to keep their progress to about fifty miles per day, and that was considered fast. However, because the ruins would be found on solid ground or not at all, they would make all possible speed across the ice. Contingencies for delays due to stormy weather had been built in, since October was the stormiest month. If they were able to avoid stopping for high winds and driven snow, they might even make it in two weeks rather than three.

At first, it was a lark. Everyone was in high spirits to be moving forward after the long weeks and in some cases months of training and preparation. A vacation mood prevailed, with LeClerc and Summers the main restraint. However, long hours traveling in a landscape that changed but little began to be wearing after only a few days. The strange night, which never got really dark, and the constant wind made it difficult to sleep at first. As the expedition began, the sun was low on the horizon, casting long shadows over the deceptively flat terrain as it circled their position, neither rising further nor setting. As the months went on, it would only get higher over the horizon, until, half-way through their expedition, it would beat down with unremitting brightness twenty-four hours a day for several weeks. Summers was confident that they'd grow accustomed to it, and fortunately LeClerc had put heavy sleeping masks in the supplies, since the two-man polar tents made of red nylon weren't particularly light-proof, even though they were double-skinned.

Nine of the pyramid-shaped tents were pitched each

night, and the occupants left to sort themselves out. Before they'd been on the road a week, it had become standard for Roosky, at six-foot-six the second tallest and at 380 lbs. the biggest, to be the odd man out with a tent to himself. JR had to sleep in a slight curl, as the edges of the walls inclined as they met the floor, an otherwise generous seven and a half feet square. Since he had the curvy Misty to curl around, he didn't mind. The others, all of average height, made arrangements according to who had been conversing with whom when they made camp for the night, or who had a bit of 'don't ask, don't tell' fun in mind for the night. Of the females, only Dr. Mendenhall and Carmen, the overqualified research assistant typically bunked together, Rebecca being uninterested in casual sex with her fellow expedition members and Carmen being interested only in the Aussie geologist, Robert Cartwright, who didn't reciprocate. Summers also held himself aloof, which meant he changed tent mates often as the others' love lives waxed and waned.

The Scott Pyramid tents had been chosen for their ease of pitching, even when the winds were fairly high, and their careful attention to ventilation. Oddly enough, next to dying of exposure without one, the most common danger of dying came from carbon monoxide poisoning, with two people breathing in a small area and the inevitable build-up of a heavy frost layer inside the tent from exhalation. Without ventilation, it was a real and present danger, not to be taken lightly. However, these tents had the latest technology to not only keep occupants snug and reasonably warm, but also to provide adequate air exchange.

In addition to the sleeping tents, when weather permitted, a cook tent was erected and Bart the cook was able to put together a hearty meal. At other times, soup from a pouch, reconstituted over an alcohol stove that was set up on the floor of one of the Sno-Cats had to suffice. The team was almost always hungry, not because the food wasn't adequate, but because of a combination of boredom and their constant shivering whenever they were outside the Sno-Cat. Even at temperatures above freezing, the wind chill would have left them cold if they stood still, a theory that had no need to be tested, since the temperature was never above freezing.

Sometimes, with the average pace only four miles per hour, the more ambitious of the team got out and walked for a while, realizing that two or three weeks cooped up in a seated position in a moving vehicle would destroy their conditioning. Others did awkward calisthenics at camp. They traveled twelve hours a day, stopping only for meals and for night camp, though the 'night' part of that phrase was merely a concept.

Eventually, the novelty of the landscape lost its luster even for the most wide-eyed of the bunch. iPads came out for video games, reading and crossword puzzles or Scrabble. Summers and LeClerc played chess on a magnetic board until they each knew all the other's moves and most games ended in stalemate. When the first slopes of the Transantarctic Mountains came into distant view, a cheer went up, until they realized that in the clear air they could see greater distances. Those peaks were still at least two days away. Worst of all, they'd have to skirt them as the mountain range ran almost parallel to the track they were following to the Leverett Glacier, which would serve as the pass through which they'd negotiate the mountains. They were at least four days away from turning south toward the pole through the mountains.

At camp on the night that the sharpest-eyed member of

the expedition had spotted the mountain range in the distance, Summers and LeClerc compared their long-term forecast document to the readings on the barometer and anemometer.

"Listen up, folks," Summers shouted over the howl of the wind. "Gather round."

Reluctantly, a few of the team crawled out of their tents, putting on coats and gloves as they gathered around him. "We're going to get some wind tonight. Real wind, in excess of 60 miles per hour. That's a little over one hundred kilometers per hour to those of you who aren't American. Make preparations to stay in your tents until it dies down; we won't be moving from this location until it does. Cook has some protein bars and other stuff you can take to your tents to eat; no hot meals before tomorrow late afternoon at best. Tell your tent mates, too, if they aren't hearing this. Let me repeat; stay in your tents at all costs. I want you all inside and your hatches battened down within half an hour."

There was a mad scramble for the sled where Bart was handing out emergency food supplies and bottled water, some people checked and rechecked guy wires to their tent sides, and a couple of hasty trades of places within the tents took place, before all human activity grew quiet within the shelters. As the wind speed increased, so did the noise, until almost everyone was put in mind of a freight train racing past a lonely country intersection, with only the shelter of a thin wall of nylon to protect them. Conversation was impossible. It was a long night. At least the driven snow obscured the weak sunlight, so that once the noise became part of the background, a few of them got some sleep.

By late afternoon the next day, the wind had reduced to half its former speed, allowing the Rossler expedition to escape from their tents. However, only eight were set up, where there had previously been nine. An alarm was raised and soon all remaining tents were empty of their occupants. Missing were Angela and Cyndi, along with any sign of their tent. Directing the others to spread out and search, Summers went to the lead Sno-Cat to retrieve the satellite phone and call for a search mission. However, as soon as he closed the door against the wind, soft snoring led him to the first two bench seats behind the cab, where the missing girls were curled up under their parkas.

"Oh, my God," he breathed. It felt as if his heart slammed into gear and started beating again when he saw them. He'd been responsible for the lives of archaeology expedition teams before, and on one terrible occasion, he'd lost a team member to a cave-in. But, he'd never lost two before the expedition had even begun. His heavy sigh of relief woke Cyndi, who opened her eyes to Summers' concerned face.

"Oh, hey, Charles. Sorry. Ange and I didn't get our tent secured, I guess. It blew away, so we had to come here. Are there any extras?"

Summers began to laugh, his relief was so great. Dropping a totally unexpected kiss on the forehead of the young engineer, he said, "We have a couple of extra tents, yes. But no extra engineers or cartographers. Thank God you're okay."

By now, Angela was also awake.

"Of course we're okay," she said. "Why wouldn't we be?"

Summers made a mental note that guide ropes would be fixed from the tent area to the Sno-Cats every time they camped from now on. It was an enormous stroke of luck that the two small women hadn't been swept across the ice with the tent, unable to stop themselves, until they either succumbed to the injuries they no doubt would have sustained, or blew far enough away that they couldn't find their way back. In fact, it was a miracle that the girls couldn't explain and didn't seem concerned about.

Since the wind was at a more reasonable twenty miles per hour that afternoon, LeClerc deemed it safe to continue, and they resolved to go ahead and travel the usual twelve hours, though that would have them making camp at about five a.m. the next day instead of their usual eight p.m. It made little difference; the daylight would be the same in any case. That they would be on a crazy diurnal schedule after that would mean nothing until they returned to McMurdo Base.

Four uneventful days later, two and a half weeks after they started their trek, the group gained the foothills of the Queen Maud Range and started making their zig-zagging route through the passes before turning nearly ninety degrees to their right and heading for Amundsen-Scott station.

Chapter Twelve

TRIALS AND TRIBULATIONS

It was at this point that the real purpose of the expedition was to begin. Rather than move along the track at all possible speed, small groups were sent out with seismographic equipment on either side of the road to attempt to map the terrain under the snow. Permission had been granted for only a few holes to be drilled for explosives that would 'thump' the surrounding terrain, the resulting seismic activity to then be recorded on geophones. Robert Cartwright had a great deal of humorous chatter about 'doodlebugs' and 'jug-hustlers', oil-field slang for the drillers and the low-level employees that strung the geophones in the array that would map the subsurface, but the others, unused to this type of physical labor for the most part, merely put their heads down and endured.

It wasn't that they hadn't been warned; just that most of them didn't have the experience to imagine what it would be like. Cold and wind that reminded them of their own winters they expected; quick hikes up ice-covered slopes in it, they hadn't. All, that is, except Summers and JR, both used to winter hiking in the Rockies near Boulder. Summers was surprised and pleased that JR took to the work with gusto, glad of an outlet for his boredom. Seeing him striding along with the petite Misty scrambling along behind him was comical, too. Their team always finished their array first, prompting Roosky to praise them every evening over dinner, and complain to the others that they slowed him down.

The Leverett Glacier is said to be about 3,000 meters, or 1.8 miles, thick; but Summers' expectation was that the rocky terrain on either side funneled the ice into the pass, leaving a thinner sheet within the rough outcroppings that they had a chance of penetrating with the seismic equipment. At least, he hoped, far enough down to detect the anomaly that a ruined city should present. However, to successfully map both sides, the seismograph equipment had to be deployed several miles from the road in either direction, as the glacier was three to five miles wide. Therefore, rather than the fifty miles per day that they'd covered on the Ross, they were making only five or so through the mountains. This created a problem for LeClerc.

"Charles, we must make better time. At this rate, we will run out of food before resupplying at Amundsen-Scott," he said one evening.

"What do you mean, we'll run out of food? You were supposed to plan enough for forty days. We've only been out here for twenty."

"Yes, but at this rate, we'll be another two or three getting through the pass, and perhaps a week and a half or two weeks to get to the Pole after that. And your crew, they eat like teenagers! They are consuming more than the allotment."

"LeClerc, I understood you to be an experienced polar

expedition coordinator. You know that calorie requirements are higher under these conditions. Explain to me exactly why you didn't calculate correctly."

"Merde! I am telling you, I calculate correctly and your crew is out of control! They demand more, the chef he makes more. I cannot make him understand that he must conserve."

"I will hold you personally responsible if we have to choose between rushing this exploration and underfeeding my team, LeClerc. I'll deal with Bart, but this better not happen again. And if you're going to swear at me, do it in English, so I can respond properly."

Summers was furious. He'd trusted the Frenchman to live up to his CV and his reputation, but something was seriously wrong. Any good leader made allowances for the unforeseen, especially in situations where an error could be life-threatening. Why hadn't this one made better calculations? Sure, one or two of his team were bigger than the norm; especially Roosky, but he supposed JR's tall frame required more calories than average as well. It should have been taken into account. Now he was going to have to impose rationing, and that wasn't going to go over well. *Too bad we aren't at the North Pole*, he mused. *We could have bagged a polar bear or something*. Where they were going, there were no potential food sources larger than microbes. There wasn't even a penguin for thousands of miles. But, at least he didn't have to worry about predators.

Summers went to the mess tent and had a talk with Bart, telling him that the food had to last for at least seventeen more days, preferably twenty, in case of a storm. After a small protest that the people he was feeding would complain if the food wasn't plentiful, and Summers' promise to let them know it wasn't Bart's fault, he went to speak to the group as a whole. LeClerc was conspicuously absent when he had gathered them together.

"Listen, guys, and that means you ladies, too. We've hit a small snag. Due to a miscalculation, we're going to have to cut back on the food a bit." Summers waited out the flurry of questions and exclamations of dismay before resuming. "It won't be drastic, but we've been eating a bit more than LeClerc planned for, and we need to make sure we aren't left a day or more from base when we run out of food. Bart's going to be serving slightly smaller portions, and the portions are going to be divided according to caloric needs. That means Roosky and JR will get a little more than me, for example."

Summers was relieved when the others began joking at Roosky's expense. "If we run out of food, we can always eat Roosky. He'd feed us all for at least a week." The laughter and elbowing quieted down when Summers continued. "Thanks for understanding, everyone, and for your cooperation. We'll do our best to correct that issue before we leave Amundsen-Scott base."

LeClerc's voice came from behind him. "It is no joke, my friends. Many an expedition has been forced to cannibalism. Do not joke of it."

Summers froze, along with everyone else. What the hell? Why couldn't the man just leave well enough alone? Everyone took it as a joke, but now a pall of uneasiness settled over the group. Charles tried to dispel it.

"Oh, come on, Paul, let's not give the kiddies nightmares. We'll be fine."

"You say that now, but if we are pinned down by storms, you may be forced to eat your words, for there will be nothing else except…"

Now Summers was angry. "That's enough, LeClerc. Go to your tent. I don't want another word from you."

LeClerc stepped out of the long shadows cast by the Snow-Cat and stood face-to-face with Charles. "Who are you to tell me what I must do? I am the leader of this expedition. You are merely a scientist. It is up to me to keep these people safe." LeClerc's hands were curled into fists, and his face was the mottled red of a man in a rage. Summers wondered what had gotten into the man. This sudden belligerence had come from nowhere, but it had to be squelched.

"Then you haven't been doing a very damn good job of it, have you, LeClerc? If I could, I'd fire you right now for gross negligence and putting these people's lives in danger. One more word and I'll have Roosky and JR forcibly remove you to your tent, and if I have to I'll have you restrained."

JR, seeing the move telegraphed, jumped to Summers' side and lashed his big arm out to forestall LeClerc from punching him. "Paul, I think you'd better go cool off," he said. Faced with a much bigger opponent, LeClerc backed down and melted back into the shadows. A shaken Summers turned to JR.

"Thanks, man."

"No problem. What brought that on?"

"I don't know. If I had to guess, I'd say he'd been drinking, but where would he have gotten any booze?"

JR flashed Summers a humorous look and shook his head. He knew where *he'd* get a drink, but it was unlikely LeClerc had found his stash, now down to one bottle. LeClerc probably had his own. But Summers should have realized that his words would rile any proud man. What JR wanted to know was why it had been necessary to insult the man. That wasn't the way to gain cooperation, any leader knew that.

"Maybe he'll be calmer tomorrow. Dude, I can live on fewer calories. Distribute my extra ones to the rest, I'll be fine," JR said.

He loped off to the mess tent, where he came out a few minutes later with a plate of stew and a hardtack biscuit.

Summers was left to stare after him. When had JR stopped being a problem and become part of the solution? Rebecca, hearing the exchange, began to understand that JR was much more complex and more of a man than she'd realized. The problem child had just acted with more maturity than either of the supposed leaders of the expedition. Interesting, but would it last?

Later that night, Misty lay snug in JR's arms, laughing about the altercation with LeClerc. "He is like a small rooster, yes? Because he is so small, he must crow louder than all the others."

JR thought it was an apt comparison, but his main concern was where LeClerc may be hiding booze. His was going to be gone soon, all the sooner because he was sharing a shot with Misty now and then. She moved in his arms, turning to look up at him with her head in the cradle of his arm and shoulder.

"JR, do you have any Scotch left?" *Damn woman must have been reading my mind*, he thought. He bent to kiss her, parting her lips with his tongue and doing his best to distract her. Until he found LeClerc's stash, he'd better conserve what he had. Misty was fun in the sack, but he didn't like her well enough to do without his daily dose of feel-good medicine. Before long, she'd forgotten about the Scotch, or so it seemed. Her hand was creeping under his thermal shirt, leaving a trail of fire where her fingertips traced the outlines of his six-pack abs. If worst came to worst, this would do to keep his mind off the booze, too.

Before they broke camp the next day, Summers had reason to take back his reassessment of JR. Everyone was eating breakfast except Misty and JR, who had yet to make an appearance. He was about to rouse them when a high-pitched scream came from the only tent that hadn't been struck yet. Summers started to run for the tent, but was stopped after only one stride by a resounding, "Oh, JR! Oh!" Half the expedition members burst out laughing, while the other half turned their backs to the offending tent, faces, what could be seen of them, flaming.

"For heaven's sake," Summers muttered. He wasn't a prude, nor were most of the expedition members. Everyone knew that casual sex was helping to break up the monotony of travel in the frozen landscape, but this was too much. If the girl couldn't control her outbursts, the camp would be in an uproar, he predicted. However, speaking to her about it might be construed as sexual harassment. The only thing to do was speak to JR instead. Summers suspected that the boy was also drinking, but he wasn't certain. That discussion had better wait until more evidence presented itself. Summers could only hope that it wouldn't do so at a mission critical juncture.

Summers found his chance to have a discussion with JR during a rest break for Misty, when JR was puttering around outside the Sno-Cats, apparently looking for something on one of the sleds.

"JR, a word, please?"

"Sure thing, boss," he said. "What can I do you for?"

"Umm, this is a bit awkward. I'm wondering if you can persuade your lady friend to be a little less, shall we say, vocal?"

JR threw his head back and laughed. "Why? Did we wake someone up?"

"No, everyone was already awake," Summers said, with some asperity. "The entire camp heard Misty praising your prowess." If he expected JR to be embarrassed he was disappointed.

"So, what's the problem?" JR asked.

"Just that in a group like this, resentments or other emotions can run high. We don't need that, in fact, it could be quite dangerous."

"Look, dude, I didn't want to come on this expedition in the first place. I don't like being here, and both Misty and I are adults. You can't do anything except send me home, which would please me just fine. So, if you have a problem with Misty appreciating what I do for her, I'd suggest you watch your own resentments, or whatever emotion that causes you." Summers was enraged at the implication, but JR was right. He could do nothing about it, except send JR home when they reached the Pole. He'd consider doing that if his behavior continued to be disruptive. The only other solution was to outlaw all conjugal activity, which would likely create a mutiny.

JR stomped off toward the Sno-Cat, while Summers, belatedly realizing that JR had indeed been searching the sled, started poking around to try to see what JR had found so interesting. However, he found nothing, and soon returned to his laptop to record where the geophone arrays had been placed today.

Later, Summers didn't know whether it was his imagination, or whether something had taken place outside his hearing, but it seemed that part of the group was out of sorts. LeClerc took his meal and went into his tent, Leaving his frequent tent mate Cecil Stone outside, talking to Robert Cartwright. Summers observed that the conversations he could see were low pitched and were taking place in groups of two or three, rather than the entire expedition gathered to discuss their days work.

"What's going on?" he asked Rebecca, after he signaled her to step aside with him so they could talk privately.

"I'm not sure," she said. "JR and Misty seemed to be arguing this afternoon and a couple of other people asked him what was wrong. I don't know what he told them. Did something happen while they were back here?"

Summers was reluctant to tell her of his discussion with JR, but as the expedition doctor, she deserved to know if there was trouble in the ranks.

"Oh, I think I know, then," he said. Rebecca glanced at him, noted the narrowed eyes above his face mask, and hesitated to ask. Finally, he said, "I thought I'd better have a talk with JR about the incident in their tent this morning. He didn't take it well."

Rebecca looked down, embarrassed. "I don't think I would've done that, Charles," she said. "It's their business after all, and if they don't care whether everyone hears, why should you?"

"You've never been on an archaeology expedition, have you, Rebecca?"

"No, I haven't. What does that have to do with it?"

"I've seen men come to blows over a woman who was too free with her favors. We're almost always in a situation where the ratio of men to women is two to one or worse. It's common to have camp romances, there's little we can do about it. But in an environment like this, I thought it was best to put as much of a damper on any future jealousies as I could."

"Do you mean, you think some of the other men could be jealous of JR's relationship with Misty?"

"Quite possibly. It's also very possible for one of the women to get jealous of Misty."

"Oh, I doubt that," Rebecca said. "JR has a reputation. I can't imagine any of the professional women having an interest. And, even though Carmen is here as a research assistant, she still has the mentality of a professional scientist. I don't think Misty will have any competition."

"I hope you're right," Summers said. "What do you think I can do about the unease this issue has caused?"

"Honestly, I think I would just ignore it. JR has probably told them that you're going to do something drastic like segregating the men from the women. When it doesn't happen, people will forget all about it."

Once again, Summers expressed his hope that she was right.

Everyone seemed to be in better spirits the next day, as Summers estimated they had only one long day before breaking out of the south end of the glacier, and having a straight run to Amundsen-Scott. So far, no one was having to go hungry, except perhaps JR, who had insisted that he not receive a larger portion than any of the others. It was going to be touch and go, however, if they didn't make good time on the rest of the journey.

At the Pole, they expected to find a new cache of supplies, and an experimental device that hadn't been ready to go when they left Colorado for Chile. The new device, built on specifications found in the 10th Cycle Library, would make the geophone arrays obsolete. It was a drone, capable of high altitude flight at low speeds with laser-like technology that would map the terrain below. With it, Summers expected to make much better progress in his search.

It wasn't quite that easy, as once again the October storms delayed them for half a day during whiteout conditions, and slowed them down on several other occasions due to high-speed winds. With an estimated two days travel left before reaching the Pole, Bart reported to Summers that he would have to serve half-rations, or they would be without food on the last day of travel. Technically, Bart should have reported this to LeClerc, but the men were still not speaking. LeClerc blamed Bart for not following protocol, while Bart insisted LeClerc had thrown him under the bus when the shortfall was discovered.

Summers felt that the entire group should be involved in the decision. If it had been even more drastic, he would probably have deferred to LeClerc's judgment. But, since they were just talking about two days, and the supplies of chocolate bars was not in shortage, he felt everyone should have an opportunity to express their opinion.

"Listen up everyone," he called, when Bart had signaled him that dinner was ready to be served. "You all know that we were running a bit short of food a few days back. If we hadn't run into these last few storms, we would have made it into the base with no further problems. But, it looks like we have a choice now between half rations for tomorrow and the next day, or we can eat as usual, and hope to make good time to the base with nothing to eat on the last day. I'm calling for a vote. All in favor of half rations for two days, say aye." Seeing a clear majority, Summers didn't feel it necessary to raise the alternative. However, LeClerc, miffed at what he considered the usurpation of his authority, objected.

"This goes against protocol," he insisted. "You must call for dissenting opinions."

With a sigh, Summers said, "All in favor of full rations until we run out, say aye." When no one spoke, he looked at LeClerc curiously. LeClerc's hand shot up, and without waiting to be called upon, he suggested another alternative —that rationing start that very night. Summers called for the vote on that, and again no one answered. Summers raised an eyebrow to glance sardonically at LeClerc.

"Satisfied?" he asked.

"No, we should begin tonight with the rationing. If we run into another storm we must have some reserves."

A cacophony of arguments rent the cold twilight until Summers, making a quelling gesture, got everyone's attention. "It has been proposed that we accept half rations tonight as well," he said. "I can't say that it's a bad idea. LeClerc is right, if we run into another storm, it could take longer than two days to get to base. That would give us a slight reserve against that eventuality. All in favor, you know the drill."

Whether because they were hungry, smelling the savory stew that was already cooking, or whether they simply couldn't conceive of being delayed again so close to the Pole, not a hand was raised nor an aye uttered. Everyone ate their portion heartily, understanding that the next two days would bring hunger, though not starvation.

At mid-afternoon on the second day according to the clock they were keeping, a hungry group rolled into Amundsen-Scott, only to discover that the barely-remembered change in their day had actually brought them to the base in the wee hours of the morning. Breakfast was still several hours away, as they had missed the midnight meal from the kitchen. However, after thirty-nine days in each other's company, they were happy just to see a few new faces. The night shift at the base quickly assigned them to bunks, occasioning only a couple of complaints that customary tent mates were being split up.

After a few hours of sleep, Summers roused his crew, knowing they wouldn't want to miss breakfast. After breakfast, he spoke to the man in charge of the base, U.S. Navy Commander Neil Anderson about whether his resupply flight had made it through.

"Yes, indeed," Anderson answered. "I must insist that you show me whatever it is that your Foundation has been keeping under wraps, with an armed guard around it."

"Oh, that," laughed Summers. "I guess I'd better find out why it's been under wraps and armed guard, and then if I can, I'll be happy to show it to you."

The satellite uplink was subject to frequent interference from the Aurora Australis, so it took a few hours to get through to Boulder.

"Rossler here," Daniel's faraway voice came through the line.

"Summers here, greetings from the South Pole."

"It's good to hear your voice, Summers. I take it everyone made the trip okay?"

"Right as rain, except for a few tiffs here and there. Nothing serious. I have a very curious Navy Commander here, who would like to see our new toy. Is there any reason I can't show it to him?"

"Find out his clearance level, but I'm sure he has one high enough to see the drone. It's classified secret right now, until the committee can assess its potential as a weapon. After that, it will probably be declassified."

"It's a sad world that we've come to, isn't it?" Summers observed.

"Just be glad you're not in my position," Daniel answered.

Summers reported to Daniel that JR's health and fitness were okay, and that his behavioral issues seemed to be under control. It had been two weeks since JR had defied his authority, and after his conversation with Rebecca, he wasn't certain he should have tried to exercise it in the first place, so he didn't mention it to Daniel. A few more routine remarks were exchanged, and then Summers rang off.

"Cmdr. Anderson, may I ask your security level?"

Anderson could see no reason not to give the information, so he answered that he was cleared at the secret level, and offered to show Summers the documentation. Summers assured him it wasn't necessary and then took him to see the drone that, if it had been properly built to the specifications, would assist him in finding any ruins that may exist on the continent.

The drone looked like a model aircraft, though it resembled no previous aircraft that Summers had ever seen. It was made of an anodized aluminum fabric that had been coated in a striking metallic fuchsia. It boasted two sets of what Summers took to be wings, giving a crisscrossed appearance to the body about two feet back from the nose and two feet forward of the tail, the whole of the body being approximately twelve feet long. At rest, the drone sat on an array of wheeled struts, one under the forward set of wings, with two others and a tripod formation under the rear set. On its back was a disc-shaped object that resembled a UFO.

"Are you going to tell me what it's for?" Cmdr.

Anderson asked, though he had a good idea. The device looked like a U.S. Navy E-2b surveillance aircraft.

"Believe it or not, inside that disc are advanced electronics that should be able to map the surface under the ice to a depth of 150 feet. Unless the ice has a significant amount of broken rock in it, this will look right through it, as if it were water. It's capable of flying a grid pattern at a slow enough rate for our computers to take the data it transmits and draw a 3-D map of the surface and down to one hundred and fifty feet below."

Cmdr. Anderson was now suitably impressed. He gave a low whistle and then observed, "I'll bet my counterparts in the other services are dying to get their hands on that," he said. "You could map a minefield with it, couldn't you? And tunnels, missile silos...submarines?"

"I suppose you could," Summers said. "However, under the terms of the treaty they'd have to give it to everyone or no one."

"Damn stupid thing, that treaty," the commander said. "Why couldn't we have retained the advantage?"

"Have you ever read or heard the greeting message that the 10th Cyclers left us?"

"No, not in full. Why?"

"They left a warning that the only way to avert a civilization-ending calamity like the one that wiped them out was to find a way to end war. I can't think of a better way to end war than to put everyone on a technologically equal basis. If everyone believes everyone else's military technology is as good as theirs, then no one will believe they can win, hopefully. That should create an environment where we talk out our differences rather than sending young men to die or to be traumatized so much that they are unable to fit into society."

Anderson had nothing to say to that. A reasonable man, he understood Summers points perfectly. But, what would a career military officer do in a world without war? It was a moral dilemma that he didn't face alone.

With a continent too vast to map, even with 10th Cycle technology, in one summer season, there was no time to waste. After a three day period, during which most of the crew was encouraged to sleep and rejuvenate, the expedition resumed with fresh supplies. It was really anybody's guess as to where an ancient city might be buried under the ice. Summers insistence that it was likely to be somewhere in the Transantarctic Mountains was based on no more than a hunch, really. If, instead it was hidden by the deepest ice, they wouldn't find it this year. East Antarctica would represent a different set of challenges to thoroughly explore, mainly, the sheer size and the depth of the ice. Even if the drone technology could find it, if it were buried under thousands of feet of ice, it would be nearly impossible to get to it for exploration.

Therefore, Summers felt justified in searching an area where, if the city were found there, it would be more accessible. An added bonus was that the mountains were closer to the South Pole, their base of operations, than the vast reaches of Eastern Antarctica. Since they would be following no established track, Summers, with Nick Rossler's help, had planned on several two or three week treks in a pattern that fanned out from the pole at approximately $15°$ segments. They would trek to the mountains, make their way into the canyons and valleys as best they could, and rely on the drone to map otherwise inaccessible areas. The resulting map would be analyzed not only for potentially non-natural structures, but would prove invaluable to geologists and other scientific communities in the future.

The first disaster struck during the return trek from mapping the first segment. It was now mid-November, and daytime temperatures were approaching 40 to 45°F. The surface was therefore prone to potholes in the ice, caused by melting of wind-driven snow that was not as compressed as the ice below it. As water seeped into the fissures in the ice, dangerous conditions could arise for the unwary.

With warming temperatures, and brilliantly sunny days that resembled eternal mid-morning, the expedition members were in good spirits despite the arduous work of sample collecting, or other planned experiments. Cindy, the electronics engineer, had less to do during the day than the others, but had volunteered to carry the Geiger counter that Robert insisted on using to take daily readings as they explored canyons and valleys in the mountains. On the fateful day, the group was anticipating heading back to the Pole, and Cindy, carrying the Geiger counter, skipped ahead with youthful exuberance. Robert turned to take a sample from an interesting out-cropping, and when he turned back, Cindy was nowhere to be seen.

"Cindy, where'd you go?" he called. When he got no answer he became concerned and moved forward cautiously. Robert was following Cindy's boot tracks when, a few feet ahead, he could see that they disappeared at the edge of a large crack in the ice. Dreading what he would find, Robert slowed down and secured himself with his ski poles before peering into the crack. A cold dread washed over him when he saw that it opened out and ran deeper than he could have imagined. Cindy wasn't where he could see her.

"Cindy," he half-moaned. Robert knew he needed help. There was no way to lower himself into the crevasse without climbing gear and someone to belay him. He left one ski pole marking the edge of the crevasse and retraced his steps until he could see someone in the distance.

"Help!" He cried. He was gratified to see the other's head jerk up, a clear indication he'd been heard. He semaphored with his arms to gain the attention of whomever had heard him. In the distance he heard a faint echo as the person passed on his cry for help. Then, the person started toward him.

"No! Go back, we need rescue gear." Robert wasn't sure he had made himself understood, as the echoes resounded through the small surrounding areas. But, the other person had stopped, so he could only hope that some of it got through. Looking back, he could see he was no more than half a mile from the edge of the crevasse where Cindy had disappeared. He started shushing slowly toward the other member of the expedition, seeing when he got closer that it was Stone. With only a few hundred yards between them, he stopped and shouted again.

"Cindy's gone into a crevasse. Can't see her. Bring rescue gear."

Stone made an exaggerated nod with the entire upper half of his body and then turned and started back towards the rest of the team. Satisfied that he had conveyed the message he needed to, Robert returned to the edge of the crevasse, and laid down spread-eagled on the ice, his head hanging over the edge in a desperate attempt to spot Cindy.

"Cindy!" He called again. Without knowing the condition of the ice upon which he lay, or what hazards might be inside the crevasse, he dare not shout any louder. For all he knew, a loud shout might start an avalanche, either inside the crevasse or on the peaks a few hundred yards away. It seemed like an eternity before Robert heard footsteps crunching on the ice behind him. He looked over his shoulder to see Stone, with Roosky and Summers, carrying ropes, ice axes and a light but sturdy stretcher with a harness apparatus.

"What happened?" asked Summers.

"I don't know exactly, I was taking samples and she was ahead of me, sort of skipping," he said, only belatedly realizing how odd it had looked, with Cindy in snowshoes. "I looked up and she had gone out of sight, so I followed her tracks to catch up with her, and they ended here." Robert pointed at the tracks leading right to the edge of the crevasse.

"Oh, bugger. She must have jumped on a snow bridge, you said she was skipping?" said Stone.

"Yeah, that's what it looked like. I know it sounds crazy."

"And you can't see her?" asked Summers.

"No, that's why I went back for help. I'll go in, but I need a belay."

Summers immediately accepted Cartwright's offer, remembering that he was an experienced climber. LeClerc was the smallest, and lightest, but he feared there was no time to return to camp for him. And besides, he may not be strong enough to get Cindy back up if she couldn't help herself. Summers and Cartwright quickly fashioned a rescue rig, with a second harness for Cindy clipped to a ring on the harness that covered Cartwright's chest. Fastening the belaying rope to the ring at Robert's waist with a figure-eight knot, Summers positioned Roosky ten feet from the edge of the crevasse, and had him dig in with ice axes to prevent sliding. He then had Stone take a similar position five feet behind Roosky. Finally, he handed Robert a bag of pitons, which he fastened to his harness.

Summers paid out the line slowly from his stance directly behind Roosky. Cartwright, in a hurry to locate Cindy, rappelled on the descent, until he reached a steeply pitched ledge, where he secured himself with a couple of pitons driven into the ice before turning around to look for Cindy. He reckoned the ledge descended about fifteen feet at an angle of close to forty-five degrees. The ledge was so steep that if Cindy had hit it in her fall, she would have slid under the overhang that would have obscured her resting place from Robert's vision from the top of the crevasse. Unfortunately, the crevasse appeared to descend further from the bottom of the ledge, as there was a dark space between the edge that he could see and the crevasse wall opposite. Cindy wasn't there.

Robert felt sick, knowing he'd have to negotiate the ledge carefully to avoid slipping and falling into the deeper crevasse himself. Without being able to see how deep it was, he didn't want to risk not being able to ascend, or worse, yanking the other men in after him. He called up, hoping the others could hear him.

"Can't see her. There's a deeper crack here, going to try to get a look. Hang on, don't let me pull you in."

Summers could hear him, all right. But, he had mixed feelings about the last sentence. If Cartwright was about to make a descent that might budge Roosky, then he had to be ready to make a quick decision. He pulled out his own small ice ax and positioned it above the rope in front of Roosky.

"Okay, ready!" Summers called. The rope went taut again, and Summers paid out more nervously. Suddenly a jerk made Roosky lean back against the loop that surrounded him and dig in his heels, though there was no more purchase to be had. Summers tensed, but no more jerks occurred. After a few minutes with no more movement, Summers told Roosky he needed to check on Cartwright. He handed him the spare ice axe, and walked cautiously to the edge of the crevasse.

"Robert, what can you see?"

"Crikey," he answered. "Cindy's about ten feet down from my location. It looks like she's wedged into a crack that keeps going, and she seems to be unconscious. I don't know if I can reach her, it looks like the only way is for me to go in head first and have you guys haul us out."

Summers hated to ask it, but he couldn't risk Cartwright without knowing. "Are you sure she's alive?"

"No, dipshit, I don't bleedin' know if she's alive, but I'm not just leaving her down there. Even if she's not."

Summers knew there was no way to win this argument. He would have to authorize Robert's plan.

"Do you need us to haul you up and re-rig?"

"No, save your strength for hauling both of us up. I can do it here. Send down the stretcher, though. She may be too injured to haul her up in this spare harness."

Cold dread squeezed Summers heart, as he realized that Robert intended to unharness and tie a makeshift rig around his ankles, so that he could lower himself arms and head first into the narrower fissure. If it gave way while they tried to haul him up, Robert would fall, no doubt pushing Cindy further into the crack and wedging himself in as well. It was extremely risky, and Summers had no choice but to stand by, as Cartwright had made up his mind. He took a spare line and lowered the stretcher. Within a few minutes, Cartwright called, "Okay, I need more line."

Summers hurried back to Roosky's position, and paid

out another four or five feet of line slowly. Just then, a single tug on the line indicated that Robert was in position. Within another few minutes, a double tug on the line let them know he was ready to be pulled out.

Roosky now stood, his feet braced against the ice axes, and began to pull, wrapping the rope around his back and securing each foot he gained before hauling again. Stone and Summers coiled it carefully as it grew. For Summers, the process took a lifetime. He could only hope that Roosky was as strong as he looked, and that the sharp edge of the ice wasn't fraying the rope as it scraped across it. After what seemed like hours, Cartwright's boots appeared at the edge of the ice. Now the trick would be getting him up and over the edge without anyone else slipping into the crevasse. With Roosky holding fast, Stone and Summers made their way cautiously to the side, and began pulling Cartwright up by his legs. When they had his legs completely free of the crevasse, they laid him down, bent at the waist, and peered into the crack to determine the best way to relieve him of his burden, the unconscious Cindy, strapped into the stretcher and dangling like a pendant on a necklace.

"She's alive!" Robert cried. "But, I don't know how injured she is. Pull her up first."

"But, that means you'll be upside down until we can get that done."

"No worries, mate. All my blood's already in my head. Just hurry."

With as much alacrity as they could manage Summers and Stone pulled in the rope that had been used to lower the stretcher, until it was in a horizontal position, secured at the other end to Cartwright's chest harness. Roosky held fast the entire time, leaning back against the loop around his back as if it were a lounging chair. When finally they had managed to get Cindy free of the crevasse and secure several feet back from it, they went back to pull Robert the rest of the way in. If Cindy hadn't been unconscious and a knot forming on her forehead, everyone would have collapsed in a heap from the long effort. However, it was imperative to get Cindy back to camp.

No one knew how long they had struggled to save her. If he had been asked, Summers would have said hours. But, in fact, it was only perhaps forty-five minutes.

In the meanwhile, Angela had discovered that several members were out of sight, and had bullied LeClerc into offloading a snowmobile that they carried for emergency transport. As the four men struggled back to camp, trying not to jostle Cindy any more than they had to, Angela met them and gave a cry of alarm when she saw they were carrying her friend.

"She's alive, but injured. Can you go get Rebecca? I'm not sure she should be moved with that thing," Summers asked.

Without a word, Angela made a tight U-turn, and headed back for camp. She was back within minutes, a white faced Rebecca Mendenhall holding on for dear life behind her. As the snowmobile came to a halt, Rebecca jumped off and ran to the group that had put Cindy down to wait for her.

A quick examination revealed that there were no broken limbs, and as far as Rebecca could tell, no internal injuries. However, the fact that Cindy had not regained consciousness was of concern. Angela ferried first Cindy, then the doctor back to camp, leaving the men to walk back. By the time they arrived, Cindy's head wound was dressed, and Rebecca said she had done all she could until Cindy regained consciousness.

Summers was torn between making the return trip to Amundsen-Scott with all due speed and waiting for the injured girl to regain consciousness so that any injuries that weren't apparent now could be determined with her help. The concern that transporting her out of the crevasse could have already worsened any injuries that Rebecca wasn't equipped to discover made him opt for the latter. If the truth were required of him, he would have to admit that the extra time to complete their grid search with the drone added weight to the decision.

While Rebecca waited and watched Cyndi, Robert asked Summers if he could spare JR to help him finish his geological sampling. It was then that he remembered Cindy had been carrying the Geiger counter. The costly, state-of-the-art device was gone, no doubt wedged dozens of feet below the place where Cindy had come to rest, for it was impossible to tell how deep the hidden crack ran below where Cindy had become wedged. Summers was philosophical. At least, what they had lost was not a human life, God willing. Though Cindy had yet to regain consciousness, Rebecca was hopeful. She was showing signs of awakening soon.

By the end of the day following Cindy's accident, the grid was three quarters finished, with no appreciable results. When Robert and JR got back from their trek into the broken strata of the range, they found the camp in a celebratory mood. Cindy had regained consciousness, and had reported no pain that gave Rebecca any cause for concern about internal injuries. In fact, she was rather enjoying celebrity status. When Robert came striding into camp with

JR at his side, Cindy scrambled to her feet and walked swiftly to meet him.

"My hero!" She exclaimed, throwing her arms around him and planting a resounding kiss on his lips through his facemask. "I've always wanted to say that," she giggled.

Robert, as delighted to see her up and apparently unharmed as she was to see him, lowered his facemask and said, "How about another then, love?" When she complied, most of the expedition members clapped and cheered. No one noticed that Carmen was less than pleased, nor that one of the other men frowned.

Since Cindy insisted she was fine, the group remained where they were for the rest of their planned mapping, a matter of a couple of days. They then made their way back to Amundsen-Scott base to rest before once again taking on fresh supplies and moving to the next section.

Amundsen-Scott was a small base, certainly not equipped, as McMurdo was, for a large number of visiting scientists. Lieut. Cmdr. Anderson was not particularly pleased to have to host this group from time to time throughout the summer. However, he had received orders to give them all possible assistance, and the orders came from far above his pay grade. Consequently, he made every attempt to overlook the inconveniently exuberant behavior of some of the members of the expedition. When JR started a food fight in the cafeteria, he merely asked that they go outside and have a snowball fight instead, since snow was more plentiful than the imported foodstuffs for ammunition. Summers never knew how JR was going to react to something like that, so he was relieved when JR laughed, and left with good grace.

It was unfortunate in a way that the next stormy weather cooped them up at the South Pole base, rather than overtaking them on the trail. On the trail, it would have been just one more inconvenience, and not unexpected. However, for it to happen on their short recreational break, disappointed everyone and made it difficult to keep their spirits up. They could only spend so many hours watching movies, reading or pursuing whatever other entertainments they could find. Sooner or later, behavior would start to deteriorate.

That the fight started over Cindy's innocent hero worship of Robert was ironic. Robert had no romantic or sexual interest in Cindy, though he thought she was cute. From the beginning of the expedition, he'd had eyes only for Rebecca Mendenhall, though she was oblivious of his interest. However, the handsome Aussie was the object of extreme interest from Carmen, Angela and Cindy. To begin with, Angela and Cindy's interest was all in good fun, though Carmen's eyes smoldered whenever she thought she was unobserved in watching Robert. Now, however Cindy had taken to following Robert around like a rescued puppy, which he was beginning to find wearing.

To make matters worse, Dan Littleton, the civil engineer, was a solitary and brooding type who kept to himself most of the time. So much so that, many times, the others simply forgot he was there. Without a word to Cindy or anyone else, Littleton had developed a possessive crush on Cindy that he had been able to conceal until her accident. Now, however he was faced with the unpleasant sight of Cindy hanging on Robert's arm, gushing about his strength and bravery, flirting shamelessly and generally making a fool of herself. Littleton hated it but could see no way to stop it, so he seethed unnoticed.

Matters came to a head when Littleton overheard Cecil

Stone remarking to Robert that Cindy's attentions must be annoying.

"I didn't mind it at first" Robert was saying, "She's a cute kid. But, it is getting on my last nerve. I wish she would find someone else to bother."

It was so uncharacteristic of Littleton to step between the men and interrupt the conversation that at first neither knew what to make of it. They were all the more surprised when he suddenly took a swing at Robert, connecting only because of the unexpectedness of the move. Robert, normally a good-natured man, nevertheless took exception to being punched in the nose by someone he hadn't even been speaking to. His response was to throw a right cross that connected solidly with Littleton's jaw, turned him halfway around and sent him crashing into the wall.

That might have been the end of it if Stone hadn't been a witness. But, because someone else had seen his humiliation, Littleton recovered his balance and charged at Robert, both arms flying in a move that resembled a playground fight between girls. Cartwright simply stepped out of the way, laughing. That, in turn infuriated Littleton even further, causing him to whirl in his tracks and charge again.

Now Robert was getting annoyed. He would either have to let the little shit hit him again to save face, or knock him out once and for all. Since he had no idea what he had done to invite the attack, his better judgment was overcome by indignation. The next time Littleton came at him he once again threw the right cross, followed closely by a left jab to the stomach. Littleton folded, looking as if he would stay down this time, but by now, the commotion had attracted the security guard nearby.

Without giving them a chance to explain, all three men were hauled unceremoniously before Cmdr. Anderson. He in turn sent for Summers and LeClerc. When they arrived, Anderson, who had been hearing the two fighters bicker in low tones, was in no mood to compromise.

"Who is in charge of this expedition officially?" He asked. When both Summers and LeClerc answered' I am', he lost his temper completely.

"All right, I don't care who is in charge. Either of you or both of you need to get your people under control. I will not tolerate fisticuffs in my hallways." To Summers, he said, "I appreciate that you are here on an officially sanctioned expedition, and that you are not yet finished with it. But, one more incident, even one, and our doors will be closed to you permanently. Do you understand?"

An abashed Summers replied meekly, "yes, sir."

"Dismissed." barked Anderson.

As they walked together away from Anderson's office, LeClerc entertained an unbecoming thought that at least it had been Summers that Anderson blamed, not himself. Even though he was miffed at Summers for attempting to undermine his role as leader of the expedition, he had no wish to be in Anderson's hostile sights.

Summers wasted no time in calling the group together. In front of everyone, he allowed his temper to show.

"Cartwright, Littleton what were you thinking? We are guests in this facility and I assume that as adults you understand that guests must behave properly. No further display of aggressive behavior among my team members will be tolerated. The next person who initiates an altercation will be sent home summarily. Have you got that?"

Summers noticed that JR, his arm around Misty, was barely restraining his glee against one wall. Still smarting from his dressing down at the hands of Cmdr. Anderson, he now turned his wrath in JR's direction.

"Just what do you find so funny, Rossler?"

"Just that someone else's getting his ass chewed for a change," JR grinned.

"Wipe that grin off your face, or you'll be next." Summers surly remark seemed to amuse JR even further, but he hastened to straighten his face.

Summers dismissed the crew, still feeling in a foul temper. He would have liked to talk out his pique with a trusted colleague, but there was no one suitable. He and LeClerc had fallen out some time ago, Anderson had just embarrassed him, and everyone else was junior to him, and therefore inappropriate. He returned to his assigned bunk, hoping that the other occupant, a stranger to him, would not be there. In that, he finally caught a break.

A few days later, the expedition was on its way to map the second section of the Transantarctic Mountains. Tempers had had a chance to cool, and even Summers and LeClerc were on speaking terms, if uneasy ones. The outbound trip was uneventful, as was the mapping operation. This time, no unfortunate incidents marred the team's progress. It was now the height of summer, and they would have the opportunity to finish this section and one more before returning to base to spend Christmas there. It seemed their bad luck was at an end.

However, the continent had one last blow to strike. On the return trip from the third mapping project, winds of unseasonal strength delayed them for a couple of days. When at last they died down, everyone was anxious to make the rest of the trek at all possible speed. They had altered their return course to avoid having to skirt a large area of surface melting, and therefore were unaware that a worse hazard existed between the location where they stopped to wait out the wind and the base.

Because they were out of the mountains, and on the relative flat of the plateau, Stone, driving the lead vehicle with JR, Misty, Antonio, Carmen and Roosky as passengers, was pushing his speed while talking over his shoulder to the others. It happened so quickly that none of them could say afterwards whether Stone had been paying attention to the route or not. Suddenly, a crevasse appeared in front of them, and Stone made a desperate attempt to turn the Sno-Cat as he simultaneously attempted to stop. The top-heavy vehicle sloughed and then toppled onto its side, throwing the passengers about and tipping the vehicle dangerously into the crevasse.

The rest of the expedition was following at a more sedate speed. None of the passengers in the other vehicle driven by LeClerc, saw what had happened to the first. Their first inkling was seeing the treads, pointing crazily toward the sky rather than planted on firm ground. Rebecca let out a sharp cry, then clapped her hands to her mouth. As the others followed her gaze, exclamations of dismay were uttered. LeClerc brought his vehicle to a stop near the other, and expedition members tumbled out to run to the other vehicle and assess the damage.

LeClerc called sharply to them, yelling, "Stay back!" Until he could see why the other Sno-Cat was canted at the angle it was, he wanted no one jostling it. He climbed out of his cab to join Summers, who cautiously approached the other Sno-Cat. What they saw made both men draw their breath in sharply. A crevasse wide enough to swallow the Sno-Cat opened under it. It was delicately balanced only because the Sno-Cat was taller than it was wide, causing the roof to catch against the opposite side of the crevasse, and preventing it from dropping into the crevasse upside down.

Inside, JR had prevented the others from moving. From the windows he could see what looked like a bottomless chasm below them. He also suspected that the current position of the Sno-Cat could shift drastically if they weren't careful. Stone had hit his head and was just coming to when the others got to their position.

"Wha..." He slurred as he attempted to extricate himself from beneath the steering wheel. Only JR's sharp exclamation stilled him. When he came to himself enough that he could understand where they were and the danger that was keeping them there, he spoke more calmly.

"Bloody hell," he said, more softly than the expletive warranted. "How are we going to get out of this?"

"The others have just arrived. Sit tight, and see if they can't pull us out. We shouldn't move until they at least have us secured with ropes. It is critical that no one move at all," JR explained.

The necessity of sitting still made everyone in the stranded Sno-Cat twitchy. First one, then another would tentatively stretch out a limb before returning to their position, with a frown from JR as incentive. They occasionally caught a glimpse of one of the members of the expedition from the other Sno-Cat as they moved cautiously around the stranded one, but there had been no communication from outside to tell them how it was going.

After what seemed like hours, a slight shift in their position made Misty gasp and Antonio utter a sharp "Mierda." Carmen giggled nervously. Another unnerving shift, and then Robert's head appeared in the doorway.

"Bob's your uncle, we've got the bugger secured so she won't drop, we think."

As the others shifted as if to rise, JR said sharply, "One at a time. Carmen, you go first." He endured an accusatory look from Misty, before explaining, "We'll go in order of size. Misty, you're next." Stone reflected with surprise that JR had taken charge so naturally, and even more surprise that everyone obeyed him without argument. When Carmen had cleared the doorway JR gave Misty the go signal, and then indicated that the slight Chilean would be next. With the first three offloaded safely, JR sent Stone next. Finally he gave Roosky the go-ahead. Roosky balked.

"You said by size," he stated. "Roosky is biggest."

"But, I'm the captain," JR smirked. "I go last."

Unable to defeat this logic, Roosky lumbered to his feet, causing the vehicle to shift and both men to tense. When the movement stopped, Roosky crept with all the grace of a grizzly bear attempting to ballet to the doorway and disappeared. Now it was JR's turn. He rose as carefully as possible, not wishing to endure a repeat of the scary movement that Roosky's escape had engendered. As he reached the doorway the delicate balance of the roof on the side of the crevasse gave way, dropping the vehicle out from under him.

JR thrust himself free with a desperate push of his feet, and grabbed the rope that had secured the Sno-Cat to stop himself tumbling after it. Summers and Cartwright lunged to catch him by the arms. As the precious vehicle dropped away, the stunned expedition members watched in disbelief. Rebecca was perhaps the most stunned. Once again, she had watched JR calmly take control of a dicey situation and the others obey him without question. What had happened to him in Afghanistan that had changed the man she just saw into an irresponsible brat? And what would it take to bring the man back, permanently?

They were still two days from the base, and now had

insufficient transportation for all of them. Furthermore, though by some miracle the lost Sno-Cat's trailer sled had remained upright and LeClerc had taken the precaution of unhitching it before the rescue was attempted, they had no way to tow it. It would have to be left behind, until they reached base, unhitched the other, and returned for it.

Summers and LeClerc quickly huddled to determine their options. The Sno-Cats could carry a driver and eight passengers. Even if they crowded another couple of people into the vehicles, there would be six left over. They had two snowmobiles, each capable of carrying two people in a pinch. That still left two. They could see only two alternatives, with a third perhaps too dangerous to consider. The first was to leave eight of the expedition members with the stranded sled and sufficient food to camp until the remaining Sno-Cat returned for them. The second was to attempt to get the entire team to base at once, by taking turns at riding in the Sno-Cat or skiing. The final alternative, they rejected. That was to offload the snowmobiles, crowd as many as they could into the Sno-Cat and onto the snowmobiles, and have two ride on the sled. However, at even a moderate speed, those two would be subjected to wind speed temperatures that would endanger their lives unnecessarily.

After their huddle, Summers and LeClerc put the options to the others. Their recommendation was to leave eight members camped, and make all possible speed to base, then return for the others. However, it meant that eight people must volunteer. Stone was the first to step forward.

"It's my fault we're in this bloody mess, I'll stay." Summers merely nodded, though he knew that any of them could have made the same mistake. They were tired, eager to have a longer rest at base, and had been lulled by the relative ease of the expedition thus far.

Summers felt that either he or LeClerc should stay, and looked at LeClerc questioningly. The other man looked away, leaving Summers to understand that he would have to make the sacrifice. To his surprise, after he announced that he would stay, JR also volunteered. Then Bart stepped forward.

"If someone must stay behind, I must stay to cook for him."

Robert, ever willing to be the hero, was next, followed of course quickly by Cindy. Carmen, unwilling to leave Cindy alone with Robert, volunteered next. Antonio shrugged his shoulders and said, "If Carmen stays, I stay."

"It's settled then," said Summers. "I suggest we move away from this crevasse and camp for the night, then in the morning we can divvy up the supplies and the rest of you be on your way."

In the morning, they realized there would be a logistics problem. Once again, there was insufficient food, considering half their number would be on the ice for an extra four days. This time, however Summers and LeClerc carefully avoided an altercation and privately came to a solution. As much food as possible would be left with the eight on the ice, and the others, in return for being first out of the dilemma, would endure short rations for the next two days. It was as equitable a solution as the two leaders could think of, with the added consideration that the members who would be left on the ice would require more calories to survive the conditions, especially if the next four days brought high winds.

To the relief of everyone, the plan went off without a hitch. Exactly four days after the first half of the expedition left the others, racing for Amundsen-Scott base, LeClerc arrived alone in the remaining Sno-Cat. He had brought enough food supplies for the trip back, which was quickly accomplished.

Summers contacted Daniel by satellite phone, to report that they had lost a Sno-Cat but that everyone was safe. He praised JR's cool head in the crisis, as well as his willingness to be one of the expedition members to be left behind. It gave Daniel hope that the little brother he had admired so much for his good nature and athletic ability before his enlistment in the Marines was on his way back to his family whole and healed. He was less pleased to learn that morale seemed to be low. When he heard about the altercation between Littleton and Cartwright, now some weeks in the past, he asked Summers if some of the crew should be sent home, particularly since they no longer had sufficient transportation for everyone.

"Let me take that under advisement, Daniel. I'm not sure if the mission can be accomplished without everyone available. Let me think about it."

"Well, you have a week there at Amundsen Scott, try to have a plan ready after Christmas. We can always bring you all home and try again next year."

The thought horrified Summers. The whole world knew of the expedition. If they came home early, who might slip in to make the discoveries first? It was the last thing he wanted. However, he didn't protest. He would hope to find a plan that would accomplish his objective and satisfy the Foundation at the same time.

Chapter Thirteen

EGGNOG AND FOIE GRAS FOR CHRISTMAS

Christmas at the South Pole should have been enough of a novelty, Summers thought, to raise morale, at least for the week they were at the base. Disappointingly, it didn't. In the first place, none of the trappings of a North American Christmas were present. No tree, no Christmas feast and no presents. But, that wasn't the real issue. After talking with several of the expedition members, Summers determined that homesickness, exacerbated by the holiday without family, was the real issue.

Summers went to Cmdr. Anderson to determine if he had any ideas about raising morale, since the man was part of the small year round cadre at the South Pole. Anderson however was no help. His contention was that it took a certain type of person to remain isolated, seeing the same people day after day and no one else. If Summers had failed to select for that trait, it was his problem.

On Christmas Day, LeClerc surprised Summers. Though no Christmas feast was laid on at the official cafeteria, he had planned all along to provide one for the expedition members. Furthermore, he had secreted a supply of rum, which not even Bart had known about, to make eggnog. Summers could almost think well of the man after this.

It did create some resentment among their hosts, however. LeClerc had not taken into account that the rest of the population of the base would have appreciated being included in the feast. By the time he realized his mistake, it was too late, as there would not have been enough of the special foods to share. It was just as well, then, that Bart had to prepare his meal in the mess tent. It was far from the chestnut-stuffed turkey and traditional thirteen desserts that he would have prepared had he been offered the use of a real kitchen, but everyone made the effort to praise what he was able to create.

The smoked salmon, foie gras and other delicacies were familiar to no one but LeClerc, but delicious nonetheless. Tinned fruit cake was met with groans from the Americans, which quickly turned to surprised expressions of delight when they realized it was soaked in brandy. The eggnog was the biggest hit of all. After the meal, the group broke up into smaller groups, among which were JR and Misty, who disappeared into their room. How JR had wangled a room shared with Misty, was an object of much curiosity and discussion. But, by now most of the team were used to their shenanigans, even if some still disapproved.

Alone in their room, JR had a surprise for Misty. For three months, he had carried a pair of tiny diamond-stud earrings with which to surprise her on Christmas. As soon as she saw them, Misty threw her arms around his neck and thanked him profusely. She immediately put them on, remarking that she wished she had an outfit to wear with them that would set them off properly, and dazzle her man.

JR had an outfit in mind, and she definitely had it with her. He smiled with a devilish gleam in his eye, and began removing her clothes until he found the outfit he was looking for. JR bore no illusions that Misty was the woman he wanted forever. In the first place, she was too much of an airhead. With his sister-in-law Sarah as the ideal he aspired to, he needed a woman of intelligence and strength as well as beauty. Someone like Rebecca, for example.

Misty, however would do for the moment. She was willing, inventive and frankly, built like a brick shithouse. As soon as he started undressing her, Misty got the idea, and cooperated eagerly. She hadn't thought to bring a gift for him, but she could think of a few things that he would consider adequate.

JR couldn't quite put his finger on it, but something niggled at his consciousness every time he made love to Misty. In the throes of passion, she seemed to have an accent. Every time he noticed it, he tried to place it with no success. Today was no different. His attention diverted by the anomaly, it took him longer than usual to complete the act, impressing Misty once again with his prowess.

With the holiday behind them, only four days remained in their R&R break before Summers would be required to propose a plan for the remainder of the expedition. Reluctantly, he consulted LeClerc, since it was logistics that was the biggest issue. The other issue was whether to send some of the expedition members home, or ask Anderson to indulge them by housing those that had to be left behind each time they went out. LeClerc pointed out that they could accommodate all but four of their members, and the two of them attempted to determine which four they could do without on any given outing. They determined that Roosky was no longer essential, since they had replaced his specialty, along with the geophones, with the drone. However, his size and strength had come in handy both times that a rescue from a crevasse had been necessary.

Of the others, Antonio seemed to be the most disposable, since they had had no reason at all to employ his biology specialty, at least not yet. Nor was it necessary to bring along two research assistants on each outing. Finally, the anthropologist would not be needed until they found some evidence of human activity or ruins. It remained only to decide whether to send them home, or whether the base could accommodate them while the rest of the expedition finished their mapping projects. Anderson was not pleased, but was still under orders to provide all possible assistance. Therefore, he reluctantly agreed that the four who weren't essential could remain at base, rather than being sent home.

One remaining hurdle had to be cleared. Which of the two research assistants would be left behind? Summers suspected that if he attempted to leave Misty behind, JR would start a mutiny. On the other hand, attempting to leave Carmen behind would suit Antonio just fine, but Carmen would be angry. It would've been so much simpler with an all-male expedition, Summers thought, quite aware that he could never express it aloud. In the end they determined that the only fair way to do it was to draw straws for the first to be left behind. After that, they'd take turns, and hang the consequences. JR could just live with two weeks of celibacy every other trip. Certainly some of the other men, including Summers himself, were enduring more than that. For that matter, Summers would have left JR himself at the base, if he could have trusted him to behave.

January passed with results similar to the previous three months. Even Summers was beginning to wonder if they were wasting their time. They had mapped the subduction zone from the west side of the Ross Ice Shelf to the western half of the 90 degree meridian since arriving at the South Pole around the beginning of November. It was still just a tiny fraction of the continent, and they had only two months remaining. As they moved from west to east toward the Prime Meridian, the trips to the mountain range took longer and longer, as it ran more or less parallel to the Prime after the mid-way mark.

Furthermore, the supernumerary members were bored to the point of rebellion at the base. They wanted to work or go home, and Summers couldn't blame them. It was all he could do to summon enthusiasm every morning himself. Another problem was the unremitting sun, now almost directly overhead for twenty-four hours a day. There was no escape from the light; even the sleeping masks that LeClerc had laid in for them barely allowed them any respite. Sleeping in their red nylon tents was like sleeping inside the sun, except not as warm. Summers, an experienced expedition leader, was beginning to wonder whether this project would defeat him.

He'd been sending optimistic reports back to Boulder every time he returned to base, and was satisfied that JR hadn't been undermining them, as he was still refusing communication with his brother. But, in the second week of January, after the first round-trip to the Transantarctics after Christmas, he decided he'd better come clean before something happened to make a liar of him and ruin his credibility with Daniel. He locked himself inside a guest office at the base and called Boulder.

"Daniel, we've got problems out here. I haven't wanted

to say anything, because I thought we could handle them. But things are deteriorating, and I could use your advice."

"I'm sorry to hear that. What's going on?" Daniel sounded cautious, as if he thought maybe JR was the only problem. Summers hastened to dispel that idea.

"I'd say it's a cross between stir-craziness and homesickness. I guess we all thought there'd be more to find, and that we'd find it sooner. Now it's looking like an endless search under less than pleasant conditions, and the team is getting bored and sloppy. I'm worried that there'll be another accident. To top it all off, we've got to leave four of our number behind on each expedition, and there are resentments. The ones who get left resent that they aren't working, the ones that go resent that they're not getting paid to sit on their asses like the others. And JR's mad as hell that one of the people we left behind on the last trip was his girlfriend. Do you have any idea how surly your brother can get when he isn't getting any?" Summers tried for a humorous tone with his last sentence, but failed.

"Actually, I do. Why isn't he hooking up with someone else?"

"Maybe he's afraid Misty will cut his balls off, I don't know. But he doesn't."

"Hmmm, that's new. Well, the only thing I can think of is to come and see for myself, try to boost morale a bit. Maybe people will air their grievances to me, and we can bring some of them home. Can you hold off on another mapping trip until Sarah and I can get there? Maybe a week?"

"I guess. But, are you sure you should bring Sarah? How far along is she?"

"Past the seventh month, but I doubt if I'd get away

without bringing her with me. I'll make sure her doc okays it, though."

"It's a brutal trip, Daniel. Even just getting to McMurdo is two long flights. Try to leave her at home."

"We'll see, but I doubt she'll let me come by myself. We haven't been apart for more than a day or two since we got married. Pregnant women are unreasonable creatures, did you know that, Summers?"

LeClerc used the down time wisely, rearranging the supplies on the two sleds so that one was all they needed now. They were traveling lighter, with some of the foul-weather gear left behind because the high summer weather was less likely to produce bad storms. Also, less food was required since the expedition was down to thirteen members per trip, although extra fuel for the snowmobiles had to be carried.

Chapter Fourteen

THE ZENITH

A bit over a week later, an excited Daniel and tired but radiant Sarah set foot on the South Pole for the first time. Summers fussed over Sarah, who waved him off saying she felt fine. She looked great, he thought, obviously near term, radiant and smiling from ear to ear. Daniel had chartered a plane for the trip, flying down the coast of Mexico and South America, landing every few hours for Sarah to be able to walk and eat properly, then taking off again. The only really long hop had been from Tierra del Fuego to New Zealand, and they'd rested in Christchurch for two days before continuing. All in all it took a little longer than the week Daniel asked for.

Cmdr. Andersen was thunderstruck when he saw Sarah. Was it possible that the South Pole would have its first birth? He couldn't imagine a doctor allowing a woman that far along to travel so far, but of course he couldn't say anything. Women tended to take offense if you missed your guess about their due date. Rebecca was also concerned, but after Sarah allowed her to perform an examination, was reassured. Sarah was in top condition aside from the pregnancy, and she had weathered the flight well. However, Rebecca wanted her home before her thirty-sixth week. She and Daniel couldn't stay long.

Daniel interviewed each member of the expedition privately. He found those with the lowest morale to be those who remained behind on the last mapping trek, except for Roosky, who seemed to find some sort of entertainment wherever he was. Santiago and Stone were disenchanted with the expedition, having become convinced that there were no ruins to be found. They were anxious to get home and resume projects they'd interrupted for the chance to be here, and somewhat bitter at what they considered the waste of time.

Others whose specialties hadn't been tapped were Littleton and Cyndi, but Cyndi was content to remain as long as Robert Cartwright did. Littleton had given up his pursuit of her, and was actively campaigning to be relieved of the obligation to stay with the expedition.

At the end of the week-long visit, Daniel met with Summers and LeClerc to inform them of his decision. It was disheartening, but Summers had to admit that it was both prudent and fair. With his agreement, Daniel called everyone together for an announcement.

"We're going to cut this year's outing short, for a number of reasons. First, we need to arrange for replacement of the second Sno-Cat so that your services can be utilized most efficiently. Second, although we thought we could leave you here until mid-March, long range weather forecasts indicate we need to pull you out by the end of February, at the latest. We can't risk having you stranded here after the winter shutdown. I know you'll be disappointed to leave if the next pass finds something, but I think we all have to be realistic in recognizing that it's unlikely that it will. There are thousands of square miles more to map, so we couldn't really expect to find what we're looking for in the first season. That would have been extraordinary luck."

"Consequently, we'll be taking a few people with us when we leave. Dr. Stone, Dr. Littleton and Dr. Santiago will accompany us home. We have room on the helicopter for one more, and those who would like to apply for that seat should see me privately no later than four this afternoon."

Several people thought hard about applying, but realized their specialties were mission-critical and they'd no doubt be denied. Angela Brown, the cartographer was one of them. She'd had it with the cold, the privation on the long treks and the lack of attention from the men, most of whom seemed to lust after her friend Cyndi. She'd like to hate Cyndi, but the bubbly girl was impossible to hate. Who ever heard of a fun engineer? It just wasn't fair.

JR was also aware that his application would be denied. His pride wouldn't let him even try. His only hope was that Misty would elect to stay, too. While the others debated what to do and whether their choice would be honored, he sought out Sarah and had a long talk with her.

"How are you holding up, JR? We're getting good reports about you from Summers," she added. She was taking a rest in the lounge, her feet up and her baby bump perched charmingly on her lap. Sarah was a believer in positive reinforcement, so she was laying it on a bit thick, but JR preened under her compliment.

"Can't complain," he said. "Though I'd like to." The irrepressible grin from six or seven years ago made Sarah's heart clench. If only they could have their sweet JR back, it would mean everything to Daniel.

"Tell me about the treks," she asked, hoping to get more than a few words out of him.

"They're actually kind of fun. But don't tell Summers I said so. We drive out to the mountain range as fast as we safely can, usually takes several days. Then we use that cool drone to map a grid pattern. Have you seen that thing work?"

"Yes, they demonstrated it for us before sending it on to you. It's pretty, isn't it?"

JR gave her a disgusted look. Who would describe a cool piece of electronics as pretty? Even though its color was bright and cheery.

"I guess. Hey, Sarah, do you guys know what you're having yet? Am I going to be an aunt or an uncle?"

Sarah laughed until her sides hurt and she had to wrap her arms around her belly to ease the strain. "You're going to be an uncle, but we aren't telling what sex the baby is until it's here."

JR had accomplished his goal. He'd deflected any more questions from Sarah, whom he didn't want to disappoint by giving her too much information about his social life, and he'd made her laugh. Making Sarah laugh was a goal that he and his older brother shared, and the reward was that her silken skin turned pink and her eyes crinkled up. It made Daniel breathless to see, and delighted JR like nothing else could. If he wasn't careful, he'd creep her out, in fact.

JR was smart enough to realize that what he felt for Sarah aside from brotherly love was admiration, but sometimes he thought that Daniel had found the last perfect woman on earth. At least, he'd thought that until the expedition had thrown him together with Rebecca Mendenhall more closely than before. Now *that* was a woman he could love. She even looked a bit like Sarah. Not that the looks were the most important thing, but damn, can't hurt, right? The other person Sarah wanted to have a private conversation with was Rebecca, not only because they were friends, but because she could trust Rebecca to give a professional and honest opinion about JR's progress. Sarah didn't know quite what to make of what Rebecca said. As she expected, Rebecca talked of JR's juvenile behavior and womanizing. But, surprisingly, she had the most to say about his leadership under pressure. Most astonishingly, Rebecca confessed that if he behaved that way all the time, she might even have a crush on him. After all, he was devastatingly good-looking, a real man in every way except his occasional childish spells.

Sarah's impression was that Rebecca already had a crush on her handsome brother-in-law, but she kept it to herself. Let Rebecca have her illusions. If it turned into something, it could only be good for JR to have a woman like Rebecca love him.

It was ironic, Summers thought, that JR had begun to behave like an adult before Daniel's visit. Now that he was here, however, JR was reverting to the juvenile behavior that had marked his demeanor before they all left Boulder. For days, Summers had detected no alcohol use on JR's part. But now, every time he encountered the boy, he appeared intoxicated. Where he was getting the booze, was another question altogether. Summers wished he had the time to search the sleds for what he thought of as LeClerc's stash. But, they'd already lost a week while waiting for Daniel and

Sarah's visit. Now it would be touch and go to make their final mapping run before their February 24th deadline. That would leave them only four days to secure what they intended to leave behind, pack and load what they would take with them, and fly out on the last helicopter to McMurdo before winter storms were expected to begin.

Summers found himself in the peculiar position of wishing that Daniel and Sarah would cut their visit short, and leave, so that he and his team could make their last trek. Maybe once Daniel left, JR would straighten up again as well. Summers was an optimist, but it was not to be.

On the next to last day of their plan to visit, Daniel encountered JR and Misty emerging from their room, with JR clearly impaired. Summers hadn't told him of the drinking, so Daniel was thunderstruck.

"JR, I hope I'm not seeing what I think I'm seeing," Daniel said.

"And what would that be?" JR demanded, too drunk to moderate his tone.

"I don't believe it. You are drunk. And Misty, have you been drinking too?" Misty eyed him boldly.

"We're not on duty, you have no business trying to control what we do in our off hours," she said. The impertinence staggered Daniel for a moment, and then he narrowed his eyes.

"You have no off-duty hours while on this expedition." He said, ice dripping from his tone. "JR, I need to see you privately, immediately. Miss Rivers you may return to your room." Misty looked at him incredulously and then flounced back into the room, slamming the door.

JR rounded on Daniel and shouted, "Why do you always have to be such an asshole? We weren't doing any harm."

Through gritted teeth Daniel answered. "The harm you're doing is to our credibility with our hosts. You're putting the entire expedition in jeopardy with your selfish and mindless behavior. I can't believe you'd embarrass me this way, no matter how sick you are."

"Sick? You think I'm sick? I'm not sick, I'm pissed off. Tell me, when did dad die and leave you in charge of the family? I never asked you for your help, and I certainly don't need your attitude. Leave me the fuck alone." JR turned and started to walk away, but Daniel stopped him with a hand on his shoulder. It was the wrong move to make. JR swiveled on his back foot and came around with a swing that narrowly missed Daniel's face, only because he dodged backward as soon as JR started to move. Startled by the hate in JR's eyes, Daniel withdrew his hand, freeing JR to run for the airlock. Dressed only in street clothes, and boat shoes that he wore for house slippers, JR raced outside into the bright but cold sunlight. In a matter of moments, he was out of sight of base personnel, running at top speed and heedless of his direction.

Inside, Daniel was stunned. He knew JR had been traumatized, and being on the receiving end of his outbursts had become commonplace. But, this was worse than anything he'd seen before. Daniel worried that this time he had pushed JR too far. Troubled, he went in search of Sarah to talk it out, not realizing that JR had run straight into potential trouble when he got out of sight of the base.

The trouble wasn't that the air was too cold for survival, given what JR was wearing. At the height of summer, daytime temperatures were about 50°F, so although he might be chilly, as long as JR could find his way back to base, he would not suffer from exposure. However, finding his way back to base was the issue. On the windswept plateau, and with the sun beating down from almost directly overhead, the glare from the snow prevented long-distance visual orientation. Not only was he not within sight of personnel at the base, neither could he see it to return. But, as he ran, JR was not thinking about getting back. His only thought was to get away.

JR had screwed up again, he had to admit it. He'd thrown away all the good will he'd built up with Summers and the rest of the expedition members, but worst of all was screwing up in front of his brother. Daniel was his hero, the big brother who could do no wrong. It was horrifying that he thought JR was sick, worthless, nothing but a failure. He couldn't face that judgment from Daniel, but he heaped it on himself. *I'm just a worthless piece of shit*, he told himself. He wanted to die.

After half an hour, the thin, dry air was no longer sufficient to fuel his run. Though he was still in top physical condition, he was thirsty, tired and had to stop. Still unaware of the danger he'd put himself in, he flopped down to sit on the ice, ignoring the cold that seeped through the seat of his pants. Now that he was no longer running, he had time to think and his more logical side woke up to how ridiculous it had been to fight with Daniel. The fact was, that he was enjoying this adventure. Even though he had resented Daniel's interference in forcing him to come, he had nothing better to do at home, and being at the bottom of the world was kind of cool when he thought of it.

JR knew he had a problem, one that he'd been denying for a long time. But he had no idea how to overcome it. Loneliness overcame him as he thought, wasn't there anyone out there who could just accept him? Acceptance would help. To ask for understanding, or for someone to like him might be too much, but if they could just accept him, maybe he could begin to heal himself.

Gradually, it entered his consciousness that his bum was getting rather cold, in fact, it was completely numb. It was only then that he stood up and turning slowly with his eyes on the horizon, realized he was lost.

"Well, shit. Doesn't that just ice the cake? Where the hell is the base?" He stood stock still, to consider his dilemma. He had about an eight to one shot at walking in the right direction, even if he could maintain a straight course. Then, he thought that he could probably retrace his route by following his own tracks, but he soon discovered that his soft boat shoes had not left much of an impression. He couldn't even sit down, because there was nowhere to sit that wasn't covered in ice, for which his jeans, even over thermal underwear as they were, were not equipped to protect him.

"You asshole, JR," he said to himself. "You've screwed the pooch this time." His only hope was that someone would miss him. A little of his self-pity crept in, leading him to conclude that no one would miss him, or that if they did, they'd be glad to be rid of him, as much trouble as he was. Still, he couldn't help but hope they'd soon send a search and rescue mission.

But without knowing how far he'd run, he couldn't imagine how many square miles they would have to cover to be sure of finding him. Then, he had a brilliant idea. It was now near the end of January, almost 6 weeks beyond the summer solstice, when the sun was truly at zenith. That meant that his shadow should be able to tell him which way to go, if he could only think about it correctly. Then he had it. Because the sun was now describing a circle around the pole from a relatively shallow angle below zenith, no matter what time of day it was his shadow should point toward the pole. At least, he thought so. All he had to do, then was to follow his shadow. It could have been a fatal miscalculation, but because it was now well past noon, he actually started in more or less the correct direction.

By now, Misty had come out of her room looking for JR, and, not finding him began to ask others if they had seen him. When it became apparent that no one had, she went to Daniel.

"What happened after you sent me to my room?" she challenged.

"That's none of your business," Daniel answered. "But why?"

"He's missing," she said, simply. Her reward was the look of consternation on Daniel's face as he seized her shoulders.

"What do you mean, missing?"

"Just what it sounds like," Misty sniped. "I can't find him. No one on base has seen him."

With that, Daniel snapped into action. At his request, Cmdr. Anderson ordered a thorough search of the base. His absence corroborated, JR's status became official. It was then that a helicopter was dispatched to run a search grid. No one knew how long JR had been out of the base, but Daniel suspected it had been two or three hours, at least. Overcome with remorse, he wished he had never spoken harshly to JR. An inventory showed that no snowmobiles were missing, and JR's outdoor gear was still in his room. He had gone out onto the ice ill-equipped for the climate, and if Antarctica killed him, Daniel would never forgive himself.

Daniel wanted to join the search effort himself, but Anderson put his foot down. "We've already got one tenderfoot out there," he said. "We don't need another." Daniel had to content himself with pacing in the lounge, Sarah's eyes following him anxiously, and the other members of the expedition also waiting nervously. It occurred to Daniel as he paced, that the demeanor of the others suggested that JR was well-liked. What was it about their dynamic that brought out the worst in both of them? As soon as he had JR back safe, Daniel intended to sit down with him and try to have a pleasant conversation, take accountability for his own ill temper, and try once again to re-establish the loving relationship the brothers had shared in their youth.

It was two long hours later, when a shaken JR was delivered into his brother's arms. The helicopter had found him traveling in a direction that would have taken him right past the base without ever seeing it, had he continued. In that case, he might have walked until he dropped from exhaustion and died on the ice in a trackless wilderness. He was also ravenous, having missed both breakfast and lunch, but at least he was now sober. In respect of his near disaster, Bart obtained permission from Anderson to go into the closed cafeteria and prepare a meal for those who had been too distressed to eat.

No one wanted to question JR about his reasons for leaving the base so ill-prepared. Misty, of course had an idea, but neither Daniel nor JR were eager to corroborate her suspicions.

While the others ate, Daniel pulled Rebecca aside and asked for her assessment of the situation.

"Daniel, JR has had some moments of extraordinary courage and leadership out here. He always seems to conduct himself like a man after them, only getting into trouble when he's under Misty's influence or the influence of alcohol. I think maybe he just needs to feel competent, and that people look up to him, or at least respect him. A little trust from you would go a long way, and maybe you could take it easy on him when what he's done isn't such a big deal."

When everyone had been fed and the commotion died down, Daniel spoke quietly to JR, asking him to remain behind when everyone else went to bed, so that they could talk. JR sat, his shoulders hunched against the lecture he was sure Daniel was about to deliver. However, he had dropped his defensive attitude, knowing he had pulled a stupid stunt, and feeling he deserved the lecture. He was surprised when Daniel, instead of yelling at him, sat down and put his face in his hands.

"Damn, JR, I thought I'd lost you." The anguish in his tone made tears start in JR's eyes, which he angrily dashed away. This was the side of Daniel he hadn't seen in years, and thought was gone in the drama and new prominence Daniel had gained with his discovery of the pyramid code. His heart softened toward his brother a little, then.

"To tell you the truth, I wasn't so sure I hadn't lost myself," JR said, with a hint of humor.

"Listen, kid don't do that again, okay?"

"Fuckin' A," breathed the ex-Marine fervently. "Next time I decide to have a hissy fit, I'll do it after I've put on my outdoor gear, and stolen a snowmobile." But, his boyish grin belied the truth of his words. Daniel was fairly confident that there would be no more incidents, and no stolen snowmobiles.

"Sarah and I are leaving tomorrow, you know," Daniel said. "If it weren't for the plea bargain with that judge, I'd take you with me. You know that, don't you?"

"Yeah, bro, I know. But, I need to admit something to you. I'm actually kind of enjoying it here."

"That's good, JR. You know, some of the crew members

have let me know that you're a valuable asset to the expedition. They like you, even when you're acting like an idiot. Most of them, anyway. Promise me you'll stay safe."

"I'll do my best, Danny boy," said JR. He was still processing what Daniel had just said. He was valuable? Really? He held his head up a little higher. Maybe he wasn't such a screw-up after all.

Chapter Fifteen

IN THE STORM

By noon the next day, having seen off those who were leaving in the helicopter, Summers and LeClerc had the rest of their crew headed out for their last mapping journey. They had further to go this time than ever before, and the race was on to finish their task and get back to Amundsen-Scott before the winter storms were upon them. The outward bound trip was uneventful for the first couple of days. But then, disaster struck once again.

Even though it was still late in January, an early storm trapped the group on the ice, forcing them to stay put and wait it out. By now, their earlier experience with heavy storms was well behind them. But, they had grown complacent to the dangers of the continent with familiarity. Robert Cartwright had noticed something interesting at the edge of the last mapping data, and he wanted to explore it more thoroughly. Therefore, they had brought the mining experts, along with Roosky, on this trip. The men had been left behind on the previous trip, due to the lack of the second Sno-Cat.

Before the storm struck, they were taking their turn on the snowmobiles. But, when the group hastily made camp, these two abandoned their rides without securing them under wraps. LeClerc was directing Roosky in affixing guide ropes between the Sno-Cat and the tents when he realized that the snowmobiles were at risk. Angrily, he shouted at the mining engineers to come out of their tent and secure tarps over the snowmobiles so that wind driven sand and ice particles couldn't make their way into the motors. He then continued his task with Roosky.

As it happened, the mining engineers had settled down for the evening, and were attempting to enjoy storm rations, along with tea they were brewing over a small alcohol stove. They assumed that LeClerc meant for them to cover the snowmobiles after they had finished their meal. When they were done, they started heating water for more tea, while one decided to go out and find the tarps on the sled. No sooner had he stepped outside, then a strong wind gust took him off his feet before he had the chance to clip onto the guide rope. He shouted as he was swept across the ice, but no one heard. Unable to gain his footing he was swept further and further from camp, until, bashed against the ice and battered by the gusts of the storm, he lost consciousness.

Inside the tent, his companion finally realized he had been gone too long, when the water began to boil. He took the water off the stove but failed to douse the flame. As he got up to look outside and see if he could see his companion, he knocked over the alcohol stove, spilling the fuel, which ignited. The nylon tent, highly flammable, was immediately engulfed in flames. Though the man frantically beat at the flames beginning to consume his clothing, he was overcome before he could escape the tent. His screams of anguish went unheard because of the howling winds outside.

It was morning before anyone discovered the disaster. As they slept the storm died down, and when Bart and LeClerc rose to organize breakfast, LeClerc spotted the ruined tent, with one body entangled in the melted nylon. Horrifyingly, they were unable to determine which of the two men who had shared the tent was the burned one. The other mystery was where the other man had gone. They couldn't imagine that he would have simply walked away from his companion's body, assuming he even got out himself. However not a trace of him remained.

Baffled, shocked and confused, LeClerc and Summers could not agree whether to go on, or to return to Amundsen Scott to raise a search party. But, with no idea where to search, Summers was in favor of going on. The others were aghast. Rebecca sided with LeClerc, and the others persuaded Summers that they must return to base, no matter how unlikely that they would find the other man alive. Accordingly, they wrapped a tarp around the remains of the miner who had burned in the tent, loaded the grisly package on the sled, and turned back.

The two day trek virtually guaranteed that anyone alone on the ice, if he had been alive to begin with, would not have survived. However, everyone felt it was imperative to return the man's body to his family if possible. By the time they got back to base, LeClerc and Summers could not utter a civil word to each other. Summers' leadership was in question, and everyone else was very disturbed by his perceived callousness. Summers felt he was being judged unfairly, because his priority was to finish the last mapping project that they could. He alone knew the outrageous cost of their expedition for this year, so much that it was doubtful that they would be able to return. And for nothing.

While Summers sequestered himself in his room to brood, LeClerc approached Anderson as the expedition leader for the first time.

"Cmdr. Anderson, I must ask for your assistance in locating the body of our confrere." After telling Anderson as much as he could about the circumstances of the man's disappearance, LeClerc reported to the others that Anderson would send a fixed wing plane to fly a grid from the position of the burnt tent, which they had left as a marker, in the direction that the wind had been blowing. It was his guess that the man had been caught by a wind gust and swept away, as that was unfortunately not an uncommon occurrence. Usually, they were able to recover the victims, especially if a witness raised the alarm. But often, they were seriously injured. Anderson had no hope at all that the missing man would be found alive, and little that his body would be found. Nevertheless, he fulfilled his promise and sent the plane to search. Some hours later, it returned to base with no results. Anderson flatly refused to waste further fuel on the search, citing their need to conserve it for the coming winter.

Even though the two men had been closer friends with each other than with any of the rest of the group, a deeper pall was cast over the remaining members of the expedition when Anderson made his announcement.

Morale among the expedition members reached an all-time low. After a few hours, Summers came out of his room and called them together.

"My friends, I'm sorry if you felt my intention to go on was unfeeling. No one regrets the loss of the team member more than I, however, stopping the work to recover a body did not seem to me to honor the sacrifice that our colleagues made. It is my intention to finish the last segment before we return home. Who is with me?"

LeClerc waited until a few hands reluctantly went up. Then he stood. "I'm afraid that this will not come to pass. I have requested of Cmdr. Anderson that he stop this foolishness, before more are lost. Furthermore, I have sent word to the Rossler foundation that we must be extracted early. There will not be time to complete another mission."

His words instantly polarized the group. Cartwright and JR, two of those who had raised their hands in response to Summers request started talking at once.

"By what right..." started Cartwright.

"You little weasel," interrupted JR. Of all the people Summers might have expected to come to his defense, JR was not one of them. He noticed that Rebecca was also looking at JR with surprise.

"What was Daniel's answer?" Summers asked.

LeClerc was reluctant to tell him, because Daniel had in fact asked to speak to Summers. LeClerc had told him that Summers was unavailable, but that he would have him call at a later time. In answer, he shrugged, with a Gallic movement that irritated more than one of the witnesses. Several, however, were looking back and forth, unable to determine which side they should take.

"In that case," Summers said, drawing himself up with determination, "it's my intention to leave immediately. Come with me or don't come, but if you don't you will get no credit for any discoveries we make, and I will report to the Rossler Foundation that you abandoned the rest of the expedition."

Those who had been on the fence suddenly found their minds made up for them. As one, everyone rose to follow Summers. Everyone but LeClerc. But, when he saw that Bart was going as well, he felt he had no choice but to go with them, though he had grave misgivings about their safety. Summers quickly organized restocking of their food, and they set out without even sleeping, and without any sort of ceremony to mark the deaths of the two miners. But, in place of the easy camaraderie they had enjoyed before was a sense of uneasiness and impending doom that most couldn't shake.

Chapter Sixteen

ITS WARM IN THERE

All along, in addition to modern maps and GPS technology, Summers had been tracking their progress on the ancient maps that had first sparked his interest. With the expedition in danger of going home without result, he pinned his hopes on this last segment. Not only had Robert seen what he thought might be a cave entrance on the last edge of the previous section, but also the ancient maps showed a valley somewhere in the same vicinity. The valley was much larger than any they had encountered previously, and therefore held some interest for him. His intention was to at least explore that valley, even if they had to cut short their mapping of the rest of the segment.

The team was still saddened and depressed concerning the absence of the miners. Few were talking, and in fact, most were sleeping. The trackless waste no longer held their interest, the victim of familiarity and featurelessness. However, JR and Cartwright had discovered some interest in common, and were talking about spelunking, much to Misty's disgust. JR was beginning to tire of Misty's constant neediness. But, with only a few weeks to go before they were extracted, he was content to leave well enough alone. Bedding her was still pleasurable, because at least then her prattle ceased, while her shouts of pleasure stimulated his passion and fed his ego, giving him a reason to stay with her. Therefore, JR ignored Misty while he learned all he could about caving from Robert.

Relieved of the necessity to reduce their speed for the snowmobiles, the Sno-Cat made good time and reached the mountains only three days behind schedule, in spite of the four-day delay. However, when they reached the coordinates that the map indicated should open into a large valley, they encountered instead a steep escarpment. Summers called a halt, and asked Cartwright to join him. Showing him the map, he asked "What do you make of this, Robert?"

Robert examined the map closely, and then laid it over a modern map. Folding the ancient map along the centerline, Robert tried to match it up to the modern map. There were too many differences, however. His best guess was that one of the calamities, probably the 10th Cycle one, had shifted the land so much that the valley had disappeared. Or, it could've been tectonic movement, since the Western half of Antarctica had broken away from Australia and crashed into the eastern half, which was what had raised these mountains.

"I'd say we're buggered, mate. You really expected to find the city here, didn't you?"

Summers sighed heavily. "I had a great deal of hope," he said. "This would have been an ideal location, except for the glaciation. I'd hoped there would be some explanation to account for the 9th Cyclers colonizing this continent."

"Didn't I hear some talk that you thought geothermal activity might account for a different climate in their time?"

"It was one theory we floated," Summers answered. "But now, I'm at a loss as to where to look. It seems as if this mountain simply fell out of the sky and covered the valley."

"Well, I've read more bizarre theories about the end times calamities," said Robert. "Some say that's how Atlantis disappeared. Come to think of it, could the civilization we're looking for have been birthed on Atlantis, and the entire continent has been transported here, to become Antarctica?"

"That's an intriguing theory that has been put forth before by the fringe element," Summers said, dismissing Robert's flight of fancy. "What shall we do about this?"

"Well, what I'd like to do is explore the cave system I thought I saw. Then, maybe it's time to go home." said Robert.

"I suppose you're right." Cartwright had never seen Summers so dejected, or defeated. His own sunny optimism couldn't help but raise his adrenaline level when he thought of the possibility of finding something within the cave system.

It took a little while to coordinate the drone-mapped segment with their commercial maps. However, once they did, it was a matter of one hours' coverage by the drone to find again the dark area that he had thought was the cave entrance. At his shout of excitement, everyone gathered round. The location was perhaps ten miles to the northwest. Summers made the decision to break camp and travel there by Sno-Cat, over LeClerc's objections.

LeClerc wanted to stay in what he considered a safer zone, far enough away from the escarpment that they would be safe from avalanches or falling ice, yet near enough to the cave entrances. By now, all discipline had been compromised. With little regard for LeClerc's leadership, Summers instead called for a vote, which was in his favor. They then struck camp and moved the Sno-Cat closer to the cave system.

Robert was eager to explore the caves, but in this regard, Summers and LeClerc were in agreement.

"You should wait until you've rested, Robert," Summers said. "You've been on your feet for more than sixteen hours."

Hearing that, Robert hurriedly glanced at his chronometer. Indeed he had. The more or less constant sunlight, coupled with the excitement of his discovery, had combined to keep him from feeling the effects of fatigue. With his agreement, the group again made camp, with the plan to support his spelunking adventure the following morning. The next morning found JR harnessed into climbing gear and ready to accompany Cartwright into the cave.

"Are you sure, mate? You're a tall drink of water, and sometimes caves get tight. Are you at all prone to claustrophobia?"

"I can handle it," JR promised.

The outcome of this day would dictate whether the expedition was over for the year, or whether a few more days' exploration was warranted.

Despite their proximity, the entrance to the cave had not yet been located. Because the drone made a 3D image of the sub-surface, it showed a rather large open area underground, but Robert was aware that the entrance could be much smaller. The group split up to comb the area, Robert and JR taking the interior of the canyon. Before they left, Rebecca stopped JR to tell him to be careful. The uncharacteristic show of concern specifically for him unsettled JR, creating a warm glow somewhere in the vicinity of his stomach.

Robert and JR proceeded up a short, narrow canyon, each examining the sides of the canyon for a likely opening. Robert was squinting into the slanted sunlight to try to make out what he thought was a dark shape when JR grabbed his arm.

"Robert, could that be it?" JR was pointing to a dark alcove situated by an overhang of ice topped by deeply drifted snow.

"Could be, but I hope there's another."

"Why's that?"

"I don't like the look of that overhang. But, we've got to take a look, at least. Would you be willing to stay outside while I go in on a rope at first? You made the discovery, but I'm the more experienced climber and spelunker," Cartwright suggested.

"Yeah, man, no problem. But you'll let me come in once you scope it out, right?"

"Sure thing, mate."

Robert harnessed up, and positioned JR where he thought he'd be safe if the overhang let go, with the rope in his gloved hands but secured around a short outcropping right behind him. Then he went in, watching the overhang to judge its stability as he went. He made it in with no mishaps, and used the light on his helmet to look around once he'd reached the limit of the rope. A less experienced caver might have unhooked from his rope and gone to explore further, but Robert knew better. No matter how tempted he was to see more, safety was paramount. Even if he were willing to risk his own life, he wouldn't risk JR's, and it would have that effect if his rope went slack and JR came in after him.

From what he could see, it was well worth bringing in some of the others and exploring further. With his flashlight on full beam, he could see at least two large passageways leading away from the main cave across from his location near the entrance. In addition, a third, closer one led out of the main room on a downward pitched slope, as near as he could tell from his vantage point. He recalled other cave systems where the main entrance, even though it led into a very large room, was tiny in comparison to the rest of the system that lay hidden below. Carlsbad Caverns in the US was one of them. This main room needed to be mapped for other exits, whether they lay hidden behind stalactites and stalagmites, were visible, or led upward from the ceiling of this room or downward below the floor.

He could do no more without more gear and more helpers. It was time to leave, let JR have a peek if he wanted, and then get back to Summers and give his report.

As he assumed, JR did want to go in and look at what they'd found. He gave the younger man a quick refresher course in the use of the rope rig and some basic spelunking advice, made him promise on his honor that he wouldn't under any circumstances remove the rope from his harness, and told him he had half an hour to get in, look to his heart's content and then re-join Robert for the short hike back to the camp.

JR was sorely tempted to un-hook and get closer to some of the passages he could see, but Robert had warned him that if he felt the rope go slack once he reached the end of it, he, Robert, would personally kick his arse all the way back to the Pole. He thought the Aussie might try to do it, too, and he'd hate to have to hurt the man. But the main reason he didn't was that he liked Cartwright, who treated him like a colleague. If only other people would treat him like that instead of like a naughty child or the spoiled brother of the Foundation director, he'd meet their expectations more often.

As soon as they were spotted coming out of the mouth of the canyon, JR and Robert were mobbed by the rest of the group, none more eager to hear of their discovery than Summers. Though it was well past lunch-time, the two had eaten nothing but a couple of energy bars since breakfast, so Bart prepared something more substantial while everyone else gathered around to hear their report. JR deferred to Robert, because of course he could give a more informed description of the cave they'd entered.

"It's a large main room with passages leading off in at least three directions. Because it was so large, we wanted to come back and get some others to help us map that main room, but I can tell you that it has formed from erosion within the sandstone and siltstone sedimentary layers that lie above the granite and gneiss of the volcanic basement. There may be more than one entrance beneath the ice at the top of the escarpment, but what we went into was an opening on the side of the canyon wall. I saw no evidence of ruins, but there was something I think will interest you, Dr. Summers. That cave was warmer than it should have been."

Summers tilted his head, looking so much like a puzzled dog that JR had to suppress a hoot of laughter. "What do you mean, warmer than it should have been."

"Most caves, certainly those with small entrances, are considered closed systems with regard to climate. The temperature tends to stay pretty close to the average annual temperature of the area. In this case, that's minus 70 degrees Fahrenheit, give or take. But, the thermometer I took in there read plus 13 after only about fifteen minutes. I suspect there's a geothermal outlet somewhere below there."

"Are you telling me that there could be habitable caves below the one you were in? We're naming it Cartwright Cave, by the way."

"Thank you, but JR spotted the entrance. It should be Rossler Cave. And yes. If you were Inuit, you'd consider that one habitable."

"Rossler-Cartwright, then. We've got to get back in there."

"Yes, that's what I'd recommend," Robert said. "There's just one problem; there's a rather delicate hazard directly above the cave entrance. We'll have to be very careful, and it would be best if Roosky were with us just in case it lets go."

"That's going to cut it close getting back and forth and still being ready to be extracted on time," LeClerc said. "I say we explore what we can now, and come back next year for a more thorough search."

"No," said Summers. "We can't risk anyone getting trapped in there. We need Roosky. We'll go back to base, drop off anyone who isn't needed and doesn't want to risk not getting back in time, pick up Roosky and make it back here with all possible speed." Summers had virtually taken over the leadership position, and LeClerc, being physically unimposing and prone to fits of temper, had lost the respect of most of the team. Summers prevailed. They struck camp immediately and headed back for the Pole, traveling as fast as they dared.

By traveling long hours and settling for quick rations

instead of the gourmet meals Bart could produce given enough time, they made record time getting back and caught everyone back at base by surprise. The plan was to turn around as quickly as possible after re-supplying, and everyone had a task to perform to accomplish it. Robert and Summers went to talk to Roosky about what they might need from him, Rebecca and Bart saw to the resupply, and the others had various manual labor tasks in support of the doctor and Bart. Meanwhile, LeClerc disappeared, but no one noticed.

As soon as he could slip away, LeClerc had hurried to the weather station monitoring room, where he studied long-range forecasts. Still worried about the early storm that had taken two of the crew, he closely questioned the meteorologists about their predictions and saw their evidence. Satisfied that he was on solid ground with his request, he sought an audience with Cmdr. Andersen.

"Cmdr. Andersen, thank you for seeing me."

"Mr. LeClerc, you're welcome, but I must ask that you state your business succinctly. I'm very busy."

"Just so. Briefly, then, I wish for you to place Dr. Summers under arrest until we can arrange for transport back to McMurdo Station." His request was stated in such a calm voice that at first Andersen thought he'd misheard.

"Excuse me?"

"I request that you arrest Dr. Summers," LeClerc repeated.

"On what charges? This is an extraordinary request, LeClerc. Please explain yourself."

"Very well. Dr. Summers is even now preparing to take the expedition back to an area we just came from. There is a large cave that must be explored; however, with travel time back and forth, a few days to explore the cave, they will not be back before the last day of February. If storms create any delay at all, we would be overwintered here. I think you'll agree, sir, that this would be a most unfortunate turn of events."

"You have easily three weeks remaining before you would have to worry about overwintering. Do you have another reason for making this request?"

"Yes, sir. Your own meteorologists are predicting a very large storm that will overtake us before we reach the shelter of the mountains. This cannot help but delay us disastrously."

"And you have been unable to persuade Summers to change his mind?"

"The man is how do you say? Derangé. He will not listen, and the others, they listen to him instead of me. I am the leader of this expedition, but my power has been usurped!"

It was LeClerc's misfortune that his agitation had gotten the better of him. Now it was he who sounded, and looked, deranged. Andersen regarded him for a moment, took in the unruly hair that his hands constantly disturbed in their fluttering, the wild eyes and the deterioration of the man's English when he was disturbed. Andersen concluded that this was a case of professional jealousy that he had no business arbitrating, and told LeClerc that he'd take it under advisement. He then dismissed the hapless Frenchman, with a refusal to take action.

With no other choice to prevent the final trek, LeClerc appealed to the two whom he thought the most influential of the Rossler Foundation group: JR Rossler and Rebecca Mendenhall. Perhaps he thought JR had his brother's ear, or that the two of them could persuade others, but in any case, he spoke to them in private and expressed his concerns.

"This storm you say they're predicting. How accurate are they in terms of when the storms hit?" asked JR.

"I believe within thirty-six hours, with a fifty percent accuracy rating," LeClerc said, pulling a number out of thin air because he hadn't bothered to ask that question and didn't want anyone to know it.

"Dude, that sounds like it's a wild-assed guess. I don't think Summers will agree to abort the mission for that," JR returned. In fact, he wouldn't have done so himself if he'd been Summers. Having seen a glimpse of the cave, and with the tantalizing information about the unnatural warmth of it, which he hadn't known until Robert dropped that bombshell in his report, he was anxious to get inside it again himself. LeClerc could expect no help from JR. Nor from Rebecca, it seemed, who had nothing to add.

Distraught, LeClerc again considered refusing to go, but at the last minute, his sense of duty along with the threat that he wouldn't receive credit for his contribution if something were discovered induced him to re-join the rest after all. Within a few hours, the expedition would leave and he'd be with them, albeit against his wishes.

JR had left the meeting with an unholy sense of glee about the fireworks that may occur between LeClerc and Summers between now and the time they were all extracted to go home. He'd had nothing but contempt for LeClerc for weeks now, ever since his error in planning for the original long trip from McMurdo to Amundsen-Scott overland. Maybe after they'd been in-country for a while, the expedition members could have adjusted, as he had, to smaller rations, but not when they were so green. JR had known Marines who would have fragged an officer for such an oversight. It was inexcusable. The leader has to be capable of protecting the troops at all times. LeClerc reminded him of a banty rooster; always crowing but without the importance he gave himself. Summers was doing a better job, even though it should have been LeClerc stepping up and it burdened Summers with having to pay attention to logistics when he was there to study and analyze what they were finding, or not finding.

JR mentally counted the remaining expedition members. Summers, LeClerc, Bart, Rebecca, himself, Misty, Carmen, the two Foundation scientists, who else? Robert, of course, Angela, the cartographer and Cyndi, the electronics engineer. Oh, and Roosky. Thirteen. At least two too many for the remaining Sno-Cat, if they crowded some of the women two to a seat. But now they needed a different set than before. Summers, Bart and Robert were essential, as was Rebecca. They'd returned to base for Roosky, they needed Cyndi to make sure the drone was in good shape and Angela to draft the maps.

That left LeClerc, himself, Misty, Carmen, the two RF researchers, at least three of whom needed to stay on base. He was going, even if he had to chase the rest on a snowmobile, and he suspected LeClerc would insist on taking his rightful place rather than be left behind, even if he was against the mission. JR went looking for Misty to see if she was willing to fight for a spot, after which he'd try to talk to Summers about it, and let him know that LeClerc was conspiring against him behind his back.

Chapter Seventeen

PLAY MISTY FOR ME

Misty wasn't in the room they'd been assigned, so JR went to the canteen and the gym. Finding her in neither of the most likely places, he poked his head into the lounge before ascertaining she wasn't there either. That left the communications room, but it would have been odd for her to be there, as the group had an assigned time to use the computers, and this wasn't it. Still, thoroughness required he check there. Mindful that some people might be using the satellite phones, JR opened the door quietly to glance around. A familiar swath of shining blond hair caught his attention. Misty. She was here after all, but why?

Thinking to startle her for a bit of fun, JR crept stealthily up behind where Misty sat, whispering 'boo' and tugging at her hair when he reached her. The reaction was as satisfying as he'd hoped. Misty shrieked, jumped in her seat and turned, but somehow managed to blank the screen at the same time.

"What are you doing, Misty?" JR asked, teasingly. Misty stood and pressed herself against him.

"Oh, just surfing the 'net," she said. JR frowned. Then why had she made sure to blank the screen? He closed his eyes briefly, trying to recall what had been on it with his last glimpse. When he opened them, Misty was reaching behind her, searching blindly for the button that would turn the computer off completely. JR's hand lashed out and caught her wrist.

"Are you being naughty, searching out porn, sweetheart?" Her guilty look almost made him believe it. Aside from the fact that it was against base policy, he wouldn't have cared, but considering their relationship, he also didn't think she'd hide it from him. "Let's see."

"No!" she cried, lunging again for the tower's off button. But JR was faster. Using the wrist that he still had trapped, he swung her into his other arm and held her fast while he hit the space bar to bring the screen back to life. What he saw confused and then enraged him.

"How long?" he demanded. Misty refused to speak. He squeezed her tighter. "Is this why you…never mind, don't answer that. We're going to go see Summers, sweetheart, and I'd rather not have to hurt you, so come along like a good girl." He asked the sergeant that was checking people in and out and assigning computers to secure the one Misty had been using. The man hadn't even noticed their little altercation, so JR told him it was a matter of national security, causing him to turn white and stammer that he'd guard it himself. As JR left, herding Misty along with him, he heard the man raise his voice and tell the other occupants that the room was now closed and they'd have to leave.

JR strode through the halls, heedless of Misty's frequent missteps and the fact that she was having to practically run to keep up with his long stride. He had her securely held in his left arm and whenever she faltered, he just kept going, holding her up and letting her find her footing on her own. He couldn't remember the last time he'd been this angry. Maybe when he ran out into the ice while Daniel and Sarah were visiting, but he didn't think he'd been this mad even then.

No, it was probably the day his squad had run amok after finding an Al Qaeda nest in a small village. They'd run into an ambush, and as soon as the first of his men dropped, the others literally shredded the village with automatic weapons fire. When it was done, not only the terrorists were down, but also several old men, a couple of women, one of them pregnant, and three children were dead.

JR had lost his lunch, breakfast and to tell the truth, most of the last week's meals when he'd seen the pregnant woman, her hands clutching an enormous wound in her belly, covered in more blood than he'd seen in both of his previous deployments put together. He'd cried, screamed, and punched out several of his men before others restrained him. He'd finally been sedated by a medic that his shaken troops called for.

One corporal, who'd stood aside when it started and refused to join in, testified at the tribunal that the squad had opened fire with JR yelling 'hold your fire', so he was cleared of any wrongdoing. But he'd never forget the sight of those innocent dead men and women, or the children. Or the baby, oh God, the baby, who'd never had a chance to draw breath. The scene became his nightmare, haunting him awake or asleep, sneaking up on him to make him break out in a cold sweat. No matter what anyone said, the blood of innocent human beings was on his hands.

This time, though, he wouldn't let it distract him from the wrong that Misty had done him, done the Foundation.

He wanted her to pay, but he was exercising a will stronger than he'd known he had, to restrain himself from exacting the punishment himself. He knew he had only himself to blame for consorting with her; he'd deal with his anger over that. But, that she was endangering the expedition by spying and reporting to someone outside the Foundation would mean she'd be subject to law. Beyond her betrayal of him, beyond his disgust with himself for not seeing her true character, and somewhat to his own surprise, he felt outraged at the betrayal of his brother's Foundation and its ideals. He hoped she'd spend a long time in jail.

His frenetic analysis was winding down when he arrived at the staging area where Summers and Robert had joined the re-supply effort. Misty was literally gasping for breath, and JR's face was both grim and red from his race through the base. Their abrupt appearance startled everyone in the area.

"Summers, I just caught this little bitch sending an email to someone, and it revealed sensitive information. She's a spy!" JR roared, still too agitated to moderate his tone of voice.

"Whoa, JR, settle down. What's all this?"

With an effort, JR quelled his desire to shout, and spoke in a more normal volume, but with his teeth still clenched and his tone still dripping with disgust and rage.

"I found her in the comms room. Sneaked up behind her to surprise her, and she acted suspicious, blanked the screen. I hung onto her and opened the screen again, and it was an email to someone, saying we've discovered that cave system, and giving a GPS location. I think it also said send someone, sorry, I didn't read it all. Too busy trying to keep her from running. One of the military guys is guarding it so you can see it. What do you want me to do with her?"

Summers could see that JR's preference would be to tear her limb from limb, so he thought it prudent to have her taken into custody by the military. In the commotion, neither he nor anyone else saw the significant looks she sent to two of the other expedition members. But, they knew they'd just been activated.

The return trek to the cave was delayed by a couple of days while Summers made arrangements for Misty to be held in a secure location, since they couldn't deal with her legal infractions until they got back to Boulder. He also read the email she'd been composing when JR caught her at it, several times. When he was done, he compressed his lips and went back to Andersen to request that the computer be taken off-line until an expert could attempt to trace the destination for this message and any others she might have sent from the guest account. He then called Boulder and reported the security breach, suggesting that Daniel have Raj call and talk to the IT people at the base, so he could direct their analysis and hopefully ameliorate any damage Misty had already done. Finally, he asked, bitterly, if Daniel would go back to the firm that had done the background checks and ask them to dig deeper. They couldn't afford another mole in their midst.

JR, devastated by this latest evidence that he was a failure, took advantage of the down time by digging out the last half-bottle of the scotch he'd brought with him. It was barely enough to get a buzz, but he needed a way to kill the mental images that were torturing him. He'd gone from killing babies to sleeping with a fucking spy, probably an OS plant. Misty laughing as he chased her, back in Boulder, or splashing him in the swimming pool while he leered at her in her tiny bikini. Misty feeding him from her plate when he took her out to dinner, daring him to taste delicacies from

Thai and Vietnamese menus, insisting he close his eyes and open his mouth so she could place some potentially disgusting morsel on his tongue with chopsticks. The delectable flavor of those morsels that he never would have guessed. Misty lying provocatively posed in his bed, her unbelievably perfect body his for the taking. Misty in his arms, her face serene below him as he...Son of a bitch! He had to stop thinking about it.

JR took another slug, sent his mind prowling for something else to think about, and shied away from the memory of that pregnant woman that he'd tried to suppress only to bring it back while wondering when he'd last been so angry. In no time at all, he'd emptied the bottle, but it hadn't had the effect he wanted, needed. Shit, he could still smell Misty's scent in his sheets. He got up to tear them off the bed and banged his head on the too-low ceiling, forgetting to duck. Swearing profusely, he ripped the sheets from the bed and headed to the laundry, bumping into Roosky on the way.

"JR, comrade! You look *ne v dukhe*, am I right? How you say it, out of sorts?"

"Roosky, buddy, I'm worse than that. I'm pissed off, and only half drunk enough. You don't have any vodka, do you?"

"Ha, of course I have vodka. I am *russkiy*, yes? *Russkiy* always have vodka. Come, together we will drink it, make big *p'yanyyi*, drunk, yes?"

JR dropped the sheets where he stood, and followed Roosky to his room, where he hugged the big Russian extravagantly when he produced two bottles of Moskovskaya, a rye-based Russian vodka that would serve to get him so shitfaced he'd stop thinking altogether. Within the hour, the two of them were bonded drinking buddies, and Roosky had taught JR several drinking songs…in Russian.

His favorite was "*Do svidan'ia, goroda i khaty*", and he'd memorized the first verse with only a few errors before he'd had more than three shots of the vodka.

> Do svidan'ia, goroda i khaty,
> Nas doroga dal'niaia zoviot.
> Molodye, smelye rebiata,
> Na zare ukhodim my v pokhod.

After that, his tongue got tangled up and he couldn't negotiate the Russian syllables. It was a jaunty song, very upbeat, and it made him happy in his drunken state. Then, he asked Roosky what it meant. Roosky translated all four verses:

> *Good bye, towns and peasants' houses,*
> *A long journey is waiting us.*
> *We are young, brave fellows*
> *And we are going in a campaign at the dawn.*

> *Girls, come at the dawn,*
> *To see off our komsomol detachment.*
> *Girls, do not be sad without us*
> *We shall win and go back.*

> *We shall scatter enemy storm-clouds,*
> *We shall disperse all the obstacles on our way,*
> *And an enemy will not avoid an inevitable death,*
> *He will not survive from finding himself in the grave.*

> *There is a great hour of a requital,*

Our people gave us a weapon.
Good bye, towns and peasants' houses, -
We are going in a campaign at the dawn.

By then end of it, with the refrain 'we are going in a campaign at the dawn', JR was morose again. "What the hell kind of a drinking song is that?" Roosky, also more than a little impaired, took offense.

"We have great songs for the drinking! None of your decadent capitalist silliness. All of our songs were made in the great war!"

This prompted JR to begin chanting, "War, *huh, yeah!* What is it good for? Absolutely nothing. Uh-huh War, *huh, yeah!* What is it good for? Absolutely nothing. Say it again, y'all", but somehow it merged into the Marine marching song, "Over hill, over dale as we hit the dusty trail, and those caissons go rolling, along." He finished with a rousing "OOH Rah!", and Roosky gave him a high-five.

"You are A-OK, my friend," Roosky said, clutching JR in a hug that was truly worthy of the term 'bear hug', and kissing him on both cheeks just before they both fell sideways onto the bed – passed out.

When Summers came to Roosky's room to ask him whether his equipment and supplies were on the sled, he found the two of them sprawled on the bed, snoring loudly, each with an empty bottle in one hand.

"Where the hell…? Did everyone but me bring liquor on this trip?"

Summers searched out Rebecca to ask her when she thought the two drunkards would be ready to travel. After a quick look at them from the doorway, the smell being too much for her to get any closer, she said they could probably leave within the next twenty-four hours, but they probably wouldn't enjoy it much.

"Serves them right," Summers said.

"I agree," said Rebecca. Privately, she was very disappointed in JR. When they started their journey, she doubted he'd be any use at all, but there had been plenty of times that he'd impressed her, especially when he refused extra rations on the trek from McMurdo to the Pole. Even though it annoyed her that he and Misty carried on the way they did, she couldn't help but admire JR's good qualities when he demonstrated them. This, however, was not one of them.

Still, in her heart, she wanted to give him a pass, knowing that his acting-out was triggered by his own demons, which arose every time he blamed himself for a mistake. She began to realize then, what it would take for him to be the man he was meant to be. He needed someone to believe in him. Could she put up with his shenanigans to become that someone?

Chapter Eighteen

NO TIME LEFT

Auster listened to her operative in disbelief. Her carefully-prepared mole had been discovered and rendered useless. A call from Summers to Rossler had been intercepted with the details. Her plans to take over leadership of the Orion Society lay in ruins, and, even worse, she had no eyes or ears with the polar expedition.

"Can you extract the girl without betraying our organization, Latet?"

"No, ma'am. She's incarcerated at the South Pole base, and won't be coming out until the expedition packs it in at the end of this month. I don't expect her to be in an exposed position at any time between now and the time she goes to trial on charges of espionage."

"Will she hold her tongue?"

"Unknown. She's young, and others we have embedded in the Rossler Foundation report her to be something of a scatterbrain. Most of them used the word 'airhead'."

"Why in the world did we send her, then?" Auster demanded, beginning to understand why the former

Septentrio had so many operatives killed, and his son even more.

"She had gained the trust of Rossler's younger brother, JR. By all accounts, he was sent on the expedition against his will, and we thought that she might be able to turn him at some point. Apparently not, however. He's the one who caught her attempting to send a communique to us and turned her in."

"Latet, this is a disaster, I don't need to tell you. Is it possible to trace her reports to you? Do you need to go underground?"

"We don't think so. I will be watching for any sign that they've been able to do so, and will take appropriate measures if they begin to get close."

"Very well. I don't need to tell you that we must know what the expedition finds, preferably before anyone else. What are you doing about fixing this problem?"

"With all due respect, ma'am, I feel it's better you don't know, so that you'll have plausible deniability if necessary. Rest assured, I *am* taking steps."

"Carry on, then, and let me know when you have anything to report."

"Yes, ma'am."

Auster regarded the screen thoughtfully after Latet had broken the connection. Was it the quality of the video, or had there been something? That one would bear watching. No sooner had the thought crossed her mind when a faint smile appeared on her lips and she chastised herself silently. They *all* bore watching. Sidus' perfidy had taught them that. Latet's predecessor had been prepared to give all of them up to save himself when they were trying to capture the Pyramid Code data before it was decrypted.

Fortunately, there were always young operatives eager to

prove themselves. Sidus had died at the hands of Septentrio himself while in CIA custody, along with one of his minders. Frankly, it had surprised her and the other two. Septentrio had always been something of a nancy-boy, according to his father. How strange that he would turn out to be even more ruthless than his illustrious parent.

Latet, got up from his desk and left, driving half an hour around the Washington, D.C. belt route to a safe house that he'd acquired and equipped on his own. He had known Sidus, and he knew what had brought him down. The same wouldn't happen to Latet, he'd make sure of it. His escape route was nearly complete, and then it only remained to secure his fortune. That he was doing so by playing both ends against the middle was beside the point. At the house, Latet picked up a clean laptop he hadn't used before. He drove to an internet cafe and purchased a block of secure data transmission before sending an email.

"S: A's operative compromised. Your two apparently undiscovered. Will report when assets are in place."

Septentrio read the missive a few minutes later, and clenched his fist. Auster's schemes had grown tiresome. He would make her pay, but the punishment must be subtle and commensurate with the infraction. Something involving her insufferable teenaged daughter, perhaps. Though he himself preferred the pretty boys his manservant acquired for him. It would be more amusing, perhaps, to watch someone else debauch the girl, before killing her. He could be patient, however. It need not occur just yet. Perhaps as an object lesson once his plans for the ruined city the Rosslerites sought were implemented, as a celebration. Yes, that would be most pleasurable, a celebration and punishing the bitch Auster at the same time. How delicious!

On the frozen continent, a hung over and subdued JR moved cautiously as he prepared to leave the base. His head felt like Mt. Rushmore—as if he had multiple heads, all pounding. Andersen had turned him out of the room he'd shared with Misty, so he had to either take all of his gear with him or move it to a storage locker until he returned. Roosky had been gone from the room where they'd both passed out when Rebecca Mendenhall came to wake him with a foul-tasting concoction she said would help his hangover. He suspected it was just a mixture of the worst stuff she could think of, a punishment for his role in delaying the expedition one more precious day. If it had just been him, they'd have left without him probably. But, because he'd involved Roosky, they all had to wait because Roosky's presence when they began to explore the cave was critical.

All of the expedition members were traveling lighter these days. They'd discovered they were too exhausted to read or play games once they'd finished their day's work and eaten dinner, even if they didn't also have to pitch their tents every night because they were in a stationary camp for the duration. JR left behind everything he could possibly spare, as had everyone else, since they needed to lighten the load on the Sno-Cat so they could make better time. It was now the fourteenth of February, and Summers wanted them back at the Pole to load out by the twenty-sixth. They could make the trek to the cave in two days if the weather cooperated, but since it never did, they expected to use eight of those fourteen days just traveling. That left four to explore the cave, a woefully short time according to Robert Cartwright.

They could afford absolutely no more delays. While

Roosky and JR recovered from their binge, Summers had made executive decisions about who would be left behind. Misty's presence, of course, was off the table. Summers decided Carmen should go, and gave LeClerc the option, which he of course took. The Foundation scientists he asked to stay at the base, since there was little likelihood they could do much, even if the city were found; there just wasn't time. They agreed. The Sno-Cat would be a tight fit, but by crowding everyone into it, they were able to leave the snowmobiles behind and more than make up for the extra weight.

Finally, they were ready to go, though LeClerc made one last plea to Andersen to stop them. The storm the meteorologists had predicted was gathering over the Ross Ice Shelf and would likely catch them before they reached the mountains and relative shelter. Andersen had made up his mind, though. These troublesome scientists could sort out their own issues. He'd be glad to be rid of them when they returned. The long months cooped up with just four dozen winter caretaker personnel were beginning to look like a good long rest to him. The only thing he wanted was to be sure they'd be back in time not to get stranded there.

Summers had asked him what the hazards were if they were delayed past the first of March. Andersen encouraged him not to think that way.

"First, if the storms start early, there's no going outside. Period. The temperature is somewhere between minus seventy-two and minus seventy-nine, not that you'd notice the difference. I don't even want to try to calculate the wind chill. Suffice it to say, it's brutal. Everyone who stays is subject to winter-over syndrome, and that's not pretty either. Insomnia is common. No one can sleep, so everyone's irritable if not outright depressed. Some develop cognitive impairment. The magnetic storms interfere with communications, so we're very isolated. Then there's polar T3 syndrome. Ever hear of the Antarctic stare?"

"Sounds serious. T3 as in the thyroid hormone?"

"Exactly. No one knows exactly why, but levels of T3 drop, and you get the more disturbing of the symptoms of hypothyroidism. We think that's what causes the cognitive impairment and forgetfulness. The Antarctic stare is a fugue state, where people just freeze, their eyes open, staring into the distance.

"Mood disorders, sub-clinical seasonal affective disorder, you can imagine when you've got such a small sampling of other people, it causes problems. People who just didn't click before become bitter enemies. We have to break up fistfights, all while we're suffering from the same symptoms.

"Now, add your crew to that, and we'll be on short rations, too. No, it's imperative you leave. You might find a short window of opportunity in the first week of March, but after that the polar vortex closes in and there'll be no escape."

"We'll be back in time. That description gives me all the incentive I need, believe me." Summers thought Andersen might have exaggerated a bit to make sure he was sufficiently impressed, but what he'd said was consistent with Summers' lay knowledge of the winter conditions. Since they hadn't intended to winter over, he'd done less thorough research about that than about the conditions he'd find during the summer, but he knew winter conditions were brutal.

Summers counted heads in the Sno-Cat and took the driver's seat for the first leg of the journey. He could hear LeClerc still complaining in the back and decided it was bad for morale.

"Knock it off, LeClerc, or get out. No one wants to listen to you complain for two days."

"Two days, *merde*. Mark my words, it will be four, if we get there at all. This is a foolhardy journey, my friends. When we are in the midst of the crap, don't say I did not warn you." Satisfied he'd had the last word, LeClerc withdrew into sullen silence, and they were off.

Rebecca was lost in thought, staring without realizing it in JR's direction, though her thoughts were turned inward and she wasn't paying attention to what she saw. Bitterly disappointed, she had thought JR was turning out to be someone she could admire after all. This latest stunt of his had dropped him in her estimation again, though she couldn't blame him for being devastated at his girlfriend's behavior. She harbored a secret that would have mortified her had anyone known.

In truth, Sarah probably suspected. She and Rebecca, whom she called Becca as the doctor's other good friends did, were very close. Rebecca was the younger sister of Sarah's best friend from high school, with whom she'd reconnected when she and Daniel moved back to Boulder. When Sarah suspected she was pregnant, Cindy recommended her sister and the three rapidly became inseparable. The bonus for Rebecca was that Sarah had a dreamy brother-in-law.

Too bad that the dream was a nightmare, Rebecca thought. JR had the looks that turned her head, but his personality was a trial. She understood, of course. Sarah mentioned he'd just come back from his last tour of duty in Afghanistan a few months before, and that he was being treated for PTSD.

That ruined so many lives, she knew. But, understanding and being able to tolerate the behaviors were two different things. She'd backed off before he even knew that she was interested.

Her thoughts drifting, Becca eventually fell asleep and slumped against Carmen's shoulder. Carmen, in turn, was sleeping leaning on Robert, who at that moment was wishing he'd sat between the two women. He'd rather have the lovely Rebecca pressed against him than Carmen, who was a little brash and forward for his taste, though beautiful in her own right.

Because they were in a hurry, Summers insisted on fewer breaks than usual. Everyone was therefore rather stiff and sore when they did stop for a meal. Bart complied with Summers' wish that it be a quick one, and they were soon on their way again, over LeClerc's protests.

"Will you please make up your mind, man?" Robert finally said to him. "First you complained that we'll be longer than we planned, now you want to slow us down. If I didn't know better, I'd say you were trying to sabotage this expedition."

While LeClerc gasped in indignation, several of the others gave him speculative looks that indicated the accusation had merit. He was left with no choice but to make haste along with the rest of them. Back in the Sno-Cat, he took the last seat in the back and withdrew into himself to avoid eye contact with anyone. He'd always been somewhat of a loner, but he'd never felt so disrespected before. He cast a bitter glance at Summers. It was all his fault. If the man had wanted to run the expedition logistics himself, he shouldn't have hired me in the first place, he thought.

As the hours passed, sporadic conversation broke out, but more often everyone slept away the boring sojourn. After more than five months together, they'd worn out every topic of conversation and more than a few had developed resentments toward each other. Watching their dynamics, Summers reflected that it would be an unmitigated disaster if they were forced to winter over. He must avoid that at all costs, even at the risk of not finding any corroborating evidence that the city existed.

The storm LeClerc had warned them about struck late on the second day, with only twenty or so miles left to cover. Gale force winds rocked the Sno-Cat, prompting LeClerc to recommend that they turn the Sno-Cat leeward and stop to avoid capsizing it. His smug expression had 'I told you so' written all over it.

Summers consulted the printout of the forecast and noted that the wind was expected to blow for four days without lessening. If it had been only one or even two, he might have taken LeClerc's advice despite their differences of opinion. However, he knew they couldn't wait it out for four days. He directed JR, who was driving at this point, to keep going on their plotted course. After only an hour, JR requested to be relieved, his arms aching from holding the course steady with a buffeting side wind to fight. Robert took over and drove until Roosky offered to relieve him, and the stronger man drove the rest of the way, managing to cover the remainder of the twenty miles in only six more hours. When they reached the mouth of the canyon, he kept going far enough that the Sno-Cat was sheltered from the wind by the high canyon walls nearby.

Everyone breathed a sigh of relief at the sudden cessation of the howling wind, though they could still hear it faintly behind them. The team dropped out of the Sno-Cat stiffly, one by one, and stretched, joints popping, before moving to set up their tents and other gear. It had been twelve hours since they slept, and once the wind hit there was no stopping. They needed food and sleep, in that order. Bart got busy right away and prepared something that was tasty and filling, but quick to cook. Almost before they were through eating, the crew were snugged into their sleeping bags inside their tents, planning on an early start the next day.

Chapter Nineteen

THE ROSSLER-CARTWRIGHT CAVE

Summers woke with a start, taking a moment to recall why he'd set his alarm. Oh, yes, this was the day they'd enter the cave system that Robert and JR had found. He needed some time to steel himself for the ordeal. He got up and dressed for the day, pulling on layers of gear that he could shed as needed. Robert said the conditions in the cave were warmer than expected, but, Summers' shameful secret meant that he'd need to stay comfortably warm, not just sufficiently. Claustrophobia was bad enough, and would make it difficult to lead the others into the cave, but that coupled with cold would unman him. No one else knew he suffered from claustrophobia, and if he had anything to say about it, no one would know when the day was over, either.

He finished dressing and went to get some coffee from Bart, who was up and preparing a large breakfast for the crew. Virtually everyone was going into the cave today, and wouldn't come out again until time to retire in the evening. Each would take a couple of sandwiches with them, tucked inside their clothes so they wouldn't freeze, as well as enough water for the day.

Robert and JR were up already, and having an animated discussion on how to best explore the cave. Robert wanted to map the main room first, and then explore each passage in turn for a methodical approach. JR, cognizant of the short time available, was arguing in favor of sending a two-person team down each passage while Angela mapped the main room. However, that plan required at least three experienced spelunkers, and this team only had one and a half… counting JR as a half because of his inexperience.

Bart would not be going into the cave, nor would Roosky unless his presence were needed to clear something inside. Instead, he'd maintain a position outside and monitor the overhang. If it gave way, he'd be able to blast his way to them and get them out. That left only eight to explore the cave, and Angela was needed in the main room. Summers thought JR's suggestion sensible, but knew he couldn't lead a team because of his claustrophobia. Therefore, Summers volunteered to stay in the main room with Angela, but added his vote to the other approach. Robert, giving in with grace, said he'd lead the way in the smallest passage, and invited Rebecca to go with him. JR opted for Cyndi's company since Rebecca was going with Robert. Carmen said she'd had some experience in Chile, but had to settle for LeClerc, who protested going at all, but gave in when Carmen's heated gaze challenged him.

With the approach settled and the teams matched up, it remained only to finish breakfast and trek to the opening. They'd scrabbled together cave gear from what they'd brought for glacier safety; harnesses and a five-hundred foot nylon climbing rope for each of them to carry coiled on their shoulders until needed, helmets, which fortunately had headlamps attached. Warm clothing, of course. In addition, each had a small waist pack or low-profile backpack for their food, water, spare batteries, flashlights (those that didn't have the kind that clipped to their belts), chemical hazard lights and various other items that Robert thought might be useful.

By ten a.m., they were at the opening. Roosky would be left behind here, studying the overhang and surrounding areas for rescue routes if there were a cave-in. Summers felt he should say a few words on such a momentous occasion, but before he could gather his thoughts, Robert was leading the way inside. Summers allowed everyone else to go first, telling them he'd bring up the rear. It fooled everyone but Roberts, who had given him a long look when he'd volunteered to stay in the main room. Roberts had seen claustrophobia before, and knew that Summers could be a liability if forced into a smaller space. He said nothing, though.

Once inside, they paused to get their bearings. Those who hadn't been there before paused to exclaim over the size of the cave, which they could sense but not fully see in the darkness. Following the main wall of the cave to the right, JR located the first opening they'd seen previously. Robert took charge and directed Carmen and LeClerc to explore that one, telling them to secure one end of Carmen's rope to a piton driven into the wall at the opening and string it out behind them as they went.

If they came to branches, they were to continue turning right each time and explore until they reached the end of both of the ropes, were blocked, or found an exit. Then they were to return unless they found an exit, and continue past the first branch to the next. When they'd reached the end of the main passage or the end of the ropes, they were to turn back, exploring the branches on the other side from the opposite end, until they'd done as much as they could.

Robert's and JR's teams would do the same in their passages, but before they headed for the easily visible ones, they followed the wall around to be sure none had been missed. Satisfied that the large ones were the only ones remaining in the right half of the cave, they drew straws, JR choosing the downward-sloping passage. He had a hunch that there was something extraordinary to be found in it, and set out eagerly, Cyndi in tow.

JR led the way, appearing more confident than he actually felt. He'd fully recovered from the party with Roosky, but he didn't really have that much experience with caving in wild caves. He'd been to Linville Caves in North Carolina, and to Carlsbad Caverns National Park, but more as a tourist than anything else. Robert had given him some pointers, and he had an eidetic memory that would serve them well when it came time to map this passageway. He had no doubt that he could get himself and Cyndi in and out safely. Whether he'd look like he knew what he was doing when it came to making the right decisions, was another question.

The passageway was wide enough for the two of them to walk in side-by-side, so they chatted as they walked for about the first fifty yards. Then it narrowed, and Cyndi dropped behind him, still chattering away. She'd become quite the expert with the drone, probably the only expert in the world at this point, since the one they were using was a prototype built from 10th Cycle plans. If the escarpment into which this cave entered hadn't been so tall, they could have used the drone to map it, she was saying. However, after entering through the canyon wall, they were at least five hundred feet underground from the top of the mountain, and the range that the drone could map under the ice was about one hundred and fifty feet.

They had paid out most of JR's rope when they came to the first branch on the right, except it actually seemed larger than the passage they'd been following. Maybe it was the main part instead. JR marked the wall with a yellow grease pencil and continued about twenty-five feet before stopping to link Cyndi's rope to his, taking the coil over his shoulder now. As they walked, they'd been going steadily downhill at a shallow angle. JR wondered idly how many feet they'd descended in their 500-foot linear journey. He reckoned maybe twenty or thirty. They hadn't gone much further when their passage opened out into another cathedral-like room, with stalactites and stalagmites forming fantastic shapes throughout. JR was beginning to sweat in his cold-weather gear, and risked removing his face mask and gloves. To his surprise, it was almost warm, really warm. If you could call about 30F warm.

"JR, I have a question."

"Yeah?"

"How did these form? Isn't it erosion dripping through limestone that makes these things?"

"Hmmm, you could be right. I'm no geologist, we'd have to ask Robert. But I seem to remember something like that from visiting Carlsbad Caverns. But what's the problem?"

"It isn't warm enough for water to flow in here," she responded. "It's all frozen."

JR looked around. She was right, of course. How could he have missed that? Wouldn't it be the same in the main cave? But Robert hadn't said anything. "I'll be damned," he remarked.

They explored the walls of the room as best they could, though the rope wouldn't reach far enough to let them thoroughly examine the back wall. Even if the passage continued back there, though, the formations were so thick that JR didn't think they'd be able to force their way through. They'd reached the end of this promising passage, and it was time to retrace their steps.

Robert and Rebecca didn't wait long after JR and Cyndi started into their passage before bidding Summers and Angela goodbye for the moment and going into the leftmost of the twin passages. Almost immediately, they were forced to crouch and then crawl as the ceiling lowered. Robert turned back to ask Rebecca whether she was okay with tight spots.

"I've never been in a small cave before," she admitted. "But, I'm smaller than you. If you can make it, so can I."

Robert was aware that he should have an experienced caver with him if he were going to go into a passage where he might get stuck. It was so important to map as much as possible of this cave before they left, though, that he admonished himself to be careful and not force his way in while forging ahead. It looked like this passage was going to be a bust, with no branches up to here, and the walls tightening around them. He eyed the way ahead before removing everything from his belt and finally the belt itself, pushing everything back behind him like a mole tunneling through dirt.

Robert knew that if his shoulders would fit, so would the

rest of him. However, the move he planned would trap his arms above his head and make them useless to pull himself out if he couldn't wriggle forward. Before going in, he asked Rebecca to see if she could pull him backward even though she was in a fairly tight spot herself.

At first, she couldn't. Then she asked if it would be smart to tie the rope around his ankles and retreat far enough that she could sit up and get a purchase to pull with more force. Robert thought about everything that could go wrong, and decided that it was worth the risk. They did a practice run first, and Rebecca was able to move him by bracing her feet against the rough walls and hauling backward on the rope with all her might. They were ready to go for it.

Rebecca stayed where she was, while Robert crept forward, as evidenced by the rope snaking forward toward his position. Each time it stopped, Rebecca held her breath, waiting for the shout that would tell her to pull him out. She kept the rope taut, so she'd know the moment Robert moved. When it went slack, her heart stopped before slamming into her mouth in an effort to jump out. What had happened? Had it broken, or the knot come untied? Should she go forward and try to help, or return to the main room and get Summers? She was in an agony of indecision when she heard Robert shout, louder and more clearly than she would have expected.

"Rebecca! Come on up! I'm through, and you're not going to believe it."

She crawled as rapidly as she could before reaching the spot where they'd almost been stopped. Robert wasn't there.

"Robert?" she called.

"Come on! It opens out in about six feet, and there's another room here. Bring the rope."

Rebecca secured the rope to her belt and wriggled into the hole, realizing immediately that she had more room to maneuver than Robert did. She was pushing herself with her toes and reaching forward with her arms when she felt him seize her hands and pull. In no time she'd popped out through the narrow passage into a room that was larger even than the main room at the cave entrance. The far reaches were in darkness as Robert's headlamp wasn't strong enough to throw the light that far.

Now they had a dilemma. Rebecca's remaining rope, with Robert's still in reserve, was more than three-quarters paid out. To reach the far side, Robert reckoned they'd need more than they had. But, without reaching the far side, they were at the end of their journey. After the difficulty in pushing through what Rebecca was now thinking of as the birth canal, it seemed a shame to waste the effort by not exploring further.

The solution was dangerous, if not difficult. Rebecca would go back the way they'd come and release the far end of her rope, then retrace her steps. There was little chance of getting lost; they'd passed no openings at all before encountering the birth canal. But it was strictly against caving protocol to leave returning to chance. It was a decision that Robert didn't want to make on his own, especially after lucking out on the last one. Rebecca questioned him closely.

"What's the danger if we do release it and secure it on this side? We know where the opening is here, and it's a straight passage back to the main room after that. How could we get lost?"

"It's never as simple as it seems, love. I don't know exactly what might happen. What if we disturbed some of the support system coming through? If there were even a small cave-in, the others wouldn't know where to find us, for example. I think it's too dangerous. We should turn back, get more rope and maybe something to widen that opening, and come back tomorrow."

Rebecca had caught the excitement of exploring, and was disappointed.

"Well, you're the leader, and I'll follow you. But I can't wait to come back! It's so beautiful!"

"That it is, love, but it could kill us. Let's do it right."

Carmen was ready to throttle the expedition leader. He'd done nothing but complain from the moment they started on their way. First, that he wasn't in the lead and then that she was following Robert's instructions. He preferred to get as far to the end of the original passage as possible, then explore coming back. Carmen explained that just because the original passage opened into the main room didn't mean it led anywhere exciting, and that the other branches could just as well be the one they were looking for. Then LeClerc complained that they didn't know *what* they were looking for and that the whole trip was a waste of time and resources.

After a while, Carmen stopped responding, which annoyed LeClerc greatly, but the more he railed at her the more silent she became, until he gave up in frustration. Then he was annoyed because she'd stopped speaking to him, which forced him to keep up with her lest she turn into a side passage and he lose her.

Despite Robert's admonition that cave etiquette decreed they not relieve themselves inside the cave, LeClerc had turned aside to do just that when Carmen did turn into a secondary passage that turned out to be a dead end. She was skirting a deep depression in the center, looking for a continuation, when LeClerc came bustling in. He was holding the rope loosely in one hand as a guide, but looking at the light from Carmen's headlamp instead of his feet, opening his mouth to castigate her for turning without warning him, when he stepped into nothingness. A thin scream accompanied a sudden jerk on the rope that almost took Carmen off her feet, but was bitten off after only a few seconds.

When she'd stabilized her own position, Carmen carefully approached the edge of the depression and pointed her flashlight toward the bottom. For at least twenty feet, the furthest reach of the light, the edges were as smooth as rock could be. She couldn't see the bottom, nor could she see any sign of LeClerc.

"Paul, are you hurt?" she called. There was no answer.

Carmen was not given to hysterics. As a scientist, she'd been trained to think things out before acting. Accordingly, she took a seat on the floor of the cave and thought. If LeClerc were alive, he must be unconscious, which indicated he'd hit his head, either on the way down or on impact. How long he'd be unconscious was anyone's guess. Without medical attention, it was possible he wouldn't regain consciousness at all, or for an extended period. She could possibly climb down to him, but then both of them would be in the hole, and she doubted she could climb back out without assistance for the distance to the bottom, assuming it was just beyond the reach of her flashlight beam. If it was deeper, there was no way. The only sensible thing to do was to return to the main room for help.

Before doing so, Carmen methodically ate one of her sandwiches and took a few sips of water. Fortified for the walk back, she left the rope secured to another piton and guided herself back the way she'd come.

Summers had brought along a device that he frequently had use for in archaeological ruins that were largely intact. Borrowed from the construction industry, it was a handheld device that used a laser beam to measure the distance between walls. The range wasn't sufficient to measure across the entire main room of the cave system, but it was coming in handy for Angela's to-scale representation of the room anyway. She was measuring from stalagmite to stalagmite as near to the outer walls as she could and entering the information into a software program running on her little Samsung eight-inch tablet, which would eventually connect the dots and accurately map the perimeter of the room. Summers had taken the opportunity while Angela was preoccupied to step to the cave entrance several times and breathe, alleviating his unease.

The last time he'd done so, he failed to see Roosky, and worried a bit about what the man was doing. Had he seen a fracture in the overhang? Detected an instability, perhaps? Summers shuddered. He could think of nothing worse than having those tons of ice and rock break loose and cover this opening, trapping them inside. It was the reason they'd deferred exploring the cave until they'd retrieved Roosky from the base in the first place. If the worst happened, Roosky would use explosives to clear the opening so they could get out. It gave Summers some comfort, but had brought up another fear.

Now as he looked up at the overhang, he imagined it falling while he was at the cave opening, crushing him. Duty called him back inside, but it took all the willpower he could muster to move in that direction rather than running helter-skelter out and down the scree to the ice pack below. Clenching his teeth, he thought of Angela alone in the main room and forced himself to return. Not without a backward look and another fleeting worry about the overhang, though.

Angela had finished the perimeter measurements and was now programming features into the map. First the passageways that the three teams had gone to explore, then the major decorations in the center of the vast space. She was humming to herself, a tuneless sound that nevertheless was somewhat of a comfort to Summers when he returned to her side.

"Charles, do you know how caves like this are formed?" she asked.

"Not really. I'm an archaeologist, not a geologist. You'll have to ask Robert when he returns.

JR and Cyndi had regained the main passage and continued beyond the first branching one to a second, even wider than the first. Cyndi's question about erosion had been nagging him. If the water couldn't flow, how *did* the stalactites and stalagmites form? He turned over every natural phenomenon he could think of in his mind. As they turned into the second room, he determined to take a sample or two of the material for Robert's examination. He'd do it in an inconspicuous place, to avoid defacing the beauty of this natural treasure.

The moment they stepped into the second room, he knew something was very different. In the main room of the cave, along the passages, and in the first room they'd discovered, the formations looked similar to those he remembered in Carlsbad Caverns. They were light-colored, and looked like quartz, a creamy white for the most part. This room was so different that he and Cyndi both stopped in wonder. Before them were formations in black, dark rusty red and orange. If they'd thought before that the rooms resembled cathedrals, they now knew it was nothing compared to this. It took a while to understand that they were seeing more than their headlamps would have revealed, so dazzled were they by the color.

Before they did, JR noticed something odd on the walls. It looked like...it *was*.

"Cyndi, look at this! What do you make of it? I'm willing to bet those are manmade."

Cyndi looked where JR was pointing, on the cave wall. There, between two thin stalactites, were marks...marks that didn't look natural. She stepped closer, casting the light from her headlamp on what looked like lines of some kind of script. There was no question that they weren't natural... they were too straight, and the ends were too even.

"Oh, my God," she breathed. "Is that what I think it is?"

"If it isn't, we're both hallucinating," he answered, his heart beating rapidly. Unless he and Cyndi were both crazy, they'd just made a major discovery; that people had been here before them. And if those people were 9th or even 10th Cyclers, they were the first to see these marks in perhaps thirty-five thousand years. A spark of his former love of archaeology kindled an elation that he could barely control. At that moment, he thought about his Grandpa Nick and how proud he would be.

Beside him, Cyndi was only slightly less awed, mostly

because she'd forgotten the vast reaches of time that they were hoping to bridge. "Do you think?"

"That we should go back for the others? Absolutely! This could be what we're looking for, although I don't see any signs of a city. I don't recognize the script; it isn't Arabic. We need to get Summers, right now!"

With slightly more presence of mind than JR was at the moment capable of, Cyndi took some pictures with her otherwise useless cell phone. Summers had teased the younger ones about being so attached to the darned things that they carried them even though there wasn't a cell tower within thousands of miles, but he would eat his words when he saw this!

Pausing only to mark the entrance to the room with another swipe of his grease pencil, JR and Cyndi hurried from the fabulous room without a backward look. A pair of eyes watched them leave, and then the watcher moved stealthily toward the wall where they'd seen the script. A camera flashed, and the watcher faded back into the passage from where he'd emerged.

Carmen was the first to reach the main room. With little emotion, she told Summers that they needed to go back to see if they could rescue LeClerc, telling him what she could of how the accident happened. Since she'd had her back to his approach, all she could do was surmise that he hadn't been watching his footing, and had stepped into the void without noticing it was there. Angela was aghast. Carmen seemed to be unaffected by the accident, and Summers was dithering as if there weren't a man in need of help. To her relief, Robert and Rebecca emerged from their passage only moments after Carmen dropped her bombshell.

It had to be clear that there was an emergency. Carmen was remonstrating with Summers, who was throwing up objections to accompanying her back to where LeClerc had been lost. Angela was about to step over to Robert and Rebecca to explain when Robert took matters into his own hands.

"What's going on?"

Carmen turned to him and began once again reciting the meager facts of the accident. Robert listened carefully, but Rebecca looked over at Angela, whose face reflected her consternation. Something was wrong here, and neither woman could understand it. Rebecca recovered first.

"We've got to go and see if we can reach him. Robert, let's go."

Robert looked at Summers for approval, and seeing that he was staring uselessly at Carmen, agreed. "Come on, Summers, it may take both of us to get him out."

Even in the gloom of the cave, it seemed Summers lost his color. "I...I don't think I can."

"Come on, mate, man up. Carmen, how tight are the passages?"

Confused, she answered. "They aren't. We walked upright the entire way."

"Summers. Av-a-go-yer-mug, we need you. Follow me."

Summers took a tentative step forward as Rebecca suddenly recognized what was going on.

"Charles, I'm right here with you," she said in a low voice, not wanting to embarrass him further. He threw her a grateful look and took a more confident step as she fell into step behind him.

"Carmen, lead the way. Angela, please stay here and let

the others know where we've gone, can you do that sweetheart?"

Angela was reassured that Robert could handle it, and nodded shyly at him. It hadn't escaped her notice that the handsome Aussie was the object of many an admiring glance, not only from herself but also from Carmen and Cyndi. That he had eyes only for Rebecca hadn't escaped her notice either, so his endearment, while just a habit, thrilled her.

"Yes, Robert. Whatever you need," she answered, putting more into the words than the immediate meaning. Robert winked at her and headed toward the passage, following Carmen.

They'd no sooner disappeared within when JR and Cyndi tumbled out of their passage, calling out with excitement.

"Hey, everybody, you've got to see this!"

When no one answered, JR looked around and spotted Angela, who was standing with both hands pressed to her mouth and her eyes wide. She was shaking. JR strode over to her and put his arm around her.

"What is it, Ange?"

"LeClerc. He's...he fell into a big hole. The others have all gone to rescue him. JR, you scared me! What were you yelling about?"

"Never mind, which way did the others go? Will I be able to catch them?"

"Yes," she said, pointing out the correct passage. "But, be careful! Watch your feet." With that, JR rushed off to catch the others, but Angela grabbed Cyndi before she could follow. "Tell me what he was yelling about!"

Cyndi stopped trying to follow JR and put her arms

around her friend. "Ange, I think we found evidence of ancient humans! We've done it!"

The two were too worried about the others, even about LeClerc who had become persona non grata on the expedition, to think much further on what the discovery would mean for the expedition. Together they waited for word.

JR hurried along the passageway, guided by the rope and the faint sounds of voices ahead. His headlamp was beginning to flicker, a sign that he would need to stop and change the batteries soon. But, if possible, he would wait until he'd caught up with the group ahead. Within minutes, the voices were louder and he could make out fragments of what they were saying.

"Turned here. LeClerc was lagging behind." That sounded like Carmen, definitely a woman, and JR knew Carmen had been with LeClerc.

"Look, he must've...disgusting. I told him..." Robert. What were they talking about?

"Never mind. Time enough to accuse him when we've rescued him. Carmen, where's ... oh!"

Rebecca's startled cry galvanized JR, who began trotting through the corridor, every jolt making his headlamp go dark for a fraction of a second. With his left hand, he had hold of the rope as a guide, and from the sound of it the group was no more than seventy-five feet ahead. Suddenly, the rope snugged tight to the wall and caught him for a moment; they had turned. He slowed and, rounding the corner, saw everyone ringed around the outside of a small terminal room, looking down.

"JR!" said Carmen. "Glad you're here."

"Can you see him?" he responded.

"No, it's too deep. He's not answering, either. He's unconscious." Rebecca didn't want to add the rest, 'or dead.' They still didn't know how deep the hole was, nor what lay at the bottom. Whether ice or rock, it would have been a terrible thing to land on it, especially if LeClerc had gone in head first.

"Robert, do you reckon you can climb down there, with Summers and me to belay you?" JR's question presented the only practical solution that he could see. He was taller and heavier than Cartwright, who was a big man himself. But, Summers' visibly shaking body indicated he'd be useless, and neither of the women would be strong enough to get LeClerc in position to be hauled up. If Robert couldn't do it, it couldn't be done. The implications staggered him, along with everyone else.

"All I can do is try, mate," Robert answered confidently. "But, maybe someone should go and get Roosky to help bring us back up."

"Too dangerous," JR countered. "If something let go with him in here, then we're trapped for good. We'll go and get him only if we can't get you back up. Fair enough?"

"No worries, mate. She'll be apples." JR correctly surmised that he had Robert's agreement. Summers had gone completely silent.

While Robert checked his harness and the knot that connected it to the rope, JR consulted Summers about how far they could reasonably expect to pull the big Aussie up, assuming he couldn't help for some reason. Summers wasn't much help, but nodded when JR concluded that if he descended as far as fifty feet without result, they'd have to pull Roosky in before a second attempt could be made. JR looked for a sturdy and thick stalagmite around which to secure the rope, since he didn't trust that pitons wouldn't pull out of the shale stratum. Then Robert was ready, and without further drama, he dropped over the edge and began to rappel down with JR paying out rope as needed.

He'd gone about twenty feet when JR called down to get a report on what Robert could see.

"Nothing, mate. It's dark as pitch down there. I can see maybe another twenty feet with my lamp on, but there's no sign of the bottom.

Dismay among the others greeted that pronouncement. Rather than pull him up prematurely, JR called down for Robert to descend another twenty feet and look again. It had the same result. Rebecca stepped over to JR and put her hand on his arm.

"Josh," she said, using the family nickname, "I doubt LeClerc could have survived a sixty-foot fall. Do you think we should risk anyone else's life to retrieve his body?"

JR stared at her. Never leave a man behind was his mantra, as it was every Marine's. But these weren't Marines around him. They were civilians, and he couldn't force them to comply with his standards. He looked around at the other faces, all looking to him for leadership, since Summers had apparently abdicated. They looked stunned, frightened and weary. It was time to cut their losses.

"We're pulling you up, Robert. Give us what help you can."

"Will do."

Even the normally cheerful and optimistic Robert was subdued as the party made its way back to the main room to join Angie and Cyndi. Rebecca detained JR to bring up the rear as they coiled the rope. "JR, do you think you can persuade Summers to pack it in, now? We need to get back to the base, and this has affected everyone, even those who didn't like LeClerc."

"Did anyone actually like LeClerc?" JR inquired.

"Are you speaking ill of the dead?" she retorted.

JR shivered, a superstitious dread overcoming him. "Man, I hope he's dead. I can't imagine being down there alive and knowing no one's coming after me."

Rebecca dropped her head. She was all but certain that LeClerc couldn't have survived, but JR's exhibition of vulnerability affected her. A glimpse of what tortures he must have gone through, mentally at least, had opened up to her, and found a crack in her defenses.

Back in the main room, an anxious pair of young women were relieved to see the party emerge from the passageway. Angela was the first to realize that LeClerc wasn't with them.

"Paul?" she asked. Rebecca shook her head mournfully. "Oh," said Angela, covering her mouth with her gloved hand. "Oh, no."

Cyndi put her arm around her friend. "What now?" she asked the group in general.

JR waited a beat for Summers or Robert to respond. When neither said anything, he spoke up. "Cyn and I found something that we think is important for you to see, Summers. It's almost certainly man-made." At his signal, Cyndi showed the photos on her phone, which were disappointingly unable to adequately convey what he and Cyndi had seen.

"Are you up to a short trek into another passage?" His

suspicions were confirmed when Summers began to shake again, and Robert made it certain.

"He's got a bad case of claustrophobia, mate. Is the passage a wide one?"

"It isn't bad. Look, if he can't go, he can't. Rebecca thinks we should head back to camp anyway, and I have pictures. Let's just get out of here."

His last couple of words were drowned by a massive *whump!* that shook the ground where they stood. More than one of the girls screamed, along with Summers. Robert widened his stance, and JR dove to the ground, his arms covering his head. When the noise died down and the ground stabilized, a fearful female voice asked timidly, "What was that?"

JR stood, a little abashed at his instinctive action. He looked at Robert, who shrugged, then said, "You're the Marine. You tell them."

Everyone looked to JR. "It sounded like explosives. Everyone stay here while Robert and I check it out. Come on, Robert, you're with me."

Cartwright fell into step side by side with JR when possible, dropping back a step when the cave floor was too cluttered with stalagmites to walk abreast. "What do you reckon Roosky was doing?" he asked.

JR shook his head. "No idea, but I don't like it. Hey, where's the entrance?"

The men had followed the guide rope to a wall, which, come to think of it, was jumbled rock, unlike the surrounding walls.

"Shit," said Robert, fear coming into his eyes. "JR, this *is* the entrance. Only that blast must have brought down the overhang. We're trapped."

"Roosky will get us out, no need to panic," JR

responded. He sounded puzzled, though, even to himself. It was definitely a blast that they'd heard before, not simply a rockslide. He'd know the sound of heavy explosives anywhere; probably wouldn't forget that sound until the day he died. Who would have been blasting?

Robert was regarding him steadily as the realization came to him slowly. *Roosky* had been blasting. He must have deliberately… Could that be right? Could his drinking buddy really have brought that overhang down deliberately, trapping them there to die? Why?

The answer hit him faster than the question had. "OS," he snarled. "The fucking Orion Society. That must have been who Misty was contacting. Roosky's part of it, too. Robert, buddy, we're SOL."

"Does that mean something like buggered?" Robert asked.

"Shit out of luck," JR responded. "Screwed, fucked, dead."

"None of us found another way out, right?" Robert asked. There was no use in giving way to panic. From the look of it, they weren't going to be able to dig themselves out, certainly not with the meager food and water supplies they had with them. But, most cave systems had more than one entrance. It only remained to find another one, and they'd be fine. At least, they would be if they found it quickly enough and it wasn't too far away from the Sno-Cat to make it back in the worsening weather. He said as much.

"We'll worry about where the Sno-Cat is when we get out. We turned back because we found the script on the wall, didn't go any further to find an exit. Maybe Summers can read the script and it will show the way. What about you and Rebecca? Why did you turn back?"

"We were at the end of our rope," Robert said, with a

sharp bark of laughter at the irony. There may be a way out through that passage, but Summers will never make it through there."

"Why do you say that?"

"There's a squeeze. He'd probably have a heart attack."

"Is a squeeze what I think it is?"

"Right, mate. A tight spot. Very tight. I barely made it through."

"Okay, let's get our story and our strategy straight. I say we tell the others that it will be easier to see if there's another opening than to dig out, but we won't say it's impossible to dig out. Agreed?"

"Sounds all right."

"I'll take Cyndi and Summers and go look at that script first. If Summers can read it, great. If not, we'll keep going until we either find another exit or reach a dead end. You and the others rest. If we don't find anything, you take Angela and Rebecca and explore what's beyond that squeeze. We need to ration what's left of the food and water starting now. Anything else you can think of?"

"That about covers it, mate. Say, glad you're along, JR."

JR wasn't so sure he was glad to be along, but the other man's implied praise felt good. He hadn't felt competent to lead anyone since his squad went amok in Afghanistan. Now, it seemed he must.

In respect of Summers' mental condition, the two men played down the nature of the rock fall, leaving the impression that they could dig out if necessary. In reality, they knew it would take heavy equipment to clear the original entrance to the cave. Since that was impossible, they kept up a front for Summers and the women, though Rebecca eyed JR suspiciously now and then. When he had led a reluctant Summers and his fellow passage explorer, Cyndi, to retrace their steps toward the script on the cave wall, Rebecca buttonholed Robert.

"What aren't you telling us?"

"I won't bullshit you, it's not good. We didn't want to panic Summers any worse than he already is, but there'll be no digging out. Our only hope is to find another way out, but that's almost guaranteed."

"Almost?" Rebecca was internally reeling at the blunt way Robert spoke, but she maintained her air of outer calm. She was the doctor, she was supposed to be unflappable. There was something about being told you were buried alive that tended to flap you, though, she thought.

"Look, there's almost always a second aperture. That's in over ninety percent of the caves I know of. But, some are too small for a person to get out, some could be behind squeezes that we can't get through, like the one you and I found but even smaller. And finally, it could be one that leads upward and it could be under a thick sheet of ice. So, almost is the best I can do for you, love."

"Thanks for the optimism," Rebecca replied, with as much irony as she could muster. So. They were likely trapped and likely to die. Well, she'd cross that bridge when she came to it. "How big do you think this cave system is?"

"No idea, why?"

"We've got at most three more days to find a way out. After that, we won't be able to get back to base for over six months. I don't think our food and water will hold out, do you?"

"Shit," was all he had to say.

Meanwhile, JR, Cyndi and Summers had made their

way to the wall of script. JR had to guide and support Summers, who seemed zombie-like as they made their way further into the cave. He reckoned that Summers had weathered too many shocks in too short a time. His mental processes had shut down. If they got any use of him for reading the script, it would be an unexpected miracle.

When they came to the area, Cyndi and JR stepped back to allow Summers free access to the wall. He stepped up to it willingly enough, but almost as soon as he saw it, Summers began to shake his head.

"What is it?" JR asked.

"This looks nothing like anything I've ever seen," Summers responded. "Not even the 10th Cycle script. But it is definitely man-made."

JR risked saying what was on his mind, hoping to shock Charles out of his stupor. "So, it's probably evidence of those 9th Cyclers you were looking for, eh, Charles? Too bad we can't get out to announce your discovery."

"What?" Charles said, simultaneously with Cyndi. "We can't get out?"

"Not unless you figure that out and it points the way. Or unless Robert can find something beyond where he'd been before." JR was tired of pretending, tired of protecting the nominal leader of the expedition and tired of being in this cave. He needed a way out almost as desperately as Summers did. Surprisingly, the truth did rally Summers.

"There's no other way out of this room?"

"Not that we've found, but as soon as we saw this, we hightailed it back. Could be we missed something."

"All right, I vote we make sure this is a dead end before going back. What's the deal with Robert and Rebecca's passage?"

"Narrow part, and then they ran out of rope," JR answered succinctly.

Summers paled, and for a moment JR thought he'd lost the man again. But, he stiffened and pulled a bit of courage from somewhere deep within him. "Let's go, then."

After a thorough search of the perimeter of the room, no way out was evident. The three returned to the main room and reported their findings.

"The good news," JR started, "is that we've succeeded in our mission. We didn't find a way out, but the script is definitely man-made, although it's something Charles doesn't recognize. He surmises that it's 9th Cycle. We've found evidence that Antarctica was once inhabited by humans before our time."

The two who had been with him had already had time to absorb the news, exciting as it was. The other three, however, reacted in different ways. Carmen, whose demeanor had remained strangely unemotional since LeClerc's loss, smiled faintly. Angela could barely contain herself, knowing what it meant to Summers, whom she admired and now felt responsible for given his claustrophobia. Robert, though he was glad, was more interested in the cave and in finding a way out of it than in the fact that they'd found what they were looking for.

"Great," said Robert. "But before we get too excited, we need to find a way out of here, so we can tell the world. Ready, ladies?" He turned without another word, leading Rebecca and Angela toward the passage he'd explored earlier.

At JR's direction, everyone had left all food and unopened water containers with the group in the main room, carrying just enough water to take a sip every hour. The good news was that the remaining team were all responsible people, not defiant or given to hoarding against the interest of the group as a whole. JR now carefully divided the food into packets of about four hundred calories each. If each person consumed one packet per day, they had enough for three more days. It wasn't enough to sustain health, nor even life for very long. Beyond that, there would be no point in prolonging their lives anyway, because they would certainly die on the ice if they did manage to get out of the cave.

In a way, it was a relief to know that he'd done all he could and that he would no longer be responsible for them after the next week or so. JR had just one regret, and that was that he wouldn't see Roosky or Misty again. He'd like to have some choice words with both of them. But, it didn't matter. Nothing mattered now except doing his damnedest to get his people out of this mess, and if he failed, well, they wouldn't suffer for long.

With nothing more to do until they heard back from the other half of the team, JR and Cyndi left Summers resting and combed the other half of the main room for another passage. Several depressions seemed promising, but each petered out much quicker than the one leading to what they were now calling the library, because of the script on the wall. It was up to Robert now, but JR wasn't looking forward to guiding Summers through the squeeze. The man seemed to be burning his last reserves of courage now. What effect would it have on him, crawling through a six-foot passage that was tighter than a coffin according to Robert? Nothing good, JR was certain. Too bad there was no more scotch and no more vodka, nothing alcoholic as far as he knew. Half a bottle of the good stuff and anyone would find enough courage to get through a six-foot tight spot.

At least they knew they could all make it. JR was taller than Robert, but Robert, aside from the traitorous Roosky, was easily the brawniest. The girls would fit easily, as would Summers. With Robert leading and JR bringing up the rear, he was certain they'd get the whole team through. But what if Summers really did have a heart attack? If so, it would be best if it killed him. They wouldn't have the resources to carry him out, nor would JR risk Rebecca's life to stay with him while they went for help, knowing that a return trip to base and back would certainly put them in polar vortex season. Summers would just have to man up; there was no other choice.

While JR was chasing his thoughts in circles around this dilemma, Angela returned alone. JR jumped to his feet, alarmed, but immediately saw that Angela's face was alight with the biggest smile he'd ever seen.

"You've found a way out?" His heart was pounding again. At that moment, JR realized that he'd expected success. He didn't know why, because he had been preparing for the worst. But somehow, he'd not been able to conceive of his own death in this place, even while speaking of it.

"Not exactly, or not yet. I mean... Well, you just have to see it, there's no way to describe it!" They could get no more out of the excited girl, who was babbling and possibly hallucinating. Something about a waterfall? Not likely. There was nothing to do but follow her. It was all they could do to keep up with her as Angela fairly flew across the main room. When she dropped to her hands and knees just a few feet into the passageway, Summers balked.

"I...I can't."

"You can, and you will. If I have to knock you out and drag you through, you're coming," JR threatened.

"Maybe you'd better go first," Summers quailed.

"Nope, you're not getting away with that. Cyn, follow Angela, and take this." With a deft move, JR looped the rope into Summers' climbing harness and handed the other end to Cyndi. "If he doesn't come through in a few minutes, get Robert and drag him," he directed. "I'll be trapped here until he's cleared the squeeze, got it?"

Cyndi, wide-eyed, took the rope as directed. She then turned and crawled into the passageway herself, following Angela. JR spoke quietly to Summers.

"I know what it's like, dude," he said. "I've never been more terrified in my life than when we were under enemy fire. I was almost shitting myself, and I saw plenty of men who did. This is nothing compared to that. But, you have to get through it. It's the only way out, and I'm not leaving you here to die. You go or I stay. What's it going to be?"

Summers gulped and nodded, unable to trust his voice to speak.

"Okay, good man. Listen, Cyndi and I are going to help you, but you have to help us, too. Cyn will help pull you through, and I'm right here to push if you need me. What's your favorite song?"

The seeming non sequitur jarred Summers' mind away from the coming ordeal. "I don't know."

"Any song, man, come on."

"O, Susanna?"

"That's fine. I want you to sing that while you're going through. If Cyndi can't hear you, she stops pulling, got it?"

Summers nodded again. On hands and knees, he crawled into the opening, a thin and badly off-tune melody accompanying him. JR decided to wait before crawling in behind him. If it took them too long to get Summers clear of the squeeze, he might get a little claustrophobic himself, waiting his turn.

"Summers, you sing like a starving puppy," he called. "Louder!"

The song grew in volume, and Cyndi, catching JR's intent, called, "Now he sounds like a donkey!" At that, Summers faltered as he laughed weakly, but hastily began again.

An eternity passed for JR before Cyndi's voice echoed down the narrow opening. "JR, where are you?"

"Is Summers clear?" he called back.

"All clear, come on! You won't believe it," she called. What the hell? Had the rest gone on without him, or was the surprise right there at the end of the squeeze? Without another thought about what he'd do if he became stuck, JR dived in, crawling until he saw the opening that Robert had told him about. Six feet of solid rock, with an opening barely wide enough to inch through, pushing with his toes. JR wondered how Summers had done it. It was daunting to him, and he'd never had claustrophobia. Maybe he would after this, though. He took a deep breath, put his arms out in front of him, and pushed.

It seemed like half an hour before JR felt someone seize his hands and pull, popping him out of the tunnel all at once. When he'd got his bearings, Robert was sitting on the ground with him, grinning like a maniac. "Welcome to Shangri-La," he said. JR rolled over and sat up, then pushed himself to a standing position, hauling Robert up with him.

"Shangri-La, what are you talking about?" He could see nothing but cave walls with the familiar stone decorations hanging from the ceiling and growing from the floor. Robert gestured, a sweeping motion that invited JR to step forward and there, beyond a particularly large stalagmite, was an opening that led…to Paradise? JR couldn't believe his eyes.

He stumbled forward, Robert at his heels, through an opening large enough to drive a Jeep through, and into a dream. Before him opened a verdant valley, with grass, vines, trees; so much green he could hardly bear to look at it. After months of nothing but white ice, gray buildings and brown rocks, he was seeing something so impossible that he literally had to pinch himself to make sure he was awake. He stripped off a glove to do it, and heard Robert laughing behind him.

"It's real, mate, though I don't have any idea how it could be."

"What, how?" was all JR could manage. His brain jittered as he remembered an old movie from illicit midnight TV watching as a kid, until the reference came to mind. 'The Land that Time Forgot.' What was next, dinosaurs?

"My best guess is geothermal activity, but we haven't had much of a chance to explore. We were waiting for you."

"Where are the others?"

"They're at the pool at the foot of the waterfall."

"Waterfall. Unbelievable," JR said, with wonder.

"Indeed," returned Robert.

Chapter Twenty

YES, COMRADE, ALL DEAD

In the Sno-Cat, Bart was napping when the thunderous noise brought him to attention with an oath of surprise. He quickly pulled on his cold weather gear and jumped down to assess the situation. Seeing nothing that could have accounted for the noise, he set off against orders to follow the tracks of the others further into the canyon. When he'd walked for about forty-five minutes, he spotted a plume of ice crystals in the air near the canyon wall, and veered toward it.

The closer he got, the more he was put in mind of avalanches he'd seen on TV news reports. A great spill of whiter snow overlaid the ice on which he walked, with the plume of crystals hanging in the air directly over it. Looking around, he saw no sign of a cave or even an overhang such as Robert and JR had described to the others.

"*Sacré bleu!* There has been a cave-in! Where is Roosky?" he said, unaware he was speaking aloud. Before he could turn again to look around for Roosky, a pair of massive hands enveloped both sides of his head.

"Wha…" was his last word. The hands twisted savagely, and Bart died instantly.

"Too bad," rumbled Roosky. "He was good cook for Cajun." His companion with the big hands shrugged. It was nothing to him. He had meant to kill the cook when he went to dispose of the Sno-Cat, but the man had been missing. After sending it into a convenient crevasse not far from the canyon entrance, he'd followed the tracks until he met up with Roosky, who pointed out the lone hiker. Now the job was done, and they could get out of here.

Together, the two started for a spot outside the canyon, where a Kamov-KA60 helicopter awaited, rotors slowly turning. When they got in, the aircraft took off and swung over the top of the escarpment, into a permanent cloud cover and on over the east side of the mountain, toward the Russian base on the coast, setting down from time to time to refuel from huge, tough plastic bags scattered strategically across the ice. *Clever idea*, he thought. It solved the range dilemma, and without sacrificing weight capacity to carry their fuel with them. He had no reason to know that the idea had originated with the Americans, who dragged similar bags from McMurdo to Amundsen-Scott, for a much more efficient way to deliver fuel to the Polar base.

Roosky made his report from the Russian base. "Yes, comrade, all dead. The way is clear."

At the other end of the conversation, Septentrio seethed at the man's familiarity. 'Comrade' indeed. He was no friend to the Russian, the man was merely a tool. He considered whether it would be enjoyable to gut the man when his usefulness was at an end. Perhaps not. As he understood it, the Russian was a giant, potentially able to overcome Septentrio and harm him. Even if not, the mess would be massive. As much as Septentrio enjoyed watching the death throes, he hated the resultant mess. Perhaps he'd just shoot the pawn and be done with it.

Septentrio picked up the videophone and called Auster.

"How are you, my dear?"

The deceptively mild greeting put Auster on instant alert. What was Septentrio up to? He never called her by an endearment.

"I'm fine, as usual," she answered cautiously.

"I wanted you to know I've cleaned up your little problem, Auster. Don't make me do it again."

Fear made a brief appearance, only to be replaced by anger. "I don't know what you're talking about."

"Your spy, of course. I trust she will take the necessary steps?"

"Septentrio, please speak plainly. I have no time for guessing games," Auster snapped, though she was afraid she knew to which spy Septentrio referred.

"All right. You sent a spy to seduce the brother of Daniel Rossler. She was discovered a few days ago. She must not live to be questioned. Is that plain enough?"

"Go on."

"I have taken care of the rest of the team. My operative will terminate your spy when he returns, if she has not already done it."

"She will. She probably already has. Won't your operative be suspect, though, as the only survivor?"

"Perhaps. He will have to be sacrificed as well. Stay out of my way, Auster. I don't need your help."

Septentrio disconnected with a sense of savage glee. So far, he was ahead in this game. He would look forward to the time he could strike the fatal blow. Literally.

As soon as Roosky had made his report, the helicopter took off again, this time toward the South Pole, using a similar hop and skip method to reach the area nearby the base. Coming in low so as to avoid radar, the last landing was within five miles of the base; too far to hear, but not too far to walk for the tough Russian. He pulled on the dirty cold gear he'd worn at the cave canyon and exited the aircraft.

"*Dosvedanya*," he called to the pilot, who raised a hand in acknowledgment of the farewell and then took off. Roosky trudged toward the Pole, using the journey to get himself into character as the sole survivor of a doomed expedition.

A few hours later, he arrived at the base and practically fell into the airlock as he acted out his part.

"Avalanche," he gasped. "Buried them in the cave." The soldier who heard that dire sentence sent for Andersen immediately, and helped Roosky to the sick bay, where he was treated for exposure and dehydration. Andersen arrived as the IV was being placed.

"Welcome back, Mikhail Stefanovich," Andersen said.

Roosky, surprised to hear the base commander address him in the Russian manner, only gaped at him.

"Can you tell me what happened?" Andersen pressed.

Roosky cleared his throat, and began to tell the lie he'd practiced.

"Everyone was in cave when avalanche buried opening. I blast, but no good. When I run out of explosive, take Sno-Cat and return." He shrugged, as if that explained everything.

"Where's the Sno-Cat?"

"She fall into crevasse, I walk rest of way."

"How far?"

"I do not know. I walk two days."

"How'd you get out of the crevasse?" Andersen asked.

"She fall in only part way, I climb out. Then she disappear."

Roosky's story was implausible, but not impossible. Still, Andersen was suspicious. He continued to question Roosky until he was satisfied that there would be no way to shake the story. However, on the off chance that there were survivors of the expedition out there, he needed to send a search and rescue mission, and it needed to be fast. Winter winds called the Polar Vortex would begin within the next several days, and then there would be no more travel for six months, minimum.

With Roosky's description of the canyon and the bearing they'd taken, Andersen sent for help from McMurdo. They needed a helicopter to get to the canyon. McMurdo had two Sikorsky MH-53 Pave Low birds, retired now in the rest of the world. One was dispatched immediately to the area where Roosky indicated the mishap had occurred. Andersen would have liked to check out his story by sending out a fixed-wing plane to locate the Sno-Cat that supposedly had disappeared into a crevasse, but the operation wasn't critical to save lives, and was therefore too expensive to mount just to satisfy his suspicious nature.

Hours later, communications from the Pave Low indicated they'd located the site of the avalanche, and that it bore the characteristics that Roosky had reported. There was no sign of survivors, and the crew was turning back, unprepared to dig for them. The Rossler Foundation Expedition was officially declared missing and all members presumed dead.

Chapter Twenty-One

WHAT HAVE I DONE?

Expedition Members Missing and Feared Dead In Tragic
Antarctic Mishap
Exclusive to The Daily Camera, Boulder, CO

Reports from the United States joint military base at the South Pole today indicate that the Rossler Foundation expedition has met with a fatal catastrophe, killing all remaining members of the expedition save two. See sidebar for information on presumed spy Misty Rivers.

The expedition was conceived by University of Colorado Boulder archaeology professor Charles Summers and funded by the Rossler Foundation and most Antarctica Treaty nations after Dr. Summers discovered an anomaly in the sixteenth century maps he was studying. On one map, he located a land mass that clearly indicated the mapmaker knew of Antarctica, though in fact there is no other record of its discovery for the next three centuries. Dr. Summers then corroborated his theory that the 10th Cyclers knew of it and perhaps passed down maps that survived the 10th Cycle catastrophe into the early centuries of our cycle. Dr. Summers and his team members hoped to find a 9th Cycle city mentioned in the 10th Cycle library owned by the Rossler Foundation.

Among the dead are Summers (45), expedition director Paul LeClerc (42), expedition chef, Bartholome Deveau (38), Dr. Rebecca Mendenhall (25), Australian geologist Robert Cartwright (32), Chilean microbiologist Carmen Hernandez (age unknown), electronics engineer Cyndi Self (23), cartographer Angela Brown (34), and Joshua 'JR' Rossler (26), brother of Rossler Foundation director and CEO, Daniel Rossler.

Several members of the expedition had been sent home earlier, thus escaping the fate of the nine who were killed when an avalanche buried the entrance to the cave they were exploring, according to the sole survivor of the last expedition mission, Mikhail S. Maxhulin. Maxhulin had been tasked to stay outside the cave in order to assist if the shelf of ice that overhung the entrance were to give way. Unfortunately, according to Maxhulin, it was not just ice and snow that gave way, but a layer of the native sandstone that broke with the weight of the ice shelf. Maxhulin said that Cartwright had been concerned about it, but certain that they had brought enough explosives to clear the entrance if the unstable formation did give way. However, after exhausting his supply of explosives, Maxhulin was unable to clear the entrance.

Maxhulin barely escaped with his own life when the team's Sno-Cat became stranded in a crevasse. He was able to extricate himself from the conveyance and walk to Amundsen-Scott base at the South Pole, where he was treated for exposure and dehydration and released.

The expedition had not been without mishap prior to

the one that took the remaining lives. Two of the original expedition members, mining experts Donald Jensen and Michael Walker, were killed in a bizarre incident that no one witnessed. The first was apparently trapped in a blazing tent during a vicious wind storm and burned to death. His tent-mate was never found, and was presumed to have been swept away by the winds, which can reach hurricane strength and cause white-outs by blowing loose snow from the surface into the air.

In a final bizarre twist, one of the expedition's research assistants, Misty Rivers, was discovered sending sensitive information to an unknown accomplice and incarcerated at the base while the final mission took place. Ms. Rivers was found dead in her cell shortly after the report of the tragedy that befell the remaining members. Cause of death is unknown, pending an autopsy when Ms. Rivers' body is returned to Colorado.

The Rossler Foundation has announced that a memorial service for their fallen colleagues will be held on Friday, February 28, in the Foundation auditorium. In lieu of flowers, the families request that donations to the University of Colorado, Boulder Archaeology department be made in the names of the dedicated expedition members, who fell in the name of science. A fellowship will be endowed in honor of Dr. Summers and his expedition.

Sarah had never seen Daniel in such a state. She'd heard how he was when she'd been kidnapped by OS operatives during their search for the Pyramid code, but she hadn't witnessed it. The family gathered in Boulder as soon as the news came through, and she appreciated the support of her parents as well as Uncle Luke and Aunt Sally, Sinclair, and Martha, who flew out from Providence as soon as she heard. Sarah was grief-stricken herself, feeling it all the more because she was so near her delivery date. However, her main concern was for Daniel, who was wild with grief and guilt. It didn't matter that even his parents and other brother, Aaron, told him that he'd had no choice but to send JR with the expedition. He took all the blame, and the burden threatened to crush him.

An emergency meeting of the Board was about to take place, and though Sarah had already put herself on maternity leave, she was on hand. The rest of the family, both her side and Daniel's, had also been invited, as well as representatives from the families of most of the expedition members. Carmen's parents had been unable to make the trip, but Antonio Santiago, who had been among the scientists that were extracted early, came as their representative as well as a concerned team member. He might have been with the missing if he hadn't opted to leave early because there had been nothing to which he could apply his specialty. Most of the people who were to attend the meeting were being served coffee and pastries while Sarah and Daniel's parents tried their best to calm Daniel down. It wasn't working.

"I might as well have killed him with my own hands! Oh, God, what have I done? He didn't want to go...I forced him to!"

It had been a variation on this theme, without much respite, for the past twenty-four hours, since the news came in. At first, Sarah just held him while he sobbed, but after several hours, she called her OB-GYN for a referral to a doctor who could prescribe a sedative. It reminded her that Becca Mendenhall had been among them and brought fresh tears for Sarah, but she had to remain strong for Daniel. Daniel refused the sedatives, saying he had to keep a clear head to determine a response.

His first thought was to race to Antarctica himself, with a rescue mission, but cooler heads had prevailed. The team had been trapped in the cave with little food and water for more than seventy-two hours by the time the Russian had made it back to base, making it unlikely they'd survived even then. Then twenty-four hours for the initial reconnaissance from McMurdo, which had taken place yesterday.

It would require another twenty-four hours, minimum, for anyone to reach Antarctica from North America. There was no chance it would be anything but a recovery mission, experts agreed. That meant there was no hurry. There was too little time before the winter conditions made travel on the continent impossible, anyway. They could wait the nearly seven months for another summer season, so as not to risk more lives. Daniel was tortured by the thought of his brother, perhaps alive still, slowly losing hope of rescue and dying of hunger and thirst with the knowledge that no one had come. Every time his thoughts turned in that direction, which was often, the power of his emotions would wring a cry of anguish and frustration from him, followed by wrenching sobs that frightened Sarah half to death.

Daniel wasn't unaware that there were others involved, but they had all signed on for the expedition willingly, eagerly even. It didn't make the circumstances of their deaths less tragic, but Daniel didn't feel as much personal responsibility for them, as he did for his baby brother. He couldn't stop thinking, didn't want to stop thinking, and the anguish wouldn't let up. After a sleepless night, Sarah was at her wits' end for how to comfort him, and his parents were now beginning to realize that they were in danger of losing their eldest to deep depression as well as having lost their baby. Only their strong Christian faith kept Ben and Nancy Rossler on their feet. Nicholas was staying strong, but Bess had been hospitalized with chest pains, and he was with her rather than at Foundation headquarters on the day of the Board meeting.

More than an hour past the scheduled time of the meeting, Daniel had finally collected himself enough to preside, though Sarah fretted that the discussions would set him off again. She had called the doctor and begged him to come to their building and stand by. With everything in as much readiness as they could accomplish, the Rosslers filed in as a group. Daniel called the meeting to order.

In their years together, Sarah had been given cause on more than one occasion to be proud of her husband, but never more so than today, when he put aside the turmoil inside him to present a calm demeanor to the Board. Only moments before, he'd been shouting that there had to be a faster way to get to Antarctica so that he could go and get his brother. Now he was reading the report from Cmdr. Andersen soberly but without any evidence that he had broken down repeatedly in the past twenty-four hours. Sarah gave a thought to the victims, especially those she'd known personally, before schooling herself to listen to what was being discussed.

Daniel finished reading the report and looked up, glancing in turn at each of the family members or their representatives who were in attendance. He cleared his throat.

"I first want to express my heartfelt condolences to each of you on the loss of your loved ones. I stand with you in grief that these bright young lives have been cut short. I particularly regret that it was under the auspices of the

Foundation that such a tragedy has occurred. Today we also remember the two lives previously lost during this expedition. As of this date, only one family has had the comfort of having their loved one's remains returned to them for proper burial. The Rossler Foundation is committed to correcting that circumstance to the best of our ability, as soon as it becomes practical.

"Before I go on, for the benefit of those who are unaware, I'll give you an overview of why our recovery mission cannot begin immediately. Antarctica is a land of extremes. Most of the continent is covered in an ice sheet that is thousands of feet deep. You may be aware of the progression of day and night there. Within the next three weeks, near-total darkness will creep over the land, deepening for some weeks and lasting for approximately six months. During this time, extremes of cold and vicious winds make travel virtually impossible.

"We understand from the reports we've received that the canyon in which the expedition went missing is approximately two hundred miles from Amundsen-Scott base. Travel to the area by ground transportation takes two to four days, depending on weather conditions, and it is already very difficult and dangerous to get there by helicopter. A rescue mission sent from McMurdo base by helicopter has already determined that there is no sign of the opening where the expedition entered the cave. We also know, thanks to the survivor, that the group entered the cave with less than one day's rations of food and water, expecting to be there only a few hours. It has now been just over six days since our loved ones entered the cave. It is extremely unlikely, if not impossible, that they have survived this long, or could survive another forty-eight hours while a rescue mission is mounted.

"The reality is that we will be unable, in all practicality, to excavate until next October at the earliest. However, rest assured that we will spare no expense in returning your loved ones to you as soon as humanly possible.

"Are there any questions?"

A subdued babble of voices ensued before the family members quieted and one voice rang out.

"What if they're still alive?" Immediately, the conference room was engulfed in noise. Sarah gasped, and then looked fearfully at Daniel. This was what had been torturing him. Would he be able to maintain his professional demeanor? She saw that he had dropped his head, bowed with the weight of the knowledge that others feared what he did. Unable to speak for several moments, Daniel allowed the noise to increase, until Sinclair stepped forward.

"Quiet, please!"

As people noticed that someone else was at the podium, they began to quiet so that he could speak. Gradually, the room became silent.

"A question was asked and needs an answer. I can speak for Mr. Rossler here that no stone has been left unturned in his desire to go to the rescue of the expedition. I'll remind you that his own brother is with them. The truth is that, if they are still alive, there isn't a way to reach them before it's too late, as Mr. Rossler has told you.

"They don't have enough water, and the cold is deepening due to winter coming on. I want to assure you that death by hypothermia would almost certainly have occurred within twenty-four hours of being sealed into the cave. Your loved ones would not have had time to get unbearably thirsty, or even painfully hungry. Hypothermia has been widely reported to induce feelings of drifting, even bliss as the body shuts down. They would not have suffered, or not for long. Does that answer your question, sir?"

"So they were dead by the time the Russian got to the South Pole for help, is that what you're saying?"

"Almost certainly," Sinclair replied. Daniel gripped his arm in a gesture of thanks and fought to compose himself once more. He had one last thing to say.

"The Rossler Foundation also stands ready to assist with funeral expenses once the remains have been recovered. Please see Miss Welch from Human Resources to provide your contact information so that we can reach you when we have further news."

Daniel dismissed the meeting; however, immediately after a catered lunch, just the Board would be meeting to discuss how they'd fund the recovery operation later in the year, and what plans needed to be made. Almost a year to the day after the first expedition was approved, Daniel would be seeking funding for a second, more somber expedition. This one he would lead himself. Nothing would stop him from attempting to recover JR's body—he owed his brother that if nothing else. Nothing would ever lessen his guilt for sending JR into that icy hell, but at least his parents would have the satisfaction of knowing that he rested safely where they could visit and mourn.

Chapter Twenty-Two

THE ARRIVAL OF NJ ROSSLER

Sarah had quietly left the meeting with some of the family members, leaving Daniel to deal with the other Board members as necessary. She didn't expect him to have much trouble convincing them that their fallen expedition members would have to be retrieved as he'd promised the families, and she wasn't feeling very well. Emma, her mother, urged her to go home and rest, since her due date was less than a week away. Ben, Nancy, Emma, Sinclair and Martha were going to the hospital to visit with Bess, since Nicholas had sent a text that she was much improved and wanted company. The emotion of the meeting was still clinging to them, so Ben and Nancy especially wanted to assure themselves of Bess's health. JR's loss was something they'd have to absorb as the days went on, but for now they turned their thoughts instead to Bess, who'd taken it very badly.

Sinclair and Martha volunteered to drive Sarah home, as she would no longer fit behind a steering wheel and still reach the gas pedal, despite her long legs. They chatted idly about anything they could think of to take her mind off JR as Sinclair drove. When they reached the house, Sarah asked them to stay with her, telling Martha she was really very uncomfortable and could use a distraction. Martha made a nest for her with a blanket and sheet in a big easy chair, and had her put her feet up on an ottoman.

Sinclair was in the kitchen getting some tea for the three of them when he heard Martha shout.

"Sinclair, come quickly!" He ran into the living room with the tea kettle still in his hand, to discover Sarah writhing in pain and Martha wringing her hands.

"What's wrong with her?"

As Sarah's agony began to subside, Sinclair remembered that Martha had never had a child. "I'd say she's in labor," he answered in a whisper. "When's her due date?"

"Not 'til next week," Martha whispered back. "That's why I was going to stay, to be here when the baby's born. Should we call an ambulance?"

"No need for that," he answered. "She's got a journey ahead, but we can get her to the hospital before the next pain hits, I think. Does she have a bag packed?"

Sarah had regained her breath, though her face was white and her eyes round and staring. "I'm right here, Sinclair. Yes, I have my bag packed." Directing Martha to the master bedroom to find it, she struggled up from the chair. "Okay, Sinclair, let's go. And would you call Daniel, please?"

A bit of confusion ensued at the hospital when the three presented themselves at the desk for Sarah to check in. The registrar asked Martha if she'd like to help her daughter in case another labor pain hit her, and Martha demurred, though she thought of Sarah as a daughter. They dispatched Sinclair to the floor where Bess was being treated, to find Emma, while Sarah calmly gave the registrar her information. It had been nearly half an hour since that first pain, and nothing in between, so she felt confident it was just a particularly strong Braxton-Hicks contraction. Nevertheless, since she was at the hospital, she might as well pre-register while waiting for her doctor to arrive and pronounce her okay to go home.

Five minutes later she was suppressing a scream. This wasn't what the classes and her doctor had prepared her for. Sarah began to worry that something was wrong. Having finished the registration process, the registrar sent for a medical assistant to take Sarah to Labor and Delivery in a wheelchair, stopping at the corridor doors for a brief moment when Sinclair returned with Emma in tow.

"Mom, something's wrong," Sarah sobbed as soon as she saw her mother. Emma went to her knees, impeding the wheelchair and hugged her daughter.

"No, honey, nothing's wrong. You're in good hands and everything's going to be fine." Emma got up, dusted her pant legs, and said to the MA, "What are you waiting for? My daughter is in pain, let's get her into a bed."

Emma and Martha followed the wheelchair, while Sinclair, feeling a bit like a fish out of water, made his way back to sit with his old friend Nicholas Rossler. He didn't know what would have become of him without these Rosslers; first his old friend had recommended him to his grandson as the linguist to help break the Pyramid Code, then the grandson, Daniel, had persuaded him to move to Boulder and become head of the Foundation translation department.

The younger Rosslers had become like family to him, but an unexpected bonus had come in the form of Sarah's dear friend Martha Simms. The lovely Martha was much on Sinclair's mind these days. They had become very close, and he was hoping to persuade Martha to marry him and move to Boulder soon. In his confusion, Sinclair forgot to call Daniel until he found the others visiting with Bess.

"What's going on?" Nancy asked.

"Oh, I think Sarah may be having her baby. Good heavens! I've forgotten to call Daniel!" Sinclair stepped out of the room to make the call, unaware of the stir he'd caused. As he dialed, Nicholas, Ben and Nancy were all trying to persuade Bess to stay in bed, rather than jump out and go to Sarah's side. When Sinclair came back in, a barrage of questions hit him.

"Only one contraction so far, that I know of," he answered. That information allowed Bess to relax and wait for her doctor to give her the okay to get out of bed. Nancy, though, left to go to Labor and Delivery, promising to send a report back for Bess's peace of mind.

Daniel had received the call while the meeting was still going on, his secretary slipping in with a portable phone and a message that it was urgent. His heart beating rapidly, he took it, thinking that he couldn't take any more bad news. What Sinclair had to tell him stunned him.

Without so much as a goodbye, Daniel tore out of the boardroom, almost taking the doorframe with him. As he ran down the hall, he was considering whether running to the hospital, less than a mile away, might be faster than going for his car. His legs took him to the car, though. A few people in the parking lot heard him utter a whoop of joy and wondered what had happened.

As he drove, with no attention to the speed limit, he had time to collect a thought or two. As long as Sarah and the baby were okay, maybe this was a blessing, that little Nicholas was apparently preparing to arrive a week early.

Daniel wondered if Sarah would be okay with them giving him a different middle name than the one they'd settled on. Instead of Nicholas Daniel Rossler, maybe the little guy would be Nicholas Joshua. It had a distinguished ring to it, he thought.

By the time he reached the hospital, Dr. Sanders had arrived and was examining Sarah. Daniel was stopped in the waiting room by his mother and told he'd have to wait. A few minutes later, Dr. Sanders stepped out and greeted him. She'd met Martha, Emma and Nancy a few minutes earlier and remarked that she was lucky to have three moms at her side.

"Daniel, Sarah's in some distress and it's causing her to feel the pain more than she should be. I've ordered a sedative that should be fine for the baby, but what would be best for her is for you all to take turns sitting with her and assuring her that everything is okay. Can you do that? I must insist that no one talk about your brother. I'm sorry for your loss."

Daniel's face had fallen when Dr. Sanders mentioned JR, but he understood. Stress over JR had more than likely brought on early labor, but fortunately a week was seldom a problem. Dr. Sanders confirmed that the baby seemed fine. If they could keep Sarah calm, her labor would go more comfortably. With an effort, Daniel put his brother into a small compartment in his mind and gave the rest to Sarah and their baby. JR was beyond his help, but little Nicholas would have a father who was present, focused, and committed to his health and safety.

Since Sarah had come to the hospital so early in her labor, it was near midnight when Nicholas Joshua Rossler made his entrance into the world, much to his mother's relief and his dad's pride. He was a robust baby, nearly 21 inches long, weighing eight pounds, and roaring his disapproval of being thrust into the cold. When he heard that lusty cry, Daniel's chest and shoulders expanded so much he thought he might burst his buttons, and possibly need a larger shirt size from now on.

Despite how tired everyone was from the long day, the baby's early arrival raised everyone's spirits and gave them the emotional strength they would need for the memorial service, set for day after tomorrow. Daniel's staff were doing all they could to prepare, so he could spend the next two days with his little family before presiding at the service.

Chapter Twenty-Three

TOVARICH JR

Roosky had flown home out of Amundsen-Scott via Vostok Station, his own country's Antarctica base as soon as the interrogations were finished. He was repatriated to Russia, where another OS operative met him personally and transferred a large sum in hard currency. After the money was stashed to his satisfaction, Roosky accepted the invitation to visit Würzburg, in Germany, to be personally congratulated by the leadership of the OS in its entirety during the quarterly meeting set for the end of March. Until then, he was welcome to rest and recuperate from his 'ordeal'. It was an arrangement that suited him well.

Roosky was proud of the execution of his assignment, with only one regret. It was too bad that the Rossler kid had to die with the rest of them. He was good drinking partner, Tovarich JR. Roosky dedicated an entire bottle of the Moskovskaya, his favorite, to the memory of the night they'd had together. Less pleasant was the memory of having to waste an entire bottle before he left the base. The girl with the ridiculous name had to be silenced somehow.

He'd bribed a corrupt American to slip her the bottle, which had *nebol'shoy syurpriz*, a little surprise. She would have felt nothing as she died.

It was a neat wrap-up; he honored Tovarich JR's feelings for the girl by killing her with no pain, and the autopsy would show nothing by the time the body was shipped home for it. By then, the chemical compound responsible for stopping the girl's heart would have been reduced by the process of decay to its component parts, none of which would cause concern if found in the body.

While Roosky was congratulating himself, Septentrio's team was already en route to secure the discovery Roosky had reported. He'd left a small and subtle marker for them, indicating where to dig to enter the cave in the wake of the expedition. Misty's ill-timed communique had reached its mark and an Orion Society satellite had been re-directed to laser scan the land area under which the cave lay, revealing a large system with a surprise at one end: a valley with a higher heat signature than anyone believed possible.

Left to themselves, the Rossler expedition might have found it. Thanks to Roosky's actions, however, Septentrio was convinced that his team would be the first to discover what the valley held. After the disappointment of the failure to keep the Pyramid Code to themselves, the possibility of finding an even earlier civilization's records was worth any expense, and he'd spared none.

Even now, they were speeding across the ice on special snowmobiles that were fitted with fairings for protection from wind and cold, or perhaps they'd already arrived. In any case, he could expect to hear from them by satellite phone that was linked to the private Orion Society communications bird making a tight orbit around the perimeter of Antarctica since Misty's message was received.

In fact, though Septentrio had not yet received the report, the team had arrived shortly after Roosky's chopper had departed. They'd watched the 'copter circumnavigate the canyon from a vantage point concealed by deep shadow cast by the narrow entrance to the canyon, and once it had left, they made haste to locate the cairn of ice that Roosky had fashioned and dig through a shallow drift of snow to reveal the blocked entrance to the cave. They blasted through the rubble that Roosky had brought down, heedless of the possibility that the Rosslerites might be behind it. It was a matter of only half a day before they found their way into the main room the Rosslerites had used as a rallying point.

Unlike the Rossler expedition, the OS team had a map of the cave system created by the ground-penetrating laser onboard the satellite. Where the Rossler team had found only one entrance, the OS team knew of three, one they would find hidden behind the colorful formations of the room JR and Cyndi had found, and one branching off from deep within what appeared to be a man-made borehole. That one would be reached by rope ladder some seventy-five feet down from the surface on the way to the bottom of the hole into which LeClerc had fallen. The team of six split up, two taking the ladder approach, and two each taking the other two approaches. Those who would have to navigate the squeeze were given a head start so that they'd all arrive in the valley near the same time.

The intruders knew that the Rosslerites had either explored further into the cave system or found the valley, since they weren't found within the large room where they'd entered. A small possibility was that they'd all been buried under the rock fall, but the leader considered that unlikely. In any event, they'd need to be eliminated. The plan was to reconnoiter in the valley to try to locate the expedition team. If they weren't found immediately outside one of the cave exits, everyone would converge within the largest of the exit rooms, the one hidden behind the strange, colorful room. From there, they would plan an ambush.

Chapter Twenty-Four

LET'S FIND A WAY OUT

It had been several hours since the Rossler party emerged into the impossible hidden valley. Their first activity had involved gathering around the pool and watching as Carmen tested the water for bacteria. When she declared it potable, in fact purer than most tap water in the U.S. the team gratefully filled their water containers. Finding a source of water would help them survive until a rescue party could reach them.

The party, to a man or woman, felt a sense of unreality as they gazed around the valley. It took a while for anyone to sort out their amazement to form intelligent questions, but when they did, an excited babble broke out. It almost made sense that the air was warm; after all, they were looking at a veritable jungle, and weren't all jungles warm? In no time, they had all stripped their cold-weather gear off. Later, they would discuss whether to carry it with them as they explored this place, or leave it where they could find it again. For now, it was simply too warm to wear it, so they took it off.

JR's earlier memory of the old movie prompted him to ask if there might be animals, particularly dangerous ones, here. Robert suggested that they stop talking and listen for the typical sounds of an undisturbed jungle. After several moments of silence, he gave his opinion that whatever animals had been here, if any, were now extinct. At the same time, he wondered what would have caused such an extinction. This whole valley made no sense, other than the warmth, which he'd already attributed to geothermal activity.

As he looked around, Robert noted the high, almost straight-sided cliffs. They'd be a bitch to climb, he realized, but they also put him in mind of a volcanic cone. Could this place have been found and cultivated by 9th Cyclers, with no natural vegetation of its own and no native animals? He set that speculation aside until a more scientific catalog of what was here could be made.

Summers was excited, too. If anywhere in Antarctica was a possibility for habitation by humans, this was it. But, there was no time to look for ruins. For now, as fascinating as this place was, it was imperative to find an escape route and get back to the Pole before travel became impossible.

Each of the others was thinking or expressing thoughts relative to their own specialties, but it was Angela whose suggestion prevailed. "We should split up and explore the canyon walls for other cave entrances. Maybe they would lead us out."

Cyndi had wandered off into the jumble of trees and vines nearby and located a tree unlike anything she'd ever seen. Her shout brought the others.

"Look, that looks like fruit growing right on the trunk," she said as soon as the first to reach her came within speaking distance.

"Ripper, that's a jaboticaba!" was the answer. Robert had arrived and had such a comical look on his face that Cyndi laughed at him.

"A jaba *what*?" she asked. By then, the others were ringed around the odd-looking tree, which had fist-sized globes of dark purple growing directly out of the trunk, some of which had burst and were dripping a dark juice onto their neighbors.

"Absa-bloody-lutely, that's a jaboticaba," Robert repeated, "but I've never seen one with such huge fruit." He reached for a fruit, tore it off and brought it to his mouth, stopping abruptly when Carmen yelled for him to.

"It could be poisonous," she explained with a sheepish look at his glance of consternation.

"But, I recognize it," he said. "They grow in Australia. And this part of Antarctica was once attached to Australia, so I'm thinking its fine to eat."

"They're native to Brazil, actually, if it's what you think. But how would it have gotten here? It was only introduced to Australia recently, certainly not before Western Antarctica broke away from Australia and crashed into the eastern part to form these mountains."

Summers spoke up, acting the part of a leader for the first time since his claustrophobia had made him ineffective as such. "If we're correct in our theories, they probably got here the same way they got to Australia. The 9th Cyclers brought them. But, Robert, how in the world can this place exist?"

Robert had been thinking about that since they first got here. There had to be a geothermal source, or more likely more than one, to create this jungle-like oasis in the midst of the bitter cold and ice of Antarctica. The rising heat filled the enclosed valley, canyon actually, and held the cold at bay. Looking up, he couldn't actually see any sign of sky, and it should be quite a bit darker. There was more to be discovered, clearly. But, for now, he was hungry and was determined to try the fruit that was there for the taking. Ignoring Carmen's protest, he bit into it, causing juice to run down his chin, and closed his eyes in delight.

"Dinkum, this is the real thing. Tastes just like at home," he announced. "Like grapes." With few exceptions, Carmen being one of them, the others reached for their own fruits. Robert teased Carmen, "Not hungry?"

"I'll wait a few hours to see whether you survive," she said with heavy irony.

"Speaking of hours," Summers said, "my watch seems to be acting up. Does anyone know how long we've been in here? If we expect to get home this season, we need to find a way out and back to base."

This pronouncement sobered the others immediately. Everyone looked at their timepieces, and it was quickly discovered that everyone was showing a different time of day, those whose watch showed the date also mismatched. Robert frowned. "There must be a strong geomagnetic source here, too. I'd like to find at least the geothermal wells, if not the magnetic source, before we leave."

"I understand. But if my perception is correct, we've been in here for more than two days already. If we don't get out soon, Roosky and Bart might give us up for dead and leave with the Sno-Cat. Then we'd be stranded here for who knows how long."

JR almost spoke his mind about Roosky's role in the cave-in, but thought better of it. Better not to speculate. It was highly likely that the Sno-Cat was already gone, along with Roosky and Bart if he was still alive. There'd be no reason to hang around if indeed Roosky was responsible for the disaster. But saying so would dishearten the others. How would they get back to the base without transportation? They damn sure couldn't walk it—that would be suicide. He suspected they'd be wintering in the valley.

Robert opened his mouth to argue his point, but JR backed Summers up. "Look, we can keep our eyes open for something like that, but the first thing we need is a way out. We should split up again and work our way around the canyon walls, three go that way and four the other way."

"Then how would we communicate with the other team if we found something?" Robert objected.

"Hey!" said Angela. "Look around. Does this all look to you like it's laid out on purpose? Like, could this straight opening through the trees be a street?"

The others stopped arguing to look, and then JR picked a tree that didn't have fruit growing inconveniently on the trunk and climbed as high as he could to get a look.

"She's right," he called down. "The gaps through the vegetation are too straight. Either we've got four-legged company of some kind, or we're standing in a place where people organized the layout."

"But, where are the structures?" Summers mused.

"We're talking, what, at least thirty-five thousand years since anyone saw them? Would they have survived?" JR asked, descending from the tree carefully.

"What about those pictures on the internet...didn't some people find a video with some crazy architecture on it?" Angela asked.

"Hoax," said Carmen.

"I don't think so," said Summers. "However, we've only seen a fraction of what's here so far. The structures could be covered in these vines. The fact remains that we don't have time to explore, and we don't have time to stand here arguing about it. We have to find another way out or go back and dig out the rock fall." He shuddered, remembering the squeeze and the feeling of doom as he'd been pulled through the short coffin-like tunnel. There are seven of us, which means two teams of two and one of three. I don't think anyone should be on their own."

"Agreed," said Rebecca. "I'll go with JR and Cyndi. That leaves one man and one woman each for the other two teams, all right?" Despite their predicament, and despite the strangeness of the valley in which they stood, JR's heart did a little stutter as he realized Rebecca had volunteered to go with him, not Summers, not Robert—him. If it came to a vote, he'd cast his in favor of that. Bringing his attention back to the planning with a shake of his head, JR assumed the leadership role again, with no protest from anyone else.

The plan that JR proposed was that Robert and Angela would cut through the center of the valley as closely as they could, while the other two teams would start at the rift where everyone had emerged and travel in opposite directions. That way, if the geothermal wells were nearer the center, Robert had a fighting chance of discovering them and Angela would be able to draft a rough map as well. If the wells were near the perimeter, the other two teams would spot them. It satisfied Robert while wasting no more time. The thought of traveling to the Pole in winter conditions, especially if they had to go on foot and without shelter, was daunting to those who didn't realize the impossibility of it. Not much less daunting was the thought of wintering over at the Pole.

They tried to synchronize their watches, but within

seconds they were all showing a different time again, so they agreed to walk until they were tired or met up, having no idea how far around the valley was. All they could tell was that the opposite canyon wall seemed very far in the distance. After the experiment with the jaboticaba tree, everyone but Carmen was willing to eat any fruit that looked familiar, so they would gather that as they found it. Carmen got the remaining food supply they'd brought with them, both meager and unappetizing, while everyone else was looking forward to some fresh fruit.

Before they set out, JR gave them strict instructions to fill their water containers with water from the pool that Carmen had tested. They were not to drink any other water from the ground under any circumstances, instead they were to quench their thirst with the fruit, or in a pinch, see if they could gather condensation from the leaves of the trees. Since they weren't sure how long their treks would be, he recommended that they conserve their water as much as possible. Carmen's group of course would have her with them to test water, so extra water containers were passed to the other groups.

He also instructed them to stay together, follow the protocols that Robert had set forth if they came to any cave openings, and above all, keep eyes and ears open.

"We don't know what lives here. Just because we didn't hear anything before, doesn't mean there isn't a giant lizard or something a few miles away that would think you're a tasty morsel." JR was still thinking about those dinosaurs. "Don't approach any animal, reptile, insect or bird. If you get stuck or run into trouble, try to come back here."

Without further discussion, they set off at a good pace, neither too fast nor too slow, everyone cognizant of the price of finding the way out too late in the year. While none had yet raised the possibility, several realized that if the winter storms were raging when they found the way out, it would probably be a better idea to stay where they were than try to get to the Pole. The only downside would be that their loved ones would think them dead if they were missing that long. With no way to tell that they'd already been missing for what Roosky had reported as several days, it didn't occur to them that they were already feared dead.

JR had Cyndi set the pace, because she was the shortest. At six-foot-ten, he had even run the legs off his Marine squadron if he set the pace, so he knew how to handle it. Rebecca was taller than Cyndi, but nowhere near as tall as he, so she would be able to keep up with Cyndi all right, and if he wanted, he could run rings around them. He used that to his advantage by stopping now and again to climb a tall tree and see what he could see, or to pick a fruit that looked familiar.

From his vantage point atop a particularly tall tree, he reckoned that the opposite canyon wall was about five miles away. That meant Robert and Angela had maybe six or seven miles to hike, allowing for the necessity of detours if the path they took didn't go straight through. Assuming the canyon was roughly circular, he and his team had almost ten. He hoped Robert and Angela wouldn't get impatient waiting for them. Cyndi was about five-six. Her legs weren't going to get them around their half any time soon. They were making maybe two miles per hour, fighting through rubble from the canyon wall and dense jungle.

At first, Rebecca and Cyndi chatted, but they soon ran out of topics as they had little in common. Rebecca fell into reflection about JR's dual personality. When he had a task to do that required him to be serious and competent, he was, and she could admire him for it. But then he would pull a stunt like that drunken binge with Roosky and lose her respect again. Right now, he was being the man she could love. With a start, Rebecca looked around. She hadn't said that out loud, had she? Where in the world did it come from? Sternly, she told herself to get a grip.

Cyndi, however, was thinking about something Rebecca had brought up when they were talking. Fascinated by the simplicity of the electronics that made up the drone they'd been using, she wondered how many more devices from the 10th Cycle would prove useful in the present day. Furthermore, she wondered whether the science could be expanded into fields like medicine, and whether she could get a Rossler Foundation grant to pursue it. To occupy her mind, she began to compose the grant request mentally as they walked. It was fortunate that her team had two others on it, because she was all but blind to the passing scenery.

JR was attempting to think of all the possible outcomes of this exercise. It was possible they would find other passageways out, but he had a hunch they would all lead back to the cave system, and he doubted that surrounded them all the way around within the canyon walls. If they did find their way back to a cave system, how would they know it was *their* cave system? They could wander for days without finding another exit to the canyon where they'd entered, and if they came out somewhere else, how would they know which direction to go to get to the base? Did they have the resources to get back to base on foot with winter storms coming on or already raging? He doubted it. It was more likely that their real problems would only begin if and when they found a way out of the cave system.

None of JR's musings gave him much comfort. The only thing that made much sense to him was that they figure out some kind of shelter here in this hidden and temperate valley until the next austral summer. But that begged the question, how would they know when that was? They might have to wait for rescue, but would rescuers come if they were thought dead?

Around and around, his thoughts chased each other until he found himself asking the same questions. Finally, he tore his thoughts from them, resolved to cross each bridge as he came to it, and firmly told himself to think of something else. His eyes alighting on Rebecca's shapely backside, he began to wonder if he'd ever have a chance with her. The chief question was whether he could ever be good enough for her, but another was how could he attract her positive attention?

She was one of Sarah's best friends, and reminded him so much of Sarah that it was as if Sarah were with them. Not only in looks, but in temperament, too. JR grinned. That meant he'd better get his act together, because he'd been on the receiving end of several of Sarah's scoldings about his irresponsibility, and he was pretty certain Rebecca would feel the same way. It delighted him, then, when she dropped back from her position beside Cyndi to tease him.

"JR, I've learned something new about psychology today," she said with a grin.

"Oh? What's that?"

"Why, that singing opera cures claustrophobia, of course." All three of them had a laugh, unfortunately at Charles Summers' expense, but they would never tell of his failing. Confessing it was up to him, and if he never did, well, they'd cross that bridge when they came to it.

In contrast, Robert and Angela were highly alert as they made their way through the center of the valley. They were looking for any sign of man-made structures, as well as the geothermal sources. The path they started out on came to an abrupt end at a broad expanse of green grass, backed by closely-planted tall deciduous trees in full leaf. At least, they assumed the trees were deciduous. They didn't look like any evergreens that either of them had seen before, and that covered a lot since Angela was North American and Robert Australian. Angela quickly sketched in the natural barrier, with the caption 'Park?' as they turned right to seek a way around. Thick mist wove its way through the trunks of the trees and rose when it reached the relatively open area where they stood.

What felt to Robert like about a mile later, their path intersected with another and they turned left to resume their cross-valley journey.

"Angela, does it seem like it's been daylight for a really long time?" Robert asked.

"Yeah, now that you mention it, it does. And what's weird is, there are no really long shadows. It's almost twilight most of the time outside of here. What's making this light?"

"I'd like to find that out myself, but I've looked up and all I can see is mist high above our heads. Can't even see the tops of the canyon walls. I'm thinking the external conditions meeting the rising heat from inside here is what's causing that. But, I can't see a light source, and you'd think we could. It's got to be coming from directly in the center of the valley to not cast shadows."

Angela looked up, stopping so she wouldn't run into something as she searched the ceiling, for that's what the mist seemed to be, for a source of the ambient light. The mist was as evenly lit as the rest of the valley.

"It's kind of creepy," she admitted.

"No more so than the Pole at midsummer, right?" Robert asked.

"It isn't like a sun. More like a huge room lit by fluorescent light. It's more white than yellow. Does that make any sense?"

"Well, it makes me want to climb these canyon walls and find out if there's actually a ceiling up there, with a bunch of tubes. Man, that would be something, wouldn't it? A fluorescent tube that lasts over thirty thousand years?"

Angela laughed at his whimsy. There had to be a different explanation, but now they'd noticed the quality of the light, they couldn't get it out of their minds that they were in an observation gallery of some kind, perhaps even now entertaining the indescribable beings that watched them. It made them look up and cringe now and then, though the notion was silly.

After another couple of miles, they came to another intersection, and decided to turn left again. If they found yet another after a mile, they'd be back on their original course by turning right. Angela wished there were time to follow each path to its conclusion, to get an accurate map of the interior, but of course there'd be time later, when the current crisis had been resolved.

Summers was much happier to be out of the cave and almost back to his normal self. Unlike Robert and JR, he took the point position and expected Carmen to keep up with him, which she did without complaint. With Summers leading and no one else to see, she had time to think and no need to guard her expression. Carmen had suspected that Roosky was OS, and she found the timing of the avalanche to be highly suspicious. What she intended to do about it remained to be seen, but if she ever had occasion to encounter him again, she'd have something harsh to say to him, at the very least.

The good news was that he wouldn't have been acting alone. Even now, it was probable that other OS operatives were on the way to their location. That would give her an opportunity to escape this enclosed valley, but she'd be back. The wealth of slightly different botanical forms hinted at an equal wealth of microbiological specimens that would bear further study and assure her a place in the history of the science for years to come. What she wouldn't give for her specimen collection kit right now!

Summers was humming tunelessly ahead. He seemed to have recovered completely from his bout of claustrophobia. However, they had traded the confined area of the cave for another enclosed area, though admittedly a much larger one. What he would do if they did find an aperture leading back into the mountain and perhaps outside was a question for which she wasn't anxious to have the answer. It would be bad enough trying to make their way through another maze like the one that had led them in, without having a quivering wreck of a claustrophobic as her only help. Carmen decided at that thought that if they did find a passage into the canyon wall, she would leave Summers behind if possible, and explore only far enough to determine whether it was worth going further before meeting the others.

Lost in thought, Carmen almost ran into Summers when he stopped abruptly. He'd started shaking, so she looked fearfully at what he had his eyes fixed on. It was an opening in the canyon wall…a possible way out, but clearly another cave. Now she knew what he'd do…he'd fall apart again. She was glad she'd figured out a Plan B.

Carmen put her hand on Summers' arm to calm him. "Charles, there's no need for you to go in there. I'll go in and see if it goes anywhere. You wait here. If it looks promising, we can go on to meet the others as planned, and then come back here."

Summers was ashamed of his weakness, but he couldn't face another cave. He hung his head. "You'll come right back out if it branches too much, or gets tight, yes? I don't want you to get lost or get stuck."

"I will. Just sit here and wait. Give me the rope, and I'll be out in less than an hour, okay? But, please don't go anywhere. I don't know what I'd do if we became separated."

That little hint that she still relied on him for something restored Summers' self-esteem to some extent, and he straightened. "Of course. I'll be right here when you come out." Looking around, he found a vine-covered protuberance about bench-high and sat down. "Right here. But, hurry!"

Carmen smiled at Summers and ducked into the cleft they'd found, delighted to learn that it opened out within only a few feet into a large room, larger than the main room of the first cave. She wondered if the two caves met up somewhere, as they hadn't traveled all that far before finding this opening. Her flashlight was growing dim, and she had only one spare set of batteries left, so she was trying to wait to change them. Something caught her eye, a movement perhaps, and she went on full alert, cursing herself for waiting on the batteries. She was peering into the gloom where she'd seen whatever it was when a person appeared, dressed in white snow gear and carrying a Kalashnikov automatic rifle, which was pointed directly at her. She raised her arms.

Chapter Twenty-Five

A RIFT IN THE WALL

A little over six hours after they parted ways, JR and the women with him rounded a large boulder to find Robert waiting on the other side. Rebecca's eyes widened to see him alone, but before she could ask, JR barked.

"Where's Ange? Why did you separate?"

"Don't get your knickers in a knot, mate. She needed a bit of privacy. She's only over there a few yards." He waved into a dense tangle of vines that were laden with something that looked like blackberries.

JR relaxed, and muttered, "Sorry."

"No worries. Did you find anything?"

"Nothing. Ran into a couple of places where the canyon walls jutted out into the valley so we had to go around them. You?"

"Nothing definite. There's a large square more or less in the center that we had to circumnavigate, but we didn't see any sign of the geothermal outlets, nor a magnetic source. I'd like to go back and explore within that square. It's about eight miles around, assuming the other side was regular, like the side we took. The trees along the perimeter were so dense that there could have been a regular power plant in there, for all we know."

"All in good time. If I'm not mistaken, we've been gone from the camp for at least a full day. We've got to get out of here."

"Agreed. It will still be here next year, I'm sure. Say, have you noticed that the light in here is weird?"

"Yeah, it's too bright for the time of year. And it hasn't varied since we've been here. It's almost artificial, isn't it? One more thing to find an explanation for when we come back."

"Can't wait for that, mate! I haven't even had time to pick up any samples of the rocks 'round here."

"Do you have a theory about them?"

"Bloody oath, it's igneous. If I had to guess, I'd say we're in the crater of a dormant volcano. That's what's keeping it warm, the geothermal source under us. But damned if I know what the light is."

Angela emerged from the vines at that point and greeted the others, giving each a hug as if she hadn't seen them just six hours before. "What now?" she asked.

Instinctively, everyone looked to JR, a fact that Rebecca didn't miss. What was it about him? No matter what kind of screw-ups he'd pulled earlier in the expedition, he was clearly their leader now. Even his bearing showed it. Instead of the lazy slouch that he affected at home, he was standing tall and confident, looking into the distance where Summers and Carmen should be.

"They shouldn't have been as slow as we were," he said, looking apologetically at Cyndi, who nodded. "They must have found something. Let's all go to meet them. It'll save time, no use making them come all the way to us."

As one, they turned and fell into walking pairs, with JR in the lead. Angela and Cyndi wanted to catch up on the sights they'd seen, and Robert was happy to be walking beside Rebecca. Rebecca, however, had her eyes on the retreating form of JR, who, forgetting his stride would soon leave the rest behind, was pulling away from the pack. "JR, wait up!" she called. He didn't turn, but he did slow down so they could keep up. He felt a sense of responsibility to get these people out and to the base in time to get them home, but time was running out.

As he went, JR's eyes roamed constantly. He'd seen no animals here, nor spoor nor tracks, large or small. He hadn't even seen any birds. If they couldn't get back to base, the best thing would be to stay in this valley where there was fresh water and fruit at least. Could human beings survive on nothing but fruit for six months? He'd have to ask Rebecca. The other question, though, was whether they could stand each other's' company for that long.

It hadn't escaped his notice that there was sexual tension within the group, or that the nominal leader, Summers, was not one of the favored males. With four women and only three men, it was likely to get dicey, especially if all the men, or at least the two younger men, wanted the same woman. He liked Robert all right, but if the man made a move on Rebecca, there'd be a price to pay.

Abruptly, he stopped. Ahead was a rift in the canyon wall, but there was no sign of Summers or Carmen. As the others caught up, he pointed ahead. They would have to explore the rift, in case Carmen and Summers either hadn't gotten here yet or were somewhere inside it. JR cataloged his options. He could go in with one of the women, send Robert in with one of the women, or leave all of the women on guard outside here and go in with Robert. He'd seen no sign of anything dangerous in the several hours they'd been in the valley, so he preferred the third option.

"You girls stay outside here, in case Summers and Carmen are still on their way. Robert and I will reconnoiter and come back out to get you one way or another. Can any of you accurately estimate when an hour has passed?" Rebecca raised her hand.

"Okay, if we're not out in an hour, two of you keep going to find Summers and Carmen, and the other stay here. Agreed?"

Nods all around assured him he was understood, and without another word he plunged into the rift with Robert on his heels. Immediately, he sensed there was something different about this one. It was tall and narrow, and he could still see the strange, white-mist-filled sky after traveling several yards. He stopped and turned to consult with Robert. "This doesn't seem to be a cave. Is it possible it goes all the way through to the outside?"

"We'll know in a little while, I reckon. If it doesn't peter out and it gets colder, I'd say there's a chance." JR grinned and gave Robert a fist-bump.

"Let's hope."

Robert wasn't as sanguine. By the rough map in his head, even if they came out of the valley and back onto the ice by this route, they were at least four or five miles from where they'd gone in, with the mountain between them and the canyon where the Sno-Cat hopefully waited for them. If the winds were high, they wouldn't survive that trek. When the rift reached a point where they were blocked from forward progress without a technical climb they weren't equipped for, he didn't know whether to be glad or sorry.

JR was definitely dejected. Robert put his hand on JR's shoulder and said, "Sorry, mate."

"No worries," JR grinned. "I'm certain Summers and Carmen have found something, otherwise we'd have met up with them by now. Let's get out of here." He took point again as they retraced their steps, arriving well before the hour was up.

Chapter Twenty-Six

A VISIT FROM THE OS

"Septentrio," Carmen blurted.

The person carrying the rifle lowered it, slowly and gave the countersign. "North"

Carmen breathed a sigh of relief and lowered her arms.

"*Ich bin froh, Sie zu sehen,*" she said.

"English, please. We don't all speak German."

"I'm glad to see you."

As she absorbed this, five more figures appeared. They could have been clones, they were all so alike. Well over six feet tall, clearly well-built even though the bulky snow gear obscured their bodies. Identical weapons. The leader questioned her.

"What are you doing here? Where did you come from?"

With some asperity, she answered. "The same thing you're doing here, except that stupid Russian brought the mountain down on us and I was trapped with the others inside the cave. Please tell me he was buried in the avalanche."

A grim smile broke the serious countenance of the OS

team leader. "I'm afraid not. He reported there was a cave and left us a marker where the opening should be. He's enjoying the fruit of his labors in Moscow by now."

"Too bad, I would have enjoyed making him aware of my displeasure. Did he not know I was OS?"

"I don't know, I haven't spoken to him. But, quickly, where is the rest of your party? We have orders to terminate them and secure this cave system. What are we going to do about you?"

A wash of fear went through Carmen, before she steeled herself to negotiate. "Take me out with you. I'll change my appearance, become a new person. No one will ever know I was rescued; they'll think I was lost with the rest of them. I'll help you with the others. What's your name, anyway?"

"Pyotr. I think we can arrange that. Tell me who is in here with us, and how we should take them."

"First, you need to know they aren't 'in here'. A few feet from here is an opening into a hidden valley. You're not going to believe what you'll see there. But, to answer your question, the science director, Charles Summers is sitting right outside the opening. Elsewhere in the valley are Robert Cartwright, the geologist and Angela Brown, the cartographer. They're progressing from the opening that let us out here across the valley through the center. Robert says there's a geothermal source somewhere. The valley is warm, you have to see it for yourself."

"Others?"

"Yes, JR Rossler, Dr. Rebecca Mendenhall and Cyndi Self. Paul LeClerc was killed by a fall in the cave. JR and the women went the opposite direction from Summers and me. We're to meet by hugging the perimeter and report what we've found in the way of an exit. I guess this one leads to the outside?"

"We're in the same cave system where you and the expedition went in. We blasted the fallen rock clear of the entry you used."

"What? How? We only found one exit into the valley, and this wasn't it."

"There are three, and we did know about the valley, though we couldn't see into it with the satellite. Do you know why?"

"Not unless the heavy clouds above interfere with the optics. Do you mean to say that we can now get out the way we came in?"

"YOU can. The rest of your colleagues are going to meet with unfortunate accidents."

"Of course. By 'we', I meant you gentlemen and myself. How can I help?"

"Is any of your party armed?"

"Not that I know of."

Pyotr ran his eyes over Carmen's slender form in a familiar way, wondering where in the world she was concealing it. Shrugging, he said, "Go out and make some excuse to Summers to wait where he is, then proceed toward your meeting point. Lead the others back here. Meanwhile, we'll take care of Summers. When you get here, suggest a search party. We'll take care of the rest."

Carmen hesitated. "There's one I'd like to leave alive." Robert would owe her his life; surely he'd be grateful.

"Which one?" Pyotr asked.

"The geologist. You'll know which one he is. The other man in the party is freakishly tall. Don't shoot the shorter man, for now. I want him for myself." If Pyotr thought she meant to torture and kill, it would go better. He nodded.

"As you wish."

Carmen turned and retraced her steps out of the opening, finding Summers seated exactly where he said he'd be. Carmen pasted a big smile on her face and bounded out of the cave, calling to Summers excitedly.

"Charles, I've found it! It's a huge passageway, and it leads directly to the outside. Whoever cultivated this valley must have made an artificial opening."

Summers started up from his seat, an expression of surprise and relief on his face. "You went all the way to the end?"

"Yes, it's just a short way. I could see the Sno-Cat. Listen, let me run to get the others, while you go out and make sure Roosky and Bart don't leave without us. It's not a tight enclosure, I promise. More like a tunnel than a cave, and it's light all the way."

Summers opened his mouth to protest that it would be better if *he* went to get the others, while she once again traversed the tunnel and alerted Roosky and Bart that they were alive. However, Carmen was already sprinting away. He'd never catch her. Seeing her speed, he thought she'd had the correct idea after all. He stood for a moment, looking at the ground before him while gathering his courage to step inside the cleft.

Summers had just heaved a sigh of resignation and looked up. Instead of the mouth of the tunnel, what he saw at first stunned and confused him. Six large figures in military gear stood before him, and every one of them was pointing a gun at him. One of them gestured upwards with his rifle. Slowly, Summers raised his hands. Despite the mistakes he'd made on this mission, Summers wasn't a stupid man. Instantly, he realized that Carmen must have met up with these men, and the fact that she hadn't mentioned it implicated her in a betrayal. He had to find a way to signal the others that they were walking into a trap, but how?

As Summers' mind worked furiously, the leader of the soldiers, as Summers thought of them, walked toward him and shoved him roughly back onto his seat. He gestured for Summers to put his hands behind his back. Summers complied, thinking that perhaps they were being taken prisoner for some unknown infraction. Could this be a remnant of the 9th Cyclers, guarding a place that was sacred to them? Or, was it a more sinister group? In any case, there was nothing to be gained by resisting. If he played his cards right, perhaps he'd be able to somehow warn the others before it was too late. He sat quietly as his hands were secured behind him by a nylon zip tie.

Once he was secure, he ventured a question. "Who are you?"

His reward was not an answer, but a powerful backhanded blow to the side of his face and head. He reeled, blood beginning to trickle from a cut at the corner of his lip. *Okay, they don't want to tell me*, he thought, with a touch of irony. He watched as the leader deployed his men here and there behind cover from anyone approaching from their right as they faced him. If they wanted to kill the expedition party, their superior weapons meant they could simply open fire as the group came into view.

But, perhaps one or two could escape by running into the jungle, away from the gunfire. Then the soldiers would have to waste valuable time hunting them down. After all, they were constrained by the Antarctic winter weather conditions as much as anyone else. Summers continued to think and analyze the situation, though his head was pounding from the blow he'd received. He wouldn't make that mistake again.

Chapter Twenty-Seven

CHARLES INJURED

Robert happened to be in the lead when Carmen reached the group three hours later. She threw herself into his arms and sobbed. Alarmed, he took her by the arms and held her away from him so that he could see her face.

"What is it, love?" he asked. Carmen knew that the endearment was merely what he called any woman he happened to be talking to, but it still gave her a thrill to hear it directed at her.

"Charles...injured," she sobbed.

"What? Where?" he shouted, bringing the others at a run. JR appeared from within the jungle ahead of the rest and quickly strode back to the group.

"What's going on? Oh, hi Carmen, where's Charles?" he said, watching her closely.

"She says he's injured," Robert said of the sobbing woman. Rebecca came forward and put her hand on Carmen's shoulder.

"Carmen, sit down here," she said, indicating a fallen

log. "Take a deep breath. Now, please tell us what's happened. Are you all right?"

Carmen took a deep breath as instructed. Then she began to speak in a shaky voice. "We found a way out," she started.

Immediately, the others broke into shouts and relieved laughter, before she held up her hand. "Charles didn't want to go in, you know how he is. Anyway, I was in the lead, and I heard a sound behind me. He had walked into something and hit his head. Somehow, I got him out, and he was bleeding from a gash on his head. I didn't know what to do, or how far away you all were, so I made him sit down, put a bandage on his head and made him as comfortable as I could and then I ran to find you."

"You left a man with a head injury?" Rebecca asked, outraged.

"I didn't know what else to do. I didn't have anything else to help him. Please, you have to come quickly."

"How far?"

"I don't know. I've been running for a long time, but I don't have a good estimate of how long. The opening wasn't all that far from where we started." No one but JR noticed that Carmen's story didn't add up. There was no blood on her clothing from Summers' wound, and she hadn't even broken a sweat in this long run she described. Nevertheless, he'd have to go along with it until he knew more. She could be dangerous to the others if she knew he suspected her of an untruth. He hadn't forgotten that LeClerc had disappeared while with her, too.

Robert and JR had a quick consult to calculate, and decided that they'd come more than halfway from their meeting point to where they had separated at the beginning. That meant there could be as much as four miles to go to reach Summers. JR looked over at the others to be sure he wasn't overheard, then told Robert of his suspicions.

"Don't let Carmen out of your sight. Something's wrong here, and I'm beginning to suspect we brought half the damned OS with us." Though he was shocked, Robert agreed that there'd be no harm in being careful.

"I want to take Rebecca with me in case she can do something for Summers, though I suspect he may be dead already. You and the other women come more slowly. I want at least an hour between us."

Their plan formed, JR stepped over to Rebecca.

"Becca, I think you and I can move more quickly if we go on ahead. Carmen's exhausted, so we'll leave her with the others here while we go ahead to help Summers. Are you up for moving fast?"

Neither of them noticed that Carmen started to object, but stopped protesting when they took no notice of her. She wanted to lead them into the ambush, but maybe this was better. Breaking them up would ensure that no mistakes were made. The OS would get them all in the end, anyway.

Rebecca, who ran for fun, gave JR a sardonic look. "Race you."

JR grinned back at her. "You don't want to challenge me like that." Without another word, he broke into an awkward lope, knowing that if he ran full-out, he'd both leave her behind and run out of steam within a mile. Rebecca was beside him in seconds, her medical kit in its backpack slapping her back as she jogged.

"How long can you keep this up?" JR panted.

"Oh, ten miles or so," she answered.

Jeez, she'll do better than I will, he thought. It couldn't have been more than four or five miles to get to Summers. At their current speed, they'd reach him in an hour or less, but it was hard to talk. And he needed to talk to Rebecca before they got there. He slowed his pace a bit and she dropped back to match it.

"Becca, were you looking at Carmen's face when she told how Summers got injured?"

"No, she was turned away from me. Why?"

"Something's off. I think she was lying."

"Why would she do that?"

"Oh, I don't know. Because she's another one of *them*, maybe?"

"Who?"

"You know, like Misty. The OS," he answered, his mouth twisted with bitterness.

Rebecca stopped running, and after a couple of steps JR managed to stop, too. He turned to face her.

"What would make you think that?" she demanded.

"For one thing, she never met anyone's eyes when she was telling that story. Whenever she saw I was looking at her eyes, they'd slide away from me. There was no blood on her from Charles' wound, and where would she get a bandage? She wasn't sweating or even breathing hard from supposedly running all that way. The whole story was just, I don't know. Weird. Incomplete."

Rebecca was quick to understand. "You're right, that's weird. I didn't notice any of it, I was so worried about Charles. Do you think he's really injured, or…" Rebecca didn't finish her sentence, not sure what the alternative might be.

"I don't know, but I don't think we should run headlong the whole distance. In fact, I'm not sure how far that distance is. She could have been lying about that, too."

"Would she have lied about finding a way out? Why would she do that? What's she up to?" Rebecca's fearful questions burned JR to the heart. He took her hand.

"Becca, I'm going to level with you. You know Misty was a spy, and I'm almost certain she was OS. I think Roosky was, too. He brought that cave down on us deliberately. That was an explosion, not the rock giving way, I'd bet my last vital organ on it. I don't know what Carmen is up to, but it wouldn't surprise me if there was an ambush waiting for us, based on the way she didn't want us to go ahead without her. We need to go carefully, see what's up there, before we run straight into it. If Charles can be helped, it won't be until after we've taken care of that danger.

"But, don't worry, sweetheart, we'll get out, even if we have to go back into that cave and dig ourselves out. We need to be smart about this. I need to reconnoiter, and right now is as good a time as any. I want you to conceal yourself in the jungle while I climb that tall tree over there, so I can see what's up ahead. All right?"

Rebecca nodded, distracted that he'd called her sweetheart, and now that she thought of it, he'd been using her family nickname ever since they got to the valley. She slipped into the dense tangle of vines and trees. When he could no longer see her, JR whistled to let her know that she had gone far enough. Then he scaled the tree as he'd been doing periodically around the entire valley. He could only see about half a mile ahead, by his reckoning, but there didn't appear to be anything out of the ordinary there.

He whistled to Rebecca to come back out as he descended, and they resumed their jog, running for about ten minutes before he stopped again to repeat the lookout process. In this way, they continued for the next two miles or so. It was at the next repeat that JR found what he was looking for. Something was definitely wrong about the scene he beheld.

Chapter Twenty-Eight

TAKE THEM OUT ONE BY ONE

One hundred yards away, JR could see Summers sitting slumped with his hands behind his back. He quickly located Rebecca, hidden from the trail but visible to him from his vantage point. She was watching him. He put his forefinger to his mouth in a shushing gesture, and she instinctively ducked, then looked up at him again. He nodded, gave her a 'stay' gesture with his palm, and descended. He'd seen no one but Summers, but that didn't mean there wasn't anyone. He needed to get closer, but for this mission, he'd make his way through the jungle.

Ten yards further toward Summers, he climbed another tree, careful not to rustle any leaves. Unfortunately, it was one of the jaboticaba trees, which meant he was going to climb down covered in purple juice, but it couldn't be helped; this was the only tree of any height where he wanted to climb again. As he reached the highest branches, he wished for more cover. Below him, perhaps another ten yards away, was a figure dressed in black military gear and holding an automatic rifle. An AK-47, he thought. The man appeared to be asleep, which would probably result in his squad leader shooting him if JR didn't take him out first.

JR was trained in hand-to-hand combat, but he had to get down from the tree without waking the man, and without Becca calling out to him. He turned around and caught her eye again, repeating the shush and stay gestures. Then he began backing carefully down the tree, squashing more fruit as he went. An idea occurred to him and he deliberately squashed some with his hands, smearing the juice over his face. Not for camouflage at the moment, it wouldn't do that, but for the startle effect. If the man woke while he was approaching, an extra second or two while he processed what he was seeing could mean the difference between life and death for JR and his party.

JR crept back to where Rebecca was waiting, anxiety written on her face. He whispered, barely making a sound, that they had been right in their suspicions. There was an armed guard not far from their current position, but he didn't know yet how many in all. He'd have to determine the force they were up against before forming a plan. Fear gripped Rebecca, but her medical training to never show it helped keep her calm. Before JR could leave to carry out his mission, she put her arms around him.

"Please be careful, Josh, I want you back in one piece." JR's heart skipped a beat. She'd called him Josh, something only his mom and sometimes Sarah did any more. Her arms around him became his total world for a second, before he gave her a confidant smile and started to camouflage himself as best he could.

Moist earth from beneath a tangle of vines joined the purple juice on his face, making it almost black. Then he wove vines and leaves into his clothing and hair, until he was satisfied it was the best he could do. Even if they saw him coming, maybe they'd think he was some sort of swamp monster, instead of a lethal ex-Marine, bent on destruction. Rebecca smiled when he expressed the thought, and told him he would certainly scare most people out of their wits, a giant moving bush being a very scary thing. Hurriedly, he put his backpack down next to her and turned to go.

Within ten minutes, he'd located three of them out of the six or eight he reckoned were in the vicinity. One was the sleeping guard he'd seen at first. The others were arrayed in a pattern that appeared to expect their party coming in from the left as he faced the canyon wall. If he could take these out without any noise, the odds would be a lot better, and he'd be able to get closer to Summers and find out if he knew where the others were. JR checked his back trail often as he crept into position, a silent and deadly soldier again. It wouldn't do to have one of them sneak up on him while he was sneaking up on them.

He crept silently through the jungle until he was behind the sleeping sentry. Shaking his head, JR hoped that the others, if there were others, were as sloppy as this man. He moved forward stealthily. He wasn't quite within reach when the man woke with a start. JR froze. Had he made a noise? If the man turned, he'd have to lunge; he was in plain sight.

JR waited, his breath held. The man in front of him seemed to relax, though his head remained upright. He was awake now, and this would be harder. But, not too hard for a Marine. JR leapt forward, his right arm sweeping around to pull the man's arm off his rifle, his left circling the neck. As soon as he'd wrenched the man's arm from the rifle, his right hand covered the guy's mouth, and, with a quick jerk,

JR broke his neck. The slight sounds of the scuffle might have been heard; JR wasn't sure the next sentry wasn't within hearing distance. With as little noise as possible, he dragged the man several yards into the jungle and then went back to retrieve his rifle. One down, two to go and how many more?

JR made his way back to Becca, whose eyes widened when she saw the rifle.

"Where? What?"

"Shh," JR whispered. "I have to go back up the tree. Take this." Showing her how to use the rifle if she needed to, JR melted back into the jungle. He knew that two more of the black-clad figures were between his location and Summers, who appeared to be unconscious. He marked their locations in his mental map of the area and crept toward his objective again. Without knowing precisely how many he was up against, or where the others might be, the better part of valor would be to take these two out silently, one at a time, rather than to go in blazing with the Kalashnikov. He went back to the first man and searched his body for a knife, finding one slid down into the soldier's boot.

Once again, JR crept up behind one of the sentries, this time knowing that this time he didn't have the advantage of approaching a sleeping man. The total silence of the valley was a disadvantage; there were no bird calls, animal or industrial sounds to mask his approach. Thanking his lucky stars for his training, JR was within a couple of feet of his adversary before the latter heard him, turning and raising his rifle.

JR's hand whipped forward, his scavenged knife finding the man's neck before he could speak or shoot. He dropped the rifle and slapped his hand to his neck, but JR was on him. JR yanked the knife from the flesh where it was lodged and jabbed it upward between himself and the other man. *Stroke of luck*, he thought, as the man collapsed in his arms. The knife had found the cleft between the ribs, just under the breastbone, and had punctured his heart.

Two down, one to go, but there had to be others he hadn't seen. He suspected there was at least one more, probably three to five, because none of the three he'd seen struck him as leader types. Certainly not the two he'd killed with little trouble. He dragged the second one into the jungle and moved toward the third.

This time, he wasn't so lucky. Fortunately, this one had put down his rifle for some reason, so when he heard JR behind him, he whirled and came after him unarmed but with a muffled shout. JR's arm whipped up and caught the guy at the hollow of his collarbone with the point of the knife. A horrible gurgle accompanied the spurt of blood as the man's eyes widened before closing forever. Three down, how many to go? Noises from his right indicated someone was coming. There was no time to drag the man away; whoever was left would now know that they weren't alone. JR fled the scene, wiping the knife on his pants as he ran straight into the jungle. If they caught him, at least he wouldn't have led them to Rebecca.

When JR had gone far enough into the vines and scrub brush to convince himself he was covered, he stopped and stilled his hard-beating heart with the iron discipline of his Marine Corps training. Now that his own heartbeat wasn't deafening him, he listened for sounds of pursuit. Hearing none, he considered his position. Were they waiting for him to reveal himself? Had they found the other two dead sentries? For long moments, he waited. Then, he heard Rebecca's cry of distress. Starting upward from his hidden position, he strained to hear what was happening.

"Pyotr, we've found a woman!" The shout carried through the still air and stabbed JR in the heart. Now there were two hostages, both Summers and Rebecca. He should never have allowed her to come with him. His training and experience gave him the discipline to analyze the situation first, rather than running headlong to her rescue, but that discipline was sorely tested. Failure was not an option. No matter what else happened, he had to make sure Rebecca was unharmed.

Quivering with stress, JR thought about what he'd heard. 'Pyotr,' the man had called, so that meant there were at least two. But, he'd also said 'we'. So, at least three and perhaps more. And they now had Rebecca as well as the rifle he'd salvaged. Even if he still had that, he couldn't go in shooting, for fear of hitting her. More stealth was called for, but now the intruders had been alerted to their presence.

He had two choices; backtrack to meet and warn the others, then bring Robert back to help him, or take out the remaining intruders himself. Robert seemed like a capable guy, but JR wasn't sure he'd ever been in combat. Furthermore, they had the problem of Carmen and what to do with her if the only ones left to guard her were Angela and Cyndi. Better to do it himself, and he'd better hurry or the rest of the party would be walking into an ambush.

JR began creeping through the jungle at near-ground level, careful not to disturb the vegetation as he passed. His first task was to locate Summers and then try to see where they were holding Rebecca, who had stopped crying out as soon as the men who found her had called to their leader. JR could only hope she was alive. A grim thought occurred to him about their intentions with her. He crept faster.

A few minutes later, he saw legs pressed against a stone

bench-like object that was covered in vines. The legs weren't moving. Was it a sentry? Or was it Summers? He thought he recalled that Summers was seated on something like it, but the angle was different. He risked raising his head, wreathed in brush, to check it out. Yes! Summers. But, he seemed to still be unconscious. Was he sleeping, or was it his injury that knocked him out? JR could see a trickle of dried blood at the corner of his mouth, and a contusion on the side of his face that looked like he'd taken a severe blow. Summers' hands were cuffed behind him. He'd be no use in a fight, but if he woke up and cried out, he could jeopardize JR's plan. JR crept as close as he could and whispered.

"Psst. Summers." The man stirred, giving JR hope that he was merely sleeping. "Summers, its JR, don't say anything."

To his relief, Summers opened his eyes slowly and made a show of stretching. He turned his head to the right, whispering softly.

"JR, I think the OS is here. They're going to kill us all."

"Not if I can help it," JR whispered back. "How many?"

"I saw six. But they knocked me out as soon as they were out. Don't know if others were behind them."

"Where'd they come from?"

"See that cleft in the rock? Carmen said it leads outside. They must have come from there."

At that moment, a black-clad figure appeared from the left and strode toward Summers. JR shrank back into the vines and stilled. He could only hope that Summers was smart enough not to give him away.

"Who are you talking to?" demanded Pyotr. Summers put on a face of surprise.

"Myself! Who do you think?" he asked sarcastically.

Pyotr reacted to Summers' tone by backhanding him again. He slumped, seemingly unconscious. Pyotr scanned the jungle, seeing nothing. A yard into the tangled vines, JR kept his head down, waiting for a shot in the back. Then the footfalls retreated and he risked looking up.

"Summers, are you okay?"

"Yeah, but let's not do that again," Summers whispered. His lip was bleeding again, and now a trickle from his nose joined it.

"Okay, hang tight. I'm going to take them one at a time."

JR didn't bother telling Summers that the OS operatives had taken Rebecca. It would only distress him, and he might reveal it if he knew it, which would again compromise JR's mission. He melted back into the jungle and resumed creeping around the perimeter, this time to the left since that's the way the leader had come. If he could take out the leader first, the troops would fold if they were like most. If they were specially trained, it could be harder, but he was now in full combat mode, a honed and focused weapon of mass destruction in his own right.

JR crawled back into the jungle and thought for a while. He needed to get higher again, try to figure out where the leader was, where they were holding Rebecca, and where the others were deployed. The trouble was, they had to know he was out there somewhere. Even if Rebecca didn't talk, and he was sure she wouldn't, they'd have found the dead men by now. If he climbed, they could spot him before he had a chance to get into the cover of the treetops where there were leaves to hide him. And if he were caught, the rest of the party would be walking into a trap.

He needed more eyes up above, or he needed bait. Carmen. If he could send her in, the OS operatives might reveal themselves, but would she betray him? The answer was almost certainly. But, maybe he could lure the leader out if she appeared to have been compromised and in danger. It was worth a try.

The rest of the party was probably no more than an hour behind, if that far, by now. He'd go back and let the others know what was ahead, then interrogate Carmen more thoroughly. After which, he'd have to do something rather unpleasant. He hoped the others would go along. He started back, keeping to the shadows in the vegetation instead of walking confidently along the path, in case he ran into the other OS soldiers.

As he walked, he scanned the path, for the first time realizing the significance of a clear pathway all around the perimeter of the canyon. Who was maintaining it? Why hadn't the vegetation overtaken it, like it had everything else in the valley? It was something to ask, when the current crisis was over. They needed to bring a botanist next time. He didn't register the fact that he'd thought 'next time' as if it were a foregone conclusion that he'd be back. Later, he'd remember.

Half an hour later, JR heard the rest of the group coming and quickly concealed himself. When he was sure it was them, he waited until Carmen was parallel with him, to keep her from screaming and perhaps alerting her co-conspirators. He stepped out of the jungle practically right in front of Carmen, who gave a startled gasp, prompting him to seize her and put his hand over her mouth before she could scream.

"JR, you startled me! What's all over your face?" Cyndi asked from behind him. Robert, just half a step behind her, came up and stuck out his hand, which JR grasped.

"Hi, buddy," JR said to Robert, still holding his right hand. "Your girlfriend here is an OS spy. Help me secure her, we've got a problem."

Robert's look of surprise accompanied a moment of indecision while he processed what JR had said. In that interval, Carmen, who was trained to be quicker on the uptake, whirled and broke JR's grip on her, starting toward the jungle, but JR was right behind her. He grabbed her around the waist and lifted her, struggling, into the air, turning and depositing her in front of Robert. By this time, Robert had figured it out, and he clasped her in his arms to quell her struggles. Together, they pinned her to the rock wall of the canyon, and JR snarled.

"How many are there?" Carmen stared defiantly at him and pressed her lips together. Cyndi and Angela had watched the events of the past two minutes with wide eyes, but Angela put it together first.

"JR, is Charles okay?" she asked fearfully.

"Yeah. He's been hit a couple of times, but he's basically okay. They took Rebecca, though, and I couldn't find where they were holding her. I need this bitch to lure them out one at a time."

Carmen pulled her lips back from her teeth. "Never."

"Oh, I think you'll cooperate. Robert, girls, this isn't going to be pleasant. I'd like you to remain here."

Robert, though he was cooperating by holding Carmen, objected. "What are you going to do to her?" he asked.

"Whatever I have to. Don't worry, she's not going to risk getting hurt for those guys, are you, Carmen?" he said, giving her a significant look. Her eyes widened as he removed the knife from his boot.

Angela and Cyndi started to protest, but JR cut them off. "Ladies, it's them or us. If she cooperates, she won't get hurt, I promise."

JR sacrificed a short length of one of the climbing ropes, which he cut to use as a restraint. He wrapped it around Carmen's wrists behind her until he was satisfied that it would hold. Angela, catching the intent, offered her bandanna as a gag. JR then took Carmen by the arm and thrust her forward down the path, back in the direction of the cleft and the danger. They walked for about twenty minutes, and then he stopped and pulled her into the jungle. Taking out the knife, he pressed the tip to her jugular vein.

"I want you to call out, "Pyotr, help." Nothing else. Anything else and this point goes in, got it?"

"Yes," she said.

"Do it now."

"Pyotr! Help!" she cried. JR snaked his arm around her head and covered her mouth with his free hand. He listened carefully. After several moments, there was nothing to indicate someone was on the way. JR shoved Carmen forward for another five minutes and then repeated the process. This time, a shout came in return.

"Carmen? Are you alone?"

"Tell him yes," JR snarled. "Say you're injured, and you can't crawl any further. Nothing else."

"Yes, but I'm injured, I can't make it any further," she called.

"Wait there, then. I'll send my men. Can you walk with someone supporting you?"

"Tell him yes," JR said again.

"Yes, I think so," she answered, risking a cut to her throat as she added unauthorized words. JR pulled back the knife with only a surface nick, which nevertheless left a drop of blood where he'd almost stabbed her.

"Good girl," he told her, before gagging her again with the bandanna. "Stay quiet and you live. Betray me and you die right after Pyotr."

Carmen's eyes flashed hatred at him, but she remained quiet while he shoved her to the edge of the path and arranged her lying down with her head away from the direction the OS would be coming. Pyotr was cautious, so it wouldn't be him, it would be one or both of the other two. He could handle two if he had to, but only with the element of surprise; no doubt they'd have their rifles at the ready. He crept some yards further along the path and back into the jungle, waiting for the men to arrive. In only a minute, they came into view, walking cautiously and sweeping their rifles back and forth. JR let them pass. He waited until he heard a cry from one of them, "There she is!"

As the two broke into a jog toward Carmen, dropping their guard as they went, JR leapt at them, arms wide, bowling them over with his weight and superior height. He jumped up immediately, drawing his knife and slashing the throat of one, before the other had recovered and was on him. Now it was a fight for control of the knife. JR was aware that his height was more of a disadvantage than an advantage when it came to a ground fight, especially if he were on the bottom as he was now. He struggled to maintain his grasp on the knife while attempting to get leverage to reverse his position so he could get up. A sharp pain along his arm alerted him that the other man had turned his knife hand back on his own arm and made a cut.

Suddenly, he felt a vicious kick at his hip. Carmen had

managed to stand up and was trying to help his assailant by kicking at him wherever she could find an opening. Within moments, his ribs, legs and backside were bruised and throbbing, and the distraction was keeping him from gaining any advantage in the main fight. With a shout of anger, he rolled toward the leg that was supporting Carmen and bit her, as hard as he could, just above her booted ankle. She screamed and went down, allowing JR to focus on the man who was slowly getting the better of him. Then an opening presented itself. The guy's face was close to his. JR head-butted him, stunning both of them for a moment.

JR was the first to recover, having steeled himself for the blow. The man's grip had loosened, just a bit, and JR pressed the advantage, flipping the guy over and pressing down on him. Now JR was on top, and the man was gasping for breath as JR bore down with all his might, pushing himself up from the legs to press into the other's chest. Gradually, the assailant's grip on the knife loosened until JR could wrench it out of his hand. He delivered the coup de grace quickly, slashing through this man's jugular as he'd done the other. A gout of blood spurted into his face, mixing with the forgotten purple juice.

He got up, breathing heavily, and turned on Carmen, who was still writhing on the ground, bleeding where he'd bitten her. With a sound of disgust, he suppressed the urge to kick her as well, and instead yanked her to her feet, howling through the gag. If Summers had counted correctly, there was just one man left. And he should be running toward Carmen's shouts, unless he was clever enough to know that JR would gladly trade the traitorous Carmen for Rebecca. In that case, he'd be marching down the path with Rebecca walking in front of him for protection.

JR yanked the gag from Carmen's mouth and used the dry ends to wipe his face. He couldn't know, but the resulting smears were more frightening than ever. He looked like a savage, a cannibal maybe, and his freakish height made the impression even worse. Tired though he was, he knew he'd better be prepared for whatever Pyotr might be bringing for battle. He shoved Carmen to the side of the path and found a tree to tie her to. Then he took both of the dead OS operatives' rifles and took up a position behind Carmen from the direction that Pyotr would come. Propping the rifles on convenient bushes for quick access, he settled into a waiting stance, drawing on his training to calm his adrenalin-fueled anxiety and take a moment's rest.

A few minutes later, JR rejoiced in Rebecca's cleverness as he heard stumbling on the path, along with a man's voice cursing at her to be quiet. He took up a rifle and pointed it in the direction of the voice. Rebecca came into view first, and gave a small cry as she saw Carmen tied to the tree. Immediately behind her, Pyotr stepped out and raised a side-arm. Without warning, he shot Carmen in the chest, nicking her heart. Rebecca screamed and threw herself to the ground in front of him, giving JR a clean shot. He took it.

With Pyotr fallen, Rebecca raced to Carmen's side, but she could see there was nothing to be done for her.

"Why did he shoot you?" she asked the dying woman.

"... chance at JR," Carmen whispered. "Tell Robert... cave is the same. Open now," she gasped with her last breath.

"Carmen!" Rebecca screamed. Then she wept. JR knelt beside her and pulled her into his arms.

"Becca, she was a spy. She was going to lead us to

slaughter. I'm sorry, but we need to get the others and collect Summers so we can get out of here."

Rebecca nodded, shaking, and pressed into JR. "I'm cold," she said.

"You're in shock," he replied. Sitting down beside Carmen's lifeless body, he leaned against the tree and pulled Rebecca into his chest, turning her head in the other direction and wrapping his arms around her. The others would be along soon. Meanwhile, he'd keep Rebecca warm.

Chapter Twenty-Nine

THE WAY OUT

JR had fallen into a stupor, staring at nothing except the scenes of bloody battle, with Rebecca wrapped in his arms, his only comfort. He came to attention at Robert's shout.

"What the hell?"

Rebecca stirred, too, and then sat up with a gasp. "JR, tell me it isn't…" She spotted Carmen at that moment and bit back what she intended to say, clapping her hand over her mouth. Robert had run to Carmen's lifeless body and noted the rope tying her to the tree. He turned on JR.

"If you did this…" he growled, tears beginning to form in his eyes. He was interrupted by Angela and Cyndi's arrival, accompanied by their own cries of distress. JR spread his hands, but Rebecca interjected her defense.

"He didn't kill her, the OS did." She pointed back along the trail where Pyotr's lifeless body lay. "JR saved me by shooting that guy." She looked over at JR with gratitude and a question in her eyes.

"I guess it all got to us," he said, frowning slightly as he tried to think how long they'd been out. Rebecca watched his face as he visibly gained control of his emotions.

"We should get to Summers. He's only slightly injured, unless they did something else to him while we were getting back here. I think the OS are all dead. Just before she died, Carmen said the entrance they found leads to the same cave. And I think she said it's open now."

"We should go for it," Robert said. "I don't know how long we've been in here, but it's got to be getting close to our deadline."

"What if our Sno-Cat's gone? Or Bart and Roosky are dead?" Angela asked. "How would we get back to the base?"

JR saw no point in repeating his suspicions. "Those guys got here somehow. Let's just get out and see what's what. Worst case scenario, we come back in here and make the best of it for six months."

JR's suggestion startled the others, but Becca immediately saw that it was the practical way to think. They would have clean water to drink and wash in, plenty of fruit to live on. Better to be trapped in paradise than risk a winter crossing near the Pole without equipment. But, maybe the Sno-Cat was there. They wouldn't know until they went to see.

JR and Robert sent the three women to see to Summers, while they took care of the bodies as best they could. With nothing to dig with, they couldn't bury them. After giving Robert a moment to collect himself after he lost his cookies, they settled for dragging them into the jungle and stacking them all together near the new exit from the canyon. They'd deal with them when they came back, if the jungle hadn't already done so. After all, it was quite warm in here.

After their grisly task, they rejoined the girls. Rebecca had treated Summers' cuts and released him from the zip tie with a snip of the surgical scissors in her kit. They were all eating fruit with the last of their trail food when the men got there. It was only then that Rebecca noticed JR's injuries under his camouflage and insisted on cleaning him up.

A lively discussion of their next move ensued, with Summers reluctant to enter the cave again, especially not knowing whether Carmen had lied about it being open, or this one being connected to the cave where they came in. Rebecca argued that they should all stay together, and the other girls were undecided, though Cyndi said she'd go along with whatever Robert wanted, while Angela was vociferously loyal to Summers as the leader, taking sides with the underdog because that was her nature.

Robert and JR made it a majority by saying they had to try for an exit. Faced with the other four squarely against them, Summers and Angela reluctantly rose to follow them into the cave, Angela's arm firmly around Summers' waist for moral support. At first, the cave they were walking through was tall and wide, easily traversed upright, even for JR. After walking about a quarter of a mile, though, they reached what at first looked like a dead end. Angela kept a tight hold on Summers, afraid he would bolt for the inner canyon, while the others aimed their headlamps around the walls at the end of the passage. They were about to give up and retrace their steps when Robert called out.

"Here." His headlamp disappeared as he ducked and crawled through a smaller hole. Cyndi followed. JR hung back, waving Charles, Angela and then Rebecca through. Then he went in on hands and knees, glad not to have to crawl on his belly. He could hear Summers singing as badly as ever up ahead. The height of the passage, at least here where it started, was barely enough to accommodate JR in this position. He hoped he wouldn't have to back out.

His headlamp was dimming, JR thought, as he crawled behind Rebecca. For the past ten minutes or so, he'd watched her shapely backside lead him further into the passage, which seemed almost like a man-made tunnel, it was so uniform. He was so tired that he thought he could close his eyes and just crawl in his sleep until they were out, if that were ever going to happen. The thought of being entombed here after all they'd been through snapped his eyes wide open again. Rebecca was gone.

JR's heart slammed against his chest as he fought panic. It wouldn't do to break down now, and there had to be a logical reason for her disappearance. No one had cried out, they hadn't fallen into a hole. He kept crawling. Suddenly his head and shoulders were out into a larger opening. He followed with the rest of his body and found the others all standing and waiting for him. Cyndi was babbling, tears streaming down her face. It took a minute for JR to understand what was happening. Then he saw it.

They were in the room where he and Cyndi had found the script; the strange material of the cave that didn't match the rest.

"I know where we are," he announced. The others turned from Cyndi, who was still not making much sense. "Cyn and I found this room when we were all looking for a way out," he said. "But we didn't see this little tunnel. Robert, this room's different from the rest. What is this stuff?"

"Its igneous rock, something the volcano threw out, I reckon."

"What volcano?" the others chorused in unison. Robert looked around in surprise. "Why? Didn't I say? I think that valley we were in was formed in the mouth of a volcano."

"An extinct one?" Angela asked.

"Oh, no. The reason it's so hot in there is that heat is rising from the active volcano underneath. It's a curious thing. I'm not sure how the surface cooled enough to support all that vegetation, in fact. All I know is there's a geothermal source under it, and from the look of this room, it's definitely volcanic. This is the inside of a giant lava bubble that cooled inside the sedimentary stuff around it."

Summers, having momentarily forgotten his fear upon seeing the script again, walked closer to it to get a better look.

"Is it 10th Cycle?" JR asked quietly.

Summers shook his head. "Not exactly, but close. I think it may be directions into that valley, but it looks slightly different. Maybe it's 9th Cycle. I need Sinclair, JR. He might be able to read it."

JR took a moment to consider the practicality of cutting some of it from the stone and taking it with them, but decided his grandpa would be very upset with him if he defaced an archaeological artifact like that.

"Anyone got a cell phone with battery left?" he asked. "Let's get more pictures."

Cyndi stepped forward and handed him hers. "What is this? I need to get one like it," he quipped, as he took several pictures of the script. JR handed the phone back, noting that it was showing the day and time as August 25th, at eight p.m. The electronics still weren't working properly, but most hadn't noticed because their batteries were all dead.

"Come on, let's get out of here," he said, taking the lead

now that he knew which way to go. How many hours had it been since he and Cyndi had found this room and retraced their steps? He looked for the grease pencil marks on the opening to the room and followed the narrower passage to the next opening confidently.

When they reached the main room, mouths dropped in confusion when they saw the opening. It was twice as large as it had been before, and they were rapidly cooling. They scrambled to get their snow gear back on, before venturing closer to the opening. The wind was howling, and the cold was pervasive, even in their gear. After Robert and JR attempted to step outside to get their bearings and were blown back into the cave, they all sat glumly as they tried to decide what to do.

"It's plain we can't stay in this room for long," Becca said, taking the lead on the discussion. "That cold will kill us, even in our suits. We've got to either find the Sno-Cat quickly, or retreat to a warmer spot and wait out the wind."

"Doesn't it blow more or less continuously for six months?" Angela asked.

"Yes," Summers answered. "But there are sometimes a few hours' respite. Up to seventy-two. The trouble is, we don't have any way of predicting them without the instruments on the Sno-Cat. I think we should go back to the valley."

"Wait a minute," objected JR. "We don't know how long we've been gone from the base. People are probably getting worried if they aren't already. I think we should try for the base."

Summers looked at him as if he were mad. "You're suggesting we trek over two hundred miles in a wind that could easily sweep us away like it did Walker," he argued.

"And in temperatures that would freeze you instantly without your suit. I'm sorry, but I don't think we can take the risk."

JR thought about Daniel, and how they'd argued the last time they saw each other. He thought about his mother, so worried about her baby boy in his post-war mental struggles, and even his grandparents, who weren't getting any younger. He weighed the risk of death in trying to get back to the South Pole to at least let them know he was alive, against letting them think for six months that he was dead. Conceding that Summers was probably right, he nevertheless decided to return to this opening every few hours to see if the wind had died down enough for him to find the Sno-Cat, assuming it was still there.

Reflexively, he looked at his watch as he turned away from the opening. It said February 26th, eight a.m. could that be the true date and time? Was it possible they could still make the pole before the last plane left for the winter?

JR grabbed for Becca's hand as she stepped away. She turned back to him, surprised. Mutely, he pointed at his watch and then hers. She looked at his and noted the time, her eyes widening. Then she looked at hers and suppressed a cry. February 26th, eight-oh-one. They matched! It had felt like weeks in the valley, though she now couldn't recall sleeping except for a few minutes after Carmen's death. Was it possible they'd been inside the cave for only a day or so? It felt like weeks, everyone was so weary. She nodded at JR, and they hurried to catch up with the others.

Summers was torn. He didn't like this cave, but at least it was a large space and he could hold his claustrophobia at bay. Here, he could re-exert his leadership of the expedition. When JR and Rebecca caught up with the rest of the group, he cleared his throat and asked for everyone's attention.

"We have a decision to make, and it can't wait any longer. We've seen from the conditions outside that trying to make it back to the base is foolhardy, even if we could find the Sno-Cat. Once again, the whiteout makes even that task virtually impossible. I say we retreat back to the valley, where it's warm and we have food and water. Yes, we'll be cut off for six months, but at least we'll be alive. Robert, I'd like you to lead the way."

"Just hold your horses, mate, let's hear what JR has to say," said Robert. Summers opened his mouth in outrage, but Rebecca added her opinion.

"Charles, you didn't see what JR did for us in there. We all owe our lives to him. I think we should hear him out, and then vote."

JR looked at Rebecca in wonder. Had she just expressed admiration for him? He'd been acting purely on instinct and training, but his self-esteem ratcheted up a notch as he caught Rebecca's eye. She nodded encouragingly. He took a deep breath, emboldened by the thought that she was looking up to him, taking notice of him, and in a good way. He quelled the butterflies that had suddenly swarmed in his stomach and spoke.

"Okay, here's the sit-rep. Right now it's true there's a whiteout. Becca and I noticed at the mouth of the cave that our watches might be working right again, because they were synchronized. You'll remember that we all had different times inside the valley, and that even though we tried to synchronize them, they just went wonky again. So, it may or may not be accurate, but we think its February twenty-sixth.

"That means that we've got a short window of opportunity to get back to the base if we can find the Sno-Cat, or some other transport out there. Without transportation, it's a death march, I agree. But, there's a good chance that some form of transportation is out there. Those OS guys got here somehow. We need to wait for the winds to die down. It's cold here, but the trip back to the valley and here again takes too long. We have to be ready if the wind dies down so we can see the Cat. We need to stay together.

I'll stay out by the mouth of the cave as much as I can, and if there's a break, we can make a run for it. If not, then I agree with Charles that we should winter over inside the valley where we can survive. We can use the time to thoroughly explore and map the interior, yes, Angela?"

Angela nodded, though she stood close to Summers.

"And what if the winds kick up while we're out on the ice?" Summers objected.

"Charles, do you have family at home? Is someone wondering whether you're alive or dead? Don't you think it's worth the risk to try to make it back to the Pole? Even if we can't get home, they can at least send word that we're safe."

"It's a four-day trek in the Sno-Cat. So risky!"

"I know it could be dicey, but we've made that trip several times, and we've done it in two days in a pinch. We know where the crevasses are, and I think we can push to make it in two days. If the wind comes up, we stop. It might be uncomfortable until the next break, but we can stay safely inside the Cat."

With everyone looking at him hopefully, Charles

conceded that it was indeed unusual for the winds to start so early in March, even though most research stations made that the deadline for leaving if you weren't wintering over.

"All right, but we don't wait longer than twelve hours. It's too cold here. We need to save our strength for the trek back."

JR agreed, and suggested Robert take the women and go back to the valley to stock up on fruit and water while he went back out to the mouth of the cave for another look at the weather. It was too bad that the opening let in so much of the outside cold. The walk back and forth from the back of the main room, around a winding passage through several very large stalagmites, took at least fifteen minutes. If it weren't well below zero at the mouth of the cave, he'd just stay there for the twelve hours, get some sleep. But, even at about thirteen degrees Fahrenheit, the main room was noticeably warmer.

His musings took him around the last barrier and to the opening, now significantly larger than when they'd entered so many hours before. Howling wind still drove snow past the opening in stinging gusts. Checking his watch, JR saw it now said February 26th, 9:20. Not quite an hour and a half to return to the main room, discuss the options and get back to the mouth of the cave. Okay, he could check at least six more times before his deadline passed. But, he'd have to stay awake. It was going to be a long twelve hours.

JR was making his way back to the rest of the group when he met Rebecca coming toward him.

"Hi," she said, smiling.

"Hi? What are you doing, Becca? Thought you were going to help gather fruit and maybe then get some sleep?" he asked.

"I thought I'd meet you, away from the others I mean. I haven't thanked you yet for saving my life."

"Oh." The quirky humor that JR had been known for as a kid had been in full retreat since his first deployment, but to his surprise it surfaced now. "No problem. I was going to kill those guys anyway." He chuckled at Rebecca's bewildered face. "Hey, don't pay any attention to me. Stress relief humor, you know?"

Becca looked relieved, then chuckled herself. "Yeah, I know. It's been intense. JR?"

He looked down at her walking beside him. "Yeah?"

"I've misjudged, I mean, damn it!"

He stopped, turning to her with puzzlement. She seemed to be struggling with what she wanted to say, so he stayed quiet to give her a chance to collect her thoughts.

"Josh, can we be better friends? I, I think you're amazing," she said. "It's like you're a different person here. One I admire." To his utter confusion, Rebecca threw her arms around him and pulled his head down to hers. With the face masks, a kiss would be odd to say the least, but she had to give him a heartfelt hug. After a moment, he returned it, wrapping his long arms around her as well and wondering if he could get a rain check on the kiss. A few minutes later, with both of their hearts beating a bit more rapidly, they resumed their walk back to where the others had made themselves as comfortable as possible.

They found Summers sleeping soundly with his head in Angela's lap, Cyndi curled up with her head on Robert's shoulder, and a spot that Rebecca had cleared of rubble for her resting place. She invited JR to join her and snuggled into his arms with a sigh of contentment.

Holding Rebecca felt like nothing else JR had ever experienced. She wasn't like the many other girls who'd lain next to him. He didn't know quite how to take it...a girl who wanted his protection rather than sex. He hoped sex wasn't out of the question, later of course. JR drifted off to sleep with visions of a radiant Becca coming to him in a vine-covered bower, the strange ambient light in the valley limning her soft skin, which was conveniently unfettered with clothing.

JR woke with a start. He took a chance on waking Becca by turning on his headlamp, which was now alarmingly dim. His watch said February 26th, 12 p.m. *Damn!* He'd missed a weather check. Gently extracting himself from the arm Becca had thrown over his chest and lowering her head to his backpack that he pulled over for a pillow, he unfolded his lanky frame and strode away toward the entrance as fast as he dared. By the time he reached the mouth of the cave, he could see that the wind had died down almost completely. He ventured a step or two outside and looked up, then almost staggered as his perspective flipped. Suddenly, instead of looking up at a million stars, he had the peculiar sensation that he was falling into them. His watch must be twelve hours off, he thought, because it was full dark, and only the stars lit the night. He'd completely forgotten that this would be the normal state of things for most of the day and night, for quite some time.

JR swept his eyes over the horizon, straining to see the Sno-Cat where they'd left it. Not seeing it, he went back into the cave, thinking it would be better to look for it when the sun came up, even though it wouldn't be very high or stay up for long. But, he'd better wake the others so they'd be ready to go as soon as they could find the vehicle. Who knew how long this lull would last?

JR hurried back to where the others were sleeping. He touched Becca first, waking her gently. "The wind's down, but I can't see the Cat, it's too dark. Should I wake the others, or wait until we've got a little light?"

She sat up. "Wake the others, I think. It should be a group decision, and if we're going to have to hunt for the vehicle in the dark, we need all of us."

JR left her to get up and get herself together while he woke the others. Angela was now splayed over Summers as if to keep him warm, while Cyndi and Robert had barely moved. JR woke them first, then Angela and finally Summers. Once everyone was fully awake, or as close to it as they could be after just a few hours of sleep, he told them that the wind was relatively still and the sky clear. Then the bad news; he hadn't spotted the Sno-Cat.

"It makes sense," Summers said. "If we've been in here for more than a day, and Roosky couldn't clear the opening in that time, they'd have assumed we were dead or unreachable and headed back to the base. We might as well go back into the valley."

It was finally time to come clean with everyone regarding Roosky, the Sno-Cat and Bart's probable fate. The three who hadn't already heard his theory were angered at being left in the dark, but none had the energy to lash out. Summers insisted that if that were the case, Roosky would no doubt have taken off in the Sno-Cat and they should still go back to the valley.

"Wait," objected JR. "Those OS guys got here somehow. There were six of them, and there are now six of us. We should be able to escape in their vehicle."

"Which could be anywhere," Summers retorted.

"They came in through here," JR countered. "They blew the rock fall and came in the same entrance we did, which is now much bigger, so you know that's what they did. Their vehicle has to be right outside, or not very far off. Let's go find it and get out of here, instead of giving up without even trying."

The others murmured their agreement, only Angela agreeing with Summers out of loyalty, though she wanted to go home as much as the rest did.

Robert said they should probably retrieve the ropes, so another half-hour was spent in reeling them in and coiling them for ease of carrying. Robert's idea was to rope themselves together while they searched for the OS vehicle, so that no one would be lost in the dark. Finally, they were ready to go. With JR leading the way, they paced themselves to the mouth of the cave, though some wanted to run. They still had an arduous task ahead. Finding a vehicle in the dark and the snow without knowing exactly what they were looking for could prove to be a challenge.

When they got to the opening, though, surprisingly there was some light. A red glow at the tops of the surrounding peaks had to mean the sun was up, but it seemed like very early morning, around two a.m. according to JR's calculations, or was it p.m.? JR was now completely confused. However, it mattered less what time it was, than that they had some light. Robert's insistence that they rope together was brushed off, but they did pair off to go searching, JR and Rebecca going left, Summers and Angela straight out from the opening to the cave, and Robert taking Cyndi to the right. Before leaving, they synchronized their watches to Rebecca's, which now said February 27th, 1:22 a.m. This time, they stayed synchronized after five minutes, so the pairs set off with instructions to walk for half an hour and return, unless they found something sooner. If so, they were to shout. Even if they weren't heard, the group would come back together in an hour or less.

JR swept the horizon again, hoping to see the Sno-Cat now that it was light. He couldn't help but remember that what Summers had said made sense. It had been two days. Roosky, and maybe Bart would have headed for the base, probably as soon as Roosky set the explosives. Was Bart OS as well? Or had Roosky murdered him, too? He couldn't recall whether he'd looked back at the Cat as they went into the cave. He thought it was located at an angle between his trajectory and Summers', but he didn't remember how far from the cave they'd parked it. He strained harder to see the white vehicle against the snow.

Rebecca, unaware of JR's musings, was looking straight ahead as they walked. Not too far away was an outcropping that they'd have to skirt, but JR hadn't turned yet. Maybe he intended to walk right up to it and then around. She looked up at him to see him looking intently off to their right.

"JR, there's an outcropping ahead," she said, thinking he hadn't seen it.

"Yeah, we'll angle out in a few yards, go around it." He knew the Cat wasn't close to the canyon wall, which was steep though pitched at a softer angle than the inside canyon's. Now that he knew what it was, it was almost comically obvious. An ash cone, if he remembered his undergraduate geology lessons correctly. Probably built rapidly as the volcano erupted, which meant that the sides would be steep, only wearing down through erosion over the centuries. How old was it? He'd have to ask Robert if that could be determined.

Rebecca's cry shook him out of his near-sleepwalking daze. They'd rounded the outcropping, and there, in front of them, were a group of odd-looking man-made objects. JR and Becca both broke into a run, though he outstripped her rapidly with his long legs. It was almost a surprise when he reached them. They were small, so the low light and lack of color in the environment had fooled him into thinking they were further away.

But what the heck were they? They were no longer than a two-seater snowmobile, but they were enclosed, all but the skis and tracks, in a hard shell that had no visible opening. JR was circling the first one he got to for the second time when Rebecca finally reached them.

"Snowmobiles," she said. "Three of them. These must be what the OS came in on."

"Impossible, they'd have frozen to death," JR remarked.

"Not with these fairings on them," Becca corrected. She lifted the shell from the right side of the snowmobile next to her. It raised easily, revealing a plush interior with plenty of room for two people and some cargo. JR sheepishly lifted the shell from his. Yeah, hinged on the left side. Otherwise airtight, and the onboard controls indicated they were heated. Realizing what it meant, he gave a whoop that echoed through the canyon.

"Let's drive two of them back to the meeting point, and then we can bring someone back to get this one," he said.

"Let's hope there's sufficient fuel to get back to the Pole," Becca said, more soberly.

"They were planning to get back to somewhere," said JR, confident now that they could get back to base and not have to winter inside the mountain. He mounted the snowmobile next to him and pulled down the fairing, sealing himself inside a cocoon that soon became almost too warm. Rebecca followed him in the second machine, back to the mouth of the cave, where she joined JR in his machine and they sat cozily, holding hands to JR's infinite wonder, until the others returned about ten minutes later.

Summers and Angela had heard JR's shout, and passed it along to signal Robert and Cyndi, so they'd cut short their routes and returned immediately. Everyone but Summers was excited to see the snowmobiles. Summers had grave doubts about making it back to base before the winds kicked up again, and these machines wouldn't be able to withstand a gale.

Everything that had happened since he insisted on this last, catastrophic, trip to the canyon had served to undermine his self-confidence to the point that he didn't even believe himself. The prospect of being left completely alone for the next six months, much less traversing the narrow tunnel entrance or the squeeze to get back into the valley convinced him he had to go with the others.

Rebecca ran Angela out to the third snowmobile in her machine, then both returned to the meeting point. Pausing just long enough to check fuel reserves and whether there was food—there was—the group wasted no time in heading for the South Pole and Scott-Amundsen base as fast as they could push the machines. That turned out to be very fast, even with JR's instructions about who should be in the lead, how far apart or close together they should stay, and to be on the lookout for new crevasses, keeping their eyes on each other at all times.

In spite of the events of the last couple of days, Rebecca couldn't get over how different this JR was from the brat who'd embarked with them at the beginning. This must be the old JR, the one that Sarah talked about with regret. How wonderful that she would be able to see her friend's eyes light up when she realized JR, the real JR, was back.

The group only slowed for the crevasse field that they'd

have to negotiate carefully, otherwise running at nearly thirty miles per hour, an unheard-of speed over the polar ice. At this rate, they'd be back at base in seven hours, give or take an hour to account for the slow-down and barring unforeseen accidents. Even Summers began to believe they'd make it, if the winds would just hold back for the rest of the night.

Chapter Thirty

THREE VEHICLES SIR

An enlisted man woke Cmdr. Andersen at seven-thirty a.m. to report three small vehicles approaching at speed half an hour from the base perimeter. The groggy commander, who'd stayed up until very late the night before to supervise the loading of the last scheduled flight's passengers and their cargo, couldn't understand at first what he was hearing. He asked for a repeat of the intel.

"Three vehicles, sir. Approaching our perimeter at an estimated speed of forty-eight kph."

"What kind of vehicles?" he asked.

"Unknown, sir. Radar profile is confused. They appear to be about the size of snowmobiles, but they have a higher profile. Your orders, sir?"

"Send an armed squad to meet them at the airlock. I'll be there directly." With half an hour to wait, Andersen indulged himself in a hot shower and leisurely shave, then strolled toward the airlock.

Visual confirmation of the vehicles once they were within eyesight revealed they were snowmobiles all right, at least, they had tracks on the back and skis on the front. The upper part, however, was just a bubble of some material that the exterior camera couldn't see through. A squad of half a dozen waited beyond the thick inside door to the airlock, rifles aimed at the door, with an open intercom giving them a move-by-move description of what was going on outside.

"Vehicles are opening, two people climbing out of each. Six total, repeat, six total. No visual recognition; all are wearing snow gear and face masks. Ready; outer door opening."

Outside, the sudden cold after hours in the relative warmth of the machines was a shock. There had been no room inside to remove snow gear, so everyone was somewhat overheated and anxious to get inside and strip down to their regular clothes. Summers led the way, hitting the large pad that would operate the outer door, unless it had been sealed for the winter. Then, he'd have to hope he could operate the intercom buttons with his gloves on. Taking them off and touching an outside surface, even for a moment, would invite frostbite at the current temperature of minus four degrees Fahrenheit. To his relief, the door began to swing open. He signaled the others to hurry. There was room in the airlock for all of them; no need to cycle the door more than once.

Inside, six men raised their rifles and aimed at the door, fingers resting lightly on the triggers. Quick reflexes would be important if the intruders came in shooting.

"No weapons in sight, repeat, no weapons in sight. Hold your fire unless fired upon."

Slowly, the inner door swung open, to the most bizarre sight the soldiers inside had ever seen. Six bulky, snow-suited figures were jumping up and down, hugging each other and giving awkward high-fives. When they noticed that the inner door was completely open, as one they rushed the soldiers and hugged them, guns and all. In the midst of the chaos, Andersen's voice rang out.

"Hold your fire!" was his totally unnecessary command. Every soldier was incapacitated in a bear hug from the strangers, one of whom snatched his face mask off to reveal that he wasn't a stranger after all.

"Commander, are we glad to see you!" Summers crowed.

Andersen, stunned, could only stare as each of the others shed their hoods and masks. Back from the dead, six members of the Rossler Foundation Expedition were alive after all.

Andersen started forward, meeting Summers halfway to clasp his hand and arm in a congratulatory greeting. "How the devil?"

"It's a long story," Summers said. "My people are tired, dirty, hungry and ready to get out of this gear. Can we save the report until we've had a chance to regroup?"

"Of course. But, my God, man, they're probably having the memorial service for you right now. Let me check." Andersen pushed a couple of buttons on his big, complicated watch, and realized that the service in Boulder would start in only an hour or so. Who could he call? Rossler wouldn't be answering his phone; no one at the Foundation would. It had been declared a day of mourning for the entire nation, with the President and First Lady traveling in person to Boulder to attend the memorial service. That was it! He would call his commanding officer and have the news passed up the line to the Secret Service, who would be able to alert the President.

Andersen was pleased. He liked this President, and

giving him the power to interrupt a memorial service with the good news that some had survived would be a feather in his cap. Maybe even move him up the line for promotion, get him off this barren rock. He returned to his office to make the call, failing to take note of who besides Summers and that freakishly tall Rossler kid had survived. It was an oversight that would delay the news reaching the President by a critical half hour.

Summers and his crew were hastily assigned rooms, with the luxury of each having one to himself or herself now that the base was almost empty of other people. Unfortunately, their effects had been shipped out with the plane that left three days before, the last scheduled plane of the season. Extra fatigues were found, but Angela, the shortest woman, had to roll her pants from both the waist and the ankle to avoid tripping over them. She opted for stocking feet, vowing to put the boots back on only to board a flight for home.

When they'd been fed, showered and sent to rest, Summers went to meet with Andersen to be debriefed.

"Summers, I've sent word to the States that a few of you have survived. I just got a communique back that they won't inform the President or the Rossler Foundation until they know who. Don't want to get the hopes of the families up, you understand."

"Of course. Well, I'm sure you recognized JR Rossler, the tall one. Dr. Rebecca Mendenhall, Cyndi Self, the electronics engineer. Angela Brown, cartographer. Robert Cartwright, from Australia, the geologist. You should probably report separately to his government. And myself, of course."

"What happened to the others?"

"Are you ready for a bizarre story?" Receiving an affirmative answer, Summers proceeded to tell Andersen about the deaths of LeClerc in the cave and Carmen at the hands of the OS attackers. Making sure that Andersen knew he was cuffed and incapacitated himself, Summers praised JR for his courage and ingenuity in taking out the OS. He was less complimentary about the young man's insistence that they return to base, but admitted that all was well that ended well. Summers' only question, barring the obvious, was whether Roosky and Bart had showed up at the base. When told of Roosky's appearance and story, Summers shook his head. "I think we'll find that the incident that trapped us was deliberate. JR believes Roosky was OS. God only knows what happened to Bart." Turning to matters of more immediate concern, he said, "I presume we aren't too late to get out of here before the winter shutdown?"

"Actually, you are. But, the weather looks calm for the next few days. Let's report your wish to be picked up, and see what happens."

"I thought the last flight wasn't until today, February 27th?" Summers objected. Andersen gave him an odd look.

"Today is March 1st, here. Still the 28th in Boulder. They're holding your memorial service as we speak."

Summers jumped to his feet, distraught. "Call them!"

Andersen made a motion for Summers to sit back down. "I did. The Secret Service will get word to the President as soon as I report who has survived, and he'll make the announcement. Come to think of it, I'd better make that report before it's all over. Wait here."

Andersen was a capable enough administrator, but there was a reason he was stationed at the South Pole, and it had just been demonstrated. A tendency to be reactive instead of proactive, to get mired in minor details and to lose track of time when it was critical to be on top of things would keep him in his current rank until he retired. He had his adjutant open a line of communications to his commanding officer and listed the names of the survivors, then the dead, and finally the cause of death for each of the dead, with the exception of Bart. That might never be known unless Roosky could be apprehended and made to talk.

A burst of agitated shouting from the other end of the phone line met the assertion that the microbiologist had been shot by OS operatives. Orders to get more details were followed by a statement to expect a flight to pick up the survivors the next day. They would need to be debriefed, all of them. A chastened Andersen returned to talk to Summers more.

Unfortunately, Summers had spent much of the time after becoming aware that they were under attack unconscious. Reluctantly, he told Andersen he'd have to get the details he needed from JR Rossler. Andersen told him that they would be picked up the next day and dismissed him to get some sleep. He decided to wake Rossler after his own breakfast, which had been delayed by the excitement.

Chapter Thirty-One

JOY AT A MEMORIAL SERVICE

In Boulder, the memorial service had been delayed by the Secret Service insistence that the auditorium be checked one last time for explosives and then setting up only one portable metal detector for the numerous attendees to pass through. Daniel would normally have seethed at the unexpected formalities, but he was too emotionally exhausted to notice it. He'd lost his brother and welcomed his firstborn child into the world in the space of less than two days. Now, the President of the United States had asked to speak at the memorial service. It was too much to comprehend, and he was operating on automatic.

Sarah, holding little Nicholas in a sling that tied over her shoulder was in better shape, and that was in spite of taking all wake-up calls since the baby had been born herself. She reasoned that Daniel couldn't nurse the baby anyway, and he was taking the burden of all the repercussions of the failed expedition. Beside Sarah, her parents on one side and Daniel's on the other were a solid barrier against the crowds crushing her and the baby.

Nicholas Rossler was already seated, with a wan Bess newly discharged from the hospital unable to stand for long. Sarah knew that Sinclair and Martha were at her back, though she didn't turn to look at them. As well-wishers filed past on their way to passing through the metal detector, she graciously greeted those who ventured to speak to her or offer their condolences. Sarah was a popular figure, not only locally in Boulder and within the Foundation, but nationally since her ordeal during the Pyramid Code search had been revealed.

Daniel appeared at her side to tell her that there was some sort of delay in the President's party again. Sarah examined his face, beloved by her like no other. Tears formed in her eyes as she cataloged the toll the past few days had taken on him. His eyes were red, deep bags hanging from the lower lids. If she hadn't known his age, she'd have taken him for ten years older. If only he would allow her to comfort him, but he couldn't get past the notion that he'd sent JR to his death. It was killing him, and the knowledge was killing her. Only little Nick could tease a smile from either of them. At last, a Secret Service agent came to them to tell them that all was in readiness. Daniel was on first. After reading the obituaries of the members, he would sit down and the President would have his say. After that, the family representative of each of the deceased would have an opportunity to eulogize their loved one, though not all had accepted. Daniel would go last with JR's eulogy and final remarks. Of course, there would be no processional to the cemetery, no graveside service, since the remains were entombed in Antarctica at least until next fall. The Rossler and Clark families took their places last, with Martha and Sinclair tagging along because Sarah insisted that they were family.

Daniel had ordered an organ to be installed in the auditorium for the music he'd chosen. The soft strains of 'Jesu, Joy of Man's Desiring' were playing as he took the stage and stood behind the podium. The organist expertly ended the piece early, lowering the volume so that it faded away before Daniel began to speak.

"Six months ago, we sent friends, colleagues and loved ones on a journey of discovery. To my everlasting regret, only a few returned. We thank God for the safe return of those who left the expedition early, and acknowledge their grief that they survived when their colleagues did not. Although he isn't here, we also thank Mikhail Stefanovich Maxhulin for his heroic efforts to rescue the trapped expedition, and also return thanks that he made it safely back to base with news of the disaster. His ordeal in doing so was devastating to his health, so he is not here today, though he sent word that he wished to be. In addition, we thank the US military establishments' joint efforts to recover the remains of our loved ones. The Rossler Foundation pledges to accomplish that mission as soon as it is practical to do so without risking more lives in the effort. I will now read the obituaries of the deceased."

Daniel bowed his head for a moment, overcome with the burden of what he was about to do. A commotion in front of him and to the right made him look up with a frown. In the front row, a seated President Harper was listening to a Secret Service agent who whispered urgently into his ear. A wave of apprehension went through Daniel as he rapidly scanned the crowd, looking for the threat. He looked back just in time to see President Harper jump to his feet.

"Daniel!" he called, a look of joy on his face. Confused, Daniel froze. The President was striding to the podium, the audience beginning to buzz with whispered questions. He gathered Daniel's body for a hug, causing the audience to buzz even louder. President Harper kept one arm around Daniel's shoulders as he grasped the microphone and pulled it lower to make an announcement.

"Daniel, ladies and gentlemen. I have wonderful news. Six members of the expedition have just been confirmed alive and well at the South Pole." His voice was drowned out by shouts from the audience, accompanied by loud weeping. As he used both hands to quell the noise with a downward motion, his face sobered. "I'm sorry to say that all remaining members besides these six have now been confirmed dead by the survivors. Please hold your displays of emotion as I read the names of the survivors. To the families who won't be receiving good news, my deepest condolences. The survivors are, in alphabetical order: Angela Brown." In spite of his request, a shriek from the second row went up as Angela's mother, unable to contain herself, reacted to the news that her daughter was alive. Daniel held his breath. At this rate, he'd die of lack of oxygen before the President got to the R's.

"Robert Cartwright," the President intoned, to a muffled scream from behind Sarah's row. "Rebecca Mendenhall." Daniel saw Sarah clap her hand over her mouth to suppress her cry, but from further back more screams let him know where Rebecca's parents and sister sat. "JR Rossler." At this, a cheer went up as Daniel's extended family jumped to their feet and began laughing, crying and hugging. His relief was so great that he could only let the tears fall from his cheeks unchecked, unable to speak or utter a sound.

Despite his joy that his brother was alive, Daniel still felt enormous grief and responsibility for the others, those who didn't make it. "Cyndi Self." By now, the President had slowed his delivery to accommodate the cries of joy after each name. There was one name left, Daniel realized. He held his breath again. "Charles Summers." At this, Daniel staggered to a chair behind him and collapsed into it. Summers was a newer friend, but a good one. Daniel was very glad that he was among the survivors.

In the audience, only one family huddled together in tears. Bart's people, brought from Louisiana by Daniel's generosity, mourned that his name hadn't been called. LeClerc had no family; Carmen's family had declined the invitation, sending Antonio as their representative, and the families of those who had died earlier had accepted their loss weeks before and knew that their names wouldn't be called. Misty's family hadn't been traced. Daniel and the FBI thought she was probably using an assumed name and might not even be American. Everyone else in the audience was celebrating, and the noise was insurmountable. The President would have liked to make a few extemporaneous remarks, but he couldn't make himself heard even with the microphone. He walked over to Daniel and grasped his shoulder.

"I'm happy for you, Daniel. We're going to slip out now. When you get them back home, let me know if you're going to throw a party. The First Lady and I could use a good excuse to party before this year's campaign consumes us." He gave Daniel a smile and a thumbs up, and then returned to his seat to collect his wife.

For a moment, Daniel remained where he was. Even though he was exhausted and overwhelmed, he needed to be with his family. He left the stage, dimly recognizing the music the organ was now playing as the recessional from his and Sarah's wedding. Trumpet Voluntary or something, he thought, though it seemed to be going a lot faster today. Then his mother was in his arms, sobbing her joy into his chest as his dad pounded him on the back. They acted as if he were the hero, when he knew somehow that JR was.

He'd get the story later, all that was important was that he had his brother back. His other brother, Aaron appeared behind their mother and wrapped both of them in a hug. Finally, Daniel looked up to meet Sarah's eyes, wet with her own tears of joy. He reached his hand out to her, unable to extricate himself from the group hug that Aaron was still holding. She took his hand and kissed it. "I'm so glad, Daniel. So very glad."

Chapter Thirty-Two

ANDERSEN WANTS TO SEE YOU

Summers woke JR before he went to bed himself and told him to be prepared to be interviewed by Andersen. JR knew that he was the best person to ask about the OS raid, but he also knew that if a military officer were involved, 'interrogated' might be a better word. He went to Rebecca's door and knocked softly.

"Becca, are you awake?"

"No," she answered.

"Oh, sorry."

"Don't be an idiot JR. Of course I'm awake. Come in."

JR opened the door and slipped in, looking down both ends of the hall as he did. He turned around and promptly lost his train of thought. Becca was sitting up in bed, the sheets drawn up under her arms because if her shoulders were any indication, she was naked underneath. As he fought to close his mouth, which had dropped at the sight of her, she realized his difficulty.

"They didn't have anything but boxers for me to sleep

in," she apologized. "All of us girls are out of luck in the jammies department." She raked her eyes over him, shirtless himself. Damn, if she'd known he looked that good… "What is it, JR?"

"Summers just told me that Andersen is going to interrogate me. Would you go with me? To back me up?" His anxiety was off the charts, but he thought he'd made it sound casual enough. Her face softened.

"Sure, JR. I'll go with you if you like. And if he'll allow it. But don't worry, I know you'll tell the truth, and my story will back yours up. Are you concerned that he'll ask you about Carmen?"

She'd hit the nail on the head. She was the only one there who had seen what happened, and it was all so fast. He never would have put Carmen in that position if he'd known. OS or no OS, it wasn't in his code of conduct to use a woman to shelter him. He'd just meant for her to be an element of surprise. That fucker Pyotr had shot first, didn't even give Carmen a chance to ask for help. He was never going to forget the sound of Becca's scream, or his reflex that had taken Pyotr out a second later. And he wasn't sure Becca would ever get over having a woman shot down just yards in front of her. If she never spoke to him again when they got back, it wouldn't be a surprise to him.

But he had more to worry about than that. It was only their word that *he* hadn't killed Carmen. With his PTSD diagnosis and a reputation for hair-trigger violence, could he actually be in legal trouble? His only hope was that Becca would stand by him, back him up.

"Yeah, I guess I am. Concerned about the Carmen incident. You know I wouldn't have wanted it that way, right Becca?" Before her eyes, the handsome, manly face melted into the little boy he must have been. Her heart lurched.

"Of course I know that, Josh. You're a good man. A little damaged around the edges maybe, but fundamentally good. Don't worry. It happened fast, but I'm clear on it. That OS guy, Pyotr shot her in cold blood, and you shot him in self-defense. You have nothing to worry about. Come here."

Mutely, he obeyed her command.

"Have you forgotten what I said to you in that cave? I admire you, and I'm beyond grateful that you were there to save our lives. My life."

"Becca, I'll never forget that as long as I live," he breathed.

She crooked her finger at him to get him to lean over, then put her arms around his neck and pulled him further down for a long-overdue kiss, not knowing or not caring that she was no longer clutching the blanket. JR closed his eyes as the blanket began to slip. He didn't think she'd want him to see, and the kiss was amazing even with his eyes closed. He sank to his knees beside the bed, more comfortable there than leaning over her from his height. His arms went around her, his fingertips tingling at the touch of her soft skin. For a moment, he forgot everything —where they were, what had happened in that cave, even the nightmare that seldom left his thoughts. Becca was kissing him! If there were never any more, he'd die happy from that one kiss, he thought. His body thought otherwise, but what might have happened next would never be known.

Only a sharp rap at the door made them break it off, Becca grabbing at the blanket quickly enough that he only got the barest glimpse of perfect breasts before she was covered again.

JR stepped to the door to open it. Outside was an

enlisted man who requested that JR follow him to the commander's office.

"Mind if I get dressed first?" JR drawled, shifting to keep the soldier from looking in at Becca.

"No, sir. That will be fine, sir."

JR stepped outside, hearing Becca call that she'd be ready to go with him when he passed by her door again, just knock. JR grinned as he led the way down the hall to his room. Maybe he would have a chance with her when they got home, after all. If he didn't blow it in the meantime. He vowed to keep his cool.

The following day, one of the big Pave Low choppers from McMurdo dropped out of a calm sky to pick them up and take them to an aircraft carrier that was standing by off Scott Island, between McMurdo and New Zealand. From there, another chopper would take them to Christchurch, from whence they would retrace their outbound flight to eventually arrive home. They'd say goodbye to Robert for the time being at Christchurch, since he'd head home to Sydney instead of returning to Boulder with them.

They'd see him again soon, no later than October, hopefully, when they mounted the next expedition to explore the valley, which they'd named Paradise Valley in a flight of fantasy. Summers was convinced that the script on the cave wall plus the organized layout of the paths through the jungle had to mean previous human habitation. They'd surely find the ruins they were expecting if they had time to explore every inch of the valley, with the right team and equipment the next time.

By the time the remaining expedition members were setting foot on the carrier, the news of their survival had reached all points of the globe. Maxhulin, otherwise known as Roosky, had prudently retrieved his hard currency from its hiding place and booked a flight to South America. The surviving members of the expedition must have put two and two together, he reflected. It was too bad. Tovarich JR, good drinking partner, but dangerous to the health of one Roosky Maxhulin. One thing he wouldn't be doing under any circumstances was attending a quarterly meeting of the Orion Society at the end of the month.

In Würzburg, Septentrio was throwing the temper tantrum to end all tantrums. And indeed, it did end his, as he suffered a stroke during a particularly strenuous game of flog the slave. His manservant, a new one who'd replaced the one who was playing the role of the slave in the game, made a discreet call to Latet, who ordered him to stand by. Latet contacted Auster, who sent a doctor to see to Septentrio. All of Würzburg mourned the passing of the prominent businessman, so soon after his father's unfortunate passing.

To make it even more unfortunate, he'd left no immediate heir, being a lifelong confirmed bachelor. A distant cousin was found to be the heir to the family fortune. She was sent for and installed in the ancient mansion that was the family seat.

"Mother, I'm here. We'll need to find a suitable match so I can start a family immediately."

"Of course, dear. Have you given any thought to your ceremonial name?" Auster replied.

"I don't see why I shouldn't keep the old one, just replace the final letter with an 'a'. How does Septentria sound?"

"Lovely, my dear, lovely. I'll have my response to the Rossler Foundation debacle ready for the quarterly meeting. Go ahead and open the meeting, introduce yourself, and then turn the meeting over to me."

"Yes, Mother."

Chapter Thirty-Three

NICHOLAS JOSHUA ROSSLER

The celebration in Boulder when the remainder of the expedition returned home was echoed in Denver and in Washington, D.C. But the facts of the miraculous escape were suppressed, so that only those with a need to know would hear of the wondrous tropical valley hidden in the Transantarctic Mountains. Cartwright had been sworn to secrecy except for a report to his government as well. Eventually, it would be revealed to the world, as the Rosslers had always intended for research coming out of the 10th Cycle Library. However, as with any new and convention-shattering knowledge, it had to be analyzed for potential misuse by criminal or terrorist organizations. In this case, a new expedition would have to be mounted.

Before meetings could be held, the returning expedition members endured speeches, parades and dinners in their honor, both public and separately among their families. The Rossler-Clarke family celebration was one of the larger, with the extended family and friends who were considered family all attending, along with an exuberant President Harper and his First Lady.

Baby Nicholas almost stole the limelight, though. Rebecca couldn't get enough of holding him. It wasn't until he overheard her praising his actions in delivering them from the OS threat inside the mountain that JR began to perk up. He positively glowed when he heard her say, "He's really rather dashing, isn't he, Sarah? I never realized how good-looking he is, or how sweet. And I think it may have gone a long way toward resolving his PTSD"

JR didn't hear Sarah's answer, and it didn't matter anyway. He didn't think you could actually cure PTSD, only learn to live with the flashbacks, the impotent anger and the depression. But, having a reason to learn to live with it went a long way toward making him fit company for human beings. And the reason he had was at that moment dangling his nephew on her knee and looking so delectable.

Even Sarah, on whom he'd had a deep crush since he first laid eyes on her, paled in comparison to his Becca. He couldn't tear his eyes away from her. In the course of a few months, he'd fallen head over heels for Becca, but only now would he admit it to himself. Only now did he feel he might even have a chance with her if he could keep his nose clean. He didn't care what it took. He'd stop drinking if he had to, talk to a hundred psych counselors, and follow her around on a leash like a pet dog, as long as she was his. It only remained to show her and prove it to her. *Starting today*, he thought, putting down the flute of champagne he'd picked up automatically. No more drinking, at least for now. Drinking was one of the things that triggered his rages. He couldn't risk it.

JR tore himself away from his vantage point, thinking that eavesdropping might be among the things he shouldn't do if he wanted to win Becca. He'd endured many tearful hugs from his mother, so he shied away from the corner where she and Sarah's mother were sitting and talking. Spying Bess, he went to visit with his beloved grandma. Her hugs were warm and sweet. He felt terrible that the news of his presumed death had sent her to the hospital with an angina attack.

"Hi, Grandma."

"Hi, my sweet Joshie. Oh, it's so good to have you here. Give Grandma another hug, sweetie."

He loved it when she talked to him as if he were a baby, unless others were around to hear. He'd always had a special place in the family, and he knew it. Since Dad was an only child, he was the baby of the Rossler family, and, while that was sometimes inconvenient, it had always been the cause of special treatment. He got away with more childhood transgressions, everyone looked out for him, and grandma babied him even though he was now a grown man of twenty-six. He knelt beside his Grandma's chair and gathered her tiny frame into his arms, holding her tenderly as if she might break.

Behind him, Grandpa's gruff voice startled him. "Trying to make time with my girl, are you, sonny?"

He got up quickly and hugged Grandpa, too. "Of course! Doesn't everyone."

"Oh, you boys," Bess said, blushing. JR knew it tickled her when Grandpa pretended people were trying to steal her away. In fact, for a grandma, she looked pretty darn good. Maybe people really were trying to steal her. He'd have to keep an eye on Sinclair. He chuckled, then had to explain the joke to Grandpa, who glowered in Sinclair's direction, though the man in question was so close to Martha Simms that they might have been fused at the hip.

After visiting for a few minutes, he wandered over to Sinclair, who was deep in conversation with Martha.

"Sinclair, has Charles had a chance to show you the script we found in the cave?" he asked, when the pair acknowledged his presence.

"No, this is the first I've heard of it. But to be fair, you guys have only been here a day and a half, and you've all been asleep for more than half of that."

"Sorry about that. We got all messed up, first staying awake for most of thirty-six hours, and then the long trip back north. Here, let me show you a photo of it." JR pulled out his cell phone and located the pictures of the script they'd taken on the way. He turned the screen toward Sinclair, who took it from him without thinking, intent on the picture.

"How do you zoom in?" he demanded.

"Put a couple of fingers in the center of the screen and spread them out," explained JR.

As the script grew larger, first a frown and then an expression of delight crossed his countenance. "Is this all of the message?" he demanded.

"It took a few shots to get all of it. Why? Can you read it?"

Sinclair had been studying the 10th Cycle script for a long time and could now read it in the clear as easily as he read English. This script was only slightly different, similar to the difference between seventeenth-century copperplate script and modern handwriting. It took a trained eye to read it, but training the eye wasn't difficult, because it was essentially the same shapes for most of the letters, the S that looked like a lower-case F being the exception. This script was that close to the 10th Cycle stuff.

"Can you bring your phone to the lab tomorrow so we

can get Raj to stitch the photos together? I think I'll be able to read the message if I can see all of it."

"Sure thing. I'll be in around nine."

"Make it eight? We've got a meeting with Summers at nine, and I'd like to surprise him with the translation."

"No problem, eight it is." Smiling and nodding at Martha, JR wandered off. Martha looked at Sinclair with admiration.

"You can really read that?"

"I think so. The section in that photo was too small to tell for sure, but if Raj can link them together correctly and project the photo on a bigger screen, I think I can at least get the gist of it."

"Promise me you won't get all caught up in this, Sinclair. I still need your help…"

"Don't worry, darling. I'm still going home with you to help you move out here."

"Have you said anything yet?" she asked, as he planted a quick kiss on her temple. "Did we do the right thing, delaying our announcement?"

"Oh, yes, I think so. They've had enough excitement around here for a little while, with the news out of Antarctica, and then little Nicholas being born. Having JR and the others back just put the icing on the cake. I don't think any of them could take one more shock."

"Silly man," Martha said fondly. "Do you really think it will be such a shock for them to learn we're engaged? We haven't exactly hidden our relationship."

"No, maybe not. But you know Sarah will spring into action helping you plan the wedding, and she's got her hands full right now," he answered.

"You're right. Time enough to announce it when we return with a moving van," she laughed. "But we'd better move the date up. I have a feeling someone around here might insist on going to Antarctica with the next expedition."

"You wouldn't mind?" he asked.

"Of course I would, but I know better than to try to stop my man from doing something his heart's set on. Just promise to come back to me in one piece. Being a widow once sucks, but being one twice would just kill me." Martha's words and tone were light, but Sinclair knew they were heartfelt. He'd have to think twice about asking to join the next expedition. After all, six months wasn't a long time to get used to being married. It really would suck if it were all the time they ever had together.

JR had circulated among the family until he felt his duty was fulfilled and was now approaching the sofa where Becca and Sarah still sat talking. More than anything, he wanted to know if Becca would talk with him privately. He had a burning question to ask her.

"Hey, Sarah, how's the munchkin?" he asked, when he was close enough.

"He's wonderful," the new mom replied. "Your mom says he looks just like Daniel as a baby."

"Don't they pretty much all look alike?" he asked, earning a severe frown from Sarah and a suppressed grin from Becca.

"No, they do not! Here, you haven't held him yet. Want to get a closer look?"

JR backed away, hands up in a warding gesture. "NO! He's cute and all, but I'm afraid I'd drop him."

Becca scooted closer to Sarah to make room for JR on her other side. "Sit down here and hold your nephew, you wimp," she said, laughing. Reluctantly, JR obeyed.

Becca got up and arranged his arms, which he held

stiffly where she put them. Then, she took the baby from Sarah and placed him in the cradle of JR's arm. His big hand wrapped around the diapered bottom, almost swallowing the entire infant. A look of wonder crossed his face as the sweet, warm bundle came to rest heavily in his arm.

Becca watched JR fondly. There was nothing in this world sweeter than a sleeping infant. For some reason, the eight or so pounds of completely relaxed baby felt both like more and like less at the same time. JR's attention focused one hundred percent on Nick's face, everything and everyone else in the room disappeared from his mind. The baby wiggled, settling himself more comfortably in his uncle's arms, and JR was lost, completely in love with this little scrap of Rossler.

JR was unaware of it, but Becca read the peace that had invaded his body. She gave Sarah a significant look, which Sarah returned. Maybe this was the cure for PTSD. Neither Becca, who had only known him since his discharge from the Marines, nor Sarah, had ever seen him this relaxed and peaceful. JR continued to hold the baby, his mission to talk privately to Becca forgotten for the moment. Sarah and Becca took the opportunity to visit the buffet table.

"Did you see that, Sarah?" Becca asked.

"I did. If you could bottle that, you'd be a billionaire," Sarah responded.

"Never mind that. Just seeing JR that at peace is worth more than money," Becca said, unconsciously revealing more than she intended about her feelings for him. "I prescribe holding Nicholas for an hour a day to cure him," she added, only half-joking.

"Any time he wants," Sarah added. Spotting Daniel, she waved him over. "Honey, look at your brother," she said, indicating with an outstretched finger where to find him.

"I'll be damned!" Daniel exclaimed, once he'd figured out what they were talking about. "We're going to have to keep him supplied with babies, so that lasts," he teased his wife.

"He should get a few of his own," she returned, looking at Becca as she said it. Becca blushed.

Chapter Thirty-Four

9TH CYCLE EXPEDITION

Summers had wasted no time in preparing his report, backed up by written statements from the other members of the expedition. There was definitely something to be found in Paradise Valley, and it seemed likely that the something would have broader implications than just the fact of its existence. The script in the cave, for example, as well as the clearly human-influenced cultivation within the valley, indicated that there had been inhabitants. It stood to reason that they were 9th Cycle, since that's what the 10th Cycle material had stated. However, there hadn't been time to explore much of the valley. The deceptively-small enclosure had still been too big to cover in detail, but they'd seen no structures. That alone bore more study. His report concluded with a pitch for a return expedition the very next fall.

On the morning following the Rossler family celebration for JR's return, Charles Summers was prepared to offer his report to the full Board. To his surprise, he wasn't first on the agenda, though. Sinclair was. Summers glanced at Sinclair as he took the podium, grinning. He thought Sinclair was looking directly at him, but he couldn't figure out the broad grin. What was he up to? He didn't have long to wait for the answer. On a large screen behind the podium but high enough that Sinclair didn't block any of the image, a large picture was being projected. It looked familiar.

Sinclair began speaking. "I'm going to ask my esteemed colleague Charles Summers to take the lead in this meeting in just a moment," he said. "But first, as a surprise to him and to help you make an informed decision on the request he will no doubt be making, I'd like to read to you the message left to us by the 9th Cycle."

His voice was drowned in the sudden babble of conversation, but he held up his hand so he could explain further. "This isn't a complete library, like the 10th Cycle message in the Giza pyramid. I haven't spoken to Dr. Summers about it, either, so I'm sure he's as eager to hear as you are. I'll just say in preparation that JR Rossler brought the image behind me home from Antarctica. He said, and I'm sure Dr. Summers will back him up, that this script was found in a room of the cave that led to the hidden valley inside that frozen mountain. Here's what it says.

"Welcome, visitor. You will find a passage to the place which you seek twenty hand-lengths to your left as you read this, between two pillars. You are free to enter. However, leave your weapons here; they are neither welcome nor needed in this valley. When you leave, we urge you to leave them behind. If you do not take them, we will dispose of them for you. We wish to spread peace and love into the world. We look forward to meeting you in a few moments."

"Dr. Summers, you may now take the podium, and welcome."

Charles made his way to the stage in a daze. He would never have expected Sinclair to be able to read the script so easily. That it made no explanation of who had left it or when was a disappointment, but it still told him quite a bit about the inhabitants of the valley, or at least about the people who had left the message. They were peace-loving. The fact that no weapons, or any other man-made artifact, had been found in the room with the message meant that they made good on their promise to dispose of the weapons, unless the visitors had taken them away with them when they left. Most curious of all, the script bore a strong resemblance to 10th Cycle language, which perhaps meant that the 9th Cycle catastrophe had been less complete than the subsequent one. That made him curious to trace the previous cycles as well, but first things first.

"Ladies and gentlemen, thank you for allowing me to address you. I have prepared handouts with the highlights of what I'm about to say. I hope they will aid you in your deliberations, for I am indeed going to make a request at the end of my presentation, as Dr. O'Reilly speculated. Without further ado, my report."

Charles took just under an hour to report every major event leading up to the discovery of the cave system that led to the valley, to which he referred as Paradise Valley after revealing the name the expedition had chosen. A few faces revealed displeasure that it had been named already, chiefly those of the representatives from the countries who claimed the area in question, Argentina, Chile and Great Britain. However, they were more interested in his conclusions and the request he'd be making than in arguing about naming rights.

When it came to describing the deaths that had occurred, Charles spoke gravely, expecting questions. The mysterious disappearance of one of the miners, and the burned body of the other, had been investigated thoroughly weeks before. It was the final mission, which claimed the lives of Bart, LeClerc and Carmen, that was in question. Unfortunately, the circumstances of LeClerc's death were called into question by the fact that only Carmen had been a witness, and now she was dead as well, discredited as a spy. Had she killed him herself? They would likely never know.

The representative from Chile was insistent that Summers explain how JR had known Carmen was with the OS, when Summers hadn't been able to tell him so. Charles replied heatedly that it didn't matter, since it wasn't JR who killed her, but the leader of the presumed OS squad, Pyotr. The Chilean representative retracted his near-accusation and sat back, muttering to himself.

The other question was Bart. He'd been in the Sno-Cat when the others went into the cave, but Roosky had told Cmdr. Andersen that he simply wasn't there when he went back there. Roosky wasn't available for questioning and was in fact suspected of being OS as well, begging the question of whether he had in fact killed Bart himself. So that discussion was also cut short. Summers had no other information. At last, the details of the expedition had been thoroughly explored, and it remained only for Charles to make his proposal for a new expedition.

"We have a clear duty to return to the site," he began. "We went there in hopes of finding 9th Cycle ruins. I submit to you that they are there, within the jungle that fills the valley perhaps. The script that my colleague has so ably translated proves that someone other than 10th Cyclers were there at some time. The resemblance to 10th Cycle script suggests that it was 9th Cycle inhabitants. Furthermore, we observed an organization to the pathways through the jungle that suggests humankind had a hand in it. The paths were straight and intersected at right angles. We've never seen anything like that in nature, quite the opposite. Before her death, Carmen identified several species of tree that had to have been imported, mostly fruit trees. That they are still bearing fruit after so many millennia is miraculous, and very fortunate for us, as we likely would have died without the sustenance it provided.

"My proposal is to take an expedition that includes those of the original crew who wish to go, as well as several archaeologists, botanists, and a linguist to translate any other messages we encounter, back to the site as soon as the weather breaks. We have six months to prepare, but the preparations won't be as rigorous as before, since we now know our excavations won't be carried out in normal Antarctic conditions. In your information packet, I have given an estimate of the cost, including replacing our Sno-Cats. Are there any questions before I relinquish the podium to Mr. Rossler?"

Several voices spoke at once, followed by one hand raised to identify one who wanted to ask a question. Summers asked him to go ahead with his question. It happened to be the representative from Chile.

"I'd like to propose we rename the valley in honor of our fallen scientist." An appalled silence followed. Summers couldn't speak to that suggestion; he didn't feel he had the authority. Fortunately, after what seemed an eternity, several other voices shouted, "No!" The representative from Great Britain won the war for attention.

"Under the circumstances, that would be most inappropriate. I propose that if it is to be renamed at all, it be Rossler Valley, in honor of the young man who saved the expedition, Joshua Rossler." Another babble of discussion followed, quelled by Daniel stepping forward to rescue Charles from the awkward situation.

"Mr. Thatcher, I appreciate the suggestion, and I know JR would be honored. However, it is not within our purview to name geographic features. That will be decided by the Antarctica Committee once we release the findings of this expedition. I suggest we continue to call it Paradise Valley for convenience until such time as the Committee meets. Are there any questions that Dr. Summers can answer?"

When none were presented, Summers stepped down and Daniel asked for a motion to consider the expedition. Charles slipped away when the deliberations started, too nervous to listen to the pros and cons. In his mind, there were only pros. He devoutly hoped that the Board agreed.

When he stepped into the hallway outside the boardroom, he found JR and Rebecca waiting to be called to testify. "I don't think they're going to need you," he said. "They're already deliberating the proposal to send another expedition."

Becca stood quickly. "Then I have patients to see to. JR, call me if they want us after all."

"I will. Hey, I'll walk you out," he added. Summers said goodbye and strode down the hall toward the translation department to consult with Sinclair. He'd have something to say to the old rascal, surprising him like that. Mostly, he wanted an experienced linguist with which to discuss the meaning of the ban on weapons; both the fact of it and why it would have been necessary.

JR and Becca went in the opposite direction, toward the main exit.

"Becca, can I ask you something?" JR ventured.

"Sure, JR, anything," she said with a warm smile.

"Would you like to go hiking with me tomorrow?"

"I'd love it! Pick me up at eight."

"You bet," agreed JR. Another early morning meant another night with no booze. He was getting used to it though, and a day with Becca all to himself was worth it.

Chapter Thirty-Five

YOU'VE DECIDED TO KEEP ME?

Four months later

"What have you decided, JR, grad school or expedition?" Becca asked, knowing the answer even as she asked the question. She was standing in the kitchen, cooking breakfast as he came in fresh from his morning shower after an early morning run. She handed him a glass of orange juice.

"Expedition, of course. You don't think I'd let you go back there without me," he said, planting a kiss on the top of her head. Becca gave him a wicked grin and reached for the towel around his waist. She loved him all the time, but she especially loved him straight out of the shower and dressed in a towel that she could steal.

"Hey, none of that, you wanton woman," he teased. "Why are you still here, don't you have a baby to deliver or something?"

"My day off. If any babies want to come today, they'll have to settle for whoever's on call. Are you trying to get rid of me?"

"Never," he declared, putting down the empty glass and pulling her into his arms, where she rested her face against the still-damp flesh. "What do you want to do today?"

"I thought I'd try to organize the spare room. It hasn't been the same since you moved in and dumped all your old stuff in there," she said, nuzzling the hollow between his pecs and his abs. "Seriously, do you still need all of that basketball equipment? And would you help me?"

"Of course. It's only fair, since it's my stuff. But that won't take all day. What else?"

"Well, you complain so much about my pink frilly bedroom, would you like to go get some paint and redecorate?"

"Does that mean you've decided to keep me?"

"I guess. You're like that puppy I rescued," she said, pointing at the St. Bernard that was overflowing the sofa in the living room. "You grew on me, and now I can't get rid of you."

JR chuckled and lifted Becca off her feet, holding her with her face just above his. "You know you love me," he said, lowering her for a kiss.

"As long as you don't break house-training," she said, twitching the towel away while he was distracted with putting her down on her feet.

"Hey!"

Becca ran for the bedroom, laughing, with JR in hot pursuit. He caught her, which she'd counted on, and tossed her lightly onto the bed. The painting and organizing could wait, he thought, as he tenderly divested Becca of the robe that hid her curves from him. If he'd been able to think, he might have considered what an impact this woman had made on his life, but thinking wasn't required at the moment.

JR skated his big palm across Becca's silky skin, which rose in goose bumps at his touch. If she had been able to think, she might have marveled at the change in JR, the new confidence, the sobriety. But, she wasn't doing much thinking either. Instead a sigh escaped her as they joined, both surrendering to the passion that claimed them, certain that they had a future together.

Next in the Rossler Foundation Mysteries Series

vinci-books.com/genetic-bullets

**A pandemic is unleashed. The world is on the brink.
Time is running out until a glimmer of hope emerges.**

When a 35,000-year-old city is unearthed, a devastating pandemic is unleashed. As world leaders point fingers and tensions escalate, humanity teeters on the edge of a global war that could eradicate half the population. With society crumbling and time running out, a select few may hold the key to preventing the catastrophe foretold by the Tenth Cycle.

Turn the page for a free preview…

Genetic Bullets: Prologue

In the Year 24,500 of the Ninth Cycle

Jaasiel walked in the gardens surrounding the hospital where his beloved had lain ill for seven turns. So many had fallen to this illness, but the doctors counseled hope, for there was nothing else to be done. Others railed against the isolation, though that was what brought them here in the first place. This was a beautiful place of peace and tranquility; a place to withdraw from the hurly-burly of business and crowds. Here there was no hunger, no violence, no striving; only peace and beauty.

But now this quiet, peace, beauty and isolation threatened their very existence. Someone had come here ill, and exposed another. That one exposed two or three others. Soon everyone whose forebears came from the lush valley of the land to the north of the sea and between the impassible mountain ranges were ill, and many had died.

Adnah would die soon, too, God willing. How she suffered! Jaasiel could see no hope for her recovery. Her body burned; she cried out for relief from the pain. It would have been an act of kindness to press her pillow to her face and let it end. He could not do it, though, and the inability was bitter. He loved her too much to be without her, and not enough to set aside his selfish wish to keep her alive by any means possible, so that, in the event of a miracle, she might be restored to him.

This agony of indecision and grief made him careless, or perhaps it was because Jaaseil himself was ill, though the symptoms had not yet made themselves known. In any case, his decision was taken from him in that moment, as his foot slipped off the path and he stumbled, then fell. Instantly, before he even had time to register the pain of being burned alive, he was swallowed by the fumarole that steamed beside the path. There should have been a barrier, but Jaaseil didn't have time to register that thought.

Not even a scream passed his lips, though an exhalation of surprise disturbed the algae on the surface. His last thought, cut off almost before it formed, was that his beloved would soon be with him in eternity.

Genetic Bullets: Chapter One

WE HAVE TO GO BACK

Professor Charles Summers was unaccountably nervous. It annoyed him, because he knew he had widespread support for what he was to present to the Board of the Rossler Foundation today. In fact, partial funding had already allowed him to begin the planning, and everything was set to go except for final funding for the expedition itself. Today's presentation was just a formality.

There was little that could go wrong, except that the expedition director, JR Rossler, was a bit of a wild card. Sometimes he didn't filter his observations, and Summers had reason to understand that he could be volatile. Nevertheless, he'd proved himself both courageous and resourceful on the last trip, and when he requested the position, Summers was happy to take him on this time. Especially since JR's older brother, Daniel Rossler, was the CEO and Chairman of the Board of the Rossler Foundation, under whose auspices the expedition would take place.

Firmly setting aside his nerves, Summers straightened his tie for the last time and stepped out of his office to head for the Board room. As he passed the next office, the door opened, and Dr. Rebecca Mendenhall joined him.

"Showtime, Dr. Summers."

"Indeed, Dr. Mendenhall. Thanks for your support."

"Charles, there's no need to thank me. I'm as eager to get back there as you are. I keep dreaming of a tropical paradise surrounded by Antarctic ice, and the secrets you might find under all those vines." She gave a light laugh. It was true, against all odds. The place she dreamed of was as real as the building the two stood in, although a place of mystery, certainly.

It was also the place where she had come to value JR Rossler as more than a troubled family friend. The dangers they had faced together had served to give JR back his self-respect, stolen by events beyond his control in Afghanistan. Her admiration had become love. Now the thought of being with him in that place again, after all that had happened since then, was like going back for a do-over to perfect an event that had gone wrong, erasing the ugliness of being attacked and having to kill or be killed.

Besides, it would help JR overcome his demons. His Afghanistan-induced PTSD had worsened in a way, though he had learned to control the self-destructive behavior. He no longer drank himself senseless, or chased anything in a skirt. Rebecca was responsible for that. More than anything, he wanted to keep her respect. He still had moments, though, when he despaired of being a normal person with nothing bothering him but the petty concerns of daily life. That occasional depression was driven by his nightmares of killing the men who had attacked them. Only going back to the place and facing the demons rationally would set him free, Rebecca was convinced. As a medical doctor with significant experience in treating PTSD patients, she had reason to believe she was right.

Summers and Rebecca arrived together just as Daniel was calling the meeting to order. They hurried to their seats. Across the table, JR winked at Rebecca, who acknowledged him with a smile. Daniel finished his opening remarks and turned the podium over to Summers.

He cleared his throat. Now that the time was at hand, his nerves were steady. He was prepared; it only remained to begin.

"Ladies and gentlemen, thank you for allowing me to speak in behalf of the Rossler Foundation's latest project. I hope you will agree with me that it is vitally important that we complete it as soon as possible. Briefly, we are seeking funding to return to Antarctica, this time to locate and excavate ruins in the hidden valley that we found during last season's ill-fated expedition. We believe that the only way to honor those who lost their lives earlier this year is to finish the job we went to do at that time.

"For those of you who have joined this august body since those events, let me briefly recount what occurred. As you all know, the body of knowledge that we refer to as the 10th Cycle Library contains accounts of a civilization that flourished thousands of years ago and was superior in many ways to our own. Their records contain statements that even earlier civilizations existed.

"Based on the momentous changes the discovery of the 10th Cycle Library has brought us, we would like to believe that you are with us in our desire to uncover the truth of any site that may contain information about those earlier civilizations. The 10th Cycle Library led us to go looking for a site mentioned in the annals, a site purported to be of 9th Cycle origin. We have reason to believe, both from those records and from inscriptions we found in the cave system that led to a wondrous hidden valley, that 10th Cyclers were quite familiar with this valley.

"The very fact that the valley exists challenges all modern day evidence that Antarctica has been covered in ice for millions of years. We owe it to the world today, as well as to the 10th Cyclers who went to so much trouble to let us know of their existence, to reveal it at last. In fact, this could be one of the most important and exciting scientific expeditions ever undertaken.

"We now know where the ruins we sought are located, although we didn't find the location in time to begin exploration last season. As you know, we were attacked by mercenaries sent by the Orion Society, and barely escaped with our lives.

"Now we are seeking funds to return to finish the job we started. Most of the surviving members of the first expedition are on board and eager to get there as soon as the weather breaks. In front of you are detailed plans for a three-stage expedition, which we hope you will have taken the opportunity to study before now. I will now accept questions."

"Why three stages?" asked the member from Australia.

"We anticipate needing a large crew of excavation workers," Summers replied. "In order to preserve any and all historically important details in the valley, we propose to house them for the most part in the canyon where we found the cave entrance that leads to the internal valley. That will require that a semi-permanent base camp be constructed for that purpose. As you can see, the first phase is construction. We are using pre-fab buildings flown in by helicopter, as well as heavy equipment that will prepare the site for the buildings. It shouldn't take longer than a month, including accounting for bad weather at the beginning of the summer season."

The member from Chile objected. "Last year you encountered heavy winds as you crossed the Ross Ice Shelf. For nearly a month, as I recall. How can you expect construction to occur in those conditions?"

"You're correct, we did," Summers conceded. "However, last year we were crossing on the ground, in Sno-Cats with trailers attached, which meant that the wind conditions were a bigger problem than they will be if we encounter them this year. The Sikorsky choppers we've chartered were built for heavy loads in heavy weather, and of course flying means they won't be exposed for as long as we were. We anticipate no problems in getting them in and out of the canyon on days when the wind is more subdued. Inside the canyon itself, the canyon floor is somewhat protected from the winds, which generally blow from a direction across, not into, the mouth of the canyon. Are there any more questions?"

"Yes," said Australia. "You've explained one phase. What about the other two?"

Someone hadn't done his homework, reflected Summers. He gathered his patience to answer.

"The second phase will be just the core group of scientists, including myself and several others, to locate where excavations should take place and begin experiments on the flora and any fauna or human remains that we might find while excavation takes place. Once we find the ruins we expect to find within the valley, we'll bring in the third phase, the excavation crews and support crew. There is no need to house and feed over fifty extra men for the week or two it will take to map the valley on our own. Does that answer your question? Are there any more?"

"Yes," came the answer from a different, and unexpected quarter.

"JR? What's your question?"

"What are we going to do about the Orion Society?"

Grab your copy...
vinci-books.com/genetic-bullets

About the Author

JC Ryan is a bestselling author renowned for his intricate espionage, archaeological thrillers, and conspiracy mysteries. With over 30 acclaimed novels, including the popular Rex Dalton K9 Thrillers, Rossler Foundation Mysteries, and Carter Devereux Mystery Thrillers, Ryan has captivated readers around the globe.

Drawing from his diverse professional background—as a military officer, lawyer, and IT manager—Ryan creates compelling narratives that skillfully blend historical accuracy with thrilling adventure. He is celebrated as a master storyteller, known for crafting riveting plots, meticulous historical details, and engaging, multidimensional characters. Ryan's meticulous research lends authenticity and depth to each story, immersing readers in richly constructed worlds filled with intrigue, suspense, and adventure.

Fans of David Baldacci, Lee Child's Jack Reacher, Tom Clancy's Jack Ryan, Nelson DeMille's John Corey, Vince Flynn's Mitch Rapp, Mark Greaney's Gray Man, Gregg Hurwitz's Orphan X, Robert Ludlum's Jason Bourne, Daniel Silva's Gabriel Allon, Brad Taylor's Pike Logan, Brad Thor's Scot Harvath, James Rollins' Sigma Force, Steve Berry's Cotton Malone, and Dan Brown's Robert Langdon will find JC Ryan's novels equally compelling and unforgettable.

When not writing, Ryan enjoys spending time with his college sweetheart, whom he married in 1978. They are proud parents of two daughters, have two sons-in-law, and are grandparents to two grandchildren.